SILENT WITNESS

SILENT WITNESS

A Laurel Highlands Mystery

LIZ MILLIRON

To my children Mary and Michael. I'm so proud of both of you.

Contents

Chapter One

Jim Duncan pulled back on the leash to restrain his Golden Retriever, Rizzo. "Okay, doofus. Slow down. It's a hike, not a sprint."

It had been a perfect weekend, the type he'd envisioned when he made the move to Criminal Investigation. For once, both he and Sally Castle, his fiancée, were free, something that rarely happened. No active investigations for him. Sally's calendar was clear, no court appearances scheduled until the end of the week, so no weekend prep work to do. They'd decided to take the dogs to Ohiopyle State Park and hit the trails. There weren't too many people around, and Duncan could have let Rizzo off his lead, but he opted not to. Sally's retired racing greyhound, Pixel, with his tendency to be distracted by any small, fluffy animal, couldn't be trusted, but he was well-behaved enough for her to keep him on a long, loose lead. A rich blue sky with a few puffy clouds overhead and a gentle breeze kept things from getting too hot.

In short, a perfect late spring day in the Laurel Highlands.

Sally walked beside him and held his hand. "Shouldn't I be the one leading the dog who wants to race?" Pixel ambled next to her, his long nose snuffling through the ground cover.

"I didn't think Pixel was truly a runner until he took off after that rabbit last week." Duncan paused while Rizzo investigated a clump of mountain laurel. "He must be the laziest dog on the planet."

Pixel raised his head, as if he knew he was being maligned, and barked once.

Sally bent to rub behind the black hound's velvety ears. "He meant it in the nicest way possible, bud."

Pixel blew out a horsey breath and turned away.

Duncan tugged Rizzo's leash. "Well, I've been put in my place, haven't I?"

After a bit, he spoke again. "How goes the wedding plans? Is your mom still giving you fits?"

Sally's contented expression soured. "You had to bring it up and ruin the moment, didn't you?"

"What now?"

"She says she needs another fifty invitations." Sally stared at her dog, as if she was afraid to look her future husband in the eye.

"Just for herself?"

She avoided meeting his gaze. "Well, um, yes."

Duncan sighed. "Tell her she can have half of mine and half of my parents' invites. There's so much overlap in names, we haven't filled our quota." He shook a finger. "And if she balks, tell her I said—"

"That's not all of it." They stood in the shade, but the blush on Sally's neck deepened.

He raised an eyebrow.

She took a breath. "She wants you to add some groomsmen."

"How many?" The words came from behind clenched jaws.

"She wants us each to have twelve, including the maid of honor and the best man." Sally rushed the words, as if getting them out would dull the impact.

"A dozen? Sally, I don't know that many guys I'd want at my wedding. Not even if I expand the field to the entirety of Troop B. Aren't they supposed to be people I'm friends with?"

"Please? She's insisting I have to ask the daughters of some of *her* closest friends. She says they'll be insulted if I don't." She sagged.

"What do you want?"

"To marry you and survive the day while enduring the least amount of drama." She paused to wait for Pixel. "I don't know these women, but hey, if they want to buy one of those awful gowns and show up for a free dinner, why not?"

Duncan could have explained why not, but he saw no point in taking it out on Sally, who was having enough *pre*-wedding day difficulty with her mother. He'd do almost anything to make the actual day easier for her. "I'll see what I can do." When he proposed, he knew Louise Castle would plan a wedding extravaganza for her youngest daughter. He'd underestimated the effort. Only the fact that neither he nor Sally were Catholic kept Louise from booking the ceremony at St. Paul's Cathedral in Pittsburgh. His determination to stick to the semblance of a budget had prevented her from arranging to have the reception at one of Pittsburgh's many museums. They were not among the Pittsburgh social elite. But that didn't keep Louise from trying to expand the boundaries they'd set. "At the risk of pouring salt on the wound, why are you letting her bully you like this? I've seen you face armed criminals. You could shut her down in a hot second."

She stopped to let Pixel examine a bush. "I'd take the armed gunmen over my mother any day. You're right; I could. Except I'd hear about it at every family event for the rest of my life. I keep hoping if I give her some of what she wants, she'll be happy."

That tactic has never worked for anyone else; why would it work for Louise? But Sally didn't need him to pile on. The shopping for bridesmaid dresses had been an epic battle, or so she'd said. Neither Sally nor Louise had gotten her first choice. It made him glad the tuxedo he already owned, courtesy of his first marriage, was acceptable. Louise had floated the idea of wearing the Pennsylvania State Police dress uniform, and he'd refused point-blank.

The problem was that Louise didn't seem to understand the day was not about her. He'd called his parents for advice. They had both said the same thing. Let Sally know he had her back and would do whatever she needed him to do.

He tugged Rizzo away from a thorny bush. Maybe it was time to shut down the circus. Grab a couple of witnesses, bundle Sally into his Jeep, and head for the nearest judge. Except he knew that would only create more headaches for both of them.

When Sally spoke again, her voice sounded tiny. "I am so sorry, Jim. I had no idea she'd be *this* crazy."

He sighed. "Don't worry. We'll get through it. It's just a day." He managed to wrap his arms around her waist, even while holding Rizzo's leash. "It doesn't mean as much as she thinks. If the size of the ceremony and the frippery led to a successful marriage, Tish and I would still be together. As long as I have you, it'll be fine. You decide on your name?"

Another point of contention. Sally had invested a lot of time and effort into building her law practice under the Castle name. It had only been a year and she didn't want to ruin the recognition that Castle & Parson had. Louise, of course, had been scandalized at the possibility Sally might not change her last name to Duncan. "I haven't. I suppose I could continue to practice under Castle but change my legal name to Duncan. Would you be okay with that?"

"Whatever you decide is fine with me." He kissed her. "It's your call. One piece of advice: Choose one or the other."

Sally furrowed her eyebrows. "What's wrong with hyphenating?"

"Nothing." He winked. "But Castle-Duncan sounds like the home of a medieval Scottish laird, not the name of one of Uniontown's most successful criminal defense attorneys."

She hugged him tightly. "I love you, Jim Duncan."

He rubbed her back. "Just remember. If it gets to be too much, a quick trip to the courthouse is always an option."

At the sound of something crashing through the greenery, Sally let go and turned her head. "It's too early for bears, isn't it? Could it be a deer?"

Duncan wrapped Rizzo's leash around his hand. "I don't think it's an animal. The dogs are too quiet." Both canines had perked up their ears, but showed no sign of distress.

The source of the noise crashed out of the trees on to the trail. It was a child, perhaps six or seven years old. She wore long pants streaked with mud, hiking boots, and a dirty long-sleeved t-shirt. Her hair resembled a bird's nest, with twigs and leaves tangled in it. Her face showed evidence of tears and streaks of dirt, the china-blue eyes wide with fear.

"Oh my God." Sally clapped a hand over her mouth. "Hey, sweetie. Are you lost?"

The girl stared at them and uttered a cry and turned, but she tripped over her feet and fell. She wrapped her arms over her head and scrunched the rest of her body into a ball.

Pixel went over to her. His long snoot wiggled as he sniffed her face. Freed from his short lead, Rizzo trotted over to inspect the newcomer and licked her hand. The child flinched, but then, overwhelmed by canine affection, unwound herself and reached out to touch both dogs.

Duncan took a couple of steps forward, and the child scuttled backward. "It's okay. I won't hurt you."

The girl got to her feet and stumbled away.

"I don't think she believes you." Sally held out a hand. "We won't hurt you. Honest."

The girl's frantic gaze went from one adult to another. She positioned herself behind the dogs.

Sally advanced, step by slow step. "Shhh. It's okay. Where are your parents? Did you lose them?"

The girl said nothing.

The dogs turned to examine their new friend. The girl ran her hands through Rizzo's thick fur. He barked. Pixel nuzzled her ear. She didn't flinch, but reached out to pet both dogs at the same time.

"What's your name?" Duncan asked.

Sally watched the scene. "Jim, I don't think she can hear. Look at her. She should have reacted when Rizzo barked, and she didn't."

"Are you sure?"

Sally moved so she was behind the girl and clapped her hands.

The child didn't move.

"I am now. She's deaf. Or has some level of hearing loss." She knelt down and held out her hand. Once again, the child backed away. "Well, she's clearly terrified. What are we going to do?"

Duncan thought. Most of the "lost" children he'd dealt with in his years on the job had been kids who'd been separated from their parents at events, not babes in the woods. "Give me a minute to think."

The child looked from one adult to the other and gestured in what had to be American Sign Language.

Duncan shook his head and shrugged. He hoped that communicated he didn't understand. Then he looked at Sally. "I don't know ASL. Do you?"

Sally stood. "I learned to sign the alphabet when I was in elementary school, but I can't remember half the letters now."

"That isn't going to help. First things first. Let's get back to the park." He pulled out his cell phone. He only had a couple of bars, but it should be good enough to get a text through. He tapped out a message.

"Who are you texting?"

"McAllister. I don't know where she is, but I asked her to meet us near the Visitor's Center. Or send someone." Duncan held out Rizzo's leash. "Can you handle the boys? That kid looks exhausted. We can't ask her to walk all the way back to the park."

Sally took the strip of nylon. "I've got them. What are you going to do, carry her? Can you get back up the trail like that?"

"I think so." Duncan knelt. He reached out to touch the girl to get her attention.

She pulled back and eyed him with a wary expression.

"Either her parents have taught her about Stranger Danger, or she's got a fear of unknown men." Sally crouched down.

"And women. She wasn't keen on you until she saw Rizzo and Pixel's reactions." Duncan tilted his head. "Maybe she'll let you hold her."

"I can't carry a child her size all the way back to the Visitor's Center, and you just said it's too far for her to walk." She pivoted to face him. "Call Rizzo."

He raised an eyebrow. "Come here, doofus." Rizzo bounded over. Duncan rubbed the Golden Retriever's ears, and the dog rewarded him by joyously licking his owner's face.

The girl giggled.

"Pixel, come." Sally held out her hand, and the black hound obeyed the command. After a few seconds, she held out her hand to the girl, who inched toward them.

"What are you doing?"

"She trusts the dogs, the dogs trust us…maybe they'll get her to warm up."

They waited a few moments. Eventually, the girl relaxed enough to come close so she could continue to pet both Rizzo and Pixel. Sally gave her an encouraging smile, which was shyly returned.

Duncan let go of his dog. "Think she'll get on my back now?"

"Give it a try. If not, we'll have to take it slow."

He faced the child, knelt again, and patted himself over his shoulder.

The girl bit her lip, but came over, climbed on his back, and wrapped her thin arms around his neck.

"Guess she believes the old adage." Sally tugged at the leashes to get Rizzo and Pixel moving. "Dogs are good judges of character. I agree. I've met more dogs I'd trust than people."

He stood and adjusted the girl's slight weight. "Me, too. However, considering our professions, we may be more than a little jaded."

Chapter Two

Sally walked the dogs in front of Jim. Where had the girl come from? She had to have been out with her parents, or another adult, and gotten separated. But if that was true, why had they not noticed anyone on the trails? Surely the child would be missed by now.

They arrived back in the park and walked to the Visitor's Center. Jim set the girl down and pulled out his water bottle. He held it out to the girl, who gulped greedily. "I'm going to guess she hasn't had anything to drink lately." He looked over at Sally. "I didn't hear or see anyone back there, did you?"

"Not a peep." Sally pulled out the collapsible water dish she carried for the dogs and filled it from her own bottle before taking a drink herself.

The dogs lapped noisily. The water splashed onto the girl, who laughed.

A slim figure in a gray State Police uniform jogged up to the group. Trooper Aislyn McAllister. "Hey, Boss, Sally. What's this about a lost kid?"

Jim nodded a greeting at his former trainee. "This is her." He laid a hand on the girl's shoulder. "We found her on the trail. We're pretty sure she's deaf. No name tag, no form of identification. Didn't hear anyone looking for her either."

Aislyn put her hands on her duty belt. "Should I call for a K-9 officer, search and rescue? Maybe someone who knows American Sign Language?"

The girl looked over at the new person. Her eyes grew wide, and she sidled back to Jim, pressing her body against his leg.

"Did I scare her? Is it the hat?" Aislyn took off the standard PSP campaign hat and shook out her curls.

"I don't think that's it." Sally thought. The girl stared at Aislyn from behind

Jim. No, not at Aislyn. At her waist, specifically, at the gun holster. "I think it's your sidearm."

Jim knelt down again. "It's okay." He shook his head. "I can't help talking to her, and I know she can't hear a word I'm saying." He glanced at Aislyn. "Sally may be right."

Aislyn frowned. "You think?"

"The only way to be sure is for you to pull it. I won't do that to her. Not in her state." Jim paused. "Move to your left. I want to watch her eyes."

Aislyn obliged.

Sally watched the girl. Her gaze stayed focused on the holstered weapon. "I think you're right. Aislyn, try shaking Jim's hand, then approaching her."

Again, the young woman complied. But at the first step, the child backed up, eyes still focused on the gun.

Jim found Sally's gaze, and she knew they were thinking the same thing. Sally spoke slowly. "She wouldn't react that way unless she'd seen a gun before. And maybe even seen it used."

His hazel eyes darkened in understanding. "McAllister, make that call. You'd better see if you can get a cadaver dog, too."

* * *

Purely based on instinct, Duncan chose to follow Trooper Devin Stallings and his cadaver dog, a shaggy mixed-breed named Merlin. Sure, whatever adult had been with the little girl in the woods might have simply been injured and unable to walk. However, the cell service wasn't so bad in the park that he, or she, couldn't have gotten a call out. Since he'd seen no response from park officials, he had to assume no message had been sent.

In his experience, that didn't bode well.

The two troopers and Merlin went back to where Duncan and Sally had encountered the child. Stallings sent Merlin off on his hunt from there. He padded briskly down the trail and nosed not only the ground but almost every tree, bush, flower, and blade of grass along the way.

Stallings bent over and picked up a brightly colored object. "Looks like a child's backpack." He handed it over.

Duncan rifled through the pockets. A child-sized water bottle was clipped to the outside. The main compartment held basic safety items, such as sunscreen and insect repellent. A couple of granola bars were tucked in the front pouch. He removed a laminated card from the same space. The name *Bronwen Lane*, her age, and the fact that she was deaf was written on it. "I think it's the kid's. She must have lost it scrambling through the woods."

"Not surprising. It's pretty dense around here." Stallings waved a hand.

After about twenty minutes of searching, Merlin alerted. Duncan spied two feet encased in hiking boots sticking out from behind a clump of mountain laurel. While Stallings rewarded Merlin for his work, Duncan phoned for the coroner. Then he fired off a text to Sally. **I think we found who we were looking for**.

* * *

Sally took the girl and the dogs back to the main street in Ohiopyle. Once the two K-9 handlers showed up, one from SAR and one cadaver, Jim and Aislyn left with them to search the trees. Sally prayed the cadaver team came up empty. With any luck, the girl's parent, or parents, were merely injured and unable to call out.

Her gut told her it was not as easy as that. The child's reaction to Aislyn, the gun, and her behavior on the trail were not the acts of someone who'd been sent to get help. And who would send a deaf little girl to do that without a written message of some kind?

Sally took the girl to get ice cream. "A small cone, please."

"What flavor?" asked the girl at the counter.

Now what? Sally picked up the child and pointed at the case of ice creams.

The girl smiled and pointed at a tub filled with a bright pink mixture.

"What flavor is that?" Sally asked.

"Cotton candy. Would she like to try it?" The server scooped up a small bit on a wooden spoon.

Sally took the sample and handed it to her young charge.

The girl tasted and smiled.

"That's a winner." Sally handed the spoon back.

Ice cream in hand, she led the dogs and the girl to a bench near the park. "We'll just sit here and wait for Jim, huh?"

The girl, focused on her treat, said nothing. She reached out to Pixel, who licked a trickle of melted ice cream off her hand.

What a sweetheart. Who was she? Sally checked the girl's clothes again for a name tag or some kind of identification, but found nothing. She wished she remembered more of the sign-language alphabet, but even if she did, there was no guarantee she'd understand the child's response.

"At least we have a nice day to sit and wait for your Mom or Dad." Sally watched as the girl licked her cone, oblivious to any noise around her. *I hope you're having more luck than I am, Jim.*

A large white van pulled into the park. Out of the corner of her eye, she recognized the markings of the Fayette County Coroner. At the same time, her phone chirped with Jim's text tone. She read his message. Damn. It would be too coincidental to have both a body and a missing woman in the same park on the same day. The victim's identity couldn't be confirmed until the coroner completed his job, but her heart already ached for the little girl next to her.

At least now she knew the child's name.

Bronwen tugged on Sally's arm. She gave the remainder of her ice cream to Sally. Then she moved her hands rapidly, probably asking where her parent was.

Sally knelt. "I'm sorry, I don't understand." She shrugged and tried to mime her confusion.

Bronwen made the same hand gestures, but slower.

"I still don't understand." Sally hugged the girl, then released her. If only she had a piece of paper and something to write with. Bronwen had to be old enough to read simple words.

She grabbed Sally's hand and pulled. She pointed toward the hiking path that twisted down past the Youghiogheny River, the direction they'd come from, where she'd been found.

Sally shook her head. She sat cross-legged on the grass and patted the ground next to her. "Rizzo, Pixel, come over here." She tugged on the leashes, and the dogs came and sat.

The girl followed suit, her obvious delight with her canine companions perhaps pushing any thought of return to the forest out of her mind. At least she stopped pulling Sally in that direction.

At some point, someone was going to have to tell the girl what had happened. Sally wasn't sure who that would be, but she made up her mind not to leave her young charge's side until it was over.

Chapter Three

Duncan and Stallings stood by the body. The victim looked to be in her early to mid-thirties. Her tousled hair was the same honey-blonde as the girl's, the unseeing eyes the same brilliant blue. No doubt this was the child's mother. She was dressed sensibly for a day of hiking, clad in cargo pants, a long-sleeved shirt under a light flannel over shirt, and sturdy boots. A heavy nylon backpack was nearby. The only thing that marred her appearance was the red stain over her chest.

Stallings rubbed Merlin's head. "It never gets any easier. I'm glad Merlin is good at his job, but I wish there hadn't been anything to find."

"I know the feeling." Duncan held out his hand. "Thanks for your help." He scratched Merlin behind the ears. "Nice job, buddy." Then he turned toward the young man working over the victim. "What's the story?"

Deputy coroner Tom Burns sat back on his heels. "Single gunshot wound to the chest. First impression, Caucasian woman, mid-thirties, good shape. No sign of defensive wounds."

"Any idea how long she's been lying here?"

Burns manipulated the woman's arm. "Rigor has started, but is far from set. Two to four hours. Maybe less? Educated guess. Livor indicates this is where she fell, so she wasn't moved after she was shot."

"Don't suppose you can tell me how long her heart kept pumping after the gunshot."

"Not until we get her on the table. A lot will depend on whether the bullet hit the heart or a major artery." Burns reached up and closed her eyes. "I'm hoping it wasn't long. Did you hear it?"

Duncan looked at his phone. He'd sent the text to McAllister around three-thirty. If Burns was correct in his guess, that meant the woman had died anywhere from eleven that morning to one in the afternoon. "We didn't hear anything. But we were in a different part of the park at midday. No reason we would have." He waved his hand. "We'll put out a call for anyone who was on this trail around the target time, but I doubt we'll get any results."

McAllister, who wore a pair of nitrile gloves, came over holding the other backpack, this one sized for an adult. "A water bottle, a box of granola bars, a cell phone, and a wallet." She held out the wallet. "The rest of the scene is exactly the kind of mess you'd expect in the woods."

"In other words, don't hold my breath for magical forensic discoveries." Duncan took it. "Glynis Lane."

"Glen-is." McAllister corrected his pronunciation. "It's a Welsh name."

"If you say so. Address is Pittsburgh."

Burns bagged the woman's hands. He retrieved a vinyl bag and maneuvered it around the body, making sure to take some of the woodland debris. "You think this is the little girl's mother?"

"Same last name, so the odds are good," Duncan replied. "But I'm not going to have a child make an ID, that's for damn sure. Not that we could."

"Ace, move the straps off the stretcher." Burns and Duncan lifted the body and placed it on a backboard. Burns strapped it down. "Why not?"

Duncan handed the wallet back to McAllister, who dropped it into an evidence bag. "She appears to be deaf."

"No problem." Burns fastened the webbing around the victim's feet.

McAllister secured the other end. "Are we gonna carry her out?"

"Nah, I've called the park service. They'll send an ATV." He checked his phone. "Should be here in a couple of minutes."

Duncan leaned against a tree. "What do you mean, no problem?"

"I know American Sign Language," Burns said.

"You do? When did you pick up that skill?"

"College. My buddy and I learned together."

"Why?" McAllister asked.

"Why else?" Burns gave her a lopsided grin. "We wanted to impress a girl."

She raised her eyebrows. "Did it work?"

"Sure did." He scanned the trail for the ATV, then turned back. "For him."

* * *

Sally watched as Tom Burns loaded the stretcher into the van. "Damn it. Would you think I was an awful person if I hoped you found nothing?"

Jim stood beside her. "No. My preference would be to find an injured adult who turned out to be the child's parent, but I'd rather come up empty-handed than with finding a DB." He looked around. "Speaking of the girl, where is she?"

"Over there with Rizzo and Pixel. I tied their leashes to a bench so I could talk to you." Sally waved her hand. "How are we going to determine whether or not she's related to your victim?"

"Burns says he knows ASL." Jim took in her expression. "Don't ask."

Tom shut the doors to the van and faced them. "Okay, let's talk to the child you found. Or who found you, as the case may be."

"Just a second. McAllister." Jim beckoned to the younger trooper. "Write up your report. Mention that I was on the scene, and you've handed everything over to me. I'll take it from here."

"Got it, Boss." She gave Tom a quick kiss on the cheek. "Do I need to cancel our dinner reservations?" She took off her hat and ran her hand through her hair.

He shook his head. "No. We won't be able to do the autopsy today. We're booked. Let me help Jim out with the girl, I'll take the victim back to the morgue, and then I'll text you." He stripped off his gloves and gear from the coroner's office and threw it onto the front seat of the van.

She waved to Jim and Sally, got into her marked Interceptor, and took off.

Tom held out an arm. "Lead on."

The threesome walked over to the girl, who sat between Rizzo and Pixel, while Trooper Stallings watched. Her position allowed her to pet them both at the same time. Rizzo and Pixel looked to be in their element.

Jim dismissed the other trooper with his thanks. Then he nodded to Tom, who sat in front of the girl.

"My name is Tom." His hands flowed through the signs as he spoke for the benefit of his hearing friends. "What's your name?"

The girl's hands moved in response.

"She says her name is Bronwen." Tom signed again. "How old are you, Bronwen?"

Bronwen responded.

"She's six and a half," Tom said.

Sally watched the interaction. Bronwen appeared comfortable with all the adults. Jim had told her about finding the backpack, so he knew this information already. But Sally understood the questions were intended to put the child at ease. She'd have done the same.

Jim took a notepad out of his pocket. "Ask her what she was doing in Ohiopyle."

Tom signed and watched as the girl answered. "She's here hiking with her mom. She's learning the names of trees and plants in Southwestern Pennsylvania at school, so her mom brought her here to see if they could find any."

"What about her father?"

Tom signed and watched Bronwen reply. "She said he's in heaven." He shot a look at Jim. "She's awfully casual about the fact, so I'm guessing he didn't die recently."

Sally dropped onto the ground near Pixel. "Does she know her mom's name?" She dreaded the answer.

Tom signed, and Bronwen answered. He glanced at Sally. "Glynis."

Sally brushed hair from Bronwen's face. She caught Jim's eye, and he gave a tiny shake of his head. She understood the silent message. Don't say anything. "Does she know where her mother is now?"

"What happened to your mom?" Tom again spoke as he signed. He watched the answer. "Back in the woods. She said Mom saw something during one of their stops and told her to go away and hide. Then the man came."

"Did the man see her?" Jim asked.

More signing. "She doesn't think so," Tom translated. "As far as I understand, Glynis made her leave before the guy showed up."

"Maybe she saw or heard the man approaching," Jim said. "Ask Bronwen if she saw anything."

Burns complied. "She says she hid behind a big tree like her mother told her. They argued, and that's when she saw the gun."

"He was holding it?"

Again, Tom signed, and Bronwen responded. "It was in his belt, like your friend. Bronwen must mean Ace."

A thought occurred to Sally. "If it was in his belt, how'd she know it was a gun?" She turned to Jim. "Aislyn's clearly scared her, or at least made her nervous. How would she know to be wary of a holstered weapon?"

"Good point." Jim nodded to Tom. "Ask her."

More signing. Tom brushed back his hair. "Her grandfather has one. He told her she must never touch any gun because they are very dangerous, and she could get hurt."

Jim nodded. "Then what?"

"She, Bronwen, got really scared because the man was yelling and waving his arms. She backtracked along the trail and stayed out of sight. She said she waited a long time."

"How long?" Sally asked.

Tom's hands moved, and Bronwen answered. "She doesn't know, not exactly." He paused. "She wants to know if her mom is okay."

Jim muttered an oath. "Not surprising. She isn't wearing a watch, and kids that young often have no concept of time. Not the way adults do." He rubbed his chin. "I don't want to lie to her, but I don't think the whole truth is the right thing to give her right now."

Sally thought. "Say her mother has to go to see a doctor. Jim's right. We need to find her family before we break the news that Glynis is dead."

"Well, a pathologist is an MD. Of a kind." Tom shifted his position.

She sucked in her breath. "Don't say that. Is that all?"

"If she could hear me, I wouldn't have. She doesn't have any hearing aids. I'm guessing her hearing loss is complete." He continued his silent conversation. "When her mother didn't appear, she went back. The man was gone, and her mom was on the ground. Bronwen shook her, but she didn't move. But she saw the blood on the victim's chest. That's when she took off. She says she lost her backpack along the trail. Eventually, she found you and Sally. She was scared of you as well, but you have nice dogs."

"I hope she learns that isn't always the case. You know, eventually." Sally glanced at the girl. "What about other family?"

Tom asked the question. "She has grandparents in Pittsburgh." He signed again. "Only name she gives is Grammie and PopPop. They live down the street, but she doesn't know their house or telephone number."

"Well, that isn't surprising. Not like she calls them, huh?" Sally glanced at Jim. "Can you get into Glynis's phone to get a number?"

"Not without a warrant, and it's locked. Besides, McAllister took it into evidence." Jim patted his pockets, presumably looking for a notepad, but had to settle for his phone. "Ask if she can describe the man."

Burns's hands were already in motion. "I know the basics of conducting an interview, you know." He watched as the girl responded. "She says he was tall, like you, but bigger. He didn't have any hair, and he had a picture of a bird on his arm."

"Bigger, like heavier?" Jim tapped the note.

Burns spread his hands. "I guess."

Jim frowned. "A man about six-three, let's say two-twenty-five, bald or shaven-headed, and with a tattoo of a bird. Don't suppose she knows what arm."

"Aw, hell, Duncan. Do you know your right from your left when you're under stress?" Burns waved him off. "Of course you do. What am I thinking? I think that's as good as we're going to get."

Jim slipped the phone back into his pocket. "I've had worse descriptions."

Sally backhanded his arm in a mock reprimand. "You're kidding, right? That's better than a lot of adult witnesses. Cut her some slack, she's a frightened child."

Jim held up his hands. "Calm down, Sally. She did great. I'm not saying she didn't."

Sally crossed her arms. "They why don't you look happy?"

"Because it's too easy. I don't like easy." He aimed a finger at her. "And neither do you."

Bronwen tugged on Tom's arm and signed some more.

The younger man smiled. "She says to tell you she likes your dogs very much. They are nice. What are their names?" Tom signed the answer.

Bronwen smiled and went back to petting her new friends. Rizzo put his head in her lap while Pixel flopped onto his side next to her.

Tom got up. "Is that all?"

Jim thought a moment. "Wait here. I'm gonna call Lieutenant Ferguson and find out how I should proceed." He pulled out his phone and walked off.

Sally eyed Tom. "Do you think it's too easy?"

He snorted. "Hell, yes. I have no doubt Duncan will find this bald-headed guy"—he snapped his fingers—"like that. I also think there's more to this. Admit it. So do you."

Sally watched Bronwen. She looked perfectly content, snuggled between Rizzo and Pixel. Unfortunately, Sally was sure the men were right.

Chapter Four

Duncan ended his call and went back to Sally and Burns. "Well, that sinks my plans for the night. Not that I expected anything else."

Sally blew out a breath. "Let me guess."

He held up a hand. "Ferguson said since I was here, it's my show to run."

"I'm not surprised. Isn't Cavendish on vacation, though?"

"Yes, but that doesn't matter. Either I get a temporary partner, or I'll work it alone." He looked at Burns. "Thanks for your help. With everything, not just the deceased."

He waved over his shoulder as he took off. "Anytime. Good luck."

Sally got to her feet. "I guess our dinner plans are off, huh?"

Duncan took her hand and kissed it. "Rain check. I'll get you and the boys home, change, and head into HQ. And we have to call Child Protective Services. Bronwen needs to go somewhere until I find out more about Glynis and her next of kin, including Grammie and PopPop."

"CPS? Are you sure?" Sally's expression fell. "There's got to be another solution."

Duncan gave her a knowing look. "There isn't, and you know it. We can't take charge of her, Sally. We aren't qualified. We don't know how to communicate with her."

"Not even for one night?"

Duncan knew how she felt. "I'm sorry. If we had the grandparents' name, I could find and call them, but I don't. Hopefully, CPS will find a nice family, and it'll be a short-lived stay." He wasn't all that happy himself. As much as Sally didn't want kids of her own, she was a sucker when it came to lost souls, and there wasn't one more lost than Bronwen.

* * *

Sally closed the back door. Jim hadn't stayed home long. Enough for a quick shower and a change into slacks, shirt, and sports jacket. He gave her a quick kiss. "I'll see you—"

"When I see you." She shooed him out.

Next, she filled the dog bowls and set them in the raised feeders. Rizzo and Pixel started gobbling before she stood up. "I can trust you two for a moment, right? I've got work to do."

The dogs ignored her.

Sally went to her home office, snapped on the light, and opened her laptop. She had no illusions that she'd find anything Jim couldn't. But her goal was a little different. The image of Bronwen's anguish when the CPS representative took her away was burned into Sally's memory. No way would she let that little girl stay with a stranger one minute longer than necessary. Sally couldn't make a notification, of course. But if she had the knowledge, she could make damn sure Jim moved heaven and hell to get Bronwen to the people who loved her.

As part of her law practice, Sally subscribed to a number of informational databases that held a gold mine of personal information. In no time at all, she had Glynis Lane's name, phone number, and address. Her marital status was listed as "married," but Sally quickly determined that Glynis was a widow. She didn't bother with that rabbit hole. Jim would take care of that.

Instead, she researched any family Glynis had. It didn't take long to locate her parents. Rhys and Catrin Beddoe were both still alive and currently lived in Philadelphia. Sally plugged the address into Google Maps. She whistled. "They live on the Main Line. Glynis comes from money." Yet Bronwen's clothes had not been designer. High quality, yes, but none of the high-end brands associated with outdoor activities.

But they couldn't be Grammie and PopPop. Not if they lived in Philly.

Sally printed out the information for Glynis's parents. She would behave herself and not dig any further into the dead woman's history. It was not her responsibility to notify Rhys and Catrin about what had happened to their daughter.

But if Jim didn't come home with news that Bronwen was on her way to her grandparents', Sally was prepared to take steps, whether it was her job or not.

* * *

Duncan unscrewed the cap on a bottle of sports drink as he waited for his computer to boot up. The headquarters at Troop B in Eighty Four, which was about an hour from Confluence, was never silent. But on a Sunday evening, it was as quiet as he'd ever heard it. While he waited, he stared at the desk normally occupied by his partner, Jenny Cavendish. He wondered how her ten-day cruise was progressing. She hadn't been hopeful. "Stuck on a boat with my parents, my sister and her husband, my brother and his partner, and five screaming kids under the age of ten? Shoot me now."

"I think you'll be glad to miss this one," he said to the empty room. He didn't have a good feeling about the murdered woman. True, he was starting with solid information. Bronwen, child or no, had provided a good description. He had the victim's name, unlike some of his previous cases. Except he knew that when the pedal hit the metal, even knowing that much meant squat. He also wondered who Ferguson would stick him with. Would he get a choice? Not likely.

Maybe she'd let him work solo.

Also not likely.

"Stop wasting time on things you can't control," he told himself. "Do the job."

He logged into the system and started the standard search for information on Glynis Lane. Shortly thereafter, he had a basic background. He'd have to get the Philly police to handle the death notification. On the one hand,

Duncan wouldn't have to do it, and since it was widely considered the most disliked duty in police work, he was relieved. On the other, he wouldn't get to talk to the parents, or observe them, first hand. He made a call and arranged for someone to visit the Beddoes and report back. There'd be more fingers in the investigation, which was not his preference. But it couldn't be helped.

Glynis was listed as married. What about her husband? Duncan ran a search on Tyler Lane. He'd died just over five years ago after only a little more than a year of marriage. He'd been a local artist. He never had a driver's license, only a state ID. According to the death certificate, he'd died of cancer at the age of thirty. His parents were still alive, living in Pittsburgh at an address not far from Glynis.

Grammie and PopPop. If only he'd known this earlier.

He glanced at the clock. Five thirty.

Duncan's stomach growled. He should have grabbed food on his way in. He tried to brush away the stab of guilt at ruining the plans for dinner in Ohiopyle. Sally would understand. It didn't make it better, but at least she wouldn't lay a guilt trip on him, unlike his first wife.

He filled out the forms necessary to get Glynis's bank information. A search of the Allegheny County property records showed her house in Point Breeze was current on the mortgage and property taxes. According to the DMV, she owned a 2014 Honda CR-V. The system showed no wants or warrants. No motive there that he could see. He filed for a search warrant, called the Pittsburgh Bureau of Police to ask them to send an officer to secure Glynis's house, and decided to stop for a quick look-see after he interviewed her in-laws.

He turned his attention to the items found on the body. She'd had gold earrings, her wedding ring, and a gold necklace with a heart-shaped charm on when she died. None of it had been damaged. Her wallet contained her license, three credit cards, and fifty dollars in cash. Whoever shot her hadn't been interested in theft.

He rubbed his chin. "Odd place for a shooting." It had been a sunny, warm Sunday afternoon. The chances of encountering witnesses on one of the popular hiking trails were high. Why had her killer confronted her in Ohiopyle?

Duncan opened his bottom drawer and took out a tie he kept for emergencies. Then he texted Sally. **Going to Pittsburgh. Will grab something on the road.**

Her response was a single emoji, a picture of a plate of pasta.

He got the message. She'd have dinner waiting for him so he wouldn't have to settle for crappy fast food. He grabbed the keys to an unmarked Ford. Now if only he could get lucky with Glynis's in-laws.

Chapter Five

Two hours later, Duncan parked in front of a graceful two-story house in Point Breeze. He took a moment to study the property. Tall with fresh paint. Wide front porch. The front yard was landscaped with greenery instead of grass. The windows on the second and third floors caught the last rays of the sun. An aged Mazda sedan was parked in front at the curb since the house, like many in the neighborhood, did not have a garage. Duncan got out of his car and straightened his jacket. He climbed the steps to a wide porch with a white two-seat swing and rang the bell.

An older woman, her gray hair cut short, answered. She left the storm door closed. "May I help you?"

Duncan held out his ID and identified himself. "Are you Eva Lane?"

"I am. I don't know what the state police want with me."

"May I come in? It's about your daughter-in-law."

Eva's hand flew to her mouth. "Glynis? Is she okay?"

"It's best if I come in."

She fumbled with the lock on the door and pushed it open. "Yes, of course. This way." The door opened into a living room. A couch covered in dark cloth took up one wall, and a matching recliner flanked it. The two pieces bracketed a low wooden table. The room was lit by a standing lamp in the corner, dark bronze with a cream-colored shade from which crystals dangled and caught the light. The brick fireplace was painted white and clearly only for decoration. A series of photographs lined the mantel, all of them featuring Bronwen. In some, she was alone; others showed her with

Glynis. A large painting of the Pittsburgh skyline at sunset filled the wall above the couch.

"Paul! Come here." Eva clasped her hands in front of her. "That's my husband. I have a feeling he should hear this."

"Yes, ma'am." Duncan's gaze swept the room. Lots of books. No TV. A few toys. Bronwen's?

A stocky man entered the room. He looked like a grandfather. Heavy around the middle, dark hair receding from his forehead. He peered over his glasses through brown eyes. "Who is this?"

She told him, and her voice trembled. "He said he's here about Glynis."

Paul took off his glasses. "Is she hurt? She was hiking with Bronwen down in Ohiopyle today. Did something happen to them?"

There was never an easy way to say it. Duncan took a breath. "Bronwen is fine. But I'm sorry to tell you that Glynis is dead."

Eva sank onto the couch. "Oh my God. What happened? Was it an accident?"

Paul sat next to her and put his arm around his wife.

Duncan shifted on his feet. "No. Glynis was shot this afternoon on one of the hiking trails in the state park."

Eva wailed. Paul pulled her close. "But you said Bronwen is okay. Is she hurt?"

"No, sir. Shaken up, but she wasn't injured." Duncan took his notepad and a pen out of his pocket.

"Where is she?" Paul hugged his wife, who cried on his shoulder.

"CPS took custody of her while we located family. Unfortunately, Bronwen was unable to give us your proper names or contact information, so we didn't have much choice. Especially on a weekend."

Eva cried harder.

"Shh, it'll be okay." Paul patted her shoulder. Facing Duncan, he said, "She's deaf. Bronwen. Is there any way we can take custody of her? Or do you have to wait until Glynis's will goes to probate? We're named as Bronwen's guardians."

"I don't think we have to wait for the lawyers." Duncan tried to give a reassuring smile. "I'm the one who found her, so I know about her deafness. I made sure CPS knew as well. Now that we've contacted you, we can make arrangements to get Bronwen home." He paused. "Although I understand Glynis's parents live in Philadelphia. They may try to assert their rights. You may want to hire a family law attorney."

Paul snorted. "No, they won't. They want nothing to do with Glynis. Or Bronwen. Haven't for years."

Is that so? Duncan flipped to a clean sheet in his notebook.

Eva recovered and wiped her eyes. "Where are my manners? Please, sit down, Officer Duncan. Is that what I should call you? Do you want coffee or water?" She pointed at the recliner.

Duncan perched on the chair, angling himself to face the couple. "Technically, it's Trooper, but really, it's not important. Don't put yourself out on my account."

Eva stood. "I want coffee. I might put a little something medicinal in it, too. Are you sure?"

"Coffee would be great. Black, please. Sadly, no extras since I'm on duty."

Her answering smile was weak, and she hurried from the room.

Paul took off his glasses. "Glynis is like our own daughter. Who killed her?"

"Details are a bit sketchy. Bronwen gave us a description of a man." Duncan repeated it. "Do you know anyone who looks like that? Maybe someone Glynis knew?"

Paul shook his head. "I'm drawing a blank. You said Bronwen told you?"

"Yes."

Eva came back with a tray holding three full mugs and a bottle of scotch. "You're sure you don't want anything in it?" she asked as she handed a mug to Duncan.

He took it. "This is fine." He looked around and placed the mug on the coffee table.

"Bronwen said there was a man with them." Paul repeated the description for his wife.

She frowned. "It doesn't sound like anyone I'm familiar with. Certainly not like anyone Glynis knew from the gallery." She clutched her coffee. "Did he see Bronwen? Is she in danger?"

"It's not certain, but we don't think so," Duncan said. "According to Bronwen, her mother told her to hide before this man arrived on the scene. It's possible the shooter never knew she was there."

The elderly couple held hands. "Possible, you said." Paul licked his lips. His voice held a note of worry.

Duncan understood. They were afraid the killer would come back for their granddaughter. "I won't lie to you. There's very little we're sure of at this point. But there's no evidence this man, or whoever shot Glynis, knows anything about Bronwen. We saw no evidence of a pursuit, and CPS has not contacted the police about any strangers hanging around. Please try not to worry too much."

"Whoever…you don't know it was him?" Eva asked as she clutched her cup.

Duncan shook his head. "As I said, we don't know much at this point."

The couple exchanged a look. Then Paul said, "Was she robbed or anything?"

Duncan consulted his notes. "It doesn't appear so." He listed the jewelry. "Did she wear anything else?"

Eva slowly moved her head from side to side. "No. The necklace was from Tyler. Our son. He gave it to her after they met. On the back are two dates. Their first date and their wedding day. That and her ring are eighteen karat gold. Not flashy, but not cheap either."

"Then we can probably rule out robbery." Duncan studied them. "Did Glynis have any enemies at work or in her personal life?"

"I don't think so." Paul took a drink. "Glynis was a wonderful person. I know, I know. You hear that all the time. She didn't have an enemy in the world." He flashed a rueful grin. "But someone shot her, so there was at least one person who didn't like her, right?" He swallowed. "I won't deny Glynis could be stubborn. And she never hesitated to speak her mind. Not about things at the gallery where she worked, not about politics, and certainly not about Bronwen."

"Yes, if she thought Bronwen needed something or wasn't getting what she deserved, she could be fierce," Eva added. "Oh, she did mention some annoying emails."

"From whom?" Duncan held his pen over the pad. "What did they say?"

"She didn't tell us." Eva sipped. "They were anonymous and from a generic address. Glynis wasn't too worried about it."

Maybe she should have been. "Was Glynis deaf or hearing impaired?" Duncan asked.

Paul shook his head. "Her hearing was perfect. But Tyler was. Bronwen's father. He was born deaf, just like her. It was part of the…disagreement between Glynis and her parents."

Eva's face reddened. "Call it what it was, Paul. They kicked her out. They didn't think Tyler was good enough for their precious princess. A girl from one of Philly's most prominent neighborhoods had no business marrying a poor, deaf artist from Point Breeze. Not in their opinion."

Duncan made a note to call first thing tomorrow and follow up personally with the Beddoes. "Clearly Glynis didn't share her parents' thoughts. Was she an artist?"

"She dabbled." Paul took another drink. "She's an associate director at The Glassworks. That's a small gallery here in Pittsburgh. But she was working at the Carnegie when she met Tyler."

"Did he work at the museum as well?"

"No, but he liked to visit and study the old masters. Glynis learned ASL specifically to talk to him. In my day, we'd say she caught his eye." Paul nudged his wife. "It was a whirlwind courtship, but they were good together. She became his art manager, too."

Eva tapped his knee. "Ned Tidwell was Tyler's manager."

Paul rolled his eyes. "Technically. But we both know Tyler didn't make a move without Glynis's approval. She couldn't get him out of the contract. I don't know why. But after he died, the first thing Glynis did was try to fire Ned. I don't understand it all, but while Ned represents Tyler's earlier work, including anything from before the marriage, Glynis has everything that wasn't already under contract when he died. And whatever money Tyler would have gotten from a sale goes to Glynis, of course."

"Are the paintings valuable?" Duncan studied the couple.

"Ned didn't think so, but Glynis disagreed. Not that they would sell for millions or anything like that, but she definitely thought Ned was low-balling the price." Paul looked at his wife, and she bobbed her head in agreement.

Duncan scanned his notes. "I don't want to be indelicate, but what happened to Tyler? Based on the records I found, he didn't live long after they married."

"You aren't being rude, Trooper." Eva sighed. "Tyler was already battling non-Hodgkin's lymphoma when he and Glynis wed. She knew what she was in for. Tyler seemed to be doing better, but then the cancer hit hard. He lived long enough to see Bronwen born. We"—she waved at Paul—"have been helping her ever since."

"She's an only child? Bronwen?"

Paul squeezed his wife's hand. "Yes. Tyler and Glynis, they wanted as many kids as possible before he passed. But Glynis had a very difficult pregnancy. She was bedridden on and off for her entire third trimester. After the birth, the doctor told her she'd find it hard, if not impossible, to have another child."

Duncan read over what he'd written so far. "Do you know if her parents disowned her?" He looked up.

Eva glanced at her husband. "I don't think they legally disinherited her, if that's what you mean. But the estrangement runs deep. I honestly don't know if she's talked to them since Bronwen was born. Glynis may have sent them one of Bronwen's school pictures when she was in kindergarten, but that's it." She sighed. "Fortunately, Glynis had a trust fund, from a grandparent or so she told us. She had money for the private school and whatever else Bronwen needed." Eva set down her nearly-empty cup.

Duncan didn't see a clear motive for the murder. Although it didn't sound like the victim was on great terms with Tyler's artistic manager. Something to follow up on. "Did Glynis have any siblings?"

Paul frowned. "A brother. I think he's younger. She doesn't talk to him either."

"One more thing, and there's no other way to ask." Duncan looked at Paul.

"Was Glynis seeing anyone?" Paul sighed. "Our son has been gone almost seven years, Trooper. Glynis is a young woman. We expected her to meet someone eventually. But if she did, she didn't tell us."

"I don't think we're being very helpful." Eva set down her cup. "I'm sorry."

"Don't be. This is very typical of an early investigation." Duncan gulped his now lukewarm coffee. Then he stood. "Here's my card. If you think of anything, please call me at either of the numbers, day or night."

Paul followed him to the door. "When can we get Bronwen? She's a brave little girl, but I imagine being with strangers right now is not pleasant for her."

"I'll call CPS in the morning and get the ball rolling. I'd love to tell you she'll be here tomorrow, but I'm sure there are things that have to be done. I'll do as much as I can to get her here as quickly as possible." Duncan shook hands and left.

As he pulled away from the curb, he mused over what Paul and Eva Lane had told him. He hadn't learned much. But at least Bronwen would be reunited with her grandparents. Sally would be happy about that, and he was, too. Right now, he'd take his wins where he could get them.

Chapter Six

Monday morning, Sally arrived at her office bright and early. She'd stayed up the previous night to wait for Jim. He'd arrived home late, exhausted, but bearing the good news that Bronwen's grandparents in Pittsburgh would be happy to take her "as soon as CPS gets their act together." As she waited for her coffee to brew, she riffled through her mental Rolodex, wondering if she knew anyone who could expedite the paperwork.

Her phone rang as she walked back to her desk. Caller ID showed Louise Castle's name. "Hi, Mom."

"Are we still on track to go dress shopping this afternoon?" Louise's brisk voice came over the line.

"Good morning to you, too. I'm good, thanks."

"Fine, good morning, pfft."

Sally rubbed her forehead.

"What about dress shopping?"

Sally put the call on speaker, laid her phone on her desk, and turned on her computer. "Yes, the plan is still to meet you at Raymond's at three-thirty so we can look at dresses."

Tanelsa Parson, Sally's partner, came into the room. She pointed at the phone and mouthed, "Mother?"

Sally nodded.

Tanelsa closed her eyes briefly, then headed for the coffee pot.

"What do you mean, the plan?" Louise snapped. "It's not definite?"

"It's an expression, Mom." Sally mentally counted to five. "Tanelsa and I will be there."

"Why are you bringing someone?"

"I may want a second opinion." Sally knew the kind of dress her mother favored. It was not likely to match Sally's tastes. After minimal arm-twisting, Tanelsa had agreed to play backup.

"You *will* have a second opinion." From the background noise, it sounded like Louise stepped outside. "Mine."

"You're the first opinion," Sally said. She chose her words deliberately, with the aim of soothing her mother's ego. "I don't count myself." Not true, but not something she was about to tell Louise.

"Oh." Her mother moved on, seemingly unable to respond to the statement. "Is *he* going to be there on Thursday for the cake tasting?"

"You mean Jim?" It annoyed Sally to no end that Louise often referred to Jim using pronouns, but it was too early for that fight. "His intention is to be there."

"What do you mean by that?"

"His job is unpredictable, Mom. You know that."

"Sarah." Another of Louise's irritating habits. She trotted out Sally's given name any time she wanted to give an admonition or sound motherly. All it did was make her sound condescending, but there was no telling her that. "Are you sure you want to go through with this? God knows I want to see you safely married, but there's still time to back out."

Tanelsa re-entered the office, raised her eyebrows, and headed for her desk.

Sally gripped her pen. "Why on earth would I want to break things off with Jim?"

"You just said it," Louise replied. "His job is unstable—"

"Unpredictable. Not unstable."

"Same thing."

Across the room, Tanelsa lifted her hands and lowered them. Sign language for *deep breath*.

Sally swallowed her retort. "It is not, and you know it. If anything, Jim has one of the most stable jobs out there. After all, it's not like crime will disappear in our lifetimes." She heard her mother start a reply and rushed on. "If he can be there for the tasting, he will. End of story."

Louise seemed to accept the finality in her youngest daughter's voice because she changed the subject. "Have you heard from your father?" Doubt laced the words.

"As a matter of fact, I have." Sally took great satisfaction in the fact Eric Castle had responded to her, but not his wife. "He said wild horses couldn't keep him from the wedding, and he will absolutely be there to give me away."

"Hmm." There was silence. Sally was sure her mother was searching for a scathing reply. Obviously, she failed because she said, "Then I'll see you this afternoon. Don't be late." She ended the call.

Sally lowered her forehead to the desk and groaned.

"You shouldn't give in to her so often," Tanelsa said. "Call this insanity off right now, make a date at the courthouse, and get it done. You know Jim and his folks won't care."

Sally had met Andrew and Grace twice, once the previous Thanksgiving and again a couple of months ago. She'd talked to Grace several times on the phone. No, her future in-laws would not mind. They were lovely people who wanted their son and his bride to be happy. Jim wouldn't care either. He wanted to be married, end of story. "I can't." She raised her head and looked at Tanelsa. "You think my mother is bad now? This is just a living nightmare. She'll be hell if I tell her we've opted for a quickie ceremony in front of a judge." Sally rested her chin in her hands. "I'll get it from my brother and sister, too. Especially Noreen. Because as soon as Mom hangs up with me, she'll be on the phone to Reen. They both will never forgive me. For different reasons. Mom for disappointing her and Reen for having to listen to Mom bitch."

"Your funeral." Tanelsa stirred her coffee. "I didn't know your dad was alive. You've never talked about him."

"He lives in Pittsburgh, but his job makes him travel a lot." Sally went back to her computer. "We email and text frequently. He knows it's easier on me if he keeps his distance."

"Then your folks are divorced?"

"Legally separated." The arrangement had puzzled Sally ever since she graduated from law school, but it wasn't her marriage. "Neither Mom nor Dad wants a divorce. Mom doesn't want to lose his money. As weird as it sounds, I think Dad still loves her. He couldn't live with her drama anymore, though. After I got my law degree, he moved out. He once told me if Mom regained her sanity, he'd come back. But he's not holding his breath."

Tanelsa tested her coffee. "But he'll be at the wedding?"

"You heard me. He wouldn't miss it. I know parents aren't supposed to have favorites, but Dad does, and it's me. If I was getting married on the moon, he'd book the next shuttle."

Tanelsa murmured something unintelligible.

Sally decided she didn't want to know what her partner had said. "Hey, do you know anyone with connections at CPS?"

"Not off the top of my head." Tanelsa opened her laptop and scrolled. "Why?"

Sally told her about finding Bronwen, her murdered mother, and the child's fate. "I don't want her languishing in the system a minute longer than she has to. She should be with her grandparents."

"Sally."

Tanelsa's stern tone made Sally look over.

The other woman pointed at her. "This has nothing to do with you or the firm. I get what you're saying, but for God's sake, let the system do its work. We have things to do this week. Where are you with the petition for the Clancy case?"

"I'm not getting involved. With Bronwen, that is." Sally went to the CPS website and looked for names she recognized.

"What else do you call what you're doing?"

"Making sure the wheels of justice don't grind to a halt."

"In other words, getting involved." Tanelsa leaned forward. "I understand your feelings. I share them, in fact. The kid should be with family. And she will be. Jim will see to that." She straightened. "Now. What about the petition?"

"It's written and in your inbox for proofing." Sally knew Tanelsa was right.

Bronwen didn't need her. Things would work out fine. Slowly, maybe, but fine.

She couldn't get the image of Bronwen's huge blue eyes out of her mind, though. Slowly wasn't good enough. Sally remembered a CPS contact from a case she'd handled when she worked for the Public Defender's office and picked up her phone.

Chapter Seven

Fueled by two cups of strong coffee, Duncan arrived at his desk early. The first thing he did was check the status of his requests from the previous night. Glynis's financial records weren't in. Neither was the information from her cell phone carrier. Not surprising. Since it had been Sunday night, he hadn't expected anything from the tech division. He also had a message from Trooper Ben Hartigan, who'd apparently performed the death notification for the Beddoes family and asked Duncan to contact him. He made a quick call to confirm the time of Glynis's autopsy, scheduled for that afternoon at three. He'd dialed the first three digits to return Hartigan's call when he noticed Lieutenant Ferguson striding toward him. Behind her was a fresh-faced younger man who looked like he'd graduated from high school last week.

"Duncan. Status report." Ferguson's staccato tone put a lot of people off. Duncan had learned it was her standard mode of operation. If the words came at you like gunfire, you were okay. If her sentences were long and involved, it meant trouble. He hadn't believed it until he saw her in action with a fellow trooper who'd failed to follow through on some field interviews.

He fervently hoped Ferguson never stopped being abrupt with him.

He opened his notebook. "Glynis Lane's autopsy is this afternoon, but right now the presumed cause of death is a gunshot wound to the chest, medium range."

"Single GSW?" Ferguson snapped out the question.

The face of the trooper behind her took on a wary expression.

"The deputy coroner observed at least two when he was on scene, but of course couldn't say much more." Duncan tried to condense his notes as he spoke. "No sign of robbery, no assault. Her daughter, who is deaf, did give us a description of a man who was allegedly with the victim. She was placed with CPS last night. I also spoke to the victim's in-laws. They couldn't give much on suspects or motives."

Ferguson frowned. "Are they taking the child?"

"Yes. I've already called CPS to get that process in motion. With luck, it won't take too long."

"Luck being the operative word. What else?" Ferguson continued to ignore the other man.

Duncan gave a subtle wait sign and continued. "I have a callback to a trooper near Philly, which is where the victim's parents live. He handled the notification. I plan to talk to the parents myself. Still waiting on financials and cell records. I'll get another warrant to search the victim's house more thoroughly this morning and head up to Pittsburgh. I only made a brief stop last night because I wanted to interview the in-laws, and it was getting late. Pittsburgh police are securing the house. I still need to call her employer." He flipped the notebook shut. "For now, that's all. Oh, and I'll circulate the description the girl gave us, see if anything comes of that."

"Good description?"

"Yes, but I don't know how much use it'll be in the short-term. Mr. and Mrs. Lane, the in-laws, didn't recognize it. On the surface, he looks to be our shooter, but I'm distrustful of easy answers."

Ferguson jerked her head. "This is Trooper Kevin Abara." She motioned the younger man forward. "He's new to the section."

Duncan held out a hand. "Pleased to meet you."

"Likewise," Abara said in a somewhat thin voice. His handshake was limp. He had a deer-in-the-headlights look about him, too. Hopefully, it was Ferguson who had overwhelmed him, not the job.

Oh God, please don't do this to me.

"With Cavendish on PTO, you'll work this case with Abara." Ferguson's words confirmed Duncan's worst fears. "Show him the ropes. Questions?"

"No, ma'am." Duncan knew she didn't want any. Her statement was a formality.

"Good. Carry on." She strode away.

Duncan gave his new partner a more thorough once-over. He was not short, but he had to look up at Duncan's face. His build was trim and solid. Not a bad-looking guy, and his off-the-rack suit was good quality. "Looks like we'll be together for a bit. Where are you from?"

"Erie. I've been on the job for five years. I want to expand my career, so when I saw the opening in Criminal Investigation down here, I applied. I thought it would look good on my resumé." Abara coughed and dropped his gaze. He recovered quickly. "Where should I sit?"

Duncan's opinion of him slipped a notch. Even if the statement was true, you shouldn't say it out loud to your new partner on day one. Judging by Abara's face, he knew it. Duncan decided to take the high road and let it pass without comment. Let Abara think his gaffe had gone unnoticed. "You heard Ferguson. My regular partner is on vacation, so you might as well use her desk. Don't go through the drawers, though. Especially the top left. That's where she keeps her emergency stash of power bars." Duncan watched him. He thought CIS would look good, huh? Investigative work was not like TV. Reality was a lot less glamorous. Duncan wondered if the guy would have the same opinion on Friday.

"What's our first move?" Abara asked. His dark eyes held an eager light.

"I want to go back to the victim's house. We'll need a new warrant. After I'm finished with the call to Hartigan, you can watch while I complete the affidavit so you can see how it's done. We'll get the signature on our way to Pittsburgh." Duncan knew a judge who wouldn't rake them over the coals but would still ask enough questions to give a good sense of the process. "While you wait, I want you to look up The Glassworks. That's the art gallery where the victim worked. Call and get a time we can meet. If the timing works, we'll run up to Pittsburgh, do the search, talk to the employer, and be back for the autopsy in Uniontown this afternoon."

Abara squinted. "Isn't that a lot of paperwork?" He sounded disappointed.

"It makes the world go round." There was no way this guy had spent five years on the job and not learned that lesson. "If you need help with anything, and I'm still on the phone, grab someone and they'll be happy to give you a hand."

Abara started the computer search, his expression still screaming doubt.

Duncan headed for a quiet conference room to make his call. Hopefully, he had covered his misgivings a little better than his partner.

* * *

Sally no longer had a number for Lena Zelinsky, but it didn't take long to sift through the agency's website and find it. As it was only eight-thirty, she hoped it was early enough to catch Lena before her day started.

Tanelsa shook her head. "Sally, it's none of your business."

"T, I found that girl. I can't stand back and let her languish in the system when she could be with family that loves her." Sally dialed the number. "Don't tell me you wouldn't do the same damn thing."

Tanelsa pressed her lips together and went back to work.

Sally's plan worked. "Fayette County CPS, Lena speaking."

"Lena, this is Sally Castle. We met a few years ago."

"The Dunbar case. Those two kids. I remember." Lena paused. "I heard through the grapevine you went private."

"I opened a criminal defense practice not long ago with another woman." Sally leaned back in her chair.

"Are you calling about a current client?"

"No, this is something different." Sally took a deep breath. "I'm looking for information on a girl named Bronwen Lane."

Lena turned serious. "Sally, you know I can't give information on an active case."

"I'm one of the people who found her at Ohiopyle. I want to make sure she's okay."

"Fine. Keep it quiet, okay?" The sound of keys clicking came over the line. "We've placed her with a good family."

"Did you know her grandparents were found and contacted? They want custody."

More tapping. "Yes, we have the report from the police. It's good, but it'll take time."

Of course it would. "But they're eager to get her home. I also understand they are her legal guardians."

"How do you know?" A note of suspicion rang clear in Lena's voice.

Jim would not appreciate Sally talking since it would almost certainly land him in hot water with the brass. "Can I just say I have an inside source and leave it at that?"

"Mmm. Unfortunately, the police didn't know that yesterday. Now there are forms to fill out, i's to dot, t's to cross." Lena paused. When she spoke again, her voice was softer. "We researched the mother because that was the name we had. I think someone is calling her parents this morning. If the other set of grandparents apply for custody, the case could get referred to family court. It might be messy. Family matters often are, even when the deceased parent's will is clear."

"I understand." How much to say? "I don't think the other grandparents will contest the situation."

"Inside source again?"

"Yes." Sally swiveled in her chair and faced Tanelsa, who seemed to be at work, but from the lack of movement, hung on every word she could hear. "I want Bronwen to be taken care of, that's all."

Lena sighed. "I appreciate your concern. But I can't ignore the rules. You *must* understand that, so why are you trying to circumvent them?"

"I do, and I'm not doing anything like that." Sally sat forward. "But I know how things are."

Lena bristled. "Meaning what?"

"That your office is backed up, understaffed, and overworked. Just like every other state agency there is." Sally lowered her voice. "I get it. I saw the same thing at the PD's office. Bronwen is an easy case to close. Or should be."

A rush of exhaled breath. "I won't deny that being able to place Bronwen with the grandparents who happen to be her legal guardians would be a help. I'd be able to work on kids who are in a much tighter place."

Tanelsa shot Sally a look. She gave her partner a thumbs-up. "I absolutely agree. Tell me. What can I do to help expedite things and get her home?"

Chapter Eight

Duncan wanted to conduct his phone call on speaker, so he set up in an empty office to call Trooper Hartigan. It took some time to connect with the Philadelphia-area officer. "I appreciate the assist." Duncan uncapped a pen. "What have you got?"

"Glad to help. I'll make sure you have everything you need for the file, but here are the basics." Hartigan took a breath. "The Beddoes family is nuts."

"Come again?"

"I've never seen people who were less reactive when I gave them the news about their daughter. If they didn't have a cast-iron alibi and no motive, I'd wonder if they were involved." He paused. "The mother twitched and shot a look of pure fear at her husband, but other than that, nada."

It was not what Duncan expected to hear. "What happened?"

"I went to the house and gave them the news. The mother fidgeted a little but kept her hands clasped in her lap. Aside from that one look, no significant reaction. The father said it was no more than they expected when their daughter went against their wishes. 'We told her nothing good would come of leaving us.'" Hartigan paused, and it sounded like he was flipping pages. "I asked what they meant. Beddoe said they'd advised Glynis not to move to Pittsburgh and definitely not to marry a penniless artist with cancer. That if she did so, they wanted nothing more to do with her."

Duncan scribbled notes. "When was that?"

"About seven years ago. They meant it, too. I asked if they'd been in contact with the victim."

"What'd they say?"

The sound of more page-turning. "The victim sent them a school picture of the kid, maybe a year or so ago. No phone calls, no texts, no FaceTime. Just a single picture." Hartigan huffed. "Can you imagine? My kids don't always do what I want, but I haven't cut them off. It's not like Glynis took up a life of crime or anything terrible. No, she had the audacity to marry for love. What century are we living in?"

"Money and status are still important to some people." Duncan reviewed his notes. "Then they knew their son-in-law was ill?"

"Oh yeah. Mr. Beddoe was quite clear. They didn't approve of…what was his name?"

"Tyler Lane."

"Right. They didn't like his background, the fact he was an unsuccessful artist, at least by their standard, or that he was likely to leave Glynis a young widow."

Duncan picked up the emphasis in Hartigan's words. "Then it wasn't that he was an artist, just that he didn't have money?"

"Definitely." Hartigan slurped something. "If Tyler had been the next Andy Warhol, I'm sure they'd have sung a different tune."

Money made almost any profession acceptable. "Did they disinherit her?"

"Beddoe refused to answer that question and told me it was none of my damn business."

It might not be Hartigan's, but it sure was Duncan's. "Did you ask about whether they wanted custody of Bronwen?"

"I did." A note of disgust crept into the other trooper's voice. "Beddoe said they have zero interest in taking the girl. Is she with CPS now?"

"Yes, but I also located her paternal grandparents. They live in Pittsburgh and are eager to have her. They said they're the legal guardians anyway."

"They won't get a fight from the Beddoes." Hartigan paused. "Maybe I shouldn't say this, but I think she'll be happier with her dad's parents. I've never met snootier people, and these aren't the first Main Line residents I've encountered."

If they were really that estranged from their daughter, it was hard to see how they'd be involved in her death. Especially half a state away. But stranger things had happened. "You said they have an alibi and no motive."

"Yes. They were at a fundraiser all Sunday afternoon for some local politician. There are about five hundred witnesses." Again, the sounds of paper rustling. "You'll confirm this, I'm sure, but Beddoe told me they aren't beneficiaries to any will the victim might have, and 'she doesn't have anything worth inheriting anyway.' I may be wrong, but my gut says you'll have to look elsewhere."

Based on what Hartigan had said thus far, Duncan wasn't surprised. He checked his notes. "You keep using 'they' but only quoting the father. Did the mother say anything?"

"Not a word." Hartigan paused. "At the time, I thought she was deferring to her husband. Now, I'm wondering. That look. It was definitely fear. What is she scared of?"

It was a good question. Duncan would have to figure out a way to talk to Mrs. Beddoe alone. "What about siblings?"

"That's where things get sticky. They have one other child, a son. Younger than his sister by three years." Hartigan made another sound of disgust. "I think he lives in the apartment over their garage. Pictures of him all over the house. I didn't get a chance to meet him, but he looks like a smarmy rich kid. Gareth. Want me to dig into him?"

"Not yet. But I'll be in touch if I need another assist." Duncan didn't like putting the work in another's hands, even though Hartigan sounded competent enough. But Duncan couldn't fly back and forth to Philly to conduct interviews.

"I'll send over my reports for your files." Hartigan hung up.

Duncan sat back. He'd seen enough situations where parents turned their backs on their children that the Beddoes' attitude didn't shock him. He was a little surprised they had no interest in Bronwen. He reviewed his notes and circled Gareth's name. Just how much money did he stand to inherit now that his sister was gone?

* * *

Duncan returned to his desk and saw Abara scrolling through an app on his phone. "All right, let's head over to the judge and get that affidavit signed. Did you make those phone calls?"

Abara didn't look up. "Don't worry about it. I called the Pittsburgh Bureau of Police. They're going to handle it and call us with the results."

"You did what? When?"

"I just got off the phone."

"Shit." Duncan snatched the phone and punched some numbers. "Hi, this is Jim Duncan with the PSP. You got a request about a search and some interviews? Yeah. There were some crossed lines. We'll do it. You've still got an officer to this address, right?" He read off Glynis's house number and street. "Perfect. Keep it locked down until we get there. Thanks. No need to send anyone to the gallery, either. Sorry for the mix-up. At least I caught you in time. Right. Bye." He hung up and dropped into his chair.

Abara set down his phone. Faint lines of annoyance creased his forehead. "What did you do that for?"

Duncan took a deep breath. *Remember, the guy is young and green.* "When possible, you do your own searches and interviews. You need to file for your own search warrants, always. Same as when you were on patrol. You need to be able to defend your actions in court."

"I never had to apply for search warrants. I helped execute them, but I didn't write them."

That was going to change. "You will now. The more people you bring in, the more fingers in the pie, the more paperwork. Plus, doing an interview yourself gives you the opportunity to observe a witness first-hand and see things others might miss. This is our investigation. We need to control the pace, what happens, and keep things as clean as possible."

"But Pittsburgh is at least an hour's drive from here. Isn't it more efficient to get help from PBP in the city? That way, we can move on to other things."

"It's not about efficiency." How could Duncan explain it without sounding like a lecture? "You're right, saying we don't want to waste time. But it's important to be on the scene. As long as you don't have to buy a plane ticket, you do your own work. As you become involved in more investigations, you'll see."

If anything, the explanation made Abara more irritated. At least, judging by the way the lines on his face deepened. "If you insist. I still think it's not the best method, but I guess you're the lead. What should I do?"

Duncan slapped down the affidavit form. "What I told you to do fifteen minutes ago. Call the gallery. Then read this over so you have an idea of what we're looking for. Remember, you have to be specific but in a way that'll let us look into every nook and cranny. Listing small things like checkbooks or jewelry means we can open drawers. If all you say is you're looking for an elephant, you can't look in a desk drawer."

Abara scoffed. "Nobody writes checks these days."

"But they exist, so we'll look for them. Call Glynis's workplace. After you've done that, read, and let me know when you're ready to go." Duncan watched as the younger trooper rolled his eyes, picked up the affidavit, and scanned it. He squashed down a wave of irritation. Had he been this way as a newbie? He didn't think so.

Duncan checked a calendar. Cavendish wasn't due back for another seven days. As he watched the other man, he feared he'd be counting to ten a lot until she returned.

Chapter Nine

It turned out there wasn't a magic button Sally could press to make Lena skip all the formalities of releasing Bronwen to her grandparents. However, the CPS caseworker did say she'd do everything she could to expedite the process. Privately, Sally decided to advise the Lanes to get a lawyer familiar with family law, just in case. But she couldn't randomly call them. She'd have to wait for the right opportunity.

She did have to drive to Pittsburgh to meet with a member of the Allegheny County District Attorney's Office about a client who'd been arrested in Fayette County. The man claimed he had information about a string of robberies in Pittsburgh, the latest of which had resulted in the death of the homeowner. Naturally, he wanted a deal. At least it was a nice day for a drive.

On the way, Louise called. Sally knew why. Her mother wanted to talk about yet another wedding detail. The day was warm and sunny, and Sally didn't want to bicker and ruin her hopeful mood. She sent the call to voicemail. She'd pay for it later, but that was later. Right now, she had more important things to focus on.

Once she'd concluded her business with the Allegheny County ADA, she checked her phone. No messages, and it was only eleven-thirty. The memory of Bronwen and her frightened demeanor on the trail tugged at Sally's heartstrings. There was no way she could be this close to the grandparents and not check in to see how their custody application was progressing. After all, she'd found the girl. Any normal human being would want to find out how Bronwen was doing.

Sally navigated the streets of Point Breeze until she reached the Lane address. Typical of Pittsburgh, she parked on the street. The houses were tall and jostled together. The front yards were small. Most did not have garages or driveways. On the surface, it didn't look like the best neighborhood for children. She admonished herself. "You have no idea what the backyard looks like or how many other kids live here." The houses were not opulent, but they weren't dumps either. She knew Frick Park wasn't far away. Based on the property records she'd researched, the Lanes had raised their son here. For all she knew, half the homes on the street had children Bronwen's age.

She climbed the porch steps and pushed the shiny brass button next to a new-looking storm door. After a moment, the door behind it, made of an attractive dark wood with inset panes of leaded glass, opened. "Good morning. Are you Mrs. Eva Lane? My name is Sally Castle."

The older woman, her gray hair in a pixie cut, smiled. "Yes. Please come inside." She pushed open the storm door.

"Don't you want to know who I am? See some ID?"

The woman blinked. "You must be a woman from Child Protective Services to talk about Bronwen. Aren't you?"

"No. I'm one of the people who found Bronwen yesterday. Down at Ohiopyle." Sally gave her most reassuring smile. "I understand she's not in your care yet, but I was in Pittsburgh on business and thought I would stop by. Check up on how things are going."

"I see. If that's the case, *do* you have ID?" Eva asked.

Sally held out her court credentials and driver's license.

Eva stepped back. "Good enough. Come in."

Sally entered a living room filled with comfortable furniture covered in a dark blue fabric. She surreptitiously brushed her hand over the back of a chair. It was soft, yet felt durable. Much like the upholstery her sister, who had three children around Bronwen's age, had chosen. A large area rug covered the shiny wood floor. A large painting hung above the couch. Like the outside, the room was cozy and welcoming. It was a place to spend time and talk. She didn't see any toys, but maybe they were in another room.

"Please, sit anywhere." The woman raised her voice. "Paul, is the coffee ready?"

A man, presumably Eva's husband, entered with a tray. "Got it right here." He set it on the coffee table. Then he held out his hand. "Paul Lane. Glad to meet you." He wore a button-down shirt, slacks, and shoes.

"This is the lady who found Bronnie yesterday." His wife fluttered her hands. "Would you like some coffee? Cream, sugar? Or maybe you prefer something else?"

Sally took in the woman's neat dress, which was not evening wear, but definitely appropriate for church. She didn't think it was a garment a woman would wear around the house. She realized they'd dressed up for the visit with CPS and that part of their solicitous behavior was meant to cover their anxiety. "Thank you so much. Coffee would be lovely. Just a little cream is fine." She sat in the recliner. "How is Bronwen? Have you seen her?"

"The caseworker, Ms. Zelinsky, arranged a video call for us this morning." Eva took the seat in the sofa corner nearest the chair. "She seems okay. But anxious to come home, of course."

Paul handed Sally a cup. "You must be the lady with the dogs. Bronnie told us about you."

"That's me. And my fiancé." Sally accepted the drink.

Understanding flooded their faces. "Then we owe you our thanks," Paul said. "I don't want to think about what might have happened to Bronnie if you hadn't found her."

"How did you find us?" Eva asked.

"I'm friends with Ms. Zelinsky. She gave me your name and address." Sally hesitated. "Have you gotten any updates?" Sally took a sip. The taste of the coffee was warm and rich.

"They're working on it," Eva said. "That woman, Ms. Zelinsky? She talked to us at length earlier. She emailed a form we need to fill out and said since Bronwen had to be released from CPS to our custody, there were some things to do. Bureaucracy at its finest." She shot a look at her husband.

"I don't understand why it's so complicated," he said. "Glynis's will is quite clear. We're Bronnie's guardians. End of story."

Sally set her coffee down. "I was only with Bronwen for a couple of hours, but she seems like a sweet kid. I mean, I couldn't talk to her. I don't know sign language. But she was so scared. I guess she made an impression on me."

"Do you have children, Ms. Castle?" Eva asked.

"No. I'm engaged now, and I've never been married." Sally chuckled. "Call me old-fashioned, but I think finding the right man should come before the having kids part."

Paul laughed. "I'm right there with you."

Sally chose her words carefully. "I mentioned I'm a lawyer. I might be able to help you. Give you names of family law experts, things like that. Should you need it." Sally folded her hands. "I can't make promises, you understand. But if the road gets bumpy, I'd like to help if I can."

Eva leaned forward. "Do you think we'll need a lawyer?"

"I hope not, but I'm also a big believer in being prepared."

"Prepared for what?" Paul asked.

For the system to royally mess things up. But Sally didn't want to alarm them, so she said, "For anything that might happen."

Eva brushed her lap. "We appreciate it. We don't understand why they won't just give her to us."

"I wish Jim, that's my fiancé, or I had known about you yesterday. We would have called you directly and skipped all the fuss."

"You don't mean Jim Duncan, do you? He's the trooper who came last night to talk with us. He said he's one of the ones who found Bronnie. I don't suppose he can do anything." Paul squeezed his wife's hand.

Jim would kill Sally if she even hinted at such a possibility. Time to change the subject. Her impression of the Lanes was a couple who loved their granddaughter. That helped her turn the conversation where she wanted it to go. "I understand your son, Bronwen's dad, died when she was a baby. Tell me about him."

"Tyler was our only child." Eva's posture relaxed. "We wanted more, but it didn't happen. He was born deaf, like Bronwen. I suppose it might have been for the best we didn't have other kids. We were able to focus on his needs."

"It was a lot harder for him than Bronnie. We couldn't afford the special school." Paul added to the story. "He did well, though. He had a lot of friends. When he met Glynis, we knew it was love at first sight. That was okay with us. She's a great girl." He swallowed. "Was, I guess I should say. She learned ASL and was right by his side for everything. Even when her folks were, well, less than enthusiastic about the match."

"They didn't think he was good enough for her." Eva didn't quite keep the scorn from her voice. "He was an artist from a working-class family, you see. Not old money. Ty and Glynis loved each other. That's all that mattered."

Sally's gaze was drawn to the painting. Although slightly Impressionist in style, she recognized the Pittsburgh skyline as seen from Mount Washington. The sky was filled with brilliant color. "Is that one of his paintings on your wall?"

"Yes. Isn't it beautiful?" Eva puffed with pride. "Ty wanted to do pictures people could recognize, not that modern stuff. But he put a twist on it. His teachers said he had a great eye for color."

"It's striking." It was something Sally would gladly hang in her own living room. "Did he ever sell any of his work?"

The Lanes exchanged a dark look. Paul answered. "He tried. He had an agent, a man named Ned Tidwell. We told this to Trooper Duncan last night."

As Sally listened to Paul talk, Tidwell sounded worse and worse. She knew Jim would feel the same way.

"Ned was forever making excuses about why Ty's work didn't fetch more money," Eva added after her husband finished. "It wasn't the style people wanted, or the subject matter, or the color palette was too strong. Glynis thought he was full of shit, pardon my language."

"Was she also an artist?" Sally asked.

"No. She did have a degree in visual art, but she worked in a gallery. First at the Carnegie as an assistant and later at The Glassworks, in a slightly bigger role. She hosted more than one show for Ty, as a matter of fact. His pictures were always popular, or so she said."

"Did she ever discuss it with the agent?"

Doubt crept over Eva's face. "We think so. She didn't talk about it much."

Sally's memory went back to the man Bronwen said she saw. "What does Tidwell look like?"

"I know what you're thinking, Ms. Castle," Paul said. "Trooper Duncan said he got a description of a bald man with a tattoo from Bronwen. That's not Tidwell. He's on the short side, long hair, and skinny. He's not the guy from the park. I doubt Bronnie ever would have seen Tidwell. Glynis wouldn't have invited him to the house to discuss business."

Sally pursed her lips. "Who gets the money from the paintings, now that Glynis is dead?"

"We hope it's Bronnie, but frankly, we don't know for sure."

Eva tilted her head. "What does this have to do with us getting custody of her?"

Sally shook herself. "Nothing. I'm sorry. It's an occupational hazard. I can't stop asking questions." She intended to find out more about Ned Tidwell. "You've been helping Glynis since your son died?"

"Yes." Eva seemed to accept Sally's glib explanation without pause.

"We've watched Bronnie, we've taken her to school, to activities, gone to her art shows. She takes after her father." Paul's pride was as obvious as his wife's. "Glynis always worked, and she has her own money, so that was never a problem. But we made sure she never had to worry about childcare."

"Would you like to see the rest of the house? The yard, maybe?" Eva asked.

"Of course." Sally stood.

The Lanes showed her Bronwen's room, a confection of pink that was fit for a princess. The neat backyard was filled with new play equipment, all of it surrounded by rubber chips that would be found on any playground. There was a room full of educational toys and videos. "Thanks to closed captioning, she can watch all the princess movies," Eva said. While the cookie jar was full, the fridge held plenty of fruit and veggies. "I make dinner every night. No fast food in this house."

An hour later, Sally was convinced Bronwen would be well taken care of by her grandparents. "As I said, this should be straightforward and you shouldn't have any problems once all the bureaucratic baloney is satisfied," she told the Lanes as she prepared to leave. "Just in case, here's my card. If things stall and you believe you need legal help giving the system a push, call me. I'll do what I can to find someone local you can trust."

Both of them clasped Sally's hand in turn. "We're so thankful, Ms. Castle," Eva said. "For your visit and for taking care of her."

"My pleasure." She shouldered her purse. "You said Glynis worked at The Glassworks?"

"Yes." Paul's forehead wrinkled. "Why? Is that important?"

"Oh, not really. But if the gallery has more of your son's art, I'd love to see it." Sally waved and left. It wasn't a lie. She wanted to see more of Tyler Lane's work.

She also wanted to find out more about Ned Tidwell.

Chapter Ten

Duncan parked in front of Glynis's house on Gettysburg Street in Point Breeze. In the light of day, he could take better stock of the property. It was located a block from her in-laws, which certainly made traveling between the houses easy. All of the homes on the street were much the same. Tall, close together, with small front yards and porches. To him, it was claustrophobic, but he understood the appeal of being close to family. He could see where Glynis's needed a little paint work, especially on the trim, but she'd done her best as a single mother. The yard needed to be cut, but wasn't completely overgrown. Flower boxes full of multi-colored blooms hung from the porch railing. One overgrown flowering shrub fronted the house. A child's bike was tucked inside the porch wall.

He approached the Pittsburgh officer standing guard at the front door. "Morning. Any visitors?"

The officer signed Duncan and Abara into the scene and handed them paper booties. "The in-laws came by earlier. Wanted to get the kid's clothes. I explained this is still an active scene. As soon as you released it, which should be soon, they'd be able to get the girl's things." The officer's gaze was stern. "I hope I didn't mislead them. They are going to get their granddaughter, right?"

Duncan tugged on a pair of nitrile gloves. "Depends on what you're talking about. I expect I'll be hearing from CPS shortly, and they'll be able to get inside today. As for custody, well, I'm with you. It should work out that way, at least based on what I know at the moment. You and I both know it doesn't always go the way we think is the most logical, but maybe we'll all be happy with the outcome this time." He beckoned to Abara, who'd put on his own booties and gloves, and they went inside.

"How do you want to do this?" Abara asked.

"You go upstairs. I'll take the first floor. I already took her computer and a few other big things." Duncan cast his gaze around the living room. "Now that we know about this art manager, the victim must have files or correspondence." He was tempted to make a snarky comment about a possible checkbook, but bit his tongue.

"Especially if they weren't on good terms. Didn't you say the autopsy is at three?"

"Yes, and I want to stop at the gallery, so get going."

"Got it." Abara climbed the stairs.

The first-floor spaces were obviously lived in. Neat, but not immaculate. Duncan sifted through magazines and old newspapers. He moved aside a pile of children's books, including several titles he'd purchased for his niece and nephew. Most of the toys were educational in nature and were far outnumbered by the books. Bronwen was a reader.

Photographs were everywhere. Many of Bronwen at various ages. Several showed her as a baby with a man who had sandy hair, blue eyes, and a welcoming smile. The same man appeared in a black and white photo in a silver frame. He wore a suit. Glynis wore a simple, long white gown and glowed with happiness. They stood under a trellis twined with ivy, hands clasped, and gazed into each other's eyes. A wedding photo. The man must be Tyler Lane. Duncan picked it up and studied it. Lane did not wear hearing aids. Duncan could see the same bone structure in his face as in Bronwen's. Lane appeared a little on the thin side, maybe a result of the treatment for his cancer. But his love for his wife and child was obvious.

The eat-in kitchen had the same level of clutter as the living room. Not dirty, but not magazine shoot-ready either. The whole house was a place where people lived, not a showroom. Most of the food was healthy, but there was a box of sugary cereal in the cabinet and one of snack-sized bags of chips under the island. The fridge was full of fruit, but also contained some chocolate pudding snacks.

A small secretary's desk in an alcove drew his attention, and he quickly determined this was Glynis's workspace. The cubbies held bills, paid ones on the right, unpaid on the left. An empty space showed where the laptop he'd taken the previous night usually sat. The white tower of the router occupied the top, and a small table next to the desk supported a wireless laser printer. Unopened mail was stacked on one side of the desktop. Duncan thumbed through it. A phone bill, mailer advertising a local restaurant, and an oversized postcard offering lawn services. "What's this?" The business-sized envelope had the address of the Tidwell Arts Management agency stamped in the upper corner. Duncan slit it open. Inside was a check for forty-three dollars and sixty-nine cents. The memo line indicated it was from a sale of one of Tyler's paintings. "Either he's taking a huge commission, or the painting didn't sell for much." He dropped the envelope in an evidence bag and remembered what the Lanes had said. Glynis had not been happy with Tidwell. Was this why?

Abara appeared in the doorway. "What are you mumbling about?"

"Check from the art agent." Duncan held it up. "Are you done already?"

"Not quite. I thought you said the in-laws told you Glynis wasn't dating."

"They said not as far as they knew." Duncan's senses sharpened. "Find something?"

Abara waved. "In the bathroom. Come on."

The two men climbed the stairs. Abara jerked his thumb toward the modest room. "Tight quarters, but take a look."

The space was just big enough for the toilet, a sink set in a repurposed table, and a tub with a shower curtain. A medicine cabinet hung over the commode. Most of the items were either generic medicines and vitamins, child's soaps, or women's toiletries. No birth control. But on the top shelf was a man's razor, a can of shaving cream, and a natural deodorant with a masculine scent. "Somebody stayed here often enough to have his own personal items." Duncan picked up the deodorant. Used, and not only once.

"Who was he?" Abara leaned on the doorjamb.

"That's the million-dollar question." Duncan replaced the stick. "You find anything in the bedrooms?"

"Negative. Well, not that would belong to a man, if that's what you mean." Abara consulted his notes. "The girl's room looks like it was painted with Pepto. So much pink. Kid's clothes, jewelry, lots of books. Some art supplies. Nothing of note in the victim's room. Clothes, some costume jewelry. Not cheap, but nothing of high value. One painting, one photo of the couple on Mount Washington. Or I think that's where they are. Take a look if you want to."

Duncan went into the main bedroom. A queen bed took up most of the space. Above it was a painting of Fallingwater. Duncan easily recognized the Southwestern Pennsylvania landmark, even though the style was not what he was used to. The lines were soft, like they'd been fuzzed out. The colors weren't, though. The iconic house had been captured at the peak of leaf season, and the brilliant reds, oranges, and golds gave power to the image. He was not really an art critic, but there was a compelling aura to the work. Lane's signature in the bottom right corner confirmed the authorship. It was something Sally would love.

The photo was across the room, above the dresser. Abara was correct. Glynis and her husband, this time in formal wear, stood on the vantage point at the top of the Duquesne Incline. It was late evening, and the lights of the city skyline glittered behind them. The picture filled Duncan with peace, but also sadness. Lane's face seemed drawn, his cheeks a little hollow. "They look very happy. I wonder when it was taken."

"It's not dated." Abara didn't appear as affected. "She doesn't look pregnant, but not like she just gave birth, either. My guess is before they got hitched. She's wearing a diamond, but neither of them have a wedding band. He's not well, you can tell that. Why a woman would marry a man knowing he's gonna kick the bucket is beyond me."

"Hey. Have a little respect." Duncan knew he shouldn't snap, but he couldn't help it. Rationally, a cop couldn't make every case personal. He'd lose his sanity. But something about this couple demanded a little more sensitivity. Maybe it was because he knew their daughter.

Abara held up his hands. "Sorry. It's a valid question."

"Yeah, but you could ask it better." Duncan turned and headed down the stairs. To be thorough, he went into the basement, which was filled with Lane's art supplies. Everything had a thick coat of dust. He wondered if Glynis couldn't bear to come down here since her husband's death. He returned to the living room.

Abara waited. "Are we done here?"

"I think so." Duncan surveyed the room once again. "Let's make a quick stop at the gallery and head for Uniontown. I don't want to miss the autopsy."

"You're the boss." Abara paused at the door. "Did you find a checkbook?"

"No. Bank statements and bills, no checks."

Abara pushed outside, a smug grin on his face. "Told you so."

Chapter Eleven

Sally pulled into a parking spot and stared at the front door of the art gallery. Suddenly, she wasn't sure this was a good idea. Jim would definitely follow up here, and she'd complicated more than one investigation for him. Perhaps it would be better to take her win from the visit with the Lanes and go home.

Except she really wanted to see Tyler's paintings.

She wandered inside the cool, quiet gallery space, pausing at the empty desk in the foyer. Several larger rooms opened off to the sides. *That must be where they hang the paintings.* She wandered through the room to the right, but while there were several exquisite works on display, none of them matched the style of the painting she'd seen at the Lane house.

Undeterred, she wandered over to the second room, where she hit pay dirt. The far wall was devoted to Tyler, right down to a small sign with his name and dates of birth and death. The paintings ranged in size from approximately twelve inches by twenty-four to as big as three feet by five feet. All of the subjects were identifiable as Pittsburgh or at least Southwestern Pennsylvania. He'd painted his subjects in all seasons. Every picture had been done in the Impressionist style, but with bold colors she was unused to seeing in the softer brush strokes.

Each painting had a small sticker affixed to the frame with the sale price. They ranged from eight hundred for the smaller works to five thousand for the biggest canvas. Sally knew nothing about how to price art, but it seemed high for an unknown artist.

A soft voice spoke at her shoulder. "Can I help you?"

Sally turned to see a mousy-looking young woman with light brown hair pulled back into a low ponytail. The lack of makeup, and the fact she wore a loose peasant-style blouse over slightly faded jeans, gave her the appearance of a person just out of college. "I was looking at the paintings." Sally waved a hand at the wall. "Perhaps you can help me. These seem awfully expensive. Why is that?"

"A couple of reasons." The young woman took out a soft cloth and wiped a frame. "The first is that they are done in oils. That immediately makes them cost more than a similarly-sized work in pastels, ink drawings, or even watercolors because the medium is more expensive. The size of the painting also plays a role. This one"—she pointed at the biggest frame—"is simply huge." She took a deep breath. "The biggest factor is that Tyler Lane is dead. You saw the plaque, I'm sure."

"I did."

"What you see is all there will ever be from him." The woman tried for a smile but didn't quite make it. "If it's popular, art can be more expensive after the maker's death." The cordless phone in her hand rang. "Excuse me a second." She walked away without giving her name.

Sally would ask when the woman returned. For the time being, she focused on the price stickers. If Glynis didn't think the royalties were big enough, just how much was Ned Tidwell taking?

* * *

As soon as Duncan pulled into the parking lot for The Glassworks, he recognized the deep red Toyota electric SUV near the door. What the hell was Sally doing here? She might be art shopping, but he doubted that. He knew she'd felt deeply for the little deaf girl. Which meant Sally was here to poke around the edges of the investigation into Glynis's murder.

Abara circled the SUV and whistled. "Sweet ride. A lot of those electric cars look weird, but this one's cool."

How was he going to explain Sally's presence to Abara? "Come on. You're the one who didn't want to waste time." Duncan entered the gallery.

Inside, he paused at the small, empty desk near the door. A plastic display full of pamphlets stood on the counter, which also held an empty cordless phone cradle. He swept his gaze around the gallery and saw that paintings of all sizes and styles covered the walls. The right-hand showroom was full of what looked like more modern pieces, abstracts, and similar works. He spotted a lone woman in the corner of the other room. There she was. "Go find the owner or someone in charge," he told Abara. Then he strode over to Sally.

She jumped when he touched her shoulder, and she nearly dropped the pamphlet she held. "God, you scared me."

"Why are you here?" He crossed his arms over his chest.

She waved at the paintings, all of which stylistically resembled the one from the Lanes' home. "Browsing for art. Do you like it?"

He wasn't fooled. "You just *happen* to be looking at art by the murdered woman's dead husband, which just *happens* to be displayed where she worked. You seriously want me to believe this is a coincidence?"

She widened those green eyes. "Hey, they come along. Sometimes."

He raised an eyebrow.

She wilted a bit. "Fine. I went to visit the Lanes." She told him about her conversation with the CPS caseworker and her talk with Bronwen's grandparents. "You know how slowly the bureaucracy works. I thought I could be a resource if they need help."

"You don't practice family law."

"But I'm familiar with the concepts, and I'm sure I could make a reference." Sally lifted her chin.

"Let's say I buy it. What does talking to the Lane couple have to do with you being here?"

"They had a painting, and I wanted to see more of Tyler's work." At his expression, she added, "I'm not lying about that. He was very talented. Did you see this one here?" She dragged him over. A landscape that had to be three feet high by five feet long hung on the wall. Cucumber Falls. Again, the lines were blurred, almost like those pastels Tish had made him go see at a show at the Carnegie years ago. But these colors were stunning. Tyler had definitely captured the energy of the water and the serenity of the foliage.

"Gorgeous," he said, keeping his voice flat.

Sally slapped his shoulder. "Don't be that way. Okay, fine." She let go of his arm. "Has the name Ned Tidwell come up yet in your investigation?"

"He has. Tyler's art agent, or former agent, I'm not too clear. That's part of the reason we're here."

"Then you know Glynis didn't like him." Sally glanced around and lowered her voice. "What if the feeling was mutual?"

He pinched the bridge of his nose. "Sally, I appreciate the fact you are invested in that girl's situation. But you can't go mucking around in an open investigation. You know this."

"I'm not mucking around. I'm—"

"Use whatever word you want. You shouldn't be doing it." He dropped his voice. "This time, you're gonna get me in trouble."

Abara came over. "Who is this?"

Sally extended her hand and gave her name. "I'm Jim's fiancée."

"Kevin Abara." He gave her the once-over. "Duncan, you didn't tell me you were engaged. Too bad. Otherwise, I'd ask you out for a drink, Ms. Castle."

Duncan clenched a fist. *New or not, I'm gonna deck him.* First, the guy said he was using CIS as a career move, and then he made a comment like that? It took the word *clueless* to an entirely new level.

Next to him, Sally must have sensed his tension because she tucked her arm through his.

He grappled with his irritation and shoved it aside. "Sally, Trooper Abara is new. He is my *temporary partner.* This is his first assignment." He hoped Sally would correctly interpret the meaning behind the stressed words.

From the slight widening of her eyes, she did. "Oh. Pleased to meet you. Always good to meet Jim's coworkers."

"Funny you being here when we are." Abara tilted his head. "Anything to do with the girl you two saved on Sunday?"

"Oh, no." Sally squeezed Jim's arm. "I'm here on a decorating mission. Jim's been on his own for too many years. The house needs a woman's touch, if you know what I mean. I saw a feature about this local artist, Tyler Lane, in a magazine. I loved his work, and the article said some was on display here."

"Then you didn't know Tyler Lane was the victim's husband and the deaf girl's father?"

"Is he?" To anyone who didn't know her, Sally's disbelief sounded genuine. "Jim doesn't bring his work home. I don't either, to tell you the truth. I'm a defense attorney. We figure we get enough crime from nine to five, so there's no reason to make it part of the home life."

Abara must have bought the act because he relaxed. "Sorry if I sounded suspicious. Being a cop, you get kind of jaded. I thought you were butting in. A murder investigation is no place for a civilian."

"I completely understand. I'm the same. Jaded, I mean. Hazard of the job, right? But don't worry. I would never dream of messing around in Jim's work." She squeezed Duncan's arm again.

He cleared his throat. "Whatever you like is fine with me. We'll talk about options tonight. Abara, did you find the owner?"

"Yeah, she's waiting in the main office." Abara nodded toward the corner. "Good meeting you, Ms. Castle." He sauntered away.

"You, too." She stood on her tiptoes to give Duncan a kiss. "Seems like he bought it. But if you think I'm leaving without doing my own interview, you don't know me very well." She raised her voice. "You don't care if I get a painting?"

He sighed. "Whatever you like, dear."

Chapter Twelve

Abara was already seated when Duncan reached the office. "Sorry. Giving my fiancée a budget." He shook hands with the handsome woman in her early forties on the other side of the desk. "Trooper Jim Duncan."

"Your partner introduced both of you. Virginia Ridgemont. I own The Glassworks." She gestured in the direction of the chairs. "So terrible about Glynis. Hell of an associate art director. I still can't believe someone shot her."

"That seems to be the general feeling so far." Duncan took out his notebook and the evidence bag with the check. "Tell us about her. I understand she was not an artist herself."

"No, but she had a great eye." Ridgemont steepled her hands. Her nails were unpolished and cut short. "She could spot talent a mile away. She was great at arranging the pieces, too. Not only what complemented what from the same artist, but how to position works from different people on the same wall. All her shows had a great flow to them. I was considering promoting her to assistant director and making her responsible for arranging her own shows."

"Considering. What do you mean by that?"

Ridgemont tapped her thumbs "I need an assistant to grow the gallery. Glynis had her good points. But she could be a little rough. I have another associate director who is a candidate. Olivia is not as great of a salesperson, but she's got a talent for wooing donors."

"Looks like the job is Olivia's by default. What's her last name?" A job at a small gallery didn't sound like something to kill over. Then again, people never ceased to amaze him.

"Mueller. And not necessarily. It's a business decision, Trooper." Ridgemont lifted her hands. "Just like I'm sure the PSP doesn't want to promote someone who can't do the job, I don't want to put a person in a position where she'd be in over her head. It's not good for her or me."

It was a true statement. At the same time, Duncan was well aware of the fact that weaker candidates got promoted all the time in every field.

"Is that all Glynis did here?" Abara asked, his own pad in hand.

"Mostly," Ridgemont replied. "I booked the artists for the shows. She helped them select the pieces for display and arranged them. With the promotion, she'd have been able to choose what artists to host. And she assisted with valuation from time to time."

Duncan rested his right ankle on his left knee. "What does that entail?"

"Most artists want to sell their work. Make some money." Ridgemont spread her hands. "Glynis would have the piece appraised and help them set a fair price. One that allowed them to be compensated well, but that a buyer would accept. It's a balance, you understand. Art is very difficult to put a price on because it's not like a mass-produced sweater or even dry goods. There's the materials, but also the artist's time."

"Plus the emotion you provoke in the buyer?" Duncan had seen enough craft and art shows in Confluence to know part of the value was set by the person forking over the cash.

Ridgemont tapped her fingers. "Exactly. Glynis was good at navigating ego and reality. Not all artists realize they aren't Picasso." She gave a wry grin.

Abara sat forward. "But you said that wasn't her primary job."

"No. We have a person on staff to do that. But occasionally she gets overwhelmed, and Glynis is happy to help." Ridgemont bit her lip. "Was happy."

Duncan waited, then said, "You look like you're trying to figure out whether to say something. I suggest you do and let us deal with it."

She sighed. "On the TV shows, the cops are always asking who disliked the victim. The response is always the dead person was so well-liked, she couldn't have had any enemies."

"I gather that wasn't true of Glynis."

"Don't get me wrong." Ridgemont sat forward. "Glynis *was* a wonderful person. She was kind, generous, smart, and passionately invested in making sure artists were paid fairly for their work. But she could be, well, prickly, I guess is the word."

"What do you mean?" Abara asked.

"She and Delia, that's our regular valuator, didn't always see eye to eye. Glynis thought some of Delia's judgments were weak, that she both over- and undervalued works." Ridgemont fidgeted with some papers. "They had a rather heated discussion a month ago. Who am I kidding?" She rolled her eyes. "It was a blow-out fight. If it had been two guys, punches would have been thrown."

"Over the price of a painting?" Duncan didn't bother to hide his skepticism.

"A little more than that." Ridgemont stood and retrieved a file from the cabinet near the wall. "One of the services we provide is to certify and value paintings. Delia's specialty is nineteenth-century art. A man brought a small painting to us a couple of months ago. He said his grandmother had it and had always claimed it was done by Albert Bierstadt. He wanted to know for sure. If it was genuine, it could be worth a lot of money."

Duncan took the file. Inside was a certificate of authenticity signed by Delia Struthers. The picture under the certificate showed a boat tied up at a lakeside dock, trees in the background. It was nice, but nothing special. At least not in his estimation. He handed back the file. "Let me guess. Glynis disagreed."

"It was more than that. She accused Delia of ineptitude, said she didn't have the faintest idea what a Bierstadt painting looked like, and couldn't possibly have earned a degree without such basic knowledge. She said she'd be looking into Delia's credentials. Delia lost it. She said she'd be damned if some upstart would question her professional opinion. She told me I'd better support her or she'd find another gallery to work with."

Abara took the file and took his own look. "What did you say?"

"That I'd talk to Glynis, we'd work it out, that it was probably a big misunderstanding." Ridgemont sagged in her chair.

"An employee gave you an ultimatum and you went along?" Abara's voice betrayed his shock.

Again, she lifted her hands. "People don't want to work for a small gallery. If I didn't have to lose Delia, I didn't want to, so I said I'd smooth things over."

"And did you?" Duncan asked.

"I tried." Ridgemont brushed hair from her face. "Glynis said she was waiting on proof, and it might be better if I let it go for the time being. Give her some time to make sure she was right. That was three, no four, weeks ago. Then we started a big show, and quite frankly, the subject got dropped."

Abara handed the folder back. "Then Glynis didn't follow up on her concerns?"

"I have no idea." Ridgemont replaced the folder in the cabinet and resumed her seat. "I guess we won't know, not that I need to. Delia tendered her resignation this morning. She said she got a job in Los Angeles and was moving back to the big city scene, where she belonged."

Duncan made a note. "Anyone else?"

Ridgemont hesitated. "There's...no, it really was nothing."

"Why don't you let us be the judge of that?" Abara asked in a voice perfectly suited for a pretentious TV detective.

Duncan fought down a sigh. "What my colleague means is that small things are often important. I understand it feels like throwing someone under the proverbial bus, but it's better to tell us everything now. That way, we can investigate and strike it off the list." *Or not*, but he didn't say that.

"I told you earlier about Olivia Mueller." Ridgemont ran her finger up and down her water bottle.

"You did. What about her?"

"If Glynis had a fault, it was the fact she was too blunt. She'd either never heard the old saw about catching bees with honey or she didn't believe it." Ridgemont sighed. "Glynis didn't believe Olivia had the credentials for the position, and she didn't refrain from saying so. Now, I know what you're thinking. That it's my decision, and why did it matter what Glynis thought?"

Duncan waited.

Abara opened his mouth, but after one look at his partner, he shut it.

Ridgemont continued. "Glynis was right. Her background is better than Olivia's. But Olivia has a softer personality, one that is a little better suited to customers who are on the fence. And she does know some very influential people who could help the gallery raise its profile. At the same time, she often puts her foot in her mouth and unintentionally put people off." She let her arms fall to her sides. "Glynis could be impatient. She expected people to know what they wanted and make decisions. It did turn some people off, and we almost lost a sale on a couple of occasions. Ironically, Olivia was the one who saved them. Glynis never quite grasped that writing a check with three or more zeros on the end could be hard for some people. Then again, I believe she grew up in a family with money, so it was probably not something she had to deal with."

"Then you hadn't made up your mind?" Duncan asked.

Ridgemont rubbed her forehead. "I told both of them I'd make my decision before the end of the month. Olivia seemed disappointed but willing to wait."

Abara shot a quick look, like he was asking for permission to speak.

Duncan gave a tiny nod.

"I take it Glynis was not as patient?" Abara asked.

"She told Olivia she'd only get the job over her, Glynis's, dead body." Ridgemont's expression was weary. "Glynis said she'd walk before she'd take direction from a nobody like Olivia. But honestly, it was talk, that's all. Olivia is the meekest creature on God's earth. I had to beg her not to quit on the spot because she was convinced she was wasting her time and would be better suited doing anything except art direction."

Duncan didn't say that even the weakest person would lash out if she thought she was threatened. "Anything else we should know about?"

Ridgemont thought, her upper teeth pressed into her lower lip. "Glynis did mention some harassing emails."

"We've heard about those. Anonymous, weren't they?"

"Yes. But I don't think they were threatening, as in loss of life." Ridgemont thought. "More of a nuisance. I don't think Glynis took them seriously. 'No one wants to work with you,' 'Why don't you quit and go back to administration,' 'You don't belong at a private gallery.' Stuff like that. They weren't signed, and she didn't recognize the email address. It was from one of those webmail providers, if I remember correctly."

"What did she do about it?" Abara asked.

Ridgemont shrugged. "Deleted them."

Duncan didn't think it sounded very promising, but he'd have the techs look for the emails. He glanced at his watch. If he wanted to make the autopsy, he had precious little time remaining. He pulled out the evidence bag. "I see you have some of Tyler Lane's work on display. Did you sell his pieces out of The Glassworks?"

"Not until very recently." Ridgemont sat back. "Which is too bad, really. Tyler's work is good, and his subject matter sells well because it's all local. Tyler had an agent. Glynis was trying to get out of the contract. She'd brought some of Tyler's newer works, things she found after his death, to us. I guess those weren't contracted with the agent. I forget his name."

"Ned Tidwell."

"Him." Ridgemont snapped her fingers. "Anyway, Glynis didn't like him when Tyler was alive, but Ned had been the first to believe in Tyler, so I guess there was a feeling of obligation there. Glynis had an artistic eye, but she was a businesswoman at heart."

"How does the sale process work?" Duncan asked. "In general."

"The artist, or the artist's agent, places the work in a gallery." Ridgemont ticked off the points on her fingers. "The gallery and the artist work out a selling price. I won't bore you with details. Upon sale, the gallery gets a cut, the agent takes a percentage, and the artist receives the rest. Payment is usually made to the agent, who then disburses to the artist. Assuming there's an agent, of course. And the artist needs or wants to use a gallery."

Duncan handed over the bag. "This is a check we obtained in a search of Glynis's home. It looks like the proceeds from a sale. Does this seem like a fair amount?"

She took the envelope and peered through the bag. "It's hard to say for sure. I don't know anything about the size of the painting or what it is." At the troopers' expressions, she added, "Oils are worth more than watercolors, for example. However, Tyler usually worked with oils, and his canvases were rarely smaller than twelve by twenty-four inches. Often, they are much larger. At first blush, this is a ridiculously small payment. One of his works here at my gallery, *Night Flowers*, is priced at twenty-five hundred dollars. There's one of Cucumber Falls that is five thousand. After the gallery commission, Tyler, and now Glynis, would get a nice check at the time of sale. Not enough to fund one hundred percent of their bills, but way more than this." She waved the envelope.

"Did Glynis ever talk to you in detail about her objections? About Tidwell, I mean." Duncan took the bag back.

Ridgemont nodded. "Oh yes. Tidwell claimed Tyler wasn't good enough for bigger galleries. She believed he was underselling Tyler's work and maybe cooking the books so it looked like the paintings were selling for less than what they really did. Based on what I know, I would have to agree."

"What makes you say that?" Abara asked.

"Glynis brought me the cancelled checks and descriptions of the paintings." Virginia's gaze was shrewd. "I know I just said it was hard to tell, but based on the information she gave me, he should have been getting amounts with at least three zeroes on them. Before the period." She took a bottle of water out of a mini fridge and opened it.

Duncan slipped the evidence bag back into his pocket. "Let me guess. She wasn't."

"Not even close." Virginia set the bottle down on a coaster. "She went through Tyler's papers after he died. He wasn't getting lavish amounts either. Tidwell said he wasn't well known."

"Did Glynis confront the agent?"

"She planned to. That's when she brought the unrepresented paintings here. *Night Flowers* is one of them." Virginia tipped her head in the direction of the gallery. "I agreed to display them and handle the sales. Glynis wanted to see if the work truly wasn't selling or if Tidwell was blowing smoke."

Duncan thought that over. "If he was?"

"She told Tidwell if that was the case, she'd ask for an audit of his books. That I know. Every sale he ever handled, and not just Tyler's. All of Tidwell's clients." Virginia smirked.

If Tidwell had been crooked, an audit would rip the cover off his scheme. He'd be ruined. "He couldn't have been happy."

"Oh, he wasn't. He came here once. He told Glynis to butt out. She didn't know what she was doing, and he wouldn't stand by and have his business ruined." Virginia paused. "I had to threaten to call the cops to get him to leave."

Duncan exchanged a glance with Abara. "How have sales been?"

Ridgemont's answering smile was faint. "I've sold three, and at higher prices than what Tidwell claimed he was getting."

The troopers exchanged a look. "Do you know if Glynis moved forward with her threat, or was it talk?" Abara asked.

The gallery owner shrugged. "She never mentioned it, no. But that doesn't mean she didn't."

Duncan checked his notes. "One final question. Did you ever see Glynis with a man? Specifically tall, bald, big tattoo of a bird on his arm?"

"Glynis kept her private life just that, Trooper. Private."

Duncan stood. "Thank you for your time, Ms. Ridgemont. If we have any other questions, we'll be in touch." He handed over a business card.

"Happy to help." Ridgemont also rose. "I will say Glynis Lane could be a pain in the ass when she had her fire up. But she was passionate. And it breaks my heart to think of that dear little girl an orphan."

As Duncan left, he didn't see Sally again, but her SUV was still in the parking lot. He got in and looked at the dashboard clock. They were cutting it close, but they'd have just enough time to get to the autopsy.

Chapter Thirteen

Sally watched from around a corner as Jim and his partner thanked Virginia Ridgemont and left. Jim's gaze swept the space, no doubt looking for her. He didn't give any hint of acknowledgment, which made her believe her strategy of ducking into another room had worked. It wasn't that she was trying to hide. He'd already seen her and would spot her SUV in the lot. But she knew he didn't completely approve of her snooping around. He wouldn't embarrass her in public, but neither did she want to face the disapprobation in those hazel eyes.

Unlike Jenny Cavendish, his temporary partner would absolutely not approve.

A woman, not the one Sally had spoken to earlier, stuck her head through the arched opening to the side room. "Oh, good. You're still here. I was afraid you'd left. Olivia told me a potential buyer was here, but then I got sidetracked. Did she come back to check on you?"

"She did, but I wanted to talk to you directly. That is if you're the owner."

"I am. Virginia Ridgemont.

Sally offered what she hoped was the smile of an overawed buyer. "I've never bought art from a gallery before. It's very overwhelming." She waved at the wall. "They're all so expensive. I guess I have a little bit of sticker shock. I want one, but I don't know if it's worth this much money."

"Yes, but we don't sell prints. These aren't mass-produced tchotchkes from overseas. Each one is a signed original work. You'd have something no one else has." Ridgemont stepped closer, and the wide legs of her navy blue pants swished. "I see you found the display of Tyler Lane's work. Gorgeous, isn't it?"

"That it is." Sally turned her attention to one of the medium-sized canvases that was maybe fifteen by twenty inches. The scene showed the Pittsburgh skyline at night from the perspective of the south side of the Monongahela. Both sports stadiums were visible along with the famed Sisters Bridges spanning the Allegheny. Fireworks exploded across the sky, fierce bursts of red, blue, white, orange, and yellow. "Call me crazy, but I see a touch of Impressionist influence. But usually those paintings use more muted colors."

"You do." The gallery owner stood next to Sally. "I asked Tyler about it once. He said he loved the Impressionist style, but his world was already soft enough. He was deaf. He wanted to bring power to his work through the use of bold colors. He called this one *Night Flowers*." She clicked her tongue. "He died several years ago. The art world lost a genius."

"He was popular?"

"I think he was on the edge of a breakout, yes." Virginia tilted her head to study the painting at an angle. "He'd been selling at shows like the Pittsburgh arts festival. His wife believed his work belonged in galleries, maybe on a permanent basis. She wanted The Glassworks to be the exclusive outlet."

"Why here?"

"She worked for me. Glynis was one of my associate directors." The other woman shook her head. "Talk about another tragedy. Their poor daughter."

Here was the opening Sally wanted. "What happened?"

"Glynis was murdered over the weekend." Virginia waved a hand over her shoulder. "That's what the police were here for. I hope they catch the bastard."

Sally pointed at *Night Flowers*. "Do you have the rights to all of Tyler's work?"

"No, only the pieces you see here." Virginia turned in a circle. "*Night Flowers*, this one of the Loyalhanna Gorge in the fall, this large one of Cucumber Falls, and those two smaller ones down there." A frown crossed her face.

"Then I can see more at another gallery."

"Only if you contact Ned Tidwell's agency, or so I understand." Virginia paused. "You said you have a concern about price. How can I help?"

"I guess I don't understand why they have to be so expensive." Sally shrugged. "These aren't Old Masters, right?"

"Not yet, they aren't." Virginia dropped her voice. "I can tell you're the cautious type. I understand. It's a lot of cash. But you should buy the painting. I have a feeling Tyler's work is going to shoot up in value."

"Why?"

"Gut instinct. I've been doing this long enough to recognize the opportunity."

Sally blinked, feigning ignorance. "I don't understand. If this agent still has the ability to sell a bunch of Tyler's paintings, how can that happen? I might get a better price from him."

"I'll be right back." Virginia hurried away.

While Sally waited, she brought her focus back to the art. Glynis had her sights on Tidwell, huh? Based on her conversation with the Lanes, Tyler hadn't been making money off his sales. If Tidwell was selling the paintings for thousands but only paying out royalties that amounted to pennies on the dollar, he stood to lose a lot of money. And that was only from Tyler's work. What if Glynis had inspired Tidwell's other clients to jump ship? He would be ruined.

Virginia returned, holding a folder. "I probably should have given this to the cops, but I didn't think about it until now. I told them, but they had so many questions, and the paperwork slipped my mind."

Sally had been reaching for the folder, but stopped. "You should, you know. Especially if you think it's related to Glynis's murder."

"I will. After I show you. I don't think there's any harm in it." She opened the folder. "I don't appreciate people like Tidwell. They're bad for artists. I don't run this gallery to make a fortune. I do it so artists have a chance to get their work out to the public. So you can call me unprofessional if you want, but I want you to see this. Glynis sold two of the pieces she brought here. She got a lot more than Tidwell."

Sally's natural curiosity kicked in. She read the folder's contents. She whistled. The paintings had gone for a couple of thousand dollars each. Even after the gallery commission, Glynis had received a nice-sized check. Multiply that times the number of paintings Sally saw on the walls, and it was decent money that Tidwell wouldn't get. It was also enough of a difference from what he sent historically that Glynis would have been able to get an auditor on the trail as easily as a Labrador went after a fallen duck. "Wow. Who will get the money now?" She needed to refer the Lanes to an attorney who specialized in this type of thing.

"I'll make sure it goes to Bronwen, even if I have to open a college fund or something for her. It's the least I can do. I told you. I'm not in this for me. Also, I may decide to ask for an audit, like Glynis planned on doing. Or, depending on who she named as her executor, I'll advise that person to do it. I might even ask Whitley."

"Who's that?"

"A friend of Glynis's. She never mentioned Whitley's last name, but I'm sure I can find her." Virginia took the folder back. "The romantic starving artist stereotype needs to die. Painters, writers, musicians, doesn't matter. Creatives deserve to be paid for their work." She gave a rueful grin. "Guess I haven't covered myself in glory as a professional. I hope I didn't turn you off, running my big mouth. It's a subject that riles me up, so it's hard for me to shut up."

"I like passionate people. I also agree with you." From a legal perspective, the situation gave Tidwell an excellent motive for murder. Sally wasn't sure how many clients he had, but between the money and damage to his reputation, maybe even jail time, the man might have taken drastic steps. She gave the folder back to Virginia. "Did you tell the police about Whitley?"

"No. As far as I know, she was never involved, so I didn't bother."

"Still. I would advise you to mention her when you tell them about that." Sally pointed at the folder.

"Advise me?" Virginia's lips twitched. "You sound like a lawyer yourself."

Sally breezed past the moment. "Do you know who will get control of Tyler's work now?"

Virginia spread her hands. "Unlike you, I am *not* a lawyer. I hope it's his daughter, but I don't know for sure."

Sally thought about the sweet girl with the big blue eyes, alone and scared on a park trail. "How much did you say *Night Flowers* is selling for?"

"Twenty-five hundred. I'll toss in free delivery to your home if you buy today."

Sally bit her lip. It was a lot of money. She wasn't sure Jim had an open wall space big enough, but she could also hang it in her Uniontown office. Plus, it was something she could do to help Bronwen. "I'll take it."

Chapter Fourteen

Duncan and Abara arrived at the coroner's office in Uniontown at five minutes past three. "Have you seen an autopsy before?" Duncan asked as they walked down the hall.

"Yes, on a video." Abara ran a hand over his head. "I've heard stories. Are they as bad as people make them out to be?"

"I don't think so, but it may take some getting used to."

"Do you attend every one? I mean, seems a waste of time when you could be doing other things." He lifted his shoulders. "We get a report, don't we?"

"We do, but this is an opportunity to make observations and ask questions." The guy was way too focused on not wasting time. "I try to get as much information first-hand as I can."

"Just like why you didn't want to use the Pittsburgh cops?"

"Exactly." Duncan pushed through the door to the observation suite. "Hey, Doc. Sorry we're late. Burns, good to see you."

The deputy coroner, already focused on the procedure, lifted a hand, eyes on the body in front of him.

"Everyone, this is Kevin Abara. He's new to Troop B CIS. Try to be nice to him. It's his first live autopsy."

Burns snickered and muttered something, almost certainly a snarky comment Duncan didn't want to hear.

"We've just started." Doctor Evans, the pathologist, resumed his narration, cataloging the conditions of Glynis's organs and general health. "She was in good shape. Healthy lungs of a nonsmoker. Based on the liver, I'd say she consumed very little alcohol."

"That tracks with what her in-laws told me." Duncan thought back to the interview with the Lanes. "Hard to be a party animal when you're a single mom to a special needs child."

"True enough." The team continued their examination.

Abara leaned over. "What exactly are we looking for?"

"We'll know it when we see it." Duncan crossed his arms.

"Then I *really* don't see the value of being here." Abara's face betrayed his doubt. "The report will tell us the important stuff. How are we supposed to ask questions when we don't know what to ask about?"

"That's the thing." Duncan kept his gaze on the autopsy team. "You'll know what to follow up on when they say it. As for the report, the family gets a copy as well. Wouldn't you like to be able to talk to them about it? Give your impressions or information that's not on paper?"

"They can ask the coroner. Doesn't his office handle that?"

Duncan suppressed a sigh. "This is also our opportunity to collect the evidence. The victim's clothing, personal effects, things like that."

"Won't they send that to us?"

Duncan said nothing. Sometimes, you had to learn a lesson the hard way. Maybe this trip wouldn't yield any new information, and Abara would decide attendance at the post-mortem wasn't worth it. Duncan was willing to bet a decision like that would bite him in the ass down the road, but his job was to teach. It was up to the student to learn.

Doc Evans held up one of the victim's hands. "You missed this part. We have some defensive wounds here. Bruising on the knuckles and skin under her fingernails. We'll send the epithelial cells for testing."

Abara wrinkled his forehead. "She fought with her attacker. Could be good for DNA."

"Yes, but what if the evidence doesn't belong to the shooter?" Duncan kept his focus on the procedure.

Abara snorted. "The kid saw him. Who else would it be from?"

"A second actor." Duncan spoke to the autopsy team. "Any burning or stippling near the wound?"

Burns shook his head. "Nope. Whoever did this was standing far enough away that the gun didn't leave marks. We'll find gunshot residue, I'm sure, but I bet it's minimal."

"See, this is why you attend." Duncan pulled out his notepad and jotted down the information.

"I don't understand what you're on about." Abara blew out a breath. "She fought with the shooter; he backed off and popped her."

Duncan faced the younger man. "That's one idea. But remember, Glynis told her daughter to hide. The girl stuck around long enough to see the bald tattooed suspect, but then she ran off. She said she hid for a *long time*. I know kids don't have a good grasp of those things, but it sounds like it is at least possible that it was long enough for Glynis to have an argument with Tattoo Guy. Could be she hit him, which accounts for the wounds and skin. The two broke apart, Tattoo Guy left, and a second actor showed up, and that's the guy who shot her." He held up his hands. "I'm not saying we shouldn't look for Tattoo Guy. But maybe, just maybe, open your mind to the possibility there's another party in the mix."

Abara gnawed his lip.

The team in the autopsy suite paused. Burns gave a low whistle.

"What is it?" Duncan leaned closer to the window.

Burns looked up. "She was pregnant."

Duncan blinked at the news. "Her in-laws said she wasn't seeing anyone." He flipped back through his notes. Yep, it was right there.

"Maybe it was a one-night stand."

Sex in the modern age. Duncan thought. There had been men's toiletries in the victim's bathroom. For one man or for anyone who spent the night? *That feels wrong. A single mother who is as protective of her daughter as Glynis allegedly was does not have one-night stands in her house.* Except babysitting was only a couple houses away. "Does she have one of those birth control implants or an IUD?"

Burns lifted one shoulder. "Nope."

Evans rubbed his chin. "The biology doesn't lie. Glynis Lane was pregnant. I estimate she was eight or ten weeks along."

As the team continued their work, Duncan glanced at the younger trooper.

Abara's eyebrows were so high, they almost met his hairline. Yes, all this information would have been in a report. But you couldn't ask questions of a piece of paper.

* * *

Sally met Tanelsa a block away from Raymond's Bridal Shoppe, the only dress store in Uniontown Louise considered good enough to shop at. "Thanks for doing this," she said.

"I still think Lisa could hook you up a lot cheaper." Tanelsa hitched her purse strap up on her shoulder. "And something more in your style."

Sally strolled toward the store. "I think so, too. But Mom insisted." She reached the shop and stared at the window display. The mannequin wore a confection of white silk, decorated with tiny pearls sewn to a skirt that was puffed up by a cloud of tulle. The sleeves were long and came to points over the wrists. The shoulders rose in a pouf that didn't quite meet the chin. Pretty, but not what Sally wanted to wear when she said "I do." She swallowed. "Um, would you tell Lisa to be on standby?"

"I already have." Tanelsa tugged on Sally's arm. "Come on. Let's get this over with."

Louise was inside, already engaged in an animated conversation with a sales clerk. "Ah, there you are. You're late."

"Mom, it's three thirty-five. We were looking for parking." Not to mention Sally hadn't exactly sprinted to the store. "I don't think you've ever met Tanelsa."

Louise pursed her lips. "Pleasure." She pointed at a half-full dress rack. "I've already pulled a few dresses I think would be suitable. Do you still wear an eight?"

Sally forced a smile. "An eight or a ten, depending on the designer." She looked at the dresses, all of which were, in her opinion, over-decorated. The skirts were too full, and all of them had full sleeves. "Do you have anything with short sleeves, or none?" she asked the clerk.

Louise's mouth tightened. "I don't think short sleeves are really appropriate for the occasion. Much too casual. Sleeveless is too…revealing."

"Mom." Sally took a deep breath. "It's going to be September. It might be hot. I don't want to pass out from heat exhaustion at my wedding."

"You won't faint. There will be air conditioning."

Sally turned to the clerk. "What do you have? I also want to see dresses in winter white or ivory."

Louise sniffed, not bothering to hide her disapproval. "Try this one on." She held out a frothy pile of white satin.

Sally went to the dressing room and returned a few minutes later. "I feel like a cake topper." She swished the giant skirt, which was held up by what seemed like a mountain of tulle.

Tanelsa said nothing.

"But you look like royalty." Louise shook out the skirt. "Add a long veil and it would be perfect. You always wanted to be a princess."

"When I was five." Sally fought the urge to roll her eyes. "T, would you hand me that one?"

Tanelsa held out a hanger with a long white dress on it. It did not have a full skirt and was a slimmer silhouette than the one Sally wore.

She again went to the dressing room and came back. "Mmm, what do you think?"

"Closer, but still not exactly what I have in mind for you." Tanelsa circled Sally, tapping her lips. "I like the minimalist decor, though."

"You look like a hooker," Louise snapped. "It's way too tight and the neckline is definitely too low."

"We could alter the bodice to give you a little more room," the clerk said. She caught Louise's dagger-like glare and bit her lip.

"The bodice is fine." Sally smoothed her hips. "I don't think the neckline is too low at all. But while I don't want to sparkle like a fashion model, I'd like a little more bling for my wedding, if you know what I mean."

"I still think you look like a streetwalker." Louise huffed. "How would you even walk in that?"

Sally had seen a lot of prostitutes as an assistant public defender. Not one of them had worn floor-length gowns. "We'll put it on the maybe pile. What else?"

The barrage of sniping and counterarguments continued for the next two hours. Tanelsa turned in a performance worthy of a hostage negotiator and kept Sally and her mother from strangling each other as a variety of dresses were tried and rejected. As Sally faced the far wall and took deep breaths, she heard her friend speaking to the clerk.

"I'm very sorry about this," Tanelsa said. "I'll help you put these away."

"Thanks, but it's no bother." A rustle of fabric as the clerk gathered up discarded garments. "These kinds of things happen all the time. This isn't even the worst I've seen."

Sally bottled up her embarrassment and went back to the mirrors. "We'll leave it here for today. Did you say you're going to get a shipment soon?"

"New dresses come in the first of the month." The salesclerk replaced the dresses on the rack.

"Good. I'll come back next month and see what's here." Sally slung her purse over her shoulder and shot a look at her mother, who stood in a far corner, a scowl stamped on her features. She lowered her voice. "Probably without my mother."

Chapter Fifteen

The troopers emerged from the morgue into blinding sunshine. Duncan blinked as his eyes adjusted.

"The Lane couple lied to us." Abara slipped on a pair of stylish, black-framed sunglasses.

Duncan put on his Ray-Bans and headed for the car. "What do you mean?" He got in the driver's side and checked the mirrors.

Abara slid into the passenger seat. "They said she wasn't seeing anyone and couldn't have any more kids." He clicked his seat belt.

"They said Glynis wasn't dating anyone *that they knew of,* and the doctor told her it would be hard to have another kid." Duncan started the car and pulled away. "I don't think that means she couldn't get pregnant, although she may have taken it that way. It would explain why she wasn't on birth control. She didn't think she needed it." He drummed his fingers on the steering wheel.

Abara groaned. "Don't tell me we're going back to Pittsburgh."

"We may have to, but not this second." Glynis may have kept her social life from her in-laws, but would Bronwen have noticed? Did he really want to question a bereaved child?

"Are we going to ever talk to the victim's parents?" Abara asked.

"Eventually. I don't want to do that from the car, though. We'll save it until we get back to HQ."

Abara checked his watch. "It's four now. How much longer are we gonna be at this? Quitting time is five."

"Only when we aren't working a homicide." Holy crap. Where did Abara get these expectations? "Get on the phone. Call the Lanes and the woman from The Glassworks, Virginia Ridgemont. Ask again about whether Glynis had talked about any men in her life, even if it was a minor fling or a one-night stand."

"On it." Abara pulled out his phone, seemingly happy not to be heading north.

While Duncan drove and listened to his partner talk, he mulled over a second interview with Bronwen. By now, someone would have told her about her mother's death. The question was whether the kid was observant enough to notice any male friends or nights where Glynis went out, especially if it was unplanned. Duncan thought she might.

Which emphasized the fact that he needed to track down Tattoo Guy. No one except Bronwen seemed to have seen him, but he had to come from somewhere. That description was so precise that if he'd been in Glynis's life, someone had to recognize it.

Abara slid his phone back into his pocket. "Negative. The Lanes and Ridgemont both say Glynis never mentioned dating, or a new boyfriend, or even a passing affair. Ridgemont said again Glynis didn't like to talk about her personal life, except for Bronwen. Proud mother and all that crap."

"Abara, I know it's only you and me in this car, and I know you're a single guy in your late twenties, so you might not realize how you sound, but you need to work on how you handle yourself." Duncan pulled into a parking lot and thumbed through his contacts.

"What do you mean?"

"Saying proud mother *and all that crap* sounds like you're dismissing it. It's an important part of who Glynis was. Understanding the victim is crucial to solving a murder. You don't want to alienate potential sources by demeaning their dead friend, loved one, or whatever she was." Duncan tapped the call icon. "Yes, hi. This is Trooper Jim Duncan with the PSP. I'm looking for information on who the foster family for Bronwen Lane is. Yes, I'll hold."

While he listened to the Muzak, he watched Abara out of the corner of his eye. Had the words made a difference? It was hard to tell. The other man might have been puzzling through them. But it was surprising that he hadn't acquired some professionalism and knowledge of how to interact with civilians during his years in uniform. The music ended. "Yes, I'm still here. The Horners. Got an address?" He snapped his fingers.

Abara shook himself and took out pen and paper.

"7346 North Avenue, Uniontown. Thanks." Duncan ended his call. "You okay with driving across the city? It's not too far out of the way for you, is it?" He knew the comment was snarky, but perhaps the sarcasm was necessary to drive the point home.

Abara said nothing.

Duncan took the opportunity to fire off a text to Sally. **Could be another long night. Did you find a dress?**

The dots indicating she was responding appeared after a couple seconds. **No and don't ask when the next shopping trip is. You making progress?**

He knew Sally well enough that she'd be heading home for a night with the dogs and taking the edge off with a large glass of her favorite Merlot. If Tanelsa didn't take her out for a drink first. **Some. Deep breath. See you later.**

She responded with a row of hearts.

"Are you ready?" Annoyance laced Abara's voice.

Instead of a verbal response, Duncan dropped his phone in the console and pulled out. If Cavendish was on vacation the next time he caught a homicide, he would personally pay for a helicopter to go get her.

* * *

Sally gave Louise a perfunctory hug, then watched as her mother drove off without a backward glance. She turned to Tanelsa. "Now do you understand? I keep thinking that if I give in, she'll be happy and cut me some slack. But no. Shoot me now."

Tanelsa clucked her tongue. "Sally, appeasement didn't work for the British with Hitler, and it won't work with your mom. If you don't fight for every inch, she'll take a mile. Soon you'll be having the wedding of her dreams, not yours. With extra bridesmaids." She pulled a mirror out of her purse and checked her lipstick. "Did you tell Jim about that?"

"Yes, but it was the day we found Bronwen and her mother, so he probably hasn't done anything about it." Sally covered her face with her hands and pressed the heels of her palms into her eyes. Jim was lucky. He only had to solve a murder.

"And he shouldn't. Neither should you. You don't even know those people. Why have them in your wedding party?" Tanelsa laid a hand on Sally's shoulder. "You don't let clients roll over you like this."

Sally dropped her hands and glared at her partner. "Clients are paying me for my skills. Besides, our toughest customer is not as bad as my mother."

"I don't know why you don't let Lisa get you a dress and take Jim up on his offer to go to the courthouse."

"Are you nuts?" Sally pushed the hands away and jabbed a finger at Tanelsa. "I told you already. Mom would be furious. She'd take it out on me. Then she'd bitch to Noreen, and my sister would turn on me. Shit rolls downhill, remember? I don't need to get yelled at by both women in my family."

"I'm so glad Lisa and I didn't deal with this." Tanelsa dropped the mirror back into her bag. "Tell you what. Come over to our place for dinner tonight. I'll ply you with wine, you and Lisa can talk dresses, then we'll eat and figure out how to salvage this mess."

"I can't get drunk and stay the night because I have to drive home to feed the dogs."

Tanelsa grabbed Sally's shoulders again. "Bullshit. I know you have a neighbor who would be more than happy to take care of Rizzo and Pixel. Merlot therapy. Now. I promise I won't let you get sloshed. Just enough to relax."

Sally allowed herself to be pushed in the direction of her SUV. Tanelsa was right. Marge would gladly take care of the boys. Sally did need the comfort of friends. A big glass of red wine wouldn't hurt either.

She called Marge on the way to Tanelsa's house. She also stopped for a bottle of their favorite Cabernet. If she was going to drink Lisa and Tanelsa's wine, it was only right she replace it.

By the time she got to the house, the smells of garlic, onions, and herbs could be detected even from outside. Sally's stomach growled. Poor Jim. Reheated pasta last night and lousy fast food tonight. Maybe she could talk her hosts into letting her take something when she left. Knowing how Jim worked when he was on a fresh case, even if he ate now, he'd be hungry when he finally got home.

"I come bearing gifts," she called out as she came through the front door and put her purse on the hall table. She found Tanelsa and her wife in the kitchen. Three generous glasses of red wine were on the island.

Tanelsa handed her one and accepted the bottle. "Thank you. Here. Drink up."

Lisa, a small Asian woman whose size belied her fierce personality, stirred the contents of a pot on the stove, then wiped her hands on a towel. "Tanelsa told me about the shopping trip. I can talk to your mother, if you'd like. In very polite, but forceful, words."

Sally savored the velvety texture of the wine and its undertones of plum and black cherry. "No, please. Nothing against you, but it would backfire. Trust me. She'd listen, nod, and thank you for your opinion. Then she'd privately tell me how rude my friends are. Keep my glass full and we're good." She slid onto a stool. "What are you making? It smells divine."

"Beef Bourguignon." Lisa picked up a glass. "Julia Child's recipe. Takes hours, but it's worth it. I've had it on the stove all day, and it's about done. As far as the dress, have it your way. But say the word and I'm on the case."

"I'll remember that. Thanks."

Tanelsa set a platter laden with thick slices of Italian bread in front of Sally, along with a dish of flavored olive oil and herbs. "You heard anything about that deaf girl? Is she still with a foster family?"

"I believe so." Sally ripped apart a piece and dipped it in the oil. She told the others about her visit to the Lanes earlier that day. "It can be a slow process. But I'll keep calling Lena until Bronwen is with her family."

"Do you think she saw her mother's killer?" Lisa picked up her own bread.

"I don't know. I hope not. I don't want her to be a target, not to mention the mental trauma." Sally swirled her wine as she swallowed and took a sip.

"Although, I'm naïve enough to hope that even if she's a witness, the person wouldn't kill a child."

Tanelsa's expression darkened. "And we're both jaded enough to know it could easily happen." She helped herself to bread and oil. "Did you learn anything useful when you were up there?"

Sally filled the couple in on everything she'd picked up from Virginia Ridgemont and the Lanes. "Shit. I forgot to tell Jim I bought that painting."

Tanelsa took a second piece of bread. "Why would you have to? You've got your own money. You can spend it the way you want. I know he doesn't give a damn about decorating."

"That may be true, but don't you think he'd want to know about a delivery of a very large box to the house?"

Tanelsa, mouth full, nodded in concession.

"It's such a weird situation." Lisa got up to check on the beef. "Why would you follow your victim to a state park, shoot her on a public trail, and risk being seen by other hikers, never mind her kid?"

It was something that bothered Sally as well. "I wonder if it was a spur-of-the-moment act. Maybe the killer went to reason with Glynis, things got out of hand, and he shot her."

"You don't take a gun if all you're gonna do is talk." Tanelsa pointed a piece of bread at her.

This was also true.

"The kid, Bronwen? She gave a pretty good description, though." Lisa tested the sauce. "Should make him easy to find."

"The police aren't convinced he's the killer. At least, I don't think they are. Jim's being a little tight-lipped on this one. Such a detailed account makes me suspicious anyway." Sally sipped her wine. "In a mystery novel, a suspect like that is almost automatically out for me. Too obvious."

"Killer in plain sight." Tanelsa dusted off her hands. "Everybody thinks the way you do, dismisses him, and he gets off scot free."

"I don't think Jim is likely to let that happen." Sally carried the platter with the remains of the bread and the little dish of oil to the table. "I want to check into the gallery and the other employees. So many people think artists are above such gritty things as murder, but they're human."

Tanelsa set down plates and silverware. "Sally, I think it's time to let it go. A second ago, you said Jim would be on it. We have no client here, no reason to be involved. I know you want to help this kid. Send her money on her birthday. Hell, take her to the zoo if her grandparents approve. But stay out of this investigation. Focus on your wedding planning and the clients we have."

"All right. No more murder talk. Dinner is served." Lisa carried the pot with the stew to the table and put it on a steel trivet.

Sally sat down and spread her napkin over her lap. "Okay."

Tanelsa put her hands on her hips. "You're giving in that easily? No way, lady. I know better. God, why do you always do this?"

"Maybe I've learned my lesson. Have you thought about that?" Sally ladled out some chunks of beef. She could tell her partner didn't believe her. Fine. Sally wouldn't do her research at work.

That's what home offices were for.

Chapter Sixteen

Duncan parked at the curb in front of the two-story bungalow-style house on North Avenue. The yard was small but neat. He could just see a small play-set in the back yard that included a couple of swings and a slide. He cast his gaze around the neighboring houses. No evidence of other kids. Of course, it was close to dinnertime. Maybe they were all inside. But he didn't see any signs warning motorists of children at play, no toys or bicycles left out for later. Did Bronwen have anyone her age to be with? If she did, did any of them know how to talk to her?

He resolved to call CPS in the morning and get a status update on the effort to place the girl with her grandparents.

"Doesn't look like there are a lot of kids around." Abara's words mirrored Duncan's thoughts.

"No, but this isn't intended to be her home forever, either." Duncan walked up to the door and knocked.

A woman in her forties opened the inner door but left the storm door shut. "Yes? I'm not interested in buying anything."

"We're not selling." Duncan held up his badge wallet. "Are you Mrs. Horner?"

"I'm Michelle Horner." The woman peered through the glass. "Is something wrong, Trooper?"

"No, ma'am. We were hoping you'd be okay with my partner and me interviewing Bronwen." Duncan jerked his thumb behind him toward Abara.

"She's already talked to the police about that horrible day. I don't think it would be good to go over it again."

"It's not about what happened in the park." Duncan paused. "I assume someone told her what happened to her mother. Correct?"

"Yes." Michelle pursed her lips. "She's been rather despondent since then."

"Understandable." Duncan threw a glance over his shoulder at Abara, who surreptitiously checked his watch. Duncan turned back to Mrs. Horner. "I understand you know ASL? Unfortunately, neither I nor my partner do."

"I do. My son has partial hearing loss. We learned ASL a long time ago. He's off to college now." Michelle seemed to make up her mind. She pushed open the door. "Come in. Maybe talking about her mother will cheer Bronwen up a little. Although she hasn't wanted to talk to me very much, so I'm not sure she'll want to talk to a stranger." She walked off before Duncan could say he wasn't unknown to the girl.

Abara unbuttoned his jacket and looked around the room. "Kind of cheerless, don't you think?"

"Keep your voice down." Duncan laid a finger on his lips. "I wouldn't say that. The home is clean, and Mrs. Horner seems caring enough. But it's not a house full of little kids, if that's what you mean."

A minute later, Michelle led Bronwen into the room. As soon as she saw Duncan, she ran to him and threw her arms around his knees, burying her face against his legs. He patted her head.

Michelle blinked. "She knows you?"

"My fiancee and I found her on the trail that day." He disengaged her arms and knelt. He brushed a lock of hair out of her face. "How do you say *how are you*?"

Michelle made the signs, and Duncan mimicked her.

Bronwen gave a shy smile in return. Her hands moved.

Michelle translated. "She says okay, but she misses her mom."

Duncan gave the girl's hands a gentle squeeze and kissed them. "Ask her if she's comfortable answering a few questions about her mother."

Michelle tapped Bronwen on the shoulder and signed.

Bronwen looked back at Duncan and nodded.

"Good." He looked over at Abara. "Take notes. I want to concentrate on her."

"That's all? You don't want anything else?" Abara took out his pad and pen, his disappointment obvious.

"Nothing against you. But let's not overwhelm her." Duncan held up a hand. "If you think of something, ask me and I'll pass it on."

Abara grumbled under his breath, sat, and clicked open the pen.

Once again, Duncan resolved to address the topic of maintaining a professional demeanor with him, but now was not the time. He shot a look at Michelle to confirm she was ready. "Bronwen, I know your dad is dead. Do you know what a boyfriend is?"

Michelle did the translation, and again the girl dipped her head.

"Did your mom have one?"

Bronwen looked at her foster mother, obviously hesitant.

"It's okay. Mrs. Horner is helping me," Duncan said as Michelle signed. "I can't talk to you without her."

Bronwen lifted her shoulders.

"Did you ever see her with a man? Maybe all dressed up?"

"She said once," Michelle answered. "She spends the night at her grandparents' house once a week. So Mommy could have alone time. But she only saw a man one time."

"Do you remember when?"

Bronwen's forehead creased. "School had started, but before Halloween."

Anywhere from last August to October. "What did he look like?" Duncan asked.

Another pause while Michelle translated. "He was taller than Mommy. He had black hair and dark eyes. He wore nice clothes, like you are now."

"Suits, not casual clothes." Too bad a child couldn't tell whether they were tailored or off-the-rack. "Do you know his name?"

"Mommy said he was Mr. Craddock, a friend."

Abara looked up. "That name sounds familiar."

It did. Something to look into when they were done. Duncan focused on Bronwen. "Did you ever see anyone else? Maybe the big man with tattoos?"

She shook her head.

Enough of that for now. Either Glynis hadn't had much of a dating life, or she'd successfully kept it from her daughter. "Have you ever met your other grandparents? The ones who live in Philadelphia."

Bronwen gave a quick shake, and her hands flew.

"Mommy had a big fight with Grandpa," Michelle said. "He didn't like Daddy, and Mommy got mad. She said unless he apologized, he'd never meet me."

He, not they. What about Mrs. Beddoe? Duncan doubted Bronwen would know, but it was worth a shot. "Have you ever visited your grandmother?"

She shook her head.

"Hell of a thing to say," Abara mumbled. "When the Lanes said Glynis was stubborn, they weren't kidding, were they? What about the brother?"

Duncan relayed the question. He expected to hear a similar answer. When Bronwen held up one finger and nodded, surprise hit him. "She's seen him once? Is that what she means? When?"

"That's what I understand." Michelle signed again. "Yes, once. He seemed nice at first, but then he and Glynis argued. Bronwen said she'd been sent to her room, but she peeked. She couldn't hear the words, obviously, but her mom was red in the face and they both looked like they were shouting. Her uncle shook a finger in Glynis's face and slammed the door when he left."

"How would Bronwen know he slammed the door?" Abara asked. "She couldn't have heard it."

"She saw him, though. She might have felt the vibration of a hard contact or something like that." Duncan was inclined to take the child's statement at face value. "Friend of mine had a deaf dog. To get the dog's attention, he'd stomp on the floor. Same concept with a door slamming."

Bronwen tugged on Duncan's sleeve. A shy smile crossed her face as she signed.

Duncan recognized one gesture from the conversation in the park. Once again, he copied the sign. "Is she asking about my dogs?"

Bronwen's face lit up.

"Yes," Michelle replied. "She asked if you would bring them here so she could see them."

It might have been his imagination, but Michelle didn't seem enthusiastic about the idea. "I don't know that you want a rambunctious Golden Retriever and a greyhound in your house." Not his imagination. The relief in her expression was obvious. "Tell her I'll talk to Sally and we'll figure something out."

Bronwen clapped her hands and hugged him tight.

What a sweet kid. Duncan stroked her hair. Learning ASL couldn't be that hard. Sally would be all-in on a play date with the dogs and Bronwen. So would the Lanes. One more reason to get Bronwen back to her grandparents.

* * *

Sally sat at her desk collating the print-outs from her research when she heard Jim come through the door. Pixel and Rizzo clattered through the living room to greet him. As usual, she waited her turn. There was a time when she'd tried to be first in line but had given up on that pretty quickly as not worth the risk of being knocked on her ass.

"Sally, where are you?" he called.

"Here. Just a minute." She powered off her monitor, closed her laptop, and left the stack of paper on her desk. Then she went to the kitchen at the back of the house to meet him with a deep kiss. "I expected you much later. Hungry?"

"I grabbed a sandwich around five, but I could eat. What do we have?"

"Leftover Beef Bourguignon. I had dinner with Lisa and Tanelsa."

He groaned in pleasure.

Sally gave him a little push toward the stairs. "Go. Change. I'll get it heated—or at least started."

A few minutes later, he appeared in the kitchen, dressed in his favorite ratty PSP sweatpants and a t-shirt. "That smells ridiculously good."

"As you can see, the boys think so, too." Rizzo and Pixel had not left her side since she poured the stew into a saucepan to reheat. "It's probably not as good as it was fresh off the stove, but it has to be better than whatever fast food you had."

"At least it was Panera, but I can tell you right now this is better." He grabbed a bowl, fork, and a bottle of Edmund Fitzgerald porter, then sat at the table. "Make sure you tell them thanks."

"I will." She tested the temperature. "It needs a few more minutes. How'd your day go?" She sat across from him.

He twisted the cap off the beer bottle. "Long. I'd still be at it if the Beddoes had been home, but after the third call rolled to voicemail, I threw in the towel. We'll try again in the morning."

"We? Oh, right, Kevin Abara. The guy I met earlier."

"That's him."

"How's that going? The temporary partner, I mean."

He took a long pull from the porter. "I wish Cavendish were here. Abara has good instincts but is rough around the edges. Fresh off patrol, but his skills around public interaction need work. He's completely lacking in the professionalism department. I haven't gotten over that comment to you."

"It kinda surprised me, to be honest."

"Yeah, well, I don't think he intends CIS to be a long-term stop in his career with the PSP. He made an off-the-cuff remark about building his resume that didn't thrill me. I could tell he immediately regretted it."

Sally cringed. Such an attitude would not endear the new guy to Jim, who took whatever job he was doing very seriously. "Do you think he'll cut it?"

"If he can take criticism and learn, and realize that hitting on another man's fiancée is not cool, possibly. Time will tell." He got up, checked the pot, and ladled the beef into his bowl.

"I was going to do that."

He waved her off. "You brought it home and warmed it. That was enough." He sat and dug in. After a few mouthfuls, he said, "Tell me what you were doing at the gallery today."

"I told you, looking at art. Oh, that reminds me. I bought a painting."

"Which one?"

"*Night Flowers*, the one of the fireworks over Pittsburgh." She watched him. "It's being delivered later this week, so if you come home and there's a big box in the living room, that's what it is. I'll need help hanging it." She waited for a response.

He thought. "Where do you want to put it?"

"My first thought was over the fireplace, but the heat might damage it. If we can't find a spot in the living room, or if you don't like it, I'll hang it in my office."

"The heat won't be a problem. We'll find a place for it. If it's the one I think it is, I liked it." He forked up another chunk of beef. "What else?"

She should have known better. "Being involved with a trained investigator is annoying." She puffed out her cheeks and let out a breath. She filled him in on her conversation with the gallery owner. "I've been picking around the edges of Ned Tidwell's personal history. Tyler's so-called agent. He's a real piece of work."

Jim didn't stop eating but beckoned with his hand. He swallowed. "Hand it over."

There were times he knew her too well. She got up and brought her research back to the kitchen. "This is everything I've found so far. His clients might be starving artists, but he's not an impoverished agent. He has a nice place in Lawrenceville and drives a brand new Grand Cherokee 4xE. Mortgage up to date. He's also a member of one of Pittsburgh's more upscale country clubs. No criminal record I can find."

"Nice wheels." Jim flipped through the reports.

"According to his website, he currently represents about half a dozen local artists. I wouldn't have thought there was a lot of money in representing lesser-known artists, but based on what I found, I'd say there's money coming from somewhere."

"What kind of credentials do you need to be an art agent?"

"Hardly anything, as far as I can tell." She pointed to a page. "He has a bachelor's degree in business from Robert Morris. No background in art, art history, fine arts, nothing. On his About page, he says he's had a lifelong love affair with the arts, nurtured by his mother, who painted but couldn't make any money. Because of that, he decided to make it his mission to help artists make a living wage off their work."

"Very altruistic of him." Jim raised an eyebrow as he handed back the paper.

"That's what I thought. I'm going to call his other clients tomorrow and maybe see if I can find some former ones." She waved away the stack. "You can keep that. I'll print another copy."

"No. I can't use much, if any, of this. You know your databases have more information sometimes than what I'm supposed to have access to." He skimmed the pages and handed the research back. "But thanks. I'll do my own work tomorrow. Actually, I'll get Abara to do it. He can file all the requests at once."

"Who else are you checking into?"

"Oh no. I'm not telling you that. Quite honestly, I'm surprised you're not a step ahead of me on this one. You talked to Virginia Ridgemont." He took another drink.

"Spoil-sport." She stuck her tongue out, then rested her chin on her hands. He'd mentioned Glynis's boss, so whoever he was running background checks on had to work at The Glassworks. Had that been a slip of the tongue? Doubtful. Jim was too good for that. "Did you learn anything you *can* tell me?"

"Some. I talked to Bronwen. By the way, she wants a visit with Rizzo and Pixel." He grinned. "We'll wait until she's with the Lanes. I got the feeling her foster mother isn't a dog person."

Sally thought about how happy Bronwen had been, petting both dogs. "When will that be?"

"I'll call CPS tomorrow." He raised an eyebrow. "This stays between us, right?"

"Of course."

"If Glynis was dating, she kept it from her daughter. Bronwen's never seen Tattoo Guy. But she did meet one man, a Mr. Craddock."

Sally sat bolt upright. "Craddock? As in Whitley Craddock, the big-shot real estate guy?" Virginia had assumed Whitley was a woman's name, and Sally had followed her lead. Learning Whitley was a man put a new spin on things.

"Could be. Bronwen didn't know the guy's first name." Jim gave her a puzzled stare. "It sounds vaguely familiar. Like I've read it in the news."

"It should, and you probably did. Craddock is a major real estate developer in Pittsburgh. His mother is related to some guy who was big in Pittsburgh's history."

"Like Henry Clay Frick or the Mellons?"

"Something like that. They're distant cousins of some sort. He trots out the connection every time he proposes a *rejuvenation* of a city neighborhood." She made air quotes.

Jim speared another bite of stew. "You say that like it's a bad thing. Some of those neighborhoods could use a facelift."

"Sure, but his form of renovation is gentrification at its worst." She got a loaf of bread, cut off a generous slice, and sat as she handed it to him. "You know, throw out the residents, raze the buildings, and put up yet another block of high-priced apartments and boutique shopping."

Jim made a face.

"He's also married."

Jim lowered his fork. "Huh."

She could tell by his expression he was debating whether to say something. "Mum's the word, I swear."

He sighed. "Glynis was pregnant. Anywhere from eight to ten weeks along."

Sally's mouth fell open.

"Makes me wonder what her connection to Whitley Craddock is."

The exact same thought that had occurred to Sally.

Chapter Seventeen

When Duncan arrived at headquarters the next morning, Abara was already there, a travel mug of coffee on his desk. He looked up. "Morning. I had an idea. Why don't we get the Philly police, or someone from Troop K, to visit the victim's parents again? Also, we could have them track down her brother. Then, I thought we could reach out to the Pittsburgh Bureau of Police and have them take another crack at her in-laws. They must know something, even if they don't think so. That'll free us up to focus on local suspects. What do you say?"

"I think it's half of a great idea." Duncan settled at his desk.

"Only half? What don't you like?"

"The part where we farm out the legwork in Philly and Pittsburgh."

Abara shot him a look of disbelief. "Don't tell me you want to drive across the state to see them. That's what, seven hours?"

"No, you're right. Any destination that requires a plane ticket, you normally get local help. But." He held up a finger. "We already have Hartigan's report. I want to talk to them personally. We might pick up on something you wouldn't get from reading a sheet of paper. I'd set up a video call if I could."

"What about the Lane couple?"

"I believe we've gotten everything we're going to get for now. But I have some new names we can run with." Duncan took a deep breath. "Before we do that, I want to talk to you."

"About what?"

Duncan had made this speech as an FTO when he was uniform. How successful it was depended entirely on the listener. "There were a couple of times yesterday when I found your level of professionalism a little on the low side. For example, when we're in front of a witness, it's important to present a united front. I'm the lead detective. If you have objections or questions, wait until we're alone to raise them."

"I didn't say anything wrong."

"It was the way you said it. When we were talking to Bronwen, I gave you a task, and your first response was to be pissed."

Abara ran a hand through his hair. "You told me to take notes. I'm not a secretary."

It didn't seem like Abara would be one of the better listeners. "If Jenny Cavendish, my partner, was here and I asked her the same, she wouldn't have blinked. The time to object is after the interview, not during it." He held up a hand. "I'm not gonna beat a dead horse here. Bottom line. Coming across as a professional can make a witness decide to talk or clam up. And I'm not just referring to when you're talking to them. How we interact is just as important. Got it?"

Abara glared but held his hands up. "Whatever."

Well, that went over like a fart in church. Duncan gave it up for the present. He didn't trust his ability to stay calm when it came to Sally. Instead, he wrote a list and pushed it to Abara. "These are the people we need to dig into."

He picked it up. "I recognize the two gallery employees. But do you honestly think Whitley Craddock is involved in this?"

"A private source tells me Glynis had a friend named Whitley, and you were there when Bronwen said Glynis brought a Mr. Craddock over once. It's a unique enough name that I'm willing to bet it's the same person."

"How reliable is this source?"

If it had been Cavendish, Duncan would have straight-out said he'd heard it from Sally. But he didn't know how Abara would react to the fact he'd discussed an open investigation with a civilian. "Very reliable. Get those background checks going. I'll call Glynis's parents again."

"The standard?"

"Yep. Wants, warrants, prior convictions. Whatever public financials are available. Property records and anything from the DMV."

"Why don't we call Struthers, Mueller, and Craddock right now?"

"Because I don't want to go in cold."

Abara woke up the computer and typed, all the while grumbling under his breath.

"Is there a problem?" Duncan suspected he knew the cause.

"There's an awful lot of paperwork involved in this job. Even more than on patrol. I kinda thought I'd be out on the street and there were, I don't know, researchers for this kind of thing." Abara focused on the keyboard while he talked.

"We do have researchers." Duncan picked up his phone. "You."

Abara scowled but continued with his task.

Duncan looked up the number he wanted and dialed. After four rings, a man with a deep voice answered. "Rhys Beddoe here. Who is this?"

"Trooper Jim Duncan with the Pennsylvania State Police."

"I already answered questions for the man who came to the house." Beddoe's voice sounded edgy and impatient, but he didn't hang up.

"I understand, sir. I have a few more. In addition, I wanted to speak to you myself and give my condolences to you and your wife."

There was a pause. "I don't recognize this area code."

"I'm calling from Washington County, sir. Troop B headquarters in a little town called Eighty Four." Aside from the name of the county, Duncan doubted Beddoe recognized the name.

"What do you want? I have ten minutes before I have to leave if I'm going to make my tee time."

Duncan had no doubt Beddoe would cut him off mid-sentence, too. "I have the report from Trooper Hartigan. If you don't remember his name, that's the trooper who visited and notified you about Glynis's death. According to your statement, you hadn't spoken to her in a while. Can you be a little more specific?"

"No, I can't." Beddoe huffed. "I made it very clear to Glynis when she married that artist that it would be up to her to mend the fences. She had no business connecting herself to a penniless man, who I thought would die within a year of their marriage. I wasn't off by much. Sad to say, she was too stubborn to admit her mistake."

Because she didn't think it was. Duncan made a note. "Then you haven't spoken to her since her marriage?"

"Possibly. I didn't keep track of dates."

"You've never seen your granddaughter, Bronwen?"

"Not in person. Of course, Glynis sent a birth announcement. We received a photograph of the girl a year or so ago, but I threw it out." A clatter of porcelain. "You have seven minutes remaining."

Harsh man. "It's my understanding that you have quite a bit of money. Did you formally disinherit Glynis? That is, is she still in your will?"

"That's none of your business."

Duncan pinched the bridge of his nose. "Mr. Beddoe, I'm investigating a murder. Your only daughter's, in fact. I think you'll find a lot more of your personal information is my business than you think. If you don't want to tell me, I'm sure I can get a court order."

"You do that. You have five minutes. Catrin, where is my five iron?" The last sentence was softer, as though Beddoe had moved the phone away from his mouth.

"I'm told Glynis had a trust from her grandparents. Is that correct?"

"Since the police rarely ask questions they don't have the answer to, I think you know it is. I advised my mother and father-in-law not to do it, but she was as stubborn as Glynis was."

From the conversation thus far, Duncan thought it was a trait that ran straight from grandmother to father to daughter. If Glynis had been as headstrong as people said, no wonder she and her father hadn't gotten along. "What about your son, Gareth? Do you know if he was in touch with his sister?"

"I doubt it. He and his sister had precious little in common."

"When was the last time you talked to him?"

"We had dinner on Friday at my club. He said he had a business trip this week and would be out of touch." A car horn sounded in the background.

"That's my ride. I'm afraid I have to go." He ended the call.

Duncan slammed down the phone. He'd had three minutes left.

* * *

Sally decided to work from home on Tuesday. There were no scheduled court appearances or meetings on her calendar, but she texted Tanelsa to be on the safe side.

Tanelsa replied quickly. **Don't forget we have to present the Carson deal on Friday.**

Sally bit her lip. **I'll have it done. If I have time, I'll go to Pittsburgh and get the signature for the Montgomery case, too. I'll see you tomorrow.**

Tanelsa's response was a line of thumbs-up emojis.

Since the paperwork for the Carson deal was practically done, the first thing Sally did after feeding the dogs and brewing coffee was call Lena Zelinsky at CPS. Sally knew Jim had said he'd do it, but she also understood the murder investigation came first. If he caught a big break in that, he might never get a chance to call about Bronwen's case.

"I'm working on it, Sally." Lena's keyboard clicked. "The more you bother me for updates, the slower it goes."

"How hard can it be? She has relatives who are willing to take custody, and they're her legal guardians now."

"If they'd known that when they found Glynis Lane's body, it would have been easier. Once a kid's in the system, it's a ton of paperwork." Lena sighed. "Look, off the record?"

"Promise." Sally leaned back in her chair.

"Should be today or tomorrow." The clicking stopped. "I won't bother to ask if that's fast enough for you, but it's the best I can do."

"Perfect. Thanks, Lena." Sally ended the call.

Satisfied that Bronwen was heading home, Sally turned her attention to finding more information about Ned Tidwell. The conversation at the gallery yesterday bothered her. It was absolutely not her area of expertise, but if she could obtain evidence of wrongdoing on his part, she would be better placed to find someone who could help.

She had the information she'd found yesterday. Whatever Tidwell was up to, he hadn't been caught in any illegal transactions. Yet. She went back to his website and clicked over to the page of clients. All of them were local to Southwestern Pennsylvania, but aside from Tyler Lane, none of the names were familiar.

After she made her list, she started at the top and called each person. In some cases, there wasn't an answer. In others, she reached a partner or spouse of the person she wanted. It seemed none of Tidwell's clients were successful enough to make a living wage from art. Because of his incompetence or something else? In every case, she left a message asking for a callback. Maybe some would come through.

As she drew a line through the last name on her list, she tapped her pen on the desktop. What next? Tidwell hadn't been happy with Glynis's decision to sell through The Glassworks. Maybe he had paid off someone at the gallery to sabotage her efforts. "Glynis can't sell Tyler's work, she gives the rights back to Tidwell, and he gets to keep doing whatever he'd been doing." Sally made a note to find out how much had Tidwell been selling the artwork for. Such a scheme only made sense if he had been inflating the price. But to get anyone to buy, he'd have to have documentation that the painting was worth the higher cost.

Last night, Jim had dangled a clue in front of her, that she'd talked to Virginia Ridgemont. He must have been referring to someone connected to The Glassworks. Was one of them Tidwell's partner? If so, what was the arrangement? She ruled out calling Virginia or visiting again. It was one thing to question the gallery owner about a painting she was allegedly interested in buying and had in fact purchased. An interrogation about her employees would certainly put the woman on edge and make her clam up.

But there were other resources. Sally pulled up the gallery website and clicked on the About page, where she saw a link for a staff listing. There weren't a lot of names, which wasn't surprising for a small operation. They might employ interns as floor staff and outsource their accounting. Aside from Virginia and Glynis, only two other women were listed. Delia

Struthers, the person who evaluated the artwork for price, and Olivia Mueller, who was also an associate director. Delia's picture looked like one of those glossy glamour shots. Her wavy blonde hair fell to her shoulders and contained bold streaks of orange. Her eyes were dark under dark brown, sculpted eyebrows. Her makeup looked professionally applied, with smoky eyeshadow and red lipstick on full lips.

By contrast, Olivia appeared mousy. Sally recognized her as the young woman she'd spoken to yesterday, albeit briefly. Brown hair pulled back in a ponytail, pale eyes, pale skin, and not a trace of cosmetics. Olivia was the complete opposite of Delia. Sally hadn't known Glynis when she was alive, but from all reports, Olivia would have shrunk in stature when compared to her as well.

Sally jotted down the names and fired up her databases. "Okay, Delia, who are you?" She sipped her coffee while she waited. Pixel wandered in, came over for a head scratch, then flopped down on his bed in the corner. After a minute or two, the search results popped up. Delia Struthers, thirty-seven years old. Originally from Paterson, New Jersey, she also rented a condo in Lawrenceville. Sally consulted a map. Delia's and Tidwell's residences were separated by a couple of blocks, but it was not impossible they'd crossed paths, especially since they were both involved in the art scene. DMV records showed a Tesla Model 3 registered in Delia's name. Sally pulled up the website for the company that owned Delia's building and clicked through the pictures. "Nice digs for someone who works for a local gallery." Delia had attended Montclair State University and graduated with a degree in Art & Design, no honors.

"Wait a minute." Sally went back to The Glassworks website. "Well, isn't that interesting." Sally took another sip of coffee. In her gallery site bio, Delia claimed to have a degree from the Pratt Institute. Sally searched for the school. Based on the articles she found, the Pratt Institute was definitely more prestigious than a New Jersey public university. The question was how had no one noticed the discrepancy, especially when the truth was so readily available?

Sally made a note and returned to her database search results. That was the only jarring thing. Delia did not have a criminal record or open warrants. Her credit rating was average, and her risk profile showed no serious debt. Her employment history before coming to Pittsburgh listed a few smaller galleries in New York City, but also a brief stint at the Metropolitan Museum of Art.

Intrigued, Sally dialed the museum's contact number. After a few transfers, she reached the department where Delia had worked for six months. After identifying herself, Sally asked whether the woman remembered Delia.

"Oh, yes. Nice girl. She was with us for a little while a couple of years ago," the woman replied. "Why are you asking about her?"

"Her name has come up in a case I'm researching."

"Is she in trouble?"

"Not that I know of. I'm looking for background." Sally hesitated. When the woman didn't hang up, she continued. "Why'd she leave the Met?"

"I don't think that I should say anything. I liked Delia. It was a real shame what happened."

"I understand completely. I'll have to talk to her about it. I'm sure it was nothing."

"She's a good person." The woman sounded like she was trying to decide what to say. "I wasn't directly involved, but I'm sure what happened was a big misunderstanding. She wouldn't be involved in anything criminal, if that's why you're calling."

Yes, the fact she completely misrepresented her educational background is a mere failure to communicate. Why jump to the assumption that Delia was in legal trouble? History, or because Sally had said she was a defense attorney? "I understand. Thank you again." Sally hung up.

Delia had falsified her educational credentials, probably to look like a more attractive employee. She may even have misled subsequent employers about why she'd parted ways with the Met. By law, a company could only say someone had worked for them during the time in question. Saying you worked at the Met and left sounded far better than you were fired for lack of performance. Had Tidwell found out? That would absolutely make her a target for blackmail if he'd been looking to undermine Glynis's efforts on her late husband's behalf.

Even worse, had Glynis discovered the truth? If so, Sally didn't see her as someone who would have kept quiet. If Delia's true background, and her lies, were revealed, it was possible—in fact, probable—she'd never work in the art world again.

Sally looked at her dog. "As they say, the plot thickens, Pixel."

Pixel opened one brown eye, blew out a breath, and went back to sleep.

She went to the kitchen and warmed up her coffee. She returned to her office to focus on Olivia Mueller. Her background was as unlike Delia's as her appearance. She'd gone to Carnegie Mellon, where she'd graduated with high honors. She drove a ten-year-old Chevy Sonic and rented an apartment in Garfield, a neighborhood that was much more affordable and not nearly as trendy as Lawrenceville, although it was the home of the Penn Avenue Arts & Commercial District. She had a second job at a coffee shop in the Strip District. Her risk profile was high due to debt, both loans and revolving credit. According to the address history results, Olivia had lived in five different places in seven years, all rentals, and had been evicted from two of them for failure to pay. The average price of an apartment had gone down with each successive neighborhood, leading Sally to conclude Olivia's income had been shrinking over time. Her expenses may not have kept pace.

If Tidwell had dangled money in front of Olivia, she might have agreed to do whatever he asked. Not only that, if Glynis was the favorite for promotion, Olivia might have seen a scheme as a way to get back at a professional rival. Except all signs indicated Olivia was on the financial edge, if not flat broke. Surely that wouldn't be the case if she'd taken bribes.

Sally debated researching Whitley Craddock but decided to leave that alone. "You are not investigating a murder. It's all about Tyler's art, and Craddock has no connection to that. Keep that in mind." Of course, if either Olivia or Delia said anything that suggested Craddock knew about Tyler's work, Sally would be on the phone in a red-hot minute. And if she happened to learn something about Glynis's death, so much the better.

Chapter Eighteen

Duncan wrote up the notes from his phone call with Rhys Beddoe and went back to his desk. "How's it going?"

"Slow." Abara pushed over a few sheets of paper. He'd been quiet since the earlier talk, but there was no telling whether it had been out of pique or because he'd taken the lecture to heart. "Nothing on any of those names in NCIC or NLETS. No wants or warrants. No drug or terrorist convictions."

"That last isn't surprising." Duncan scanned the printouts. The FBI's National Crime Information Center and the National Law Enforcement Telecommunications System were useful, but not all-powerful. "Although I suppose had anyone been involved in the drug scene and Glynis found out, that would be motive."

"Well, that's a dead end as far as I'm concerned. Especially Mueller. She doesn't have enough cash. If she was dealing, she wouldn't have the credit problems she does." Abara picked up his coffee cup but set it down immediately. "I suppose she could be hiding it. She drives an old car, lives in a lower-socioeconomic-level neighborhood, and none of her financials make her look like a good candidate for that scene."

Duncan found the report on Olivia Mueller. Abara was right. She had all the signs of a woman living practically hand-to-mouth. In his experience, those in the drug trade, even lower level, appeared a little more well-off, even on paper. He scanned her background. "She got a quality degree, though. CMU is pricey. The student loan debt must be crushing." He flipped to Mueller's credit report. It wasn't as high as he'd thought, but high enough to eat a good chunk of her income every month. "Maybe you were classmates."

Abara gave him the stinkeye. "I was a senior when she was a freshman. Besides, I never took an art class, not even as an elective."

No, Duncan was sure that career-focused Abara would not have wasted time on frivolities such as art. Too bad, because it might have helped his personality. Duncan pulled his thoughts back to the job.

Delia Struthers, however, looked to be sitting pretty. Better looking, better credit history, better ZIP code. Better car. He furrowed his forehead. "Struthers's bio on the website. Where does it say she went to school?"

"You saw that, too." Abara's voice held a note of satisfaction. "Don't bother looking it up. What's in her bio and what's in her educational history doesn't match. Now, I suppose someone who graduated from a New Jersey state school might know just as much as someone from…I forget the name of the school, but I know it wasn't the same."

"The Pratt Institute, I think it was." Duncan pulled up The Glassworks' website and went to the Staff page. Then he Googled the Pratt Institute. He whistled. "Yeah, no wonder she claimed to have graduated from Pratt. Much more elite."

Abara consulted his notes. "Ridgemont told us Struthers quit her job at The Glassworks. Think they found out and showed her the door? The old 'leave quietly and we won't make a fuss' deal?"

"Something to ask. We'll set up interviews with both women." Duncan twirled a pen. "What do you have on Craddock?"

"Whitley Craddock, age forty. Married, lives in Pittsburgh, the Highland Park area. Two kids. Wife's name is Aline." Abara read from the screen. "All his public record financials are healthy. There is a new Porsche Cayenne registered in his name. Owner of Craddock Designs, LLC."

Duncan opened a browser and typed it in. The Craddock Designs website was slick. He recognized several of the neighborhoods and developments Craddock had backed. It was pretty much what Sally had told him. "Another company making money off upscale apartments. That'll make him popular or unpopular, depending on who you ask."

"But he must be successful based on the number of projects he's done."

Abara lifted a shoulder. "The price tags on these places are not cheap, and he keeps winning bids. If he's losing money, he's an idiot or someone's fleecing him."

"Got an address for the main office?"

Abara recited it. "I'm looking at the company's social media sites now. Every time they post about a new project, I'd say half the comments are about how it's about time the area saw new growth. The other half are from people either condemning the destruction of historic buildings or forcing lower-income residents out of their homes." He clicked and scrolled. "What do we have here?"

Duncan rolled his chair over to the other trooper's desk. "Show me."

"This post is all about the grand opening of some apartment complex. It's dated six months ago." Abara enlarged a photo. "The woman standing next to Craddock. Look familiar?"

It was Glynis Lane. Dressed in evening attire, she hovered at Craddock's elbow. What did she have to do with the opening of a high-rise? "Are there any others?"

Abara clicked through the shots associated with the post.

"Stop." Duncan pointed at the screen. "There she is again." This time, she and Craddock were closer. Glynis, wearing impossibly high heels, spoke into Craddock's ear. He leaned over, a grin on his face.

"They look awfully cozy." Abara clicked the print button on the browser. "I don't see any pictures of Mrs. Craddock, either."

"No pending divorce filing or evidence she and Craddock might be separated?"

"Nope. I wonder what she's saying to him? Glynis, I mean."

"Good question." Given the absence of any type of painting, Duncan very much doubted it had anything to do with art.

* * *

Sally arrived in Pittsburgh around eleven. Getting the signatures she needed only took twenty minutes. After she was done, she decided to make an unannounced visit to Delia's Lawrenceville address. Her building was a block of condos just across the 40th Street Bridge on Willow Street. Sally parked up on 43rd and walked back to the building. The neighborhood, once home to working-class families, now boasted a mix of luxury condos and apartments interspersed with old homes, all of which looked to be renovated. Sally was sure the interiors no longer contained their original decor or appliances.

Which meant the houses sold for way above their original prices and attracted a completely different demographic.

In the lobby, she scanned the mailboxes looking for Delia's name. The label on the box for 304 said D. Struthers in bold, black letters. Sally pressed the buzzer.

At the same time, a clean-shaven young man pushing a bicycle with wide tires, dual side bags, and a serious suspension came through the locked interior door. "Excuse me. Can I help you? Who are you visiting?"

"I'm looking for Delia Struthers." Sally handed over a business card.

"Castle & Parson? Did someone leave her money, or is she being sued?"

"I'm not at liberty to say." Sally hitched up her purse. "Do you know if she's home?"

"No, but I doubt it. She goes for a run every morning."

"It's almost noon."

"But technically still morning."

Damn it. Sally didn't fancy camping out and waiting. What were the chances Delia would call if she left a card? Slim, if history was any guide.

"You could try The Juicery on Butler Street." The young man leaned his bike against the wall while he checked his mailbox. "She sometimes stops there. I've seen her with their cups."

"Where is that?"

"Block between 43rd and 44th. They make a pretty good cleansing smoothie. You should try it." He shoved the mail into one of the holders on the bike and pushed it outside.

Sally decided to take his comment as a simple recommendation, not a judgment on her physical appearance. She set out at a brisk pace. The weather was good, and while she hadn't worn shoes designed for a long walk, a couple of blocks wouldn't hurt. She might even get some ideas for the wedding from the local stores.

She didn't pass any bridal shops, but The Juicery was easy to spot thanks to a bright green awning with orange lettering. She stepped back to allow a trio of young women in brightly-colored workout attire to exit before she went inside. She took off her sunglasses and scanned the dozen or so people inside the café. Delia stood at the bar, focused on her phone. Her color-tipped hair was pulled back in a knot, and she wore black running gear with a hot pink stripe down the side of the racer-back top and snug leggings. Matching designer running shoes completed the look.

Sally loitered near the back of the store as she planned her approach. Her normal straight-on tactic wouldn't work. She couldn't use Glynis's murder as an excuse. She wasn't representing a client. She didn't know Glynis, so she couldn't claim she was involved because of a friendship. She also didn't want to sound accusatory and push Delia into storming off without saying anything.

But she had bought one of Tyler's pictures. That was the perfect conversation starter. Sally made her way up to the bar and placed her order. Then she moved over to the pickup area and made sure to stand close enough to Delia that conversation would be natural, but not so close as to crowd her.

Sally took out her phone and checked the time. "I hope the service is quick. Seems kinda busy. Maybe I should have gone elsewhere."

Delia's gaze flicked up. "Nah, it's not so bad. You have to be somewhere?"

"Yes, I have a meeting in forty-five minutes, and I have to walk two blocks to get there. City parking at its finest."

"You'll be fine." Delia waved a manicured hand. "The longest I've ever waited was ten minutes, and it's not nearly as busy today."

"Oh, good." Sally pretended to read something on her phone. "I've never come here. How's the Antioxidant Elixir?"

Delia smiled. "Everything is good. I stop on my way home after my run for the Green Goddess, but I've never had anything bad."

"Awesome." Sally wrinkled her forehead. "Do I know you? You look familiar."

"I don't think so." Delia returned her interest to her phone.

Sally snapped her fingers. "You work at The Glassworks. I saw you down there at the latest show. Someone told me you do the painting valuation." She paused. "I love your hair, by the way. That kind of color would never work on me."

"Oh, I don't know. You'll never find out unless you try it." Delia slipped her phone in the side pocket of her leggings. "It's just hair, right?"

Sally took a moment to picture Jim's expression if she walked through the door with Delia's flame-orange coloring. It might be worth doing just for that. "I always wondered what a valuator does. Is that your job title?"

"Not exactly, but that's okay." Delia shot her a look. "Why do you want to know?"

Crap. Sally didn't want to make her suspicious. "Just making small talk. Although." She bit her lip. "Maybe you can help me."

"I quit my job at The Glassworks yesterday."

Sally put on what she hoped was a crestfallen expression. "Damn. I bought a painting, and I think I might have overpaid. It was one of the ones in the second gallery. You know, the Impressionist style with the bold colors."

"Tyler Lane's work."

"That was the name." Sally glanced around. "The prices seemed kinda high, but the owner convinced me it was a good deal. Now I'm not so sure. I wondered if you had anything to do with that and could, you know, set my mind at ease. Or give me a reason to go back and demand a partial refund. But if you quit, well, don't worry."

"Since you brought it up, I can let you in on something, especially since I don't work there anymore." Delia checked her phone. "I didn't set retail prices; at least I didn't for those pieces. I worked with people who brought their pictures in and asked for help deciding how much they're worth. But I'm not surprised you found Tyler's work overpriced. Don't get me wrong. He's a good artist, or at least he was. He died some years ago."

"Oh, I didn't know that." Sally frowned. "Maybe that's why the paintings are so expensive?"

"That's not it. Or not all of it." Delia lowered her voice. "His widow set those prices. If you ask me, she's out of her mind. That's not even her job. She's supposed to design the exhibits, not meddle with pricing. Or at least that was what she used to do."

"Did she quit?"

"No. I read in the paper she was killed over the weekend." Delia examined her manicure. "Maybe now the paintings will go back to her agent. If so, hopefully he'll set a fairer price. One that smart people might pay. The paintings really aren't half bad." She seemed oblivious to the fact her words implied she thought Sally was dumb for paying what had been on the sticker.

"Do you know the agent?"

"I've worked for him a couple times, but I don't know him all that well. He represents several artists in the area. In fact, I might call him about Tyler so he can make some money now Glynis is out of the way." She checked her phone again.

"Sounds like you didn't like her very much."

The girl at the counter called two names. Two women claimed their drinks. Delia took a step forward. "It's not popular to speak ill of the dead and all that, but she probably poked the wrong bear. I'm sorry for her kid, though."

Sally followed. "What do you mean by that? Poking the bear."

"Glynis had an attitude. She thought she knew more than she did, if you get my drift. For example." Delia faced Sally. "A woman brought in a painting she claimed was painted by Albert Bierstadt."

"Was it?"

"Yes, but it was small and obviously hadn't been well cared for so, the value wasn't as high as it might have been. I called the lady and gave her what I'm sure was disappointing news. When Glynis found out, she went off. She told me I didn't know what I was talking about. I have a degree from the Pratt Institute." Delia waited, possibly expecting a reaction.

Sally gave it to her. "Impressive."

"I know. Where was Glynis's art degree from? Not the Pratt." Delia sniffed.

"She told me I couldn't possibly be a Pratt grad, and she'd prove it. She said not only would she get me fired from The Glassworks, I'd never work in the art world again if she had anything to say about it."

"Ouch." Sally could only imagine the humiliation of being fired and blackballed would rankle enough. But if Glynis exposed Delia as the fraud she was, every valuation she'd ever done would come into question. It might even make her the target of expensive lawsuits. "What happened?"

"Nothing, and it doesn't matter now."

"Right, because she's dead."

"Virginia Ridgemont thinks she's all that and a bag of chips, but when LACMA calls, you pick up the phone." After a glance at Sally, Delia elaborated. "Los Angeles County Museum of Art. You know what I'm saying?"

"Mmm." Sally tried to look suitably impressed. Delia's words held a note of pride. No, not pride. Desperation? As though she wanted to impress a total stranger. "You sound like you know your way around the art world, that's for sure."

Delia flipped her hair. "Art is all I've ever wanted to do. I mean, I can't do it myself. But this is my dream. I want my own gallery, to be my own boss. I want every artist out there, in whatever medium, to be calling me, begging for space. I'm going to be the next Gertrude Stein."

"Didn't she have the saying about how women need men like fish need a bicycle?" Sally didn't see the connection.

Delia waved her hand. "She didn't originally say that, but I'm not talking about the feminism. I mean her art collection. She had one of the most impressive collections of art of her time. Picasso, Matisse, Cézanne. All the heavy-hitters of the day."

Delia's passion was obvious. But if her false education claims were known, she'd never make it. The lie would follow her for life, and no matter how good her artistic eye was, she would be forever known as a fraud. The departure for LA was too convenient for Sally. She'd never heard of LACMA, but she'd be willing to bet they had a more robust HR department than The Glassworks.

The question was how far Delia would go to perpetuate her lie.

Before Sally could respond, the girl at the counter called Delia's name.

Delia grabbed a plastic glass full of a green drink, a few napkins, a straw, and returned to Sally. "I gotta run. I'm sorry to say you probably did overpay for Tyler's painting. I would have suggested you try to haggle down to half the listed price. That's my opinion, probably the last valuation I'll do in Pittsburgh. Enjoy your drink." She pushed her way through the door and the knot of people outside without a single word to the people she'd jostled out of the way.

Sally watched her go. "And she thinks Ridgemont is full of herself." Delia hadn't tried to mask her dislike of her former coworker. But would she have said the same thing if Tidwell had represented the paintings?

A thought occurred to Sally. Did Tidwell know about Delia's false credentials? Had he blackmailed her into working with him? But that didn't make sense. If Delia wanted to protect her reputation, she would have eliminated Tidwell, not Glynis. Unless there'd been some kind of accommodation. Help him get control of Tyler's work back, and he'd forget about Delia's fraud. Until the next time he needed something from her, of course, but she wouldn't necessarily know that.

"Sally?" The girl at the counter called out, then smiled when Sally approached. "Enjoy."

Sally grabbed her deep pink smoothie and took a cautious sip. "Not bad." She might not have learned enough to identify Delia Struthers as Tidwell's accomplice, but at least she hadn't completely wasted the seven dollars she'd spent on the Antioxidant Elixir.

Chapter Nineteen

t eleven-thirty, Duncan finished filing the last of his warrant applications for Glynis's phone records and personal financial data. "You ready for lunch?" he called over to Abara, who stood by the copier.

"I thought you'd never ask." He tapped his papers together and tossed them on the desk. "What's around here?"

"There's a pretty good sandwich shop in town. We can grab something and then go over to get these taken care of." Duncan signed the last form. "I'll buy."

Abara stiffened. "No need for that. I have money."

Is he still insulted from our talk earlier? If so, Duncan needed to smooth things over. "No, I should have done it yesterday, it being your first day and all." He slipped all the papers into a manila envelope. "I also should have taken you to Whiskey & Rye for drinks. But we were on the road. We'll do it tonight. First round's on me."

"I told you I can pay my own way."

What was the guy's problem? "It's tradition. Cavendish did it for me when I started at CIS. Now it's my turn. Didn't you do something for the new people when you were in uniform?"

Abara's neck reddened. "I didn't hang out with the other troopers very much. They thought I was stuck up."

Probably because you didn't go out with them. Also, you can be a dick. Police work could be a very cliquey job. The camaraderie was one of the best aspects—at least Duncan thought so. But on the flip side, if the men and women in the barracks believed you weren't pulling your weight or thought too much of yourself, they would cut you out without the slightest regret. It seemed like Abara had done something to find himself on the outside.

Could be they'd seen the same lack of professionalism Duncan had and didn't want to spend their off-hours around it.

"New job, new start." He patted his pockets to check for his keys, phone, and wallet. Then he stood. At that moment, his desk phone rang. Caller ID showed a number with a 215 area code. Someone from near Philly, but not from the PSP. Rhys Beddoe calling back? Doubtful. Besides, it wasn't the number from earlier. "This is Trooper Duncan. How can I help you?"

"Trooper Jim Duncan with the state police?" a woman's voice asked. It wavered and sounded hushed, as though she was trying not to be overheard.

"Yes, ma'am. Can I help you with something?"

"You talked to my husband this morning."

Duncan tapped the desk to get Abara's attention. He pointed toward an empty interview room.

Abara nodded in understanding.

"Ma'am, I'm going to place you on a brief hold." He pushed the button and replaced the receiver. Duncan hurried to the room, waited for Abara, then closed the door. He picked up the handset of the phone on the table and pushed the blinking hold button. "Are you still there?"

"Yes," she said.

"Are you Catrin Beddoe, Glynis's mother?"

"Yes. I...I would have called you sooner, but I had to wait for Rhys to leave. Then I had visitors from my golf group come by to offer their condolences." Catrin took a breath. "They just left. I need to speak with you."

"Mrs. Beddoe, I'm going to put you on speaker so my partner can hear. Is that okay?"

"Yes."

"Good." Duncan did so, then took out his notebook and pen. "I gather this is about your daughter."

"Yes."

Duncan waited, but the silence stretched on. Catrin either couldn't speak or didn't know how to start. "You said you couldn't call until your husband left. Did you want to contradict something he said?"

"No. He told you the truth as far as he knew it." Catrin sucked in some air. "But it's not the whole truth, either."

"I see. Let's start with something easy. When was the last time you spoke to or saw Glynis?"

"I haven't seen her in person for years. The last time was, oh, when Bronwen was two? I went to Pittsburgh for a girls' weekend, or so Rhys thought. But really, I visited Glynis and saw my granddaughter." Catrin sniffled. "But we spoke every week. Rhys played in a golf league every Sunday morning. I would call when he left. Glynis taught me how to use video calling so I could talk to Bronwen, too."

What did Bronwen say? Duncan flipped back to his notes. He'd asked if she'd ever physically met her grandmother. Not had she seen or talked to her. His mistake. He could verify with Bronwen, but Catrin was most likely telling the truth.

"What about when your husband wasn't golfing?" Abara asked. "He must have known, even if you shut yourself into an office or another room in your home."

"When the group doesn't golf, they meet for drinks," Catrin said. "You don't understand, Trooper. Armageddon would not keep Rhys and his friends from their Sunday get-together."

Duncan could only imagine. Four well-dressed, wealthy men of privilege would not let a little thing like weather or life events interrupt their schedule. "Then you know sign language and everything about Bronwen." This was why the pronoun discrepancy had bothered him. Bronwen was right. Her mother and grandfather were on the outs. Catrin may have let her husband speak for her publicly, but privately was another matter.

"Oh yes. It was something else I had to hide from Rhys, but I used an app Glynis told me about. Bronwen is such a dear girl. A perfect blend of her mother and father. She would show me pictures she'd drawn. Glynis would have mailed them, but she couldn't risk Rhys finding out." Catrin paused. "Do the Lanes have her?"

"They will. We had to bring in CPS since we didn't immediately have their names, but I know they want custody." Duncan checked his notes from the previous interview. "They don't think you have much interest in her. In fact, I don't think they knew you and Glynis were in touch. Are you saying you want custody?" That would crush the Lanes.

"I'm sure they didn't. Glynis wouldn't have told them anything for fear it would get back to Rhys. He'd never allow Bronwen to come live with us. She's better off with them." Catrin's sadness was almost tangible. "They must think I'm awful. Not that it was likely they'd contact Rhys, but they might have if only because they were concerned about Bronwen. I'm sure you are all too aware of that, doing what you do."

He brushed by her assumption about the Lanes. "Yes, ma'am. We are."

Abara cleared his throat. "I take it you weren't the one with the objection to Tyler Lane."

"He adored Glynis. What more could a mother want for her child?" Catrin sighed. "Of course, I knew he was sick. I did ask Glynis if she was sure she wanted to marry him. The heartbreak, you know. But Glynis was stubborn, just like her father. No wonder they didn't get along well. Two peas in a pod, as the saying goes."

"What about your son?" Duncan flipped more pages. "Gareth. Would he and Glynis have talked?"

"I doubt it very much." Catrin's voice turned scornful. "Gareth shared all his father's opinions, and I do mean all of them. He thinks it makes him look like the dutiful son. No, the only reason Gareth would have called Glynis is to ask for money."

"Bronwen said he visited once."

"Yes, Gareth told me about it." Catrin paused. "He said she turned him down and told him not to bother asking again. He claims he didn't. He accused Glynis of having an exalted opinion of herself and he didn't need her."

"Doesn't he have his own cash?" Abara asked. "After all, Glynis had a trust from her grandparents, or so we were told."

"That's right. Rhys's mother and father settled money on both of them.

Gareth spent his before he was thirty." Catrin hesitated, then continued. "He's a terrible spender. It's why he lobbied Rhys so hard to cut Glynis out of the will."

"Then Rhys did disinherit her?" Duncan glanced at his partner, who frowned.

"No. Rhys loves his son, but he loves money more." The sounds of fabric rustling came over the line, as though Catrin had shifted. "He disagreed with almost everything Glynis has done with her life, but he still thinks she'd be a better steward of his estate. He's right, of course. Which is why Glynis continues to be the heir of most of Rhys's assets. Some is set aside for me and some for Gareth, but the bulk of the money will go to Glynis or would have."

"Why does it even matter?" Abara drummed his fingers. "Rhys sounded awfully healthy when we talked to him. I don't see him kicking off any time soon."

Duncan gave him a withering glare. The guy had all the tact of a blunt axe. Had no one ever counseled him on how to conduct an interview? "What my colleague means is, normally the potential of a large inheritance would be considered motive. In this case, it seems it would be years before that happens."

"Not as long as you think." From the sound of her voice, Catrin had become worried. "Rhys has stage 4 melanoma. Too many years golfing without sunscreen. He tried treatment, but it made him so sick, he couldn't golf and it wasn't doing much good. So he stopped. The doctors say he has anywhere from four to six months to live, maybe less. It's another reason he refuses to miss his Sunday get-togethers."

"He's that ill and still golfs?" Abara asked. "He told us earlier he couldn't talk to us because he'd miss his tee time."

Her answering laugh was bitter. "My husband hasn't golfed in months. But he can still drink. He waits for his friends at the clubhouse to socialize after they finish."

"Mrs. Beddoe, my next question will sound indelicate, and I apologize." Duncan cleared his throat. "How much money are we talking about?"

"I understand. You have to ask." Catrin's voice dropped to a near whisper. "After taxes, Glynis could have expected to inherit almost five million dollars. If Rhys changed his will, it might go to Gareth. He talked about it once or twice."

Abara let out a low whistle.

"But, right now, wouldn't it go to Bronwen as Glynis's surviving heir?" Duncan asked.

"I don't know. I'm not a lawyer, Trooper Duncan. Rhys blustered, but I have no idea if he actually got around to making the change." Catrin sucked in a breath. "Frankly, I'd rather it go to Bronwen, at least in a trust for when she's older. To be quite honest, I'm afraid of what my son would do with so much money."

That didn't seem right. Duncan made a note to ask Sally that night.

"Mrs. Beddoe." Abara broke in, voice a little harsh. "Where is your son now? Your husband said he was on a business trip. And where was he last Sunday?"

When she spoke, Catrin sounded near tears. "I don't know. He didn't say anything to me about traveling this week, but he's not home. He told me he was going to Hilton Head last weekend with friends, but I saw Mrs. Templeton, the mother of one of the boys, and she said the trip was next weekend."

Duncan and Abara exchanged a look. Finding Gareth Beddoe had just jumped to the top of the to-do list.

Chapter Twenty

Sally sat in her SUV, drumming her fingers on the steering wheel as she mulled over Delia's words. It struck her as odd that Delia had fooled everyone about her educational credentials. Maybe Virginia Ridgemont hadn't done the deepest dive into a prospective employee, but surely the Met had.

Maybe Sally should find the owner of that painting, the one Delia had said was genuine, but worthless. What was the artist's name? Bierstadt. Sally took out her phone and searched. According to the article she found, Bierstadt was an American painter of some note. If the owner would allow Sally to get it evaluated again, it would expose Delia's fraud. It wouldn't explain how Tidwell and Delia had worked together, if that had been the case.

But it would give her a motive for murder.

Before Sally could do anything else, the phone rang. Caller ID showed a local phone number. "This is Sally Castle."

"Oh, Ms. Castle. This is Eva Lane." The older woman sounded near tears. "I'm sorry to bother you, but I don't know who else to call."

A cold stone settled in Sally's throat. "No worries, Mrs. Lane. It's why I gave you my card."

"Call me Eva, please."

"Eva." Sally took a deep breath. "Is something wrong with Bronwen's case? Are Glynis's parents contesting your custody?"

"Oh, no. Nothing like that. In fact, we're picking her up this afternoon. She'll be so happy to be home, and we can help her get past the trauma of losing her mother. We haven't heard anything from the Beddoes. Sadly, that's not a surprise."

Relief flooded Sally. "I'm glad to hear it. What else can I help you with?"

"It's Tyler. Well, not him, but his paintings." Eva sniffled. "It's so complicated. I don't know how to start explaining."

"I happen to be in Pittsburgh right now. How about I come over and we'll talk?" If whatever the problem was involved the artwork, it most likely had something to do with Tidwell.

"Oh, would you? We're at our wits' end here." Eva's gratitude came through clearly.

"Give me"—Sally checked her GPS—"half an hour." They said goodbye, and Sally hung up. She stopped at a bookstore in Squirrel Hill that was on the way and bought a book about dogs as a welcome-home present for Bronwen. Then she drove over to the Lane house.

When Eva opened the door, her red eyes and pale face were mute evidence she'd been crying. "Oh, thank goodness you're here. You'll know what to do."

"I brought something for Bronwen." Sally stepped inside and handed Eva the book. "I hope I live up to your expectations."

"You will." Eva ushered Sally through the living room and into a bright, cheery kitchen. The blue motif from the family room continued on the walls, but in a lighter hue. The honey-colored cabinets matched a square, sturdy table that could seat four. The front of the retro-style refrigerator was adorned with a child's artwork. Sally recalled the Lanes saying Bronwen was a budding artist, and the drawings were much better than anything Sally produced at the same age.

Paul sat at the table, his glasses perched at the end of his nose. A pile of papers was strewn in front of him, and he held a sheet in each hand. He glanced between them and occasionally looked at the paper on the table. He wore the expression of a man trying to understand the information he had, but not quite accomplishing his goal. He looked up. "Thank heavens you're here. I can't make heads or tails of this mess." He nodded toward an empty chair.

Sally put her purse on the table and hitched the seat closer. "What's the trouble?"

"This." He thrust the papers at her.

"What am I looking at?"

"That's just it. We don't know." Eva set a mug of coffee next to Sally, along with a small pitcher of half-and-half and a plate of shortbread. "It arrived in yesterday's mail. All we understand is that it's from Ned Tidwell and the phrase *cease and desist*. Other than that, he uses such big words that we're lost."

Sally skimmed the paper. She hadn't dealt with anything like this since her first year of law school, but she got the gist of the message. "He's ordering you to stop selling Tyler's artwork through The Glassworks. He claims he's the only person with the right to sell it, especially now that Glynis is dead." She wrinkled her nose. "He's also claiming you owe him money for anything that's been sold and damages in the amount of…holy shit, five hundred thousand dollars." She glanced at the horrified couple. "Excuse my language."

Eva moaned and pressed her hands to her cheeks.

"That's preposterous." Paul's skin paled, but his voice had a harsh edge. "Glynis sold the paintings for more than what Tidwell did; at least she said so. But half a million? It wasn't that much. We don't have that kind of money. Not if we sold the house, emptied our retirement, and Bronwen's college savings."

Sally held up a hand. "Let me read this." She flipped back to the first page of the document and read again, this time pummeling her brain for what she'd learned all those years ago. After a few minutes, she set it down. "Okay. At first glance, this doesn't look great. My slightly educated guess is that he threw out a high sum to frighten you and has something else in mind."

"He got the frightened part right." Paul took off his glasses and rubbed his eyes.

"You can fight it, right?" Eva asked as she wrung her hands.

Sally sighed. "I'm not a contract lawyer. I know just enough to suspect he's bluffing, but not enough to help you." She drummed her fingers on the table. "Did Tyler name a person responsible for his artwork in his will? Like an artistic executor?"

The couple exchanged a helpless look. "We don't know. If he did, it would have been Glynis. She had to have a copy of his will in her house. She was very organized."

Of course. Sally would ask Jim if he had found anything in his search. "What are the terms of her will?" she asked. "Broadly speaking."

"Paul's the executor." Eva laid a hand on her husband's shoulder. "Everything goes to Bronwen. Well, there are a few small bequests, including one to us. She named us as Bronwen's guardians. All the money is in a trust until Bronwen turns twenty-one. That's all we're aware of."

"How much cash are we talking about?"

"I don't know." Paul took off his glasses and pinched the bridge of his nose. "Six figures, at least. We know Glynis had a trust, but she never told us exactly how much was in it. The will does specify that Bronnie gets all Glynis's liquid assets. What about the artwork? Does she get that?"

"Maybe." Sally sifted through the pages. "I don't do wills or estates, either. If you needed a defense attorney, I'm your girl. But this?" She waved a hand over the table. "You need someone for the will and someone for contracts. Preferably someone who does intellectual property and knows about art."

Eva buried her face in her hands.

Paul patted her head. "We don't know anyone like that. Well, we can call the guy who did our wills. But the other? Where would we even start?"

Sally took the opportunity to study the couple. To say they looked like lost lambs was an understatement. She had to do something.

"Tidwell better hope he doesn't come by the house, the vulture." Paul took off his glasses. "He's doing this because Glynis is dead and he knows we don't have the first clue, isn't he?"

"Maybe." Sally swept up the paper. "He thinks if he bullies you, you'll cave and give him what he really wants, which is the rights to Tyler's artwork. I doubt he really thinks you can cough up the money. It could be a scare tactic."

"But why?" Eva asked.

Sally debated how much to say. "It's possible he was lying about the sale of Tyler's work, giving your son pennies on the dollar and pocketing the majority of the sale. I've spoken to the owner of the gallery where Glynis worked. She said it's possible Glynis threatened him with a lawsuit or audit, although the owner isn't sure Glynis ever took action. If anything, it could very well be that it's him who owes you money, not the other way around."

"Can you prove that?" Paul's eyes glinted. "Or is that what the cops are investigating?"

"The police are concerned with Glynis's murder. If they uncover anything as a result of that investigation, they'll hand it off to the proper authorities." Which might be the same department of the State Police, but maybe not. It was something else to ask Jim. "But if you're asking if you should call them over this, I'd say no. This is a civil matter."

Eva sighed.

"That brings us right back to the beginning." Paul heaved himself to his feet. "Ms. Castle, can you do it? Prove this Tidwell character is a fraud?"

Sally locked her gaze on his. "It's not something I usually do."

"But can you? We'll pay you for your time."

Money wasn't Sally's concern. She was an attorney, not a private investigator, something Tanelsa would be quick to point out. She had no experience in this area of law. She didn't want to make promises she couldn't keep. Even so, she had more knowledge and resources than the Lanes. "I'll tell you what I'll do. First, I'm going to scour my list of contacts for a good IP lawyer. Someone who can help you respond to Tidwell's claims. If I don't know someone, my partner may. That'll address the immediate concern. For now, do not respond to this." She shook the paper. "Do not talk to him on the phone. If he shows up at the house, tell him to leave, and if he won't, call the police and have him arrested for trespassing. You have nothing to say, and above all, do not sign anything. Got it?"

The couple nodded. Eva's eyes shone with tears, probably of frustration considering her personality, and she clenched her fist.

"I'm not a private investigator, either. But I do have some resources. Let me do a little digging. Based on what I find, I'll be able to advise you on how to proceed." She stood. "You can pay a retainer for our services for now. Let's see where this goes. Sound fair?"

Paul grasped her hand. "First, you save our granddaughter's life, and now you're doing the same for her father's legacy. Thank you."

Sally offered her best confident smile in return. Bronwen hadn't really been in danger, and Sally had no idea if she could do anything about Tidwell. She wasn't going to say anything to the Lanes, though. Not when they were clutching her as tightly as if she were the last life vest on a sinking ship.

Hopefully, she wouldn't drown with them.

Chapter Twenty-One

Duncan gave Abara the job of tracking down Gareth Beddoe's location. At the same time, Duncan ran Gareth's name through NLETS and the NCIC database. He also ran the standard credit and background checks. By mid-afternoon, he had the framework of a picture, and it wasn't necessarily pretty.

Abara dropped the phone receiver into its cradle. "Does anybody like this guy except his mother?"

Duncan's gaze flicked up. "What do you mean?"

"I called his landlady, his boss at his last job, and a guy whose name the landlady gave me as a friend. Or at least that was her impression, since he visited frequently. None of them have anything good to say about Gareth Beddoe."

Duncan set aside his work. "What've you got?"

"He's three months behind on his rent. The landlady said if she sees him and he doesn't have her money, not only is she changing the locks on his place, she'll sell his stuff and sic a collection agency on him." Abara drank from a bottle of sports drink. "According to her, he's not home much, even when his rent is up to date. When he is, he has a habit of hosting loud parties that annoy the other tenants. The cops have been there more than once. She doesn't think much of his so-called friends, either. She described them as a collection of Main Line brats and hangers-on looking for a good time, which Beddoe seems more than capable of providing. However, she's also seen past-due mail in the trash with the empty bottles for top-shelf booze. She swears there was a guy in the parking lot last month looking for

Beddoe's car. He kept comparing all the cars there with a piece of paper in his hand. He made a phone call, swore a lot, and left."

Duncan looked through his findings. "Beddoe drives a new Audi RS5." He opened a browser and whistled. "Those things start at eighty grand, and I'm sure he got one with all the options."

"Nice ride." Abara flipped a page. "Until last month, he worked at Rogers & Gunn Investments."

"He has a degree in finance from St. Joseph University, so that makes sense."

"Yeah, well, he sucked at it. His manager said he was always late, his work was sloppy, and he spent more time on the golf course than in the office. They finally let him go after he botched one of their big accounts. Client lost money, lawsuit threats, the works."

Duncan paged through the pile until he found Beddoe's education records. "He graduated without distinction after five years."

"Maybe daddy paid for it. I'm not talking about tuition." Abara took another drink.

St. Joe's had a good reputation. Duncan doubted that was the case. Then again, money talked. He made a note to find out if the elder Beddoe had made any significant financial contributions around the time of his son's graduation. "Either that or the school granted him a degree because he'd met the minimums. You don't need straight As to get a diploma." He would try to get Beddoe's transcript or the name of his advisor. "What about the friend?"

"Nathan Osterman. He and Beddoe went to college together and were in the same fraternity. According to him, he loaned Beddoe money on a couple of occasions after college because Beddoe was afraid to ask his father."

"How much?"

"Almost fifty grand." Abara tossed the notebook on his desk. "Allegedly, he hasn't seen Beddoe in three weeks, which was when Osterman demanded the amount be paid, in full, 'or things would get ugly.' The last bit is a direct quote."

"Well, at least those descriptions match what I've found." Duncan read from the screen. "No current wants or warrants, but he was busted several times in college for misdemeanor possession of marijuana, public indecency, and public intoxication. Separate charges. Each time he pled out and got community service."

"Thanks to daddy, I'm sure." The edge in Abara's voice could have cut rock. "I knew guys like that at CMU. They thought the world owed them everything because their parents footed the bill. The rest of us, the ones who put in the work, were social chumps but they sang a completely different tune when they needed help finishing a paper or studying for an exam."

That's right. You're a Carnegie Mellon grad. Duncan knew the school by reputation. It was known for the quality of its engineering school, but also had top-notch programs in other disciplines, all of which came at a premium price. Abara would have seen a lot of entitled rich kids. If he'd spent four years trying to fit in with them, that might explain his more annoying traits. But the knowledge made his habit of cutting corners even more puzzling.

Abara didn't seem to notice that Duncan's attention had wandered. He finished his sports drink and threw the bottle in the recycling bin. "I bet he has a whole wallet full of platinum cards."

Duncan wrenched his thoughts back to the task at hand. "Nope. He has almost no credit history. The only card I can find is an American Express Centurion, but the account is in his father's name, not his."

"You need major income to qualify for that." The younger man's eyes narrowed. "Daddy gave him a card on his account? Why?"

"It may be a way for the elder Mr. Beddoe to keep track of his son's spending. Might even be so he can tighten the purse strings if junior gets out of line. At the same time, he can quietly pay off the balance and keep his son out of trouble. My guess is that Gareth doesn't qualify for an account on his own."

Abara tilted his head. "Then why is he behind on his rent, and there's a guy looking to repossess his car?"

"My guess? Gareth hasn't told his father, and Beddoe Senior isn't listed as a co-signor on either the lease or the car loan."

"How much did Mrs. Beddoe say Glynis would have inherited?" Abara frowned.

"Somewhere in the neighborhood of five million dollars."

"Definitely worth killing over, but why now?" Abara paused. "Why not wait until the old man was dead?"

Duncan raised an eyebrow. "Think about it. We haven't seen a copy of Glynis's will yet, but based on what you know of her, would she have left her money to her brother?"

It only took a moment for Abara to connect the dots. "No way. She'd leave it to her daughter. Which means Gareth would need his sister out of the way before his father kicked off."

"Not only that, Rhys would have to change his own will." Duncan aimed a finger at his partner. "I was going to ask Sally, but I looked it up myself. Under Pennsylvania law, if Glynis predeceases her father, guess who would get her inheritance?"

Abara wrinkled his forehead, but then his expression smoothed. "Presumably her heir, who we assume is Bronwen. That's how my grandfather's will worked. If mom died before he did, her portion would go to her surviving issue or whatever the legalese calls it."

"Exactly. Whoever left skin under Glynis's fingernails got close enough for her to scratch him." Duncan paused, watching as his words sank in.

Abara bobbed his head slowly. "Which might mean she knew the person and trusted him. Or her. Or at least didn't consider the person a threat." He locked eyes with Duncan. "Like her screw-up of a brother."

"We can't completely discount the possibility of self-defense. Or wanting to defend her daughter. Both are pretty powerful instincts." Duncan thought. "But I agree that your scenario is more likely."

Abara jiggled his mouse to wake up his computer. "All of a sudden, I really want to find Gareth Beddoe."

Duncan watched with satisfaction as Abara typed furiously. That was the work ethic of a CMU grad and a successful investigator—as well as someone who wanted to prove himself.

* * *

133

Sally arrived back in Uniontown and spent almost half an hour bringing Tanelsa up to speed on the Lanes' situation, including the cease-and-desist letter from Ned Tidwell. Her notes and the legal papers the Lanes had received were spread out on the small table in the main office while the lawyers sat facing each other. "That's about the size of it." She swept hair from her face.

"What an asshole." Tanelsa picked up the cover letter. "These poor people have to be shell-shocked."

"They are." Sally sat back and twisted a piece of her hair around her finger. "This is Tidwell making a money grab, pure and simple. I didn't say that, but you and I both know it. He's taking advantage of the fact the Lanes are ignorant of contract law, and he's betting they can't afford a good lawyer even if they could find one."

Tanelsa's eyes moved back and forth as she read another document. "He'd never have tried this with Glynis, that's for sure. She wouldn't let him get away with it. Not if she was the kind of person who took no shit, like everyone says she was." Tanelsa tossed aside the paper. "You think he had anything to do with Glynis's murder? Step one, get her out of the way. Step two, hit up Tyler's parents."

The thought had occurred to Sally while she drove home, but she'd brushed it aside. "Possibly, but that's not our problem. I know this is gonna shock you, but we have no business investigating Glynis's death."

Tanelsa clasped her hands to her chest. "Be still, my beating heart. Sally Castle backing down?"

"I'm not backing down from anything." She looked up. "I have to help the Lanes as best I can. Otherwise, they'll get stripped of everything they have. The best way for me to do that is to focus on this lawsuit and let Jim handle finding their daughter-in-law's killer. I understand if you don't want to get involved, though. This isn't in our lane."

"It's not, but from what you said, we aren't litigating this one. We're hand-holding and giving emotional support." Tanelsa got up and went to her desk. "Maybe in the process, we can pin criminal charges on this sleazeball. That wouldn't make me sorry."

"Nor I." Sally watched her partner sit and scroll through her phone. One of the reasons she'd asked Tanelsa to join her in private practice was their shared sense of justice. It hadn't been a sure thing, but Sally would've wagered a good bottle of Merlot that Tanelsa would be on board. "We need to find a good contract attorney."

"That's what I'm doing." Tanelsa waved her phone. "I have one name to start. If he can't help, I'm sure he'll be able to recommend someone else. I want to find someone who just doesn't do contracts, but who has worked in the art world." She tapped the screen and held the phone to her ear.

While Tanelsa made her calls, Sally went back to her computer. She logged into her databases and searched for Ned Tidwell. Where he lived, what kind of car he drove, his credit history, and any criminal charges. On the last, he was clean except for a slew of traffic violations on top of a pile of unpaid parking tickets from the City of Pittsburgh. How he'd avoided racking up enough points to warrant a license suspension, or avoided having his car booted, was anyone's guess. His credit history was average, and he lived in a condo in Lawrenceville, which he'd purchased a few years ago for three hundred and fifty thousand dollars. He lived in the same neighborhood as Delia. What were the odds they knew each other? "How many clients does he have?" Sally asked herself in a low voice.

Tanelsa paused in what she was doing. "Did you say something?"

"Talking to myself. Any luck?"

"I'm on my second referral. Keep your fingers crossed."

Sally turned back to her computer. She pulled up a browser, entered *Tidwell Arts Management* in the search bar, and went back to his website. He claimed to represent the best of the Pittsburgh art world and help them get "top dollar" for their work. She went to the clients' page, where there were at least a dozen names. She used the online Yellow Pages to find phone numbers for each one of them and started calling.

"Tidwell? That ass wipe," the first man said in response to her question. "I fired him over a year ago. Made all sorts of claims he never delivered on. I go to the Arts Festival every summer and make twice what he brought in, if not more."

"Do you know his website still lists you as a client?" Sally asked.

"I'll kill him. Part of the agreement was he had to take my name down."

Tidwell's slimy tactics extended to his marketing as well. "Tell me, did you know an artist named Tyler Lane?"

"Lane, Lane." The man paused. "Deaf guy, died about five years ago?"

"Maybe a little more, but yeah, that's him."

"He did great work. In fact, Tidwell used him as a reference. I only met him a couple of times before he died. Seemed like a good guy."

It was unlikely Tidwell shared information between clients, but maybe the two men had talked. "Did you ever compare your sales results with Tyler?"

"We were at different parts of our careers, but we emailed." The artist swallowed. "I do remember him saying it was a long game, and you had to be patient. Does Tidwell still have rights to his work? I hope to hell he doesn't."

"That's what I'm working on. Thanks for your time." Sally ended the call.

Two other artists she contacted had fired Tidwell anywhere from a few months to a couple of years ago. A third was in the process of terminating her contract. All had similar stories of work selling below expectations with Tidwell and much better success selling on their own.

Tanelsa knocked on her desk to get Sally's attention. "Thank you. Tomorrow at nine. See you then." She ended her call and set the phone down. "Got one. Nithya Patel. She's a specialist in artistic intellectual property law and contracts. We have a meeting with her at her office in Pittsburgh tomorrow at nine."

Sally bit her lip. "The Lanes are gonna blow through our retainer if we have to keep driving to and from Pittsburgh."

"We'll cut them a deal." Tanelsa waved her hand. "You find anything?"

"Plenty." Sally relayed all the information she'd learned from her research and her phone calls. "Sounds like he's a serial shyster with terrible driving habits. Not quite a con man, but definitely taking advantage of general ignorance surrounding contract law."

"In other words, a grade A creep." Tanelsa sat back. "Sally, I have to be honest. Usually, your jaunts into these little moral crusades drive me a little loony. This time, I hope to God we find some dirt on Tidwell and nail his ass to the wall."

Sally liked the sound of that.

Chapter Twenty-Two

Duncan hit the Send button on the last request for background information on Gareth Beddoe. As he did, his attention snagged on movement at Cavendish's desk.

Abara had stood and shrugged into his jacket. "See you tomorrow morning."

"Where are you going?"

"Home. You said something about drinks, but it looks like you're busy." Abara waved a hand in Duncan's direction.

He wasn't wrong. Fifteen minutes earlier, Glynis's cell phone records had arrived. The plan had been to go over them, then hit Whiskey & Rye for the aforementioned drink. "We still have work to do."

Abara made a show of checking his watch. "But it's after five. If we aren't going drinking, I do this online MMPORG, and it starts at six."

"A what?"

"Massively multiplayer online role-playing game."

Duncan raised an eyebrow. "I would have thought you'd know by now we don't have a job with regular hours."

"Well, yeah, but...that was on patrol and only if a call came in late." Abara shifted on his feet. "We can't move on Beddoe until we get the info we requested. And those cell phone records will still be there tomorrow. I thought this job would be a little more predictable." He scrubbed his hair.

"We work the case until there's nothing left to work." Duncan held up the paper. "Looks like work to me."

"But you don't need me for that, right?" A pleading note entered Abara's voice.

Duncan blew out his breath. He could play hardball and insist Abara stay. But would he wind up working with a sullen partner who put forth a half-assed effort? It wasn't worth the possibility. "Fine. See you tomorrow. However." Duncan aimed a highlighter at his partner. "I advise you to tell anyone else you planned on meeting after hours, even if it's online, that you might not make it. Got it?"

Abara cheeks darkened, and he swallowed. "Yeah. Thanks." He scurried out, almost as if he wanted to be gone if Duncan changed his mind.

A moment later, Lieutenant Ferguson walked up. "Status?"

Duncan gave her the run-down of the day's activities. "Needless to say, I'm very interested in finding where Beddoe was last weekend."

Ferguson nodded once. "Partner in the bathroom?"

"He left for the day. Said he needed to leave to go play some online game."

Ferguson scrunched her face. "Did you tell him this is a fresh homicide? And that unless you had no further leads for the day, you don't go home?"

Full sentences. *That can't be good. Hope she's not pissed at me.* "I did." Duncan shrugged. "I'm not his boss. I'm not even his permanent partner. I can't make him stay. Besides, working with a guy who clearly wants to be elsewhere isn't pleasant. Not for me. I can examine the phone records alone."

Ferguson crossed her arms and tapped her fingers on her biceps. "I'll have a talk with him in the morning. Carry on." She left.

He let out a deep exhale. He was sure that if Ferguson had a serious problem with his actions, she would not have left without a more in-depth response. But he didn't want to be anywhere near her tomorrow when she gave Abara his talk.

He sent a text to Sally. **Working late again. Hopefully not too long**. He set it down, and a moment later, it sounded her text tone.

Understood. I'll keep a plate for you. The words were followed by a kissy-face emoji.

Duncan debated getting a cup of coffee from the break room but opted for a Coke instead. He grabbed a highlighter and turned his attention to

Glynis's phone records. As expected, there were a lot of calls to and from her in-laws. A week ago, she'd received a call from her mother that lasted almost ninety minutes. He scanned through the list, but that was the only recent call between the two, which backed up what Mrs. Beddoe had told him. He highlighted almost a dozen calls in the last two weeks from a different 215 number. A reverse lookup told him the number belonged to Gareth Beddoe.

Duncan checked the message history retrieved from the phone. The last one was from her, telling him to stop pestering her and that she wasn't going to change her mind. "Change her mind about what?" Duncan mused. Beddoe would have known his sister was their father's primary beneficiary. Did he want her to back out? Or had he been angling for a loan once the older man died?

Duncan checked the phone's contact list. No entry for Gareth Beddoe. Was there so much antagonism between the siblings that Glynis didn't even list her brother as a contact?

Even more reason to find out where Beddoe was last weekend.

Next, he highlighted multiple texts to a 724 number. No voice calls. Another reverse lookup revealed it belonged to someone named Christopher Janssen. Duncan put down the phone company records and went back to the history from Glynis's phone. But there wasn't any message data from Janssen. The entire conversation had been deleted, and they'd been simple SMS text messages, so there was no way to see the content from the provider records. Why would she do that? Only two reasons made sense. Either the conversation wasn't important, or she didn't want anyone to see it. No contact for him on her phone. Duncan made a note to research Janssen. *Tomorrow. Save something for Abara to do. After Ferguson is done with him, he's gonna need it.*

What Duncan didn't find were any phone calls or texts to or from Tidwell, which surprised him. He grabbed her landline phone records and scanned them. No calls to or from Tidwell there, either. They must have communicated primarily by email, which would make sense if they were in a fight over Tyler Lane's art rights. In any legal battle, Glynis would want a written record. Duncan made a note to have Abara call the tech guys tomorrow and get the status on the laptop analysis.

Duncan looked at the pages covered in highlighter marks and realized there was one other number that was conspicuous by its absence. There was no communication between the victim and Whitley Craddock. Why not? He'd come to the house at least once. When he'd talked to Sally, he'd gotten the feeling she thought Glynis and Craddock might be involved as lovers. They had found men's toiletries in the house. Craddock's, or were they for someone else? Sally had also mentioned Craddock in the context of her conversation with Virginia Ridgemont. Perhaps he had been giving advice on the artwork situation. But if that were the case, why no communication between the victim and Craddock? It seemed odd that such conversations would only occur face-to-face. She didn't have a contact entry for him either.

Duncan picked up the phone and dialed the Lanes' house. "Good evening. Is this Mrs. Lane? It's Jim Duncan with the PSP. I hope I'm not interrupting your dinner."

"We're about to leave," Eva said. "We picked up Bronwen earlier today and we're going out for Thai to celebrate."

"I'm so sorry. I should have checked the time."

"It's fine. If you're calling about Glynis, I'm happy to take a minute." Her voice caught over her daughter-in-law's name. "Have you found the person responsible?"

"Not yet, but I'm working on it." He typed the name Whitley Craddock into his browser search bar. "Quick question. Two, in fact. One, did Bronwen sleep over at your house ever?"

"Oh yes. We had a standing arrangement. She spent every Friday night here." Eva chuckled. "That was Glynis's night to herself. She loved Bronwen to death, but every woman needs a break."

Which corroborated Bronwen's statement. "Do you know what she did on those nights?"

"She rarely said. I assumed she was with friends."

Or one special friend. "Next question. Did Bronwen ever talk to you about any men at the house? Anyone in particular?"

"No." Eva drew out the word. "I can't say she did. At least not that ever registered with me. Why do you ask?"

"Just following lines of inquiry. Thank you. Enjoy your dinner." He hung up.

He stared at the phone number for Christopher Janssen. Who was he? Based on the data Duncan had, his guess was a business associate of some kind. "What the hell," he muttered and did a quick search. Nothing. Nobody had mentioned the man's name up until now, and Glynis had made lots of other calls to people she didn't have as contacts. Given the facts in front of him, he had to prioritize, and Janssen didn't make the top three. Not yet.

He checked his watch. It was six o'clock. He'd fill out the paperwork necessary for background information on Whitley Craddock, then head home. After all, he had to leave something for Abara to do.

* * *

Sally heard the crunch of tires on the gravel drive outside and looked up. Quarter after seven. Not too bad. When Jim was in the early stages of a homicide investigation, she'd known him to not get home until ten. Seven was downright early.

A car door slammed shut. Rizzo and Pixel sprang to their feet and raced to the back door. Sally followed at a more leisurely pace. By the time she made it to the kitchen, Jim had entered and given Rizzo and Pixel their expected attention. She walked up and kissed him. "Welcome home. Early night, huh?"

He squeezed her butt. "Only you would describe getting home at seven-thirty as an early night."

"It's why you love me."

"One of the reasons." He inhaled. "Smells fantastic."

"Baked ziti with mozzarella, and I made garlic bread." She tilted her head up to look into his eyes. "I've learned to make things that are easily reheated."

"Good call. Let me get out of this suit. I'll be right back."

While Jim went to change, Sally set out a plate and silverware, took the pasta dish out of the oven where it had been staying warm, and opened a bottle of Edmund Fitzgerald porter. She popped the garlic bread in the toaster oven to heat it up.

He came back dressed in his off-work clothes, a T-shirt and sweats. "Thanks." He took a deep drink of the beer. Then he sat, spooned a generous helping of pasta onto his plate, and dug in.

Sally set the bread next to him and let him eat for a couple of minutes. "What kept you this time?" she finally asked.

He held up a finger, swallowed, and took another drink. "The victim's phone records." He gave her a brief synopsis of his day.

"Abara left early? Why'd you let him?"

"Like I told Ferguson. I'm not his boss." Jim loaded up his fork with ziti. "It'll be taken care of."

Sally bit her lip. "It doesn't sound like this guy is cut out for investigative work."

"He might not be." Jim shrugged. "Not everyone is. Time will tell." He ate another mouthful, then asked, "Did Ridgemont definitely tell you the victim was involved with Whitley Craddock?"

Sally thought back to her conversation with the art gallery owner. "No. In fact, I don't think she even knew Whitley was a man. It is kind of an androgynous name." She drummed her fingers on the table. "Yeah, now that I think back, I believe Virginia referred to Whitley as a she. You think Glynis kept the toiletries for him?"

"If Bronwen spent every Friday with her grandparents, Glynis wouldn't have to worry about entertaining company." Jim took a pull on the beer bottle. "Anyone mention the name Christopher Janssen?"

"Never heard of him. Who's he?"

"A guy Glynis texted. It's feeling more and more like a business contact. She didn't have his name in her phone, no voice calls, and no one else has mentioned him."

Sally considered the information. Glynis had tried to be discreet. But Jim was right. It was hard to hide a close relationship from every single person in your life.

"What are you up to?" He eyed her. "Please don't tell me you spent all day on a murder that has nothing to do with anything you or Tanelsa are working on."

"I didn't." She took a deep breath. "The Lanes hired me for another matter." She proceeded to fill him in on the threatened lawsuit.

Jim stared, fork in midair. "You're kidding me. Tidwell seriously sent them a letter like that?"

"Yep." Sally stood up, got herself a slice of garlic bread and a glass of water, and retook her seat.

Jim studied her. "You don't think this is over your head? Why not give them the name of this new lawyer and bow out?" He chewed as he watched her.

"Because Eva and Paul don't know her. She may be fabulous. She probably is. But." Sally took a bite of bread, chewed, swallowed, and wiped her hands with a napkin. "They do know me, and they trust me. All I'm doing is holding their hands. Think of me as a human security blanket."

He grinned. "You make me feel safe all the time."

His expression was a little too sly. She swatted him lightly. "Stop it. That reminds me. Has Bronwen been delivered to their custody yet?"

As Jim wiped up sauce with the last bit of bread, he nodded. "This afternoon. I talked to Eva earlier. Time to arrange a playdate?"

"I'm going up there tomorrow for the meeting with Nithya." Sally picked up the dirty dishes and took them to the dishwasher. "I'd take Rizzo and Pixel to play with Bronwen while the adults talk, but she'll be at school. We'll set something up." She bent over to put a tab in the dishwasher before she closed the door.

"What you're telling me is you'll be too busy to look into Glynis's murder, correct?" Jim came up behind her. She faced him, and he brushed hair off her forehead.

"I decided I don't have any skin in this game. I'm not representing anyone accused of the crime or who is involved in any way." She placed her hands on his chest. "Yes. I'm sitting this one out. I think I'll have my hands full with the bogus lawsuit. Plus the other open cases Tanelsa and I have. And plan our wedding. I ignored three calls and four texts from my mother today. She's going to bite my head off when I see her next."

He laid his hand over hers. "Mark your calendars, ladies and gentlemen. Sally Castle is deciding *not* to pursue a murder investigation."

"For now, at least." She wagged a finger at him. "If I get even a whiff that Ned Tidwell is responsible for Glynis's death, all bets are off."

He kissed her forehead. "I'd expect nothing less."

Chapter Twenty-Three

When Duncan arrived at HQ on Wednesday, he saw a go-cup of coffee on Cavendish's desk, but no sign of Abara. Ferguson's office door was closed. Duncan snuck a glance in the window. Sure enough, the younger trooper stood in front of the lieutenant's desk, hands clasped behind his back, and a look on his face that said he was unhappy with what he heard. But he seemed to be smart enough to take it on the chin, since he was doing a lot of listening and not much talking.

Duncan greeted a few other troopers and went to his desk. Several manila envelopes were there. He slit them open. Inside were the requested financials for Glynis as well as for Gareth, Olivia Mueller, and Delia Struthers. Between analyzing the new information and attempting to track down Gareth, it would be a busy day.

A door opened. "Glad we had this conversation." Ferguson's voice cut the air. "Any questions?"

Abara replied, "No, ma'am." Moments later, he appeared by Duncan's desk and cleared his throat. "What's on the agenda for today?"

Duncan studied him. Aside from a red tinge on the skin inside his ears, he appeared unruffled. Duncan decided not to mention the meeting with the boss. "We have a bunch of paper to go through. I also want to find out where Gareth Beddoe spent the weekend if he wasn't off with his friends, and where he is now if he's not in Philly."

Abara grabbed an envelope, sat, and began to read. He didn't say a word and gave the impression that he didn't want to engage in conversation.

All right then. Let's see how this goes. Duncan briefly wondered if he should give a mini pep talk, but decided against it. Let the other man process what he'd heard. Instead, Duncan found the phone number he had for Gareth's cell and called. After several rings, it went to voicemail. "Mr. Beddoe, this is Trooper Jim Duncan with the Pennsylvania State Police. Please call me back." He gave his number and hung up.

He picked up Glynis's bank statement and financial records. She made regular payments to the Pittsburgh School for the Deaf. Almost certainly Bronwen's tuition. Two store credit cards had small balances. She also had a Visa and an Amex, but neither of those showed any current charges. Historical payments looked like they had been prompt. She had two bank accounts, checking and savings. Every two weeks, she transferred money into the savings account, and the amounts varied. What she hadn't spent out of her paycheck? There was also one deposit of three thousand dollars a month. Cross-references told him it was a regular payment out of her trust. He looked at the trust balance and whistled.

Abara looked up. "What?"

"Remember that money Glynis had from her grandparents?"

"The trust? Yeah."

"The balance on it is close to three-quarters of a million dollars." Duncan handed over the page. "If I'm reading that right, Glynis received a monthly stipend. But based on the interest it earns, that money will last a very long time."

"That's before any inheritance from her dad." Abara raised his eyebrows. "Lady had cash, that's for sure."

Duncan sat back. "Based on what I saw, she lived well within her means. She drove a ten-year-old Honda CR-V. She lives in a nice neighborhood, but she could have afforded much more. The biggest expense is her daughter's school tuition."

"The exact opposite of Olivia Mueller." Abara returned Glynis's information and picked up his notes. "She's working two jobs to pay off her school loans. A CMU education is expensive. Her bank balance goes almost to zero before her salary comes in."

"Not much money in working at an art gallery, either. Not a small one."

Duncan wondered how much the promotion at The Glassworks would have been. Probably not much, but to a woman living paycheck to paycheck, every penny counted. "What's the second job?"

"She's a barista at Uncommon Coffee." Abara typed. "It's an independent coffee shop on Smallman Street in Pittsburgh. Nice reviews. Looks hip and trendy. One of those places where they roast the beans on site."

The pay couldn't be much there, either. But maybe the patrons were generous tippers. "You said her degree was from Carnegie Mellon?"

"Yes. She double-majored in art, with a concentration in painting, and finance."

Duncan looked for Glynis's education credentials. University of Pittsburgh. "We should ask Olivia how she felt about Glynis potentially being promoted over her."

"Noted." Abara went back to his pile of paper. "But I can't see that as much of a motive. The promotion. It would be what, a couple hundred a month? At most? Maybe even less."

"It might not be all about the money. Could be prestige. Did Glynis rub Olivia's nose in the fact she might be passed over?" Duncan wrote as he talked. "It's true that money and sex are very common motives for murder, but there's also injured pride, bitterness, and revenge."

"It seems pretty thin. Shooting someone because she got a promotion and you didn't."

"To you and me it is. So is killing someone for their sneakers, but that's happened plenty of times. When I first started on the job, my FTO told me it didn't matter if I thought something was a good motive. What mattered is if the shooter did."

Abara crinkled his forehead.

"However, yes, it's the weakest motive among our suspects. I'll grant you that." Duncan twiddled his pen. "Do we know if Olivia has a registered handgun?"

"No, but I'll find out." Abara typed some more. "Nothing in the statewide registry in her name."

Which didn't mean Mueller didn't have a gun, only that it wasn't registered.

Duncan checked the time. Almost quarter to ten. "I'm going to call Gareth again. Keep going. We've got information from Delia Struthers in that pile, too. You didn't see anything on Glynis's laptop, did you?"

Abara nodded and picked up the phone. "No. I'll call and get a status update."

"Good. I want to know if she kept those anonymous emails and where they came from." Duncan dialed Gareth's number again. This time, it went straight to voicemail. Turned off? Dead battery? Or had Gareth listened to the first message, recognized the number, and deliberately ignored it? "Mr. Beddoe, it's Trooper Duncan again. You need to call me back, or I'm going to come looking for you. One way or the other, we're going to talk."

Abara glanced up. "Not making it easy for you?"

"No." Duncan tapped his desk. He could track the phone, but he'd need a warrant, which meant he needed probable cause. He could argue that Gareth stood in line to inherit a small fortune if his sister was dead. Good motive, but supposedly Gareth hadn't been anywhere near Ohiopyle State Park when Glynis had died. He went back to his notes from his conversation with Mrs. Beddoe. Templeton was the last name of the friend Gareth should have been in Hilton Head with. He'd obtained the mother's name and phone number when he talked to Mrs. Beddoe. A quick call to her produced her son's contact information.

Duncan called. "Hello, is this Ryan Templeton?"

"Uh, who'd like to know?" The voice sounded like that of a younger man but held an obvious note of caution.

"My name is Jim Duncan, I'm with the Pennsylvania State Police."

"Am I in trouble?"

"Assuming you are Ryan, you're not in any difficulties with me. I'm calling about a friend of yours. Gareth Beddoe."

"Yeah, I'm Ryan." A long pause. "Is Gareth in trouble?"

"I can't say. Right now, I'm only looking for him." Duncan waited, but when he didn't hear anything, he continued. "I understand he was supposed to be in Hilton Head with you this past weekend."

"He canceled last Thursday. Said he wasn't feeling well."

"Have you talked to him since then?"

"Um." Templeton drew the word out. "I don't know if I should tell you that. Cops, you know? I don't want to cause a problem for him."

Duncan pinched the bridge of his nose. "Are you aware that his sister was murdered on Sunday?"

Templeton's voice climbed a notch. "Murder? Gareth wouldn't kill her. That isn't his scene."

"Maybe not, but I have to talk to him." Duncan waited a beat. "Have you spoken with Gareth since Thursday?"

"We texted on Saturday. I sent him a picture, said he was missing a killer weekend." Templeton's words tumbled over each other. "He said he was bummed, but there'd be another one. That was all. I swear. Look, Gareth might not have liked his sister, but he wouldn't kill her."

Duncan grasped the words. "They didn't get along?"

"Not really. Not even before she took off to marry that artist guy. Different personalities, you know? Gareth liked the fast lane. Glynis was more uptight and responsible." Templeton hesitated.

Duncan's instinct said the hesitation meant an internal debate. "If you know something, you should tell me. I'll find out anyway. Better I hear it now and avoid any confusion."

Templeton blew out a breath. "You know their dad is real sick, right? Well, Glynis is supposed to inherit a lot of money. Gareth, he always felt it was unfair. Especially since she hadn't talked to the old man in years. When Gareth was drunk, he'd go on and on about how he was going to make his sister see reason and decline the inheritance. Or at least share it."

"Do you think he would have tried?"

"I'd like to say it was the booze talking. But Gareth lives an expensive life. His dad is willing to foot the bill, but I don't think Glynis would, and Gareth knew it." Templeton paused again. "Maybe I shouldn't tell you this, but I don't believe he was sick at all. I think he went to Pittsburgh to talk to her."

"Why do you say that?"

"I was at his place earlier in the week. His phone was on the table, and I saw a notification pop up from an airline, a reminder about a trip to

Pittsburgh on Friday. I asked, and he stuffed the phone in his pocket. He said it was nothing." Templeton sounded dejected, as though he had made these arguments to himself and lost. "Who else does he know in Pittsburgh? No one, as far as I'm aware. He must've gone to see her, right? But that's all it would be. Talk. Gareth is kind of a pussy. He's got a big mouth, but no guts to back it up."

Until he reached a breaking point. Duncan didn't know if Gareth had come to Pittsburgh, not for sure. But the new information might be enough for a warrant.

Chapter Twenty-Four

At ten-thirty, Sally and the Lanes arrived at Nithya Patel's office, which was in PPG Place. Tanelsa had stayed behind to "mind the store," as she put it, and make sure they didn't fall behind on their other cases.

The secretary invited them to sit, but Sally and her clients didn't wait long before a woman emerged from the office. "I am Nithya Patel. It is a pleasure to meet you." She shook hands with everyone, her grip firm and warm.

Sally nodded at the Lanes. "This is Eva and Paul Lane. Thank you for taking the time to see them on such short notice. My name is Sally Castle. I'm helping them navigate the intricacies of the legal process."

Nithya led them back to her office, where they all sat. She was about Sally's height, but had an ageless quality to her face that meant she could have been anywhere from her late twenties to her early forties. There were a few strands of silver in her jet-black hair, which was twisted back in an elegant chignon, yet the date on the framed law degree said she was a few years older than Sally. She wore a white silk blouse and deep red pencil skirt, her jewelry simple and gold. "Please have a seat." Her voice was musical, with the barest hint of an accent that enhanced the pleasant sound.

"I've heard your name, Ms. Castle." Nithya's dark eyes looked thoughtful. "You handled the Alec Wilson murder appeal last winter. I followed the trial. You did excellent work, but why is a defense attorney involved in a contract dispute?"

Sally had anticipated the question. "I'm not. I fully admit my knowledge of contract law is thin, and it's even worse when it comes to contracts for creative work. However, Mr. and Mrs. Lane are unfamiliar with legal matters and terminology. We know each other from a prior situation. My job is to guide them through the process of hiring the kind of person they need."

"My responsibility would be handling the dirty work, is that it?" Nithya raised a thin eyebrow.

"I'm not sure I'd put it that way, but you would definitely be in charge of crafting and presenting a response." Sally held up her hands. "I have no intention of getting in your way. All decisions are between you and the Lanes."

The other lawyer smiled. "I understand. You are a guide in a strange land, is that it?"

"Just so."

"I see. Now then." Nithya held out a hand. "You brought all the paperwork relating to your son, his artwork, and this man Ned Tidwell?"

Paul handed over an expandable folder crammed with papers. "This is everything. At least we think it is. Glynis, that was our daughter-in-law, she kept the records for Tyler's work, even after he signed with Tidwell. Tyler's our son. He did the paintings."

"Why are they not here?" Nithya accepted the folder.

"Tyler died a little over five years ago," Sally explained. "Glynis was murdered last weekend."

The statements garnered raised eyebrows from Nithya, but nothing more. She took out a pad and pen. "Before I start reading, tell me your story. From the beginning."

Eva and Paul did so as they spoke in turn and covered everything from Tyler's early career to signing with an agent, right up to receiving the lawsuit from Tidwell. "That's when Ms. Castle suggested we consult a professional, and she recommended you," Paul said.

"I see. Let me read these." Nithya put on a rectangular-shaped pair of reading glasses. She scanned each page, turning them over slowly and putting them in separate piles as she finished. She took notes as she did, occasionally making a soft clucking noise with her tongue. When she finished, she took off the glasses. "I will be honest. Your son did not make a very wise decision by signing this." She gestured at the paper. "I see this often with creatives. They are so eager to get their work out to the public, whether it be a gallery or a book publisher, they do not take the time to consult a professional who can spot the areas of trouble."

Eva's face crumpled. "So we have no chance at fighting?"

"I did not say that." Nithya held up a hand. "The contract itself is amateurish. This Tidwell, I do not think he used an attorney to craft it." She focused a sharp-eyed gaze on Sally. "You have suspicions, too. Why?"

Sally liked this woman. She was direct and avoided loading her words with legalese. She'd listened to the Lanes and read through the paperwork. Sally was sure it wouldn't be the last time she would do so. That law degree was from Northwestern. Nithya knew her business. "I told you I'm no contract law expert. What bothers me is the timing." Sally consulted the timeline she'd written for herself. "Glynis listed the first picture at The Glassworks over a year ago. It was one that was not covered by the contract with Tidwell. Three months later, she listed another two." Sally set her notes down. "Why did Tidwell wait so long? He could have sent the cease and desist, and filed his lawsuit, back then. By all expectations, he should have. My belief is he waited until he saw an easy mark. Someone he could bully and who might cave. Mr. and Mrs. Lane know very little about this sort of thing."

Nithya gave a slow nod. "Glynis Lane, she would not have been so intimidated, is that it?"

Eva spoke up. "Glynis never rolled over for anyone. She would have cleaned Tidwell's clock. I wouldn't be surprised if by the end of it, he owed her money. That was our Glynis."

"Whereas you, he would see you as sheep. Easy prey." Nithya smiled. "But sheep are usually protected against the wolves by a loyal sheepdog. I agree with Ms. Castle. This Tidwell, he is most likely looking to bowl you over with big words and scare tactics. He does not know you have a very capable sheepdog on your side."

"Then you can help us?" Eva clasped her husband's hand.

"I can and I will. People like Tidwell should not be allowed to get away with things like this." Nithya took out a contract. "I will have my secretary fill this in after you read it and agree to the terms. If you have questions, please ask. I will explain."

Sally picked her purse up off the floor. "It looks like you're in good hands. This is where I bow out gracefully."

Nithya held up a hand. "Please, stay. I have a feeling that as we dig deeper, we won't only find bad contracts. We may uncover illegal tactics. I would welcome your opinion as a criminal law specialist."

Sally set her purse down. Ned Tidwell wasn't going to know what hit him.

* * *

Duncan wrote up the affidavit for the geo-location of Gareth's phone. Abara had offered to do it, but Duncan didn't want rookie mistakes with this one. A lot of citizens didn't like the fact the police could and did track people's phones. A fair number of judges didn't like it either, which required a crystal clear argument about why such action was necessary. It wasn't something Duncan would hand off to just anyone.

Abara watched with as much attention as a rabid Steeler fan would on fourth and goal with the game on the line. "Think a judge will buy it?" he asked.

"That's why I'm making the application. If I thought otherwise, I wouldn't bother." Duncan read and reread his argument. It was as tight as it was going to get. If he'd been working with Cavendish, he would have let her look it over. Abara didn't have the depth of experience needed to even give a thorough critique. He'd get Ferguson to give it one last read. He set the form aside. "In case we don't get approval, we should think of Plan B."

"You mean other ways to prove Gareth was in the Pittsburgh area last weekend." Abara shrugged. "Why not wait until after we hear what the judge says? It might not be necessary."

"Because I like to be prepared."

"You're a real Boy Scout, you know that?"

It wasn't the first time Duncan had heard that, and he was sure it wouldn't be the last. What people failed to understand was that the statement didn't bother him. "What would you rather do? Have a contingency plan that lets you make progress or stand there with your pants around your ankles until an idea strikes you? Figuratively speaking, of course."

Abara opened his mouth, then closed it. After a second, he spoke. "Templeton wouldn't say exactly where his buddy was?"

"I don't think he knew for sure." Duncan put a mark in the win column for him.

"We could call the airlines." Abara twirled a pen. "Only problem with that is there might be a dozen flights from Philly to Pittsburgh on a single day if you consider every one."

"We could ask Templeton if he noted the carrier on the alert."

"We'd still need a warrant for the airline records, though. Wouldn't we?"

"Yes, but getting a passenger manifest is a lot less intrusive than geo-location. Or so people think." Duncan rocked in his chair. "We could check EZPass records, in case he drove instead of flying. Speaking of records, let's see if Gareth has a registered handgun."

"On it." Abara pulled the keyboard closer and typed. He mumbled to himself as he read. Finally, he said, "No records for Gareth Beddoe. However, Rhys Beddoe has a Colt .45, a Smith & Wesson .38, and a Glock 9mm." He frowned. "You can't fly with a gun. Can you? I mean, unless you're, like, law enforcement."

"If it's unloaded, completely secured, and you're over eighteen, you can." Duncan sat up. "Not in a carry-on, but you can declare it in your checked bags."

Abara chewed over that fact. "He wouldn't have to travel with the ammo. He could buy it locally."

Duncan aimed a finger at him. "Now you're thinking. That nugget gives us motive and means. I think I'll add that to the warrant affidavit." He wrote it down. "Which means we can check stores in Allegheny County and closer to Ohiopyle to see if a man matching Gareth's description bought ammunition for any of those weapons."

"What was the victim shot with?"

Duncan shuffled the papers on his desk as he looked for the autopsy report. "Unknown. No bullet was found in the body or at the scene. Any of those three could have made a through-and-through wound at a range that wouldn't leave stippling."

Abara blew out a breath. "You know, this is a lot easier on TV."

Duncan bit back a comeback. Yes, he'd had similar thoughts about the comparison between Hollywood and reality. He didn't know Abara well enough yet to be able to tell whether he was being serious or sarcastic. "You get anything on Delia Struthers while I was on the phone?"

"What? Oh, right. The other chick from the gallery." Abara snapped his fingers. "I did. Hold on. Yeah, here. On the surface, she looks pretty normal. No criminal history, no debt, good job, drives a newer Tesla, has a condo in Lawrenceville."

Duncan sensed a *but* coming. He waited.

"She's also a liar. We already knew, or at least suspected, she faked her educational credentials, and we were right." Abara found the sheet he was looking for. "Moreover, she listed her last employer as the Metropolitan Museum of Art. But she didn't work there. She was an intern. They found out about the school thing and fired her ass. Quietly, of course. God forbid it get out that they were duped."

"They told you that?"

"Not in so many words." Abara passed over his notes. "I called them. The minute I identified myself as a cop, the young woman on the phone started babbling about how HR didn't know, she was an intern and slipped through, it wasn't their fault, on and on. I think I lucked out by getting a junior staffer who happened to hear the water cooler gossip. I'm pretty sure if I talked to the museum director, Delia's former boss—or shit, anyone in charge of anything—I'd have gotten the run around."

It was entirely possible. Duncan couldn't fault his partner for taking advantage of the employee's knee-jerk reaction. He'd have done the same. "Do you think Virginia Ridgemont at The Glassworks knew?"

"No. But I believe Glynis was suspicious. I went back to my notes." Abara held up his notebook. "Ridgemont told us about a painting, something Struthers gave a value on, and Glynis didn't believe it. I didn't write down the exact details, whether it was too high or too low, but that doesn't matter. I think that caused her to dig into her coworker's past. She might even have found out about the fraud and blackmailed Struthers over it."

"No, she wouldn't do that. From everything we've learned about the victim, I don't think she was the type." Duncan rubbed his chin. "But she would have blown the whistle, no doubt. I don't think she would have stopped at The Glassworks, either. She'd make sure the word got out."

"She'd have black*balled* Struthers?"

"That's a strong word, and I don't know if Glynis had that kind of clout. But the art world is, I'd imagine, a big clique. It wouldn't put Struthers in a good position when she went looking for another job, that's for sure. A small independent gallery might take a chance, but a big one, like the Met or even the Carnegie, wouldn't touch her with the proverbial ten-foot pole." He looked up. "Any gun registrations for Struthers?"

"Already checked. No. But as we've said for others, that doesn't mean she didn't get her hands on one." Abara took a moment to study his partner, then sighed. "We're going to Pittsburgh again, aren't we?"

"Eventually." Duncan picked up a phone. "Let's tackle the warrant application first. Then we'll decide how to deal with Ms. Struthers."

Chapter Twenty-Five

Duncan stood in Judge Kirkland's office, watching as he read the affidavit. His thick black eyebrows were pulled down so far they nearly touched the tops of his wire-rimmed glasses. He tapped the edge of his desk with a thick forefinger. Without the black robes, Kirkland looked more like a grizzled military veteran than a judge. Fitting, since he'd spent twenty years in the Marines. No matter what Duncan had told Sally in the past about his dislike of judge shopping, Kirkland wouldn't have been his first choice to review this particular affidavit. The man had publicly and loudly proclaimed his dislike of using technology to track suspects. However, it was lunchtime, and he also had a widely known habit of eating at his desk, something other judges did not do. Beggars could not be choosers.

Duncan knew better than to rush Judge Kirkland. Pressing the case might piss him off and make him deny the warrant application out of spite. Duncan remained still, hands clasped behind his back and ready to answer any questions that might be thrown his way.

Abara did not. Whether it was his personality or lack of experience, the longer the wait, the more he fidgeted, shifting his weight from foot to foot and biting at a hangnail. Once or twice, it looked like he would speak—until he caught Duncan's look. He sighed and checked his watch.

Can't you see he's enjoying making us wait? Duncan wanted to shout at his partner. But he couldn't. Not only was it unprofessional, it wouldn't help his case.

Judge Kirkland laid the application on his desk. "As a rule, I don't like

GPS surveillance, Trooper. I've made that perfectly clear from the bench."

"Yes, your honor. I know."

"Yet according to this, you think it's necessary." Kirkland gave him a beady-eyed stare. "I'm not the only one with a reputation. You've got your own."

"I'm aware of that."

"Behind closed doors, you're known as a man who does his homework instead of bothering us with a half-assed Hail Mary throw. They say you know your stuff." Kirkland tapped the page. "Why should I sign this?"

Abara interrupted. "It's in the affidavit, isn't it?"

Duncan shot him a quelling look and wished he believed in ESP. *Shut your damn mouth.* "There are a few things. One, the suspect in question has a compelling motive, the possible inheritance of five million dollars."

Kirkland, who'd spared Abara a swift glance, focused on Duncan. "He doesn't know that, does he?"

"But he may believe it. That's all that matters, at least to him. He's hard up for cash. We know that from his mother's statement and his outstanding debt to his friend, Nathan Osterman. We know he's argued with his sister in the past, based on the testimony of Mrs. Beddoe, Ryan Templeton, another of the suspect's friends, and the victim's daughter."

"Who is a deaf six-year-old girl, isn't she?"

"Yes, but she gave us a solid description the day of her mother's death," Duncan countered. "She may be a child, but she's observant."

Kirkland favored him with a begrudging nod.

"Also, the suspect lied. He told his mother he was going to Hilton Head. He didn't. He told his father he had a business trip this week, but no one seems to know where, and he was fired from his last job."

"He may have changed his mind," Kirkland said.

"But why not tell Mrs. Beddoe? Ryan Templeton told us not only did the suspect back out of the trip to Hilton Head, but he had booked another one, by plane, to Pittsburgh for last Friday."

Abara again opened his mouth to speak.

Duncan gave a quick head shake. "Finally, the suspect had access to firearms. True, the autopsy was unable to definitively identify the caliber of the weapon used to kill Glynis Lane, and no ballistics evidence was gathered from the scene. However, of the three handguns we know are in the Beddoe house, any of them is a sufficient caliber to be the murder weapon. He's failed to return multiple phone calls. If we put all of these facts together, I believe they fulfill the requirements of probable cause. Gareth Beddoe is a solid suspect, and we need to find him as soon as possible. Before he harms someone else."

"Like who?"

"We have reason to believe whoever shot Glynis knows, or believes, Bronwen was there and is a witness. It's entirely possible the shooter will be looking to eliminate any threat, which puts her in grave danger."

A gleam of appreciation showed in Kirkland's eyes. "If I were to deny this warrant, do you have other options?"

Before Duncan could answer, Abara spoke. "We do, but none of them are as expeditious or efficient as GPS location."

Kirkland's gaze, now hard enough to cut stone, swung in his direction. "This office does not exist to make your job easier, Trooper Abara. In fact, just the opposite. You need to prove the necessity of this action, and telling me it means you can work faster is not good enough."

Abara's face darkened.

Why can't you shut up? "Your honor, please excuse my partner," Duncan said. "He's new to CIS and doesn't have much experience in these matters. In fact, this is his first major investigation. He's still learning."

Kirkland grunted.

"What he meant to say is that yes, we do have other options, and we will use them if you deny the warrant. However, if Gareth Beddoe is the killer, he hasn't quite gotten what he wanted by murdering his sister. What he would need is for his father to die. Rhys Beddoe is terminally ill, according to his wife, but Gareth may not wait that long. I've already mentioned the potential threat to a six-year-old girl. It's in the public's best interest that we find him and either make an arrest or clear his name so we can focus on other suspects. The best way to do that is by using geo-location technology."

Kirkland stared at Duncan for what seemed like minutes but was probably much less time. He picked up a pen and signed the affidavit. "Here." He handed it to Duncan. "And you." He aimed a finger at Abara. "I was leaning toward approval before you spoke. Then I thought maybe I should deny the request, just to teach you a lesson. You're lucky your colleague is making this argument. Next time, keep your trap shut and maybe you'll learn something." He picked up his sandwich, a clear sign of dismissal.

Duncan took the hint and hustled Abara out of the judge's chambers. After all, nothing said Kirkland wouldn't change his mind if Abara put his foot in his mouth a second time.

Chapter Twenty-Six

Sally remained in Nithya's office and read over everything they'd compiled during the meeting while Nithya escorted the Lanes out. They'd talked for almost two hours. Nithya's soothing voice and ability to answer every question had definitely gotten their clients off the ledge. It also made Sally feel better about handing off the case to someone more prepared for the fight ahead. She glanced up at the wall clock. It was twelve-thirty. She sent a text to Tanelsa. **Meeting went great. Going to see if I can catch Olivia Mueller for an interview.**

There was no immediate answer. Tanelsa might be at lunch or in a meeting. Sally dropped her phone in her purse. At least she wouldn't have to come up with a story to justify talking to Olivia. She'd agreed to support Nithya, which meant she could go back to acting in an official capacity. It was much more comfortable. Sally would suck at being a private investigator. She hated making up stories.

Nithya returned. "They are lovely people, the Lanes. I hope we are successful." She took a seat at her desk.

Sally leaned on the desk. "Lawyer to lawyer. What are their chances of winning?"

"You know there is always a risk of failure. But this contract." Nithya held it up. "It reads like a template from the internet. No doubt, Tyler Lane should not have signed it. But I believe we have a good chance of at least defeating this lawsuit. If I can wrest control of all Tyler's work from this so-called agent, I will."

"Good." Sally gathered up her papers. "I'd like to go talk to Olivia." She told Nithya about Glynis's success selling above the asking price Tidwell had claimed was the best he could do. "Virginia Ridgemont, owner of The Glassworks gallery, previously mentioned doing something like an audit. We need to know if she took action. I'll call her back, of course, but I also want to know if Olivia knew anything about the situation."

"Agreed. Will Mrs. Lane's records be at the gallery? I am talking about the widow."

"Even if it was, the police will have it by now as evidence for the murder investigation." Nithya frowned, and Sally continued. "I know the lead investigator. We've worked together in the past. I think I can get him to either let us make copies or at least read Glynis's stuff and take notes."

"Good. Let me know your progress. Meanwhile, I will call these other clients."

"Will do. Thanks again." Sally left. Her stomach growled, reminding her she hadn't eaten since early that morning. She'd stop for a quick bite and call Olivia.

She didn't answer her phone, but a quick call to The Glassworks confirmed the woman was expected by one. After Sally ate, she drove over to the gallery, went inside, and asked for the associate director.

A couple of minutes later, Olivia appeared. "May I help...I know you. You were here the other day." She halted a few steps away. "Is something wrong with the painting?"

No wonder Virginia wanted to promote Glynis instead of Olivia. She's not a very good saleswoman if her first assumption is negative. "I'm here on a related, but different matter." Sally held out a business card.

Olivia read, lips moving. "Criminal defense as in broke the law? I didn't do anything illegal."

Not what is this about or who's in trouble. Interesting. "What wasn't you?"

"I thought you were going to accuse me of something. Forget it. What do you want?"

Olivia's statement was definitely something to tell Jim about. "I'm not here to accuse you of anything." At least not yet. Sally looked around. "Is there somewhere we can talk?"

Olivia chewed her bottom lip. "I don't know if Virginia would like me talking to a lawyer. Besides, what business would a defense attorney have here at the gallery?"

"I've already spoken to your boss." It was technically true, although Sally intended to ask Olivia slightly different questions. "I need to follow up on a few things, no major issues. I'm sure Ms. Ridgemont won't mind. She is considering promoting you, right? Clearly, she trusts your judgement."

The answer appeared to put the young woman more at ease, at least a little. "Oh, well, um." She glanced behind her. "I guess we can use the room where we put food for events. This way."

Sally followed her to a small conference room, with a table for six and a sideboard. Sally set her briefcase down and opened it while she indicated that Olivia should also sit. "I'm working with another attorney on litigation surrounding Tyler Lane's artwork."

"I didn't do much with Tyler's stuff." Olivia crossed and recrossed her legs. "That was Glynis's pet project."

"I understand. Did she ever talk to you about it?"

"A little." Olivia picked at her ragged cuticles. "She didn't like his agent, I know that much."

"Did you know the agent?"

"Kinda. I mean, I knew who he was." Olivia shrugged. "He came in to see Glynis one day. He was pretty pissed off. You could tell the feeling was mutual."

Sally took notes as they talked. "Meaning Mr. Tidwell didn't care for Glynis."

"Yeah." Olivia craned her neck to try and read Sally's writing. "I really think you're better off talking to Virginia."

"As I said, I've already spoken to Ms. Ridgemont. Based on that conversation, I believe Glynis was attempting to sell some of her late husband's work through this gallery as part of her attempt to prove misconduct on the part of Mr. Tidwell." Sally fixed the other woman with a stare. "Is that correct?"

"Yeah, I think so. I told you, I don't know much about it. Glynis didn't talk to me." A note of bitterness crept in the last words.

Sally feigned surprise. "As an associate director, she didn't talk to you about her plans? Didn't the two of you get along?"

"It wasn't that." Olivia must have sensed she'd misspoke. Her words sounded rushed, as though she wanted to correct Sally's understanding. "We got along okay. Like I said, Tyler's sales were her thing. She didn't ask for much help from anyone, aside from getting permission from Virginia to list the paintings."

"Then you weren't involved in pricing anything?"

"No, she did it all herself. Delia was majorly ticked off."

Olivia's statement contradicted Delia's supposed indifference. "Why was that?"

"Delia thought pricing was her area, you know? That Glynis should have asked." With the focus off herself, Olivia sounded more relaxed. "Glynis said she didn't want help from a wannabe like Delia. Whatever that meant."

Sally knew, but assumed the statement meant Olivia was ignorant of Delia's false claims about her credentials. "Is it possible to speak with Delia now?"

"No, she quit earlier this week. Something about a job offer in LA." Olivia waved a hand. "Personally, I don't think she's ready for a market like that. After all, the Met canned her before she came here. My degree is just as good as hers, but whatever."

Words of envy, or did Olivia suspect something? Sally threw out a verbal lure. "I thought she left the Met to come here."

"Oh, that's what she likes to say." Olivia leaned forward, a gleam in her eye. Clearly, the opportunity to trash-talk her former colleague was irresistible. "They fired her ass. I don't know what it was about, but a classmate of mine got an internship there this winter. Delia was gone by then, but there was enough gossip for her to know something happened. When she, my classmate, found out Delia had come to Pittsburgh, she called me for deets, but I don't know anything. Except Delia thinks she's God's gift to the art world."

Interesting, but not relevant to Sally's case. She wondered if Jim had interviewed Olivia yet. "Would Delia know if Glynis took any action against Mr. Tidwell?"

"I doubt it. Those two definitely did not get along."

Time to put Olivia back on the defensive. "I understand from Ms. Ridgemont that you and Glynis were in competition for a promotion. With her death, is it yours?"

The change was instantaneous. Olivia broke eye contact and gave a tiny shrug. "I don't know. Virginia hasn't said anything, but there's no one left but me."

Sally pretended to study her notes. "Are you sure Glynis didn't talk about any difficulties? I understand from Ms. Ridgemont Glynis had received some threatening emails."

Olivia stared at the wall and touched her tongue to her upper lip. "I wouldn't know."

"Did Glynis leave any papers here at the gallery?"

Another nervous twitch. "The cops took a bunch of stuff with them. Maybe those were part of it." She paused. "You should talk to Chris."

Sally scrunched her forehead. "Who?"

"Chris Janssen. Glynis's boyfriend."

This was news. Sally put on a confused expression. "What boyfriend? From everything I know, Glynis wasn't dating."

Olivia's expression became gleeful, as though she was happy to pass on a bit of gossip. "Oh, she didn't like to talk about him. But I overheard her on the phone, and he came to the gallery once. Scary-looking, but to each her own. Glynis rushed him out the door quickly enough. I guess she didn't want us seeing her with a guy like that."

"Like what?"

"Tall, broad, lots of tats. He'd be good-looking if he hadn't shaved his head. I figured him for someone who belongs to a biker gang. "

Sally's neck tingled. "Why do you say that?"

"Who else dresses like that?" Olivia crossed her arms. "I gotta say, though. The phoenix on his bicep is a work of art. If I was ever going to get a tattoo, I'd go all out on something like that."

"Well, thanks for your time. I'll see myself out." Sally stood and left. She needed to call Jim. Immediately.

* * *

Duncan slipped the signed warrant in his pocket and strode down the hallway, looking for an empty room. Even an empty courtroom would do. It was time for an intervention.

Abara had to half-jog to keep up. "Who do we have to see about the GPS stuff? The tech division? Is that why you're in a rush?"

Duncan stopped in front of a partly open door. A quick glance indicated it was some type of meeting room. "Not quite. In here." He nudged Abara inside, then closed the door.

The younger trooper tugged his jacket. "What is your problem?"

"You." Duncan took a deep breath. *Stay professional.* "If you ever do something like that again, I will go to Ferguson and personally have you transferred from this section. Am I clear?"

Abara crossed his arms. "You can't do that."

"Watch me." Duncan took a step towards him. "A judge does not give a rat's ass about making your life easier. In fact, the whole point of getting a warrant is that it's hard. You have to prove probable cause to do what you want, whether that is to arrest someone, search private property, or, yes, have them tracked. Saying it makes your job easier to violate a citizen's rights is not going to impress a judge. It sure as hell doesn't impress me."

"Get over yourself." Abara shifted his gaze so he was looking over Duncan's shoulder. "You've had a problem with me since day one. You don't even know me. You're just like all the other sanctimonious jerks I've worked with. Jealous much?"

It took all of Duncan's self-control not to grab him by the shoulders and shake him. "No, I'm not. You waltzed in and basically announced this job is nothing but a stepping-stone in your career. You've been unprofessional with almost every witness we've interviewed. And you hit on my fiancée. In front of me."

CHAPTER TWENTY-SIX

"That was a joke. Sheesh."

"I didn't think it was funny, and neither did she. My point is, I see nothing to be jealous of." Duncan took a breath. "A fancy college degree means shit. You may have decent skills once you decide to put forth some effort, but your attitude sucks. Last warning. Shape up or you'll be out of here so fast, you'll get whiplash." He waited. When Abara didn't respond, Duncan added, "Understand?"

"Yes." Abara bit off the word and stayed angled away from Duncan, gaze fixed on the corner.

Duncan could see his partner was annoyed, but he didn't much care. He'd tried the velvet glove approach. It was time for tough love. Hopefully, no one outside the room had heard. Before he could say anything else, his phone buzzed in his coat pocket. He took it out. It was a text from Sally.

You need to talk to Olivia Mueller. She's hiding something. Also, Chris Janssen may be the guy Bronwen saw. He's Glynis's boyfriend.

How Sally had found that out, Duncan didn't know. He'd ask her later. He yanked open the door. "Come on."

Abara glowered as he passed his senior and stepped into the hallway. "Now are we going to the tech division?"

"Yes, but we have to hurry." Duncan pulled the door shut. "We may have found Tattoo Guy."

Chapter Twenty-Seven

After leaving the Washington County Courthouse, Duncan and Abara returned to HQ and immediately went to the offices of the tech section.

"Why don't we call the provider?" Abara asked.

"It's likely a service provider will fight the court order." Duncan pushed through the door and looked around. "It'll get caught up in months of red tape. We, and by that I mean the guys here, can use triangulation. Less accurate, but we don't need the precision of GPS. I only need to know if Gareth Beddoe is in this general area. At least for now." He spotted his favorite technician. "Andy. How's it going?"

"Not that bad." The bespectacled man came over. "I was about to call you. I have news."

"And I have something for you. You first."

Andy picked up a stack of paper. "I retrieved a bunch of deleted emails from the victim's computer. Her boss was right. I found a bunch of messages all along the same line. Glynis was a bitch, she had no business at the gallery, get out while she had a chance. All from a webmail provider with a completely meaningless username, realart7348."

Duncan thought. "I can't think of what that stands for, which is almost certainly the point." He read the emails, all of which were fairly short and exactly what Andy said. "Got an IP address?"

"They came from a lot of different ones, and I'm still working on it. Most are from various open WiFi networks in downtown Pittsburgh."

"Like what you'd find in a coffee shop?" Abara accepted the pages and read.

"You got it. I'm still working on it, and I'll let you know if I find anything significant." He folded his arms. "Now, what have you got for me?"

Duncan handed over the warrant. "Need to locate this cell phone."

"And hopefully the person carrying it, huh?" Andy tipped his head at Abara. "Where's Cavendish?"

"Vacation. Sorry I didn't introduce him sooner. This is Kevin Abara. He's new to CIS." Duncan introduced the two. "Always good to make a friend down here."

"Pleased to make your acquaintance." The tech held out his hand.

Abara gave the emails back to Duncan and stuffed his hands in his pockets.

Andy checked with Duncan and raised an eyebrow in a wordless question.

Duncan waved it off. "Triangulation. How long?"

"It depends." Andy went back to his desk, sat, and spun his chair so he faced his computer monitor. "Is the phone on?"

Duncan followed and heard Abara behind him. "The first time I called, it rang a few times before I got voicemail. I think the owner recognized the number the second time and declined the call."

"You need to stop identifying yourself in your messages." Andy jiggled his mouse to wake up his computer. "At least don't mention who you work for."

"I'll keep that in mind for the next time." Duncan pulled over a chair. "Can you find him?"

"The phone? Yes. Assuming it's still on." Andy typed. "Will your suspect be carrying it? That I can't say."

"Good enough." While Andy worked, Duncan glanced at Abara and pointed at another empty chair.

Abara shook his head. "I, uh, have to make a call. Be right back." He left.

Andy spoke, still focused on his work. "He's a bit of a cold fish. The new guy."

"I came down on him pretty hard earlier. Maybe more than I should have. I'll apologize later."

"Jim, of all the people I work with—in fact, of all the people I know—your temper has one of the longest fuses." The tech typed again. "If you unloaded on this guy, he deserved it."

"I can't believe he's so clueless, though. It has to be an act."

Andy paused in his work and caught Duncan's gaze. "I take it you had good mentors when you started the job."

Duncan nodded. "Some of the best."

"Well, maybe this Abara guy didn't." Andy went back to his screen. "Getting a wakeup call from you might be the difference between his success or failure." He continued to work.

Duncan thought about it. He'd assumed Abara had the benefit of a good FTO. Maybe not. Fitz, Duncan's first training officer, had been no-nonsense, and he believed he was a better trooper for it. He resolved to be more patient, but no less strict, with his temporary partner.

"Got it." Andy leaned back.

Duncan snapped back to the task at hand. "Where?"

"Based on the triangulation, Donegal or somewhere within a three-mile radius of there."

Duncan took out his phone. Donegal was right off the Turnpike. There was a Holiday Inn Express near the exit. More importantly, it was only twenty miles from Ohiopyle.

* * *

It was a little after three when Sally returned to the Castle & Parson office in Uniontown. She found Tanelsa in the kitchenette, brewing an afternoon cup of coffee.

Tanelsa handed over a mug. "How'd it go?" She waited for the last spit of water from the one-cup brewer, popped out the used pod, and dropped in one for Sally.

"Very well. I think Nithya is going to knock this out of the park." Sally put down her cup and pushed the button. While she waited, she told Tanelsa everything that had happened with the contract attorney that morning.

Armed with caffeine, the two women returned to the main space. "What's the next move? Are you going to look for this Janssen guy?"

"No, that's Jim's purview. Unless I find something that makes it look like Janssen has information about the art situation, I have no reason to call him." She snapped her fingers. "That reminds me. I need to ask Jim if he has Glynis's records of her late husband's artwork." She fired off a text.

"Will he let you have them?"

"Do you mean will he let me bring them here? Probably not." Sally set down her drink and took her seat. "I'm sure we can work something out if I demonstrate I really need to see them. Right now, I want to talk to Mr. Tidwell." She picked up her phone and dialed his number. She felt a jolt of surprise when he answered.

"This is Tidwell."

She gripped her pen. "Yes, hi. My name is Sally Castle. I'm looking for information on an artist you represent. His name is Tyler Lane."

"I'm sorry to say Tyler died some years ago."

"I'd read about that." She glanced at Tanelsa. "Do you still have some of his pieces?"

"I represent some of his earlier works, yes."

"So there are more with someone else?"

He paused. "What's your interest, Ms. Castle?"

Time for a bluff. "Buying. A friend of mine has one of his paintings, and I love it." Out of the corner of her eye, she saw Tanelsa cover her mouth, which didn't quite hide her grin. "She recommended I get in touch with you to see if there are any more."

"He was a real talent." Tidwell sounded relaxed as he moved into his spiel. "Fabulous eye for color and great appreciation for the local landscape. Are you looking for anything specific? I'm talking about size or subject."

"The space I have to fill is pretty big." Sally tried to remember the dimensions of the largest painting she'd seen at The Glassworks. "Do you have anything in the three feet by five feet range?"

"I don't think he painted anything that large. Hold on." There was a pause while he typed, the sound of the keys clicking audible. "The biggest I have in my inventory is twenty-two inches by thirty-two. Why don't you come by my office and see it?"

"Where are you located?"

"Lawrenceville, over on Butler Street."

Sally checked the time. "Unfortunately, it's too late for me to do that today. I live in Uniontown. And I work tomorrow."

Tidwell let loose a theatrical sigh. "Tell you what. I'll be in Connellsville tomorrow, meeting with a potential client. I suppose I can carve out some time to see you. I'll bring my sales book so you can see a picture. If you're serious about buying, that is."

"Oh, I am." Sally waved at Tanelsa to get her attention. "How about eleven? Or does that conflict with your meeting?"

Tanelsa checked her computer and gave a thumbs-up.

"No, I'll be done by then," Tidwell said. He gave her the address of the meeting location in town and hung up.

Tanelsa steepled her hands. "I gathered you wanted to know if I was free at eleven. Are we going art shopping?"

"I think the place could use something, don't you?" Sally checked her notes from the visit to The Glassworks. She'd written down the prices of several paintings other than *Night Flowers*, the one she'd purchased.

Time to find out exactly what Tidwell was charging.

* * *

After leaving the tech division, Duncan went back to the CIS office in search of Abara, who had disappeared. He found his partner at Cavendish's desk, a pile of paper at his elbow. "Look, about earlier—"

"Don't mention it. You're right. I was an ass." Abara swiveled around in the chair. "Tell your fiancée I'm sorry."

"Will do." Duncan decided to drop what he had been about to say. "What have you been up to?"

"Christopher Janssen." Abara held up the sheets. "Thirty-seven years old. Formerly lived in Pittsburgh. Current address is Bear Rocks. Works year-round at a local HVAC company. In the summer, he has a weekend job running white-water raft tours. No priors, no wants, no warrants."

Duncan skimmed the information. "You did all this while I was down with the tech guys?"

"Seemed like a waste of time for both of us to watch a dude type on a computer, so I came back." Abara gave a twitch of his shoulders. "You said we had to find Janssen, didn't you?"

"Yes. His number is in the phone records from Glynis's service provider, but only texts. He's not a contact. I thought it was a business relationship. Guess I was wrong." Duncan wondered if he should lose his temper more often. "If he lives in Bear Rocks and works down here, I wonder how he met Glynis?"

"I did, too. But the move to Bear Rocks is recent, only in the last six months. Prior to that, he was employed by a real estate company in Pittsburgh, one of the ones that owns apartment and condo buildings all over the city."

"What did he do?"

"Same thing: maintenance. Far as I can tell, he has a technical certification in HVAC, but no college degree." Abara leaned back and chewed the end of his pen. "It could be that he was called in to do something for The Glassworks. Won't know until we talk to him."

Duncan read Janssen's employment history. "Or he worked for one of Glynis's prior flings." He handed the sheet back to Abara and tapped a line.

"Craddock Designs. Damn, I missed that." Abara's mouth twisted in a sour expression. "Isn't Craddock the guy we think the victim slept with or was sleeping with? The one who is responsible for all the new construction."

"That's him. If Janssen does HVAC, he may have helped with that portion of the projects. Could be how he met Glynis." Duncan went to his desk and picked up the phone. "Don't fret the miss. It happens. Good work."

"Thanks. Who do we tackle first?"

"Beddoe. He may bolt. Janssen lives here and has ties to the area through work." Duncan picked up the receiver on his desk phone.

Abara nodded at it. "Who are you calling?"

Duncan held up a finger. "Hi. I'm meeting a guest of yours for dinner. Gareth Beddoe. I called him, but he isn't answering. Has he checked in yet? I understand. I'll keep calling." He dropped the phone in the receiver.

"Damn it. Just once, can't someone be trusting and helpful?"

"Won't tell you, huh?"

Duncan mimicked the voice of the girl who'd answered at the Holiday Inn. "We aren't allowed to give out that information." He didn't want to drive all the way to Donegal for nothing. They'd be better served moving on to Janssen and taking another crack at Beddoe tomorrow.

Abara snapped his fingers. "I have an idea. Give me the hotel number." Duncan recited, and Abara dialed. "This is Trooper Kevin Abara of the PSP. We're tracking a stolen vehicle, and our information indicates it may be somewhere along the Turnpike. Is there an Audi RS5 in your parking lot? What color? Can you see the license plate? Yes, that's it. No, please don't approach the driver. We'll handle it. Thanks." He hung up. "He's there. Or at least his car is."

"Slick." Duncan checked the time. "It'll take an hour to get to Donegal. What are the chances we catch Beddoe at the hotel and he doesn't go to dinner?"

"Let's find out." Abara stood and held out his hand. "Let me drive, and I bet I'll get us there in less than an hour. Even without the lights and siren. If I'm wrong and we miss him, we might still be able to go find Janssen."

Duncan tossed him the keys. He didn't know if this was a temporary spurt of productivity, but he would go with it as long as it lasted.

Chapter Twenty-Eight

Duncan looked at his watch as Abara pulled the unmarked Interceptor into the lot of the Donegal Holiday Inn Express. "Forty minutes; not bad. You cheated, though. You said no lights or siren."

"How else was I going to get through the construction zone on 70?" Abara opened the door. "It was one whoop. That doesn't count."

Duncan got out and tugged his sports jacket over his sidearm. "Fair enough. There's the Audi. Run the plate."

Abara leaned over the onboard computer. A minute later, he exited the car. "Yep, that's his. But seeing as the receptionist wouldn't tell you jack when you called, I doubt she's going to give up his hotel room just because you flash your badge. How do you plan to find him?"

Duncan scanned the parking lot. The Audi was parked next to the door on the side of the building. People with room keys would be able to enter without being seen by anyone at the front desk. Beddoe had lied to his mother and friend about his whereabouts, so Duncan was willing to bet he'd want to avoid being noticed. At least no more than necessary. Which meant he might be in a room near the door. The hotel had three floors. It wasn't exactly the size of the Omni William Penn in downtown Pittsburgh, but it was still a lot of knocking.

Except Duncan didn't care what room his suspect was in. He wanted to talk to the man, not a door.

He walked over to the Audi. The windshield and grill were spattered with bugs from the ride along the Turnpike, but the vehicle still looked new and expensive. He peered through the window. As he expected, the car was loaded. A red light flashed from the dashboard. "Fancy ride, huh?" He glanced at Abara.

"More than I can afford on a trooper's salary, that's for sure."

"Car like this must have an alarm, right?"

An evil grin spread over Abara's face. "Absolutely. We should check and make sure it works."

Duncan made a fist and banged on the front bumper. As expected, the Audi's lights flashed, and an ear-splitting screech from the alarm filled the air. It took less than five minutes for a man to appear, a key fob in his hand. He clicked the button, and the alarm stopped. He took two steps toward the car. Then he noticed the two troopers and ran for the door.

Abara was faster and blocked the hotel entrance. "You couldn't get a room with a line of sight to the parking lot, huh? Otherwise, you might not have had to come outside."

The man turned around to find Duncan in his path. "Are you Gareth Beddoe?" He held up his badge wallet. "If so, I've left a couple of messages for you. You haven't called back. Makes me wonder why. If you're not Beddoe, why do you have his key?"

"I'm not—" The man stopped. "I've been busy. I meant to call you back."

Duncan wondered if Beddoe had about to claim he was someone else and realized the futility of the act. "Lucky for you, I'm here now. We can chat in your room. Or I'm sure I can call the local police department and they'll be happy to lend us an interrogation room. Your choice."

Beddoe licked his lips. "Am I under arrest?"

"Not yet," Abara said, voice steely.

Beddoe's gaze flicked from one trooper to the other. "I don't want to be seen in a police department and have it get back to my father. You might as well come up." He went to the door, unlocked it with his room key, and went inside. He led the troopers to a second-floor room at the end of the hall. "On TV, this is where I offer you something to drink, but I don't have anything non-alcoholic. There's not even a second chair." He sat on the edge of an unmade bed.

"We're not thirsty and we'll stand." Duncan studied the room. The Do Not Disturb sign hung on the outside of the door. One queen-sized bed had been slept in. Clothes littered the other. A half-empty bottle of scotch was on the desk, a used plastic cup to one side. On the other was a gun. "You got a license for this?" Duncan slipped a pen through the trigger guard and lifted it. A .38 Smith & Wesson revolver. If this was the murder weapon, that would be another reason the crime scene crew hadn't found spent cartridges.

Beddoe flushed. "I have a concealed carry permit." He reached for his wallet.

Abara pulled an evidence bag from his pocket, and Duncan dropped the gun in. Abara sealed and marked the bag.

"Hey!" Beddoe half stood. "I told you I have a permit."

"You'll get it back. If the ballistics comparison to the shot that killed your sister doesn't match, that is." Abara finished writing.

"You can't take that without a warrant."

Duncan put his hands on his hips. "Would you like us to get one? We will. Don't even need to go anywhere because we can get approval over the phone. Exigent circumstances. You might flee with potential evidence."

Abara swiped to unlock his phone. "I've got a judge on speed dial for cases like this.

"Fine. Take it." Beddoe stalked to the desk and poured a splash of whiskey into a glass.

"Mr. Beddoe, where have you been since last Thursday?" Duncan asked. "Your mother thought you were going to Hilton Head. Your buddy said you bailed on them, but didn't give a reason. Although he did see the reminder about your trip to Pittsburgh on your phone."

Beddoe swallowed hard but said nothing.

"You came to talk to your sister, didn't you?" Duncan pressed. "Why else would a high-flier such as yourself be holed up in a Holiday Inn Express in Donegal?"

"What I can't understand is why you're still here," Abara added. "You must know about your sister's murder by now. Why not hightail it back to

Philly?"

Duncan watched the suspect sweat. "You don't know what to do, is that it? If you stay, it looks bad. If you run home, it looks worse, especially since you lied about being here in the first place. You're caught between a rock and a hard place, as the saying goes."

Beddoe hung his head.

"How much money did you ask for?" Abara crossed his arms. "From your sister. That had to be why you came. Did Daddy cut you off?"

"The bastard won't give me another dime." Beddoe dashed a hand across his mouth. "He took away my Amex and canceled it. It was on his account. He told me I was a disgrace, and he was done supporting my profligate lifestyle." He deepened his voice on the last two words and made air quotes. "He doesn't understand. I need that cash. Cut me off later, but without it now, I'm a dead man."

Duncan didn't know if the statement was literal or dramatic. "What did you do?"

"At the time, I didn't think it was anything." Beddoe stared at the carpet. "I went to Atlantic City for New Year's and got into a high-stakes poker game. I was hammered. I didn't know what I was doing. The next morning, once I was sober, two guys came to my room. The collections department, they called themselves. Turned out the game was run by a minor player in a local organized crime syndicate. I'd signed a pledge at the game the previous night and lost. Honest to God, I don't even remember doing it."

He's not exaggerating, Duncan thought. "How much?"

"Two-hundred and fifty." Beddoe buried his face in his hands.

Abara squinted. "That doesn't sound like a lot."

"Thousand," came the muffled response.

Abara whistled.

Duncan knew what came next. "You didn't have the money. So you made an arrangement with the guys who came to collect, maybe signed another note. Except this time, Dad wouldn't come to the rescue. You flew to Pittsburgh, hoping your sister would have pity on you. But she didn't."

"Laughed in my face." Beddoe's hollow voice aged him by at least ten years.

"It's worse than that. Dad said he was cutting me out of his will. He's not well, but you probably know that if you've spoken to my mother."

Duncan inwardly winced. The opposite of what Caitlyn Beddoe thought. Gareth wouldn't benefit from his father's decision; he'd lose. Big time.

"Yeah, we know." Abara shot a look at Duncan. "I don't get it. Your dad and your sister didn't get along. Why not lobby him to make you the heir? That would make more sense to me. Given what we've learned about your sister, it definitely had a greater chance of success."

Beddoe's laugh sounded sharp. "You don't know my old man. He loves his money. More than his wife and definitely more than either of his kids. He'll leave the cash to the person he thinks will take the best care of it. Personal feelings don't figure in."

It was pretty much what Mrs. Beddoe had told them. "Your record of responsibility to date hasn't impressed him," Duncan said. Small wonder. It didn't impress him, either.

Beddoe stared at the wall.

Abara put his hands on his belt. "What were you hoping to get from Glynis?"

"A loan. Glynis still has her trust fund money. I swore I'd pay her back. Hell, she could deduct the cash from my share of the inheritance once Dad pops off, which won't be long. Assuming his threat to cut me out was hollow, of course." Beddoe raised his gaze to the ceiling. "She wouldn't hear of it. She said I'd made the mess and it was mine to clean up. Last Sunday, I followed her to Ohiopyle. I figured I'd give it another shot." He winced. "Poor choice of words. Anyway, she had her kid with her. She wouldn't make a scene in front of her child, right?"

Duncan hefted the evidence bag. "Did you take the gun with you?"

"Yes, but I've been carrying it since the goons in Atlantic City made their intentions clear. It's protection. I didn't shoot her."

"You confronted her on the trail." Abara tilted his head. "She said no. You got mad. Things got heated. Maybe you didn't mean to. Accidental discharge or something like that."

Duncan offered a second idea. "Or you were drunk, like you were on New

Year's, and you can't remember clearly."

"I didn't shoot her!" Beddoe leaped to his feet. "I didn't even get to talk to her. I was coming up the trail, maybe fifty yards behind her. I could see she'd stopped. I was going to call out, but then this big guy appeared. Shaved head, lots of tats. They argued."

Chris Janssen. "About what?" Duncan asked.

"I don't know." Beddoe dropped down onto the bed. "My business was private, and I didn't want to clue him in, whoever he was. So I hung back. I could hear voices, but I was too far away to make out the words. I didn't know if he was a friend of Glynis's who'd side with her even though they'd been arguing, and the last thing I needed was to get in a fight with a guy twice my size. Especially since I thought he was carrying."

"Why?"

"I thought I saw a holster on his belt, but I'm not sure. I didn't stick around. I turned around and went back the way I came."

Duncan studied the man and his defeated posture. "Did you know your sister had gotten poison-pen emails threatening her?"

"No." Beddoe didn't look up. "Glynis and I were never on great terms, even as kids. I was the last person she spoke to about anything like that. If she even told me at all."

Abara folded his arms. "Just what were you planning next? You know, after she shut you down?"

Beddoe rubbed his face. "The only thing I could do. I planned to visit Glynis that night and try one last time. But when I heard on the radio she'd been shot, I panicked. It was like you said." He nodded at Duncan. "If I stay, I look bad. If I run home, I look bad. Especially if you found out I was in the park on Sunday. I'd decided to go home and take my chances with the old man when you set off my car alarm. And yes." He glared at Abara. "I tried to turn the damn thing off from the hall, but it didn't work, so I had to come outside."

It was a story that sounded desperate enough to be true. Duncan thought it over. Too much time had elapsed for a gunpowder residue swab to show anything. It was down to ballistics. "Okay, Mr. Beddoe. Here's the deal.

We're going to take your gun. We're going to test it. If it turns out your .38 fired the shot that killed your sister, you'd better have a lawyer on hand because next time a cop shows up at your door, he'll be holding an arrest warrant."

"You aren't going to tell me not to leave town?" Beddoe locked eyes with Duncan.

He waved the question off. "No. But believe me. The next time I call, you better answer the damn phone."

* * *

Sally heard the crunch of tires on gravel as she stood at the sink, washing up after dinner. She shook water off her hands and reached for a towel. Behind her, Rizzo's and Pixel's nails scrabbled on the floor as they raced to the back door.

A moment later, Jim entered. "All right, all right. Back it up." He gave each dog the obligatory head rub and pushed them aside.

"You're home early." Sally took in the rumpled shirt, tie slightly askew, and haggard expression. He was exhausted. Maybe not physically, but mentally. Odd. From what she understood, nothing about Glynis's murder was out of the ordinary. Maybe it was the strain of running the investigation alongside a partner he didn't know. He and Jenny had a rocky start, but now trusted each other in ways most people didn't understand. Sally did. It would be like preparing a defense with someone other than Tanelsa. When you constantly had to check the other person's work, the strain was twice as high. "Hungry?"

"Yes, but don't go crazy. A sandwich and a beer, and I'll be good." He came over to give her a kiss.

"Go change, and it'll be on the table when you get back."

He trudged upstairs.

Sally waited until he'd returned, downed half of the Edmund Fitzgerald, and demolished the roast beef on marble rye she'd made before she spoke again. "Rough day?"

He wiped mustard from his chin. "Yes and no. It was harder than it should have been, at least this morning. Not because of anything I had to do but…"

Sally nodded. "Because of who you had to do it with. Abara isn't getting any better, huh?"

"Well, that's the tricky part. This morning, he really put his foot in it."

She took the empty plate to the sink. "Worse than him coming on to me?"

"Professionally, yes." Jim leaned back and took a long drink. "Although I reminded him of that little faux pas when I unloaded on him."

"You lost your temper? I don't think I've ever seen that happen." It was one of the things Sally admired most about her fiancé. His ability to stay calm and in control when things were really hitting the fan.

"It happens. Not frequently, but it does. Thanks for the tip about Janssen, by the way." He told her about finding the phone number in Glynis's records. "I wish I'd followed up on him sooner."

"Hey, I would have thought the same, that he was a business contact, not a boyfriend. What about Olivia?"

"We'll get to her. Anyway." He set the bottle down. "After that, Abara seemed…chastened, I guess is the word. Even apologized to me. And you. I'm supposed to relay that." He rubbed his face. "His work later was damn good. I'd say there may be hope yet. But it's draining, watching him and investigating, you know?"

"I do. You need to trust your partner." She came back to her seat. "Tell him his apology is accepted. Maybe you should lose your temper more often."

"Not my style. Anyway, after that, we made some progress. I could have kept at it for another couple of hours, but frankly, I'm beat." He rubbed her left hand. "What about you?"

She intertwined her fingers in his and watched the lights catch at the solitary sapphire in her engagement ring. If Jim had been surprised at her choice of stone, he hadn't shown it. "Good. Bringing Nithya in was the right call. Speaking of that, what are the chances I can get a copy, or at least look at, Glynis's records for the sale of any of Tyler Lane's artwork?"

"Why do you need it?"

She told him about the upcoming meeting with Ned Tidwell. "I suspect he's charging higher prices than what he told Glynis, and a whole lot more than she sold for. I can't say why. Just a gut instinct. I'd like to see her sales records before I talk to him tomorrow."

"When is that?"

"Eleven, but I have to go to Connellsville."

Jim ran his thumb over her knuckles. "Come in with me tomorrow morning. If you really need it for the lawsuit, we'll work something out. It shouldn't jeopardize our investigation." He watched her. "Something on your mind?"

"Nope. Well, Mom sent me a text earlier to remind me, for the umpteenth time, of the cake testing tomorrow." Sally stared into Jim's eyes, the hazel color deepening as he thought.

"I plan to be there. You know that."

"I do. I'm just…" She hesitated, not sure she should speak her mind.

But as usual, Jim knew them. "Having second thoughts?"

"Yes. Not about marrying you." She rushed to make that clear.

He grinned. "Glad to hear it. Let me guess. This party is getting a bit bigger than you planned on?"

Her shoulders drooped. "I thought I was prepared for what Mom would throw at me. Joke's on me. When I was little, I figured I'd get married someday. After law school, it didn't feel as important. I was satisfied being single, and none of the guys I dated struck me as marriage material. I didn't think I'd ever tie the knot. Not until you asked. After that, I pictured a nice church ceremony, friends, family, the usual deal."

"And now it's an event with a capital E." He squeezed her hand. "This is your wedding, Sally."

She pointed at him with her free hand. "Our wedding."

"Fine. But men generally don't plan weddings. If we did, most of us would get hitched at the courthouse." He got up. "Don't let your mother have her dream wedding. Unless her dream happens to be yours."

"You sound like Tanelsa."

"I always said she was a smart woman." Jim pulled Sally to her feet. "Come on. No more talk of wedding stress, murder, or art fraud. There is a mindless comedy adventure movie on Netflix that is calling our names. You make the popcorn. I'll get it fired up."

Rizzo and Pixel leapt to their feet, perhaps recognizing the word popcorn. They didn't need any convincing.

Frankly, neither did Sally.

Chapter Twenty-Nine

Sally followed Jim to the State Police headquarters the next morning. It might have been more economical to carpool, but they'd be going in different directions afterward. If both of them missed the damn cake testing that afternoon, she'd never hear the end of it.

Once at the building, Jim signed her in and led her to a conference room. "Want a crappy cup of coffee?" he asked. "I called on the way in, and Ferguson said it was okay to show you what we collected from the victim."

"I figured. Otherwise, you would have called and told me to turn around. And the java can't be that bad." She set her briefcase on the table and removed writing materials.

He leaned on the doorframe. "Tell you what. When I bring the files, I'll bring a cup, and you can make your own decision." He left.

"Such a coffee snob." She arranged her workspace and waited. The room was bland and utilitarian, but at least didn't have the intimidating aura of an interrogation room.

Jim returned with a paper cup with a lid and a plastic bag filled with folders. "Here's the coffee, plus a couple of artificial creamers. The PSP doesn't do half and half." He set down the hot drink. "This is everything we obtained from the victim's home and office. You cannot take anything with you. If you want copies, holler and I'll try to make it happen." He marked the bags and slit them open.

She flipped off a half salute. "Yes, sir. Got it. Thank you, sir."

"Smart ass." He ran a hand through his hair. "I assume you want some privacy, and I have some things I have to see to. Text me if you need anything else." Once again, he left her alone.

Sally glanced up at the camera in the corner. She didn't know who was watching on the other end, but she waved. She picked up the cup, added some artificial creamer, and sipped. "Meh." She added a little more creamer. It wasn't the worst she'd ever had, but not as good as what she'd come to enjoy in the morning since moving in with Jim.

The first pile was Glynis's personal bank records. She'd been scrupulously neat. There were two accounts in her name. One showed all the usual activity of salary deposits, bill payments, and the assorted minutiae of household finance. The other appeared to be a business account. There was a modest balance. There weren't a lot of outgoing payments, but it had occasional deposits ranging from five hundred to a few thousand dollars. All of the transactions were dated in the current year. The deposit memos listed what Sally thought had to be the names of paintings. "Sales from Tyler's work," she murmured. Absently, she wondered when she had picked up the habit of talking to herself so much.

She ran down the list. It amounted to what she considered a nice side hustle, but Glynis wasn't buying a house on Pittsburgh's Millionaires' Row with her sales of her late husband's art. She searched for printouts of Glynis's inventory and sales receipts, but it wasn't among the information she had. She sent Jim a text. **Need information on paintings Glynis sold. Not here. On her computer maybe?**

A moment later, he responded. **Busy, but I'll ask Abara to look and print for you.**

After taking copious notes, she put the bank records aside. In the second pile were inventory records and price sheets, but not Glynis's. The logo at the top of the paper was for Ned Tidwell's agency. "These must be the works Tidwell was selling."

There was one sheet listing every piece currently for sale. Another showed what had been sold and the final price. Each painting had its own sell sheet that included information on dimensions, subject matter, and asking price. In each transaction, Tidwell reported receiving a lower price than the items Glynis had sold by herself.

"He's either a lousy publicist or the market was soft." Sally laid out Tidwell's records next to the bank information. The deposits were not these sales, all of which were lower amounts. "Significantly lower. Where are these deposits?" Sally paged back and pursed her lips when she found them. They were even lower than the sale price. For a moment, she wondered why, then realized the money that came to Tyler would be minus his agent's cut. She did some quick math. Tidwell was taking fifteen percent. It didn't *seem* outrageous, but she wasn't familiar enough with the business to know.

She called Nithya. "I've got a quick question for you. Is there a standard fee for an agent?"

"Ten to fifteen percent is reasonable," Nithya said. "I have seen contracts where agents take more, but they are not ones I'd recommend signing. Why do you ask?"

Sally brought her up to speed. "It doesn't look like Tidwell was skimming. He's taking his percentage and no more. But I still think he could be falsifying his records. I wonder what made Glynis suspicious?"

"There is nothing in her records?"

"Not what's in front of me. I've asked if I can see her electronic files. All I have is paper." Sally tapped her pen against her chin. "I may find out more when I meet Tidwell later. I'll let you know." She clicked off.

Kevin Abara came through the door. "Duncan said you wanted these." He held out another sheaf of paper. "Printouts of the spreadsheet the victim used for tracking sales. Also, I found this email chain. You might be interested in it." He set it down and hesitated.

"Thanks." She tilted her head. "Do you want to say something?"

"About the other day. At the gallery. I was out of line." He ran his tongue over his teeth. "Sorry about that. I'm not good with people."

"You've already apologized via Jim, and I told him to tell you it was accepted."

"I know, and he did. But you're here, so I wanted to tell you in person."

"Understood. You do know you're not in a great job if your people skills are rough, right? Why'd you get into law enforcement?"

He shrugged. "Seemed like a good choice at the time. You need anything else?"

"I'm good for now." What a strange answer. Most cops she'd met had a very definite calling for the job. Abara clearly did not. "Thanks."

He jerked his head in what might have been a nod and left.

He's an odd duck. No wonder Jim was having trouble with him. "Back to work, Sally." The first thing she studied was the spreadsheet. None of the paintings from Tidwell's transactions were listed, so they must have been the ones Glynis found after Tyler's death, the ones that hadn't been covered by the agent's contract. The sizes were not very different, but the prices were. In every case, Glynis had charged ten to twenty percent more than Tidwell for a similarly sized painting. The one Sally had purchased, *Night Flowers,* was almost twice as much as one of the same size in Tidwell's inventory.

Not only that, several of the paintings were marked as sold.

Sally sat back and processed what she saw. It wasn't proof that Tidwell was deliberately underselling or doing anything dishonest, but Sally would call it strong circumstantial evidence.

She picked up the printed emails and read. "Now we're talking." It was the record of an exchange between Glynis and Tidwell. In it, she told him about her pricing experiment and demanded to know the reasoning behind his strategy. Tidwell brushed her off, calling it "luck" and the results of a stronger market. Glynis fired back, letting him know she intended to contact an auditor to go over his sales records. The last message in the exchange was from Tidwell. "You're in over your head. Take the win and stay out of my business. Or you'll regret it."

Sally laid down the emails and sent another text to Jim. She hadn't intended on asking for photocopies. But based on what she read, her notes were not going to cut it.

Chapter Thirty

Two hours later, Duncan returned to the conference room. "I talked to Lieutenant Ferguson. We're getting you those copies of what you need. Did it help?"

Sally shook out her hair, which had come free from its twist, and pulled it back again. "Define what you mean by help. Did it answer questions? Yes. Did it raise a hell of a lot more? Of course. A lot is going to ride on this meeting with Ned Tidwell." She checked her phone. "Crap. Which I'm going to be late for if I don't leave now."

Before Duncan could offer to go hurry the copying process, Abara entered the room holding a folder. "Here you go." He gave it to Sally.

"Thank you." She stuffed the folder in her briefcase. "Gotta run. Thanks." She paused on her way out for a brief kiss with Duncan. "Don't forget."

He laid a finger on her lips. "Cake testing. Three o'clock. It's on my calendar."

She smiled and left.

Abara watched her go. "Is a cake really that important?"

"Not to us." Duncan led the way back to the bullpen. "But it is to Sally's mother. Keeping Louise happy *is* important to Sally."

"And making Sally happy is important to you."

"Yep." Duncan grabbed a set of keys. "Got Craddock's address?"

Abara waved his phone.

"Then let's go."

There was no discussion for nearly fifteen minutes. Abara stared out of his window. Duncan wanted to go over how they were going to approach the interview, but he held back. He sensed that Abara had something on his mind. Duncan didn't know if it was related to the investigation, but he'd had previous success letting silence do its work and waiting until the other person was ready to talk. He relied on the same approach now.

Finally, Abara spoke. "I had a stutter as a kid."

Not what I was expecting. "Yeah?"

"It was pretty bad." Abara shifted in his seat but continued to gaze at the passing scenery. "When I was really young, I had trouble getting a single sentence out. I went to speech therapy for most of elementary school. By the time I hit middle school, it was better, but kids can be..."

When he trailed off, Duncan supplied the missing word. "Assholes."

Abara glanced at him. "I was looking for something more diplomatic, but yeah. Anyway, I had it mostly under control. Unless I got mad or frustrated. Kids would deliberately provoke me. Try to make me sound like the village idiot, you know?"

"The middle school jungle is a harsh place."

"Yep. My response was to quit talking. To anyone. I'd answer questions from teachers or other adults, but my classmates? Hell no. I pulled back. It didn't get any better in high school. As a result, I didn't have a lot of friends. Actually, I didn't have any friends. I haven't kept in touch with a single person I went to school with."

Duncan had been one of the more popular kids throughout his school years, but he'd seen enough to sympathize with the other man. He remembered more than one occasion where he'd been in a situation where he'd had to step in between a bully and his target. "That had to suck. What about college?"

"Nope." Abara faced him. "My parents tried to convince me it would be easier. I wasn't buying it. I saw the stupid shit my classmates did on the weekends, drinking and partying and generally being dorks. Why would they be different? I didn't socialize much my freshman year. Within my classes, I got a reputation for being a loner at best. Worst case, people said I was stuck up. I didn't care. I didn't need them. At least that's what I told myself."

"That was a mistake." Duncan risked a look in his direction. "You would have found someone you could relate to at a school as big as CMU. Maybe a couple someones."

"You're right, and I know that now, but at the time it seemed like a good idea." Abara blew out a breath. "I'm sure you can figure out what happened from there."

"You did the same thing at the academy. And then again, when you got your first assignment." Duncan didn't need to pose it as a question. "You've been deliberately ostracizing yourself for most of your life. Why stop now?"

Abara nodded. "You're the first person I've told this to. Basically, I think I forgot how to act like a real person, or at least how to talk to others like one."

"Why'd you pick me to confide in?"

Abara caught his eye. "I don't know. You strike me as a trustworthy kind of guy. Like you're really interested in helping. Aside from my folks, I haven't seen that from others in a long time." He looked away again.

Duncan thought of McAllister, back when he'd been her FTO. She'd said the same thing. So had others he'd mentored. He didn't think he'd done anything special. He liked to help people be successful. That was all. "You haven't given them a lot of chances. You know that, right?"

"And it's probably too late. I know that, too."

"Well, I wouldn't say that. You're what, thirty-one?"

"Turned thirty last November."

Duncan checked his side mirror and changed lanes. "Then you've got at least ten, maybe fifteen years at least. And that's only until you think of retiring from this job. You may move on to something else. Lots of guys do. Plenty of time to make up for past mistakes. Hell, you've already started."

Abara cocked his head. "How so?"

"You opened up to me, didn't you?" Duncan changed lanes again. "What are you afraid of?"

The answer was immediate. "That a witness or suspect will piss me off and I'll start stammering like I used to. Or even another trooper. I'll lose their respect."

"Here's my advice. In any interview, remember you're in charge. People will try to make you mad. They'll be belligerent either to cover their fear or try to intimidate you. Don't let them. Stay cool and in control. You're the one with the badge." Duncan checked the GPS and made his turn. "As for other troopers, I've got your back. That's the benefit of having a partner. Most people I've worked with are good, with a few exceptions." He thought of his old corporal. "And the exceptions don't matter. Not in the long run."

"Thanks."

"No charge." Duncan focused on his driving, but out of the corner of his eye, he could see Abara's face had darkened, and the inside of his ears turned red. He wasn't sure if it was gratitude or embarrassment. Just in case it was the latter, he kept his attention on the road. "On to business. Let's talk about how we should deal with Mr. Whitley Craddock."

Chapter Thirty-One

Sally pulled into the parking lot of the diner where she'd agreed to meet Tidwell at exactly eleven o'clock. She grabbed her briefcase and hurried inside. Tidwell sat in a corner booth, hunched in front of an open laptop, looking much the same as the photograph on his website. Sally took a moment to study him. The sandy blond hair was longer than in the picture. He wore a pale green button-down shirt open at the neck and a pair of dark slacks. A sports jacket rested on the bench next to him. On his wrist was a large watch. The face was dark, which suggested it was some kind of wearable device. Her first impression of him was of a successful man, but not lavishly so.

She walked over. "Excuse me, are you Ned Tidwell?"

He looked up. His eyes were a pale blue, so light as to be almost gray. "That's me. Sally Castle?" He stood and extended his hand.

She shook it. "Yes. Sorry I'm a bit late. I got hung up at my last appointment."

He tapped his watch to check the time. "No problem. I was working on something. You need coffee or anything?"

"I'm going to grab a cup and I'll be right back." She didn't really want anything to drink, but having something might make the conversation more relaxed. Besides, while she hadn't said anything to Jim, he was right. Normally, he wasn't an "I told you so" kind of guy. On this subject, he probably wouldn't be able to resist.

Cup in hand, she returned to the booth. "That's better. What was keeping you so busy?"

"A little of this, a little of that." Tidwell closed the laptop. He removed a folder from a messenger bag next to him. "You were looking at some of Tyler Lane's work, is that right?"

Why the evasive answer? It might have been an opportunity to sell something else. Sally blew on her drink. "Yes. As I told you, a friend has one of his paintings and I'd love to have one for myself."

"Which one does she own?"

Shit. She hadn't anticipated he'd ask for the name of a specific painting. "It was called *Night Flowers*." She couldn't remember the names of the other pictures she'd seen, but that one definitely wasn't in his portfolio. "Fireworks in the sky over Pittsburgh. I'm looking for a similar size."

"Your friend bought it from The Glassworks, didn't she? All of those are, unfortunately, not mine to sell." He shook his head a bit theatrically. "This is the advantage of using an agent. We know the market. Not to speak ill of the dead, but Glynis didn't have my experience. Because of her stubbornness, she did her husband, and herself, a disservice."

Why did people always use that phrase right before doing exactly that? "I don't understand. Why do you say that?"

"Her pricing was way off."

"Too high?" Based on what Sally knew of Glynis's suspicions and what she'd seen in the deposits, Tidwell had been underselling. Why he wouldn't be trying to make a maximum profit was unknown, but Sally hoped this conversation would help shed some light on the matter.

"Oh no, quite the opposite. Too low. Far too low." He made a show of disappointment, sighing and shaking his head.

Sally gave herself time to think by taking a drink. Too low? *So that's your game.* He was falsifying his reported sales. It didn't look like skimming because he reported taking exactly his fifteen percent. But he'd pocketed one hundred percent of everything above the listed price. The only remaining question was how much.

"Let me show you. You said you're in the market." He pulled a three-ring binder from his bag. "I haven't seen *Night Flowers* personally. How big is it?"

Sally thought. "I'm bad at these kinds of guesses. Let's say eighteen to twenty inches by no less than thirty, but no more than thirty-six inches."

"It's a ballpark. Good enough. Let me see." He flipped the pages, which were encased in plastic sheets. "Here, this one is comparable. It's of a covered bridge down in the Laurel Highlands. Great composition. The dark red of the bridge contrasts beautifully with the dark green foliage. I believe he captured the scene in mid-summer. It would look fantastic in a room with complementary colors."

"It's beautiful." Even in the printed picture, Sally could see the details and the bold colors. She recognized it from a sell sheet in Glynis's records, which must have been provided by Tidwell. "How much are you asking for it?"

"This one is at the upper end. Twenty thousand. But if you like it, I might be able to negotiate."

Sally nearly choked. What the hell? She was sure there was one more zero on the number Tidwell quoted than what was on the record Glynis possessed. Nothing she'd seen on the works in Tidwell's inventory had been priced over two thousand. She suspected he was charging a higher price than he reported, but not by that much. If Glynis had found out what Tidwell was up to, small wonder she was pissed. Fifteen percent of twenty grand was a nice chunk of change. If Tidwell was pulling the same scheme with all his clients, the money coming in would be significant.

"Are you okay? Do you need a glass of water?" He half rose.

"I'm fine. Swallowed down the wrong pipe." She waved him back to his seat. "That's pretty steep for an artist who isn't known outside this area."

"As I said, he's dead. That raises the value." Tidwell oozed confidence, not unlike a used-car salesman going for the sale. "This is an oil on canvas, a high-quality piece. You pay for what you get."

"I'm quite sure my friend didn't pay that much for *Night Flowers*."

"And that, as I said, is the real shame." Tidwell pulled a face. "It's exactly why I say Glynis had no business trying to sell her late husband's work. It's obvious she had no idea of the true value."

Or you were running a scheme on her. She glanced at the name of the picture. *Summer Serenity.* She would look in the copies she had, for the sell-sheet to see what price he'd given to Glynis. What confounded her was how Tidwell justified such a high number. Surely there had to be some rules or standards for art. Otherwise, people could slap any dollar amount they wanted on the sticker. How would a buyer know she wasn't being ripped off? She didn't know much about the subject, but there were a lot of dead artists whose work didn't fetch such high amounts. "Let me ask you a question." Sally steepled her hands. "As I've told you, I don't know much about art. As a buyer, how do I know that's a fair price? I mean, do you set them yourself, or is there a valuation process?"

"Oh no. I have nothing to do with pricing. But I assure you, I work with a very qualified expert. I bring her in to evaluate the piece, and she gives me what she considers the fair value. From there, she and I work together to determine a price that will fit the market and give me a reasonable commission for my efforts."

"And pays the creator."

"Of course." His expression became serious and earnest, his eyes wide and no trace of mirth. "My mission is right on my website, which you no doubt read."

"I did." Sally rolled the information around in her head. "This woman who does the valuation. Who is she? What are her credentials?"

"She attended one of the premier art institutes in the country. Her name is right at the bottom of the sheet." He tapped the line.

Sally looked at the print. Delia Struthers.

* * *

Locating Whitley Craddock turned out to be more complicated than Duncan had anticipated. Craddock wasn't at his office, and his secretary refused to divulge his whereabouts without a warrant. When the troopers went to the Craddock house, Mrs. Craddock swore her husband was at work. Duncan's call to Craddock's cell rang several times before it rolled to voicemail. Frustrated, he dropped his phone in his jacket pocket. "You have two phones, right?" he asked Abara.

"Work and personal. The two should never mix." Abara held them up. "Why?"

"Call Craddock from your personal phone." Duncan rattled off the number.

"I don't think he'll answer. I wouldn't. Not an unknown number." However, Abara dialed.

Duncan didn't either, but it was worth a shot. To his surprise, Craddock must not have cared, or maybe he had been waiting for a call, because Abara spoke.

"Mr. Craddock, this is Trooper Kevin Abara of the Pennsylvania State Police. Yes, that was my partner. Yes, we really do need to talk. In person. Sir, calling from an unknown phone number is not entrapment." Abara rolled his eyes. "We're grateful for any time you can spare. Three this afternoon?"

The cake testing. Duncan glanced at his watch. It was one-thirty. Everything depended on the location. "Where?" he asked.

Abara repeated the word, then he met Duncan's gaze. "Oakland, Pittsburgh."

Duncan pinched the bridge of his nose. Damn. But it couldn't be helped. He couldn't send Abara on his own, and he couldn't very well tell Craddock to pick a different time and location. Witnesses rarely adjusted their schedule to fit the investigation. He gave the okay sign.

"We'll see you then." Abara put his phone away. "We found him. I thought that would make you happy. Why the glum look?"

"I swore to Sally I'd be at the wedding cake testing at three in Uniontown."

Abara furrowed his forehead. "Are you sure her mother will be that pissed?"

"Oh, I'm fairly confident she'll go through the roof." Duncan opened the car door. Damn, damn, damn.

Chapter Thirty-Two

Duncan pulled into a parking space on Craft Avenue, about half a block from his destination. The location was a construction site that took up at least three city blocks. Steel girders framed out a building that advertised soon-to-be high-end condos and apartments with first-floor boutiques and a coffee shop. Duncan surveyed the site and snorted in disgust. "Like this is what Pittsburgh needs. Another damn luxury high-rise."

Abara came around the car. "People keep renting them. Anyway, why do you care? You don't live up here."

"It's the principle of the thing." Duncan put his hands on his hips. "True, I prefer to live in a little less densely populated area."

Abara chuckled. "Is that what you call it?"

Duncan ignored him. "But Pittsburgh has a proud history and some gorgeous architecture. Every neighborhood has its own character." He waved a hand. "All these sleek steel and glass buildings are out of place. Why can't developers renovate what exists instead of chucking out the long-time residents, razing it all to the ground, and building these monstrosities?"

"You, my friend, are out of touch." Abara's arm twitched, as if he was about to clap Duncan on the shoulder but thought better. "Those old buildings may be beautiful, but I bet they aren't set up for what modern residents want. Hard to make a building that's over one hundred years old brand spanking new." He pointed. "Come on. There's the site office."

Duncan trailed as his partner led the way. That movement. Had Abara been about to be chummy? A shoulder slap was something he would have expected from Cavendish, a gesture of camaraderie between two people who worked closely together. *So close.* Then again, Duncan thought, maybe it was a sign Abara was making an effort. It was unrealistic to expect a complete turnaround so quickly. After all, Rome wasn't built in a day.

At the office, they were given hard hats and directions to where they would find Craddock. He stood by the structure of the nearest building, poring over blueprints with another man. "Okay. Let's do it that way," Craddock said as he rolled up the paper. When his companion nodded, he turned around. "Who the hell are you?"

In concert, the troopers opened their badge wallets. The other man slipped away. "You're a hard person to pin down, Mr. Craddock," said Duncan. "We need to ask you a few questions."

Craddock glanced at Abara. "Regarding?"

"Don't play games." Duncan put away his badge. "I've left two messages, and you've spoken to Trooper Abara. Glynis Lane."

"What about her?" Craddock's tongue touched his upper lip, and a worried light danced in his eyes.

Playing coy wouldn't work with this guy. Duncan hoped Abara had caught the signs and would hit the man head-on.

He must have because the first statement was straight to the point. "To start with, she's dead." Abara removed his notepad and pen from his breast pocket. "She was shot last weekend while she was hiking in Ohiopyle with her daughter."

"I saw that in the paper. Tragic." Craddock tapped the rolled-up paper on his palm. "But it has nothing to do with me. I hope the child is okay."

"She's fine." Duncan watched his suspect closely. "How well did you know the victim?"

"Not all that well. She did some interior design work for us."

Duncan removed the newspaper photo. "You two look pretty chummy in this picture. Would you like to change your answer? It'll go better for you if you're honest."

"Yeah, because based on that shot and what we found in her house, we think you might have been *very* good friends." Abara raised his eyebrows.

"The kind who have adult sleepovers. Were you having an affair?"

Craddock glanced around. "Not here. This way." He led them to a trailer office. Once inside, he shut the door and pulled down the window blinds. "Yes, all right? No one in my company knows. At least I don't think so, and I don't want the news to get back to my wife. Obviously."

Duncan crossed his arms. "How did you meet?"

"I told you, Glynis did some interior design work for one of my buildings last summer. Art consultation, mostly." Craddock took off his hard hat and ran a hand through his hair. "Long nights led to going out for drinks, which led to sex. Glynis was an intelligent woman. I enjoyed talking to her. My wife is not very interested in anything beyond our kids, her charity work, and the next social event. Sometimes I think they're the same thing to her. It was nice to be around a person who could talk about more than who wore what designer or the details of the latest PTA gossip."

"Did you ever meet Glynis's daughter?" Abara asked.

Craddock stuffed his hands in his pockets. "No. Glynis was very careful who she allowed into Bronwen's life. She didn't want the child to get attached to someone who was not going to be a permanent part of the family. I understood. Our relationship was never going to be a long-term arrangement."

Sensible, Duncan thought. He didn't know whether Bronwen remembered her father, but she was too young to watch people flit in and out of her mother's bedroom. "You weren't going to stick around?"

"Glynis and I broke things off right before Christmas," Craddock said. "It was mutual. We enjoyed each other's company, but—"

Abara cut in. "You didn't have plans to leave your wife? Why not? You can't love her that much or else you wouldn't be sleeping with another woman."

A pained expression crossed Craddock's face. "It's complicated."

"Believe me, we've heard it all in our line of work. You can uncomplicate it." Duncan raised an eyebrow.

"I'd lose a lot of money in a divorce. Aline, my wife, staked fifty percent of the startup costs in my business." Craddock spread his hands. "She'd get half if we divorced. Especially if she found out I was, um, less than faithful. Truthfully, I don't think she's held her vows all that sacred, either. We both get a lot out of this marriage as a business arrangement. There's no good to come from upsetting the boat."

Duncan got the feeling that Glynis was not Craddock's first mistress. But that didn't matter. "You said you broke up before Christmas. Are you sure?"

"Yes," Craddock replied. "Why do you ask?"

Abara answered. "Because Glynis Lane was pregnant."

The words were blunt, but Duncan didn't mind. The baldness of the statement might provoke a reaction.

Craddock blinked. "That's not possible. She said she couldn't have children."

"Maybe she didn't think so, but she could." Duncan tapped his thumbs on his belt. "Did you use protection?"

"Never. She made me get tested, of course, to make sure I didn't have any diseases." Craddock glanced wildly from Duncan to Abara. "It's not mine, I swear. I haven't been with her since early December. I think she'd have told me by now, wouldn't she?"

He spoke as though he believed Glynis was far along in her pregnancy. "Would you be willing to give us a DNA sample for a paternity test?" Duncan asked.

"I told you it's not mine." Craddock spoke defiantly, but with a note of fear in his voice. "You want my DNA, you're going to have to get a court order."

"Okay." Duncan took a step, as though he intended to leave, but stopped. "There might have been a witness to the shooting. Did you know that?"

Confusion crossed Craddock's face. "Who?"

Abara's answer was smooth. "We aren't at liberty to say. But where were you last Sunday between noon and three?"

"Not in Ohiopyle." The confusion left Craddock's face, replaced with a closed expression.

"Where?" Duncan pressed.

"None of your damn business." Craddock opened the door. "Good afternoon, gentlemen. You can return the hard hats on your way out. I'll get someone to escort you."

"We can find our way." Duncan held up his hands. "Then we'll call your wife. Maybe she'll tell us where you were."

Craddock reddened but didn't move as the two troopers left the trailer.

* * *

Sally stood outside the bakery and read Jim's text. **Won't make it. I am so sorry. I like chocolate, but that might not be right for a wedding cake. Whatever you want is okay with me. I love you.**

She rubbed her eyes. Jim missing the cake testing did not make her angry. She didn't particularly care about the flavor herself. No, what irritated her was that she knew her mother would unleash another round of sarcastic comments about his absence. *Jim, couldn't you have spared me that? Just once?*

The thoughts were unfair. If he could have been there, he would have. She knew this about his job when she agreed to get involved with him.

Tanelsa joined her on the sidewalk. "You look upset."

"Jim can't come." Sally showed Tanelsa the text.

"Shit." Tanelsa sucked in her breath. "This won't be good. Your mother is going to be furious."

"Tell me about it." Sally slipped her phone into her purse. "Here she is now."

Louise bustled up, fussing with her handbag. "Where is he?"

"Jim is tied up with his investigation." Sally deliberately didn't look at her mother. "He sent his regrets and his cake flavor preference, but said whatever I choose is okay." She went into the bakery before her mother could retort.

Sally introduced herself to the young woman at the register, who called back to the special order coordinator. A middle-aged woman came out and led them to a small room where tiny cake samples were laid out on dessert plates. Sally smiled. None of them were chocolate.

The coordinator explained each variety, and they tasted. "Too sharp,"

Louise said after a nibble of the lemon. "Fine for a garden party, I suppose. But not a wedding."

"I liked it." Tanelsa polished off the sample, pressed her fingers to the crumbs, and licked them off.

"I did, too." Sally licked frosting off her fingers. "But I'm afraid a whole cake of it would be overwhelming."

The bakery woman nodded. "How many guests?"

"One fifty," Sally said at the same time her mother said, "Two fifty."

Tanelsa pulled over the next option.

Sally turned to her mother. "We agreed on one fifty."

"I already told you I need more invites." Louise examined the next plate. "Is this plain yellow?" She pressed her finger to the plate to pick up a crumb.

"It's vanilla," the coordinator said. "But instead of pure white, it's a pale yellow for a little color variety."

Louise frowned. "It looks like a child's birthday cake color."

Sally held up a hand. "Don't mind her," she told the coordinator. "Mom. The number of guests. That's a rather important detail to lock down because it'll affect a lot of things. Including the cost of this cake."

"I said two fifty. What's to discuss?" Louise ate a forkful of the yellow cake, wrinkled her nose, and pushed it away. "Too plain. Although I suppose he'd like the childish color. What else?"

Sally opened her mouth, but Tanelsa laid a hand on her arm. "Pick the cake first. Then argue about people," she murmured.

The coordinator pointed at a third sample. "This is a white almond layer with a raspberry filling. It's one of our most popular options. We can do a white buttercream frosting and accent colors in whatever you want."

The cake was pretty. Sally tried it. "Delicious. I think this is a winner."

Louise shook her head. "Raspberry filling? Are you insane? You get a drop of that on your dress, and it'll leave a stain." She turned to the coordinator. "Don't you have a plain vanilla that is white in color?"

"White vanilla? Boring." Tanelsa drew the word out. "White almond has pizazz. As long as your guests aren't allergic, but you can always have a second option. Besides, when is Sally ever going to wear her wedding dress again?"

"You would say that," Louise snapped in reply.

Why something as insignificant as cake flavor should be the final straw, Sally didn't know. But it was. She forced a smile at the coordinator. "Would you excuse us for just a minute?"

The woman fled.

Sally took a deep breath. "All right, Mom. Let's get a few things straight. In your admirable desire to be helpful, you seem to have forgotten one important thing. This is *my* wedding."

Tanelsa inched her chair away.

"Of course it is." Louise waved a hand. "Next, I suppose you'll tell me it's his, too. He didn't even get you a decent engagement ring." She cast a disparaging look at the sapphire on Sally's hand.

"Yes, it is. I got the ring I wanted. And that's another thing. *He* has a name, and it's Jim. You'd better start using it." Sally took a deep breath and summoned her "opening arguments" voice. Lay out the facts with conviction and no room for debate. "The maximum number of guests at this shindig is one fifty. You will not get another fifty or one hundred invites, so you better trim your list to the essentials. I am not asking Jim to add another six groomsmen to his party, either."

Louise gasped. "You'd let those girls be unaccompanied?"

"They won't be alone because I'm not going to ask them to be bridesmaids." Sally's pent-up frustration flowed out as she spoke. "I don't know them, and they don't know me. Why make them spend money on a dress they'll wear once?"

Louise laid a hand on her chest.

"As far as today's errand, we're going with the white almond with raspberry. Tanelsa is right." Sally took her mother's half-eaten piece of cake. "I won't wear the dress again, and that's what dry cleaners are for. Getting out stains. Jim will like this one." She ate a generous piece. As good as chocolate. Well, almost.

Louise stood. "I don't know what's gotten into you." She grabbed her purse. "We'll come back to taste another day. Call me once you've calmed down and regained your senses." She swept from the room, past the befuddled employees outside the door.

"Nicely done." Tanelsa looked at the rest of the cake samples. "No sense letting these go to waste." She grabbed another plate.

"I hope my mother doesn't wait by the phone," Sally said. She glanced at the women outside. How many of these scenes did they see every month? One of them smirked at Sally. *Lots of them.* Sally ate another piece of cake. "Yep, this one." She called the coordinator back and placed her order.

Sally's phone rang. She wiped her hands and pulled it out. "Yes, Paul. What can I do for you?"

"I need you to come to Pittsburgh." Paul's anguish flooded over the connection. "Eva's been hurt."

Chapter Thirty-Three

Duncan pushed through the doors of the Emergency Department at UPMC Shadyside a little after five and went straight to the desk. He held out his badge. "Eva Lane?"

"Follow me." The nurse led him back to a curtained-off cubicle. Sally sat with Paul, speaking to him in a hushed voice, her hand on his back. The man's ashen face and shriveled posture made Duncan wonder if the news was worse than he feared. "Hey."

She looked up. "I didn't expect to see you here. Aren't you busy chasing down leads on the threatening emails and that other thing?"

"Pittsburgh police called me right after I got your text." His gaze flicked to Paul. He didn't want to say it out loud. *Because there might be a connection to Glynis's murder.* He'd gotten the bare details from the Pittsburgh officer. Eva and Bronwen had been walking down the sidewalk when a dark sedan jumped the curb, knocked them to the ground, then sped off. The officer was inclined to think it was a drunk driver. Duncan feared it was more than that. The timing was too coincidental. "Where's Bronwen?"

"CT. She's scraped up, no broken bones, but they want to check for concussion. Don't worry; she's surrounded by people." Sally understood his concern. Hell, she probably shared it. She stood. "Is Abara here, too?"

Duncan shook his head. "We were questioning…never mind. He dropped me off and headed back to the barn. I said I'd get a ride with you. If that's okay."

"Of course." She glanced at Paul. "Let's talk it over outside. Paul, I'll be right back."

He mumbled and buried his face in his hands.

"He's a mess." Sally walked to a quiet corner where they'd be out of the way, yet close enough that if something happened, they'd be able to respond quickly. "Eva's in surgery. She has a broken clavicle and a compound fracture of her right leg. I think I heard something about pins, but I was trying to distract Bronwen at the time. Eva shoved Bronwen aside before she was hit, and the car missed the girl completely. Paul isn't able to put three words together." She shook out her hair. "What do you know?"

"Right now, not much more than you do." Duncan flipped open his notebook. "Nobody got a good look at the driver. Nobody got a full plate number. Might have started with a B or a D. Some witnesses swear it was a Ford Taurus, others a Dodge something-or-other. All agree it was a beater, though. The responding officer from the Pittsburgh police thinks it was a drunk."

"Not you, though. I can tell."

"I can't dismiss the fact that Bronwen was with her grandmother. The girl might have been the target."

Worry lines creased Sally's forehead. "The killer, looking to eliminate a witness."

"Or another beneficiary to her grandfather's estate. It's possible." Duncan glanced back. "Is Paul up to answering questions?"

"I think he'll try, but don't expect too much." She went back to the cubicle. "Paul? Trooper Duncan would like to talk to you. Are you able to?"

Paul turned a hollow gaze on Duncan. "Will it help?"

Duncan lowered his voice to try and sound soothing. "It can't hurt." He sat next to the distraught man. "I got the bare facts of the accident from the cop who was at the scene. When did Eva and Bronwen leave school? I assume that's where they were coming from. Same neighborhood, right?"

"Bronnie had a half day today." Paul ran the back of his hand over his nose. "Glynis always took her to lunch on those days, so Eva wanted to do the same. Give Bronnie a bit of consistency in her life. She needs it right now."

"I understand. Where did they go?" Duncan handed the other man his handkerchief.

"La Camiseta. It's only a block or two from the school. Bronnie likes it." Paul grasped the hankie, but didn't use it. "The parking is tight in the middle of the day, so they would have walked. Once Eva gets a spot, she doesn't like to give it up, you know what I mean?"

"I do." Duncan nodded. "Would it be public knowledge that the school was letting out early?"

"It's on their website. No security on it that I know of. No login or anything. So yeah, I guess it would be."

"Bronwen went back to school yesterday, correct? Has she mentioned seeing anyone hanging around? Someone she doesn't know?"

Paul's answering look was sharp. "Why all the questions about Bronnie?" His eyes widened. "You think the maniac who killed Glynis did this? Maybe he was aiming that car at my granddaughter? What kind of animal tries to run over a six-year-old girl?"

"I'm not saying that's what happened, but I can't ignore the possibility. I'm too cynical. It's a hazard of my job. Ask Sally." Duncan laid a hand on the older man's knee. "Did Glynis ever mention the name Christopher Janssen?"

Paul shook his head. "Never heard of him."

Before Duncan could ask another question, he felt his phone buzz in his pocket. He glanced at the screen. "Excuse me. I have to take this." He got up and paused beside Sally at the door. "Stay with him."

She nodded.

He gave her arm a squeeze and left the room.

* * *

Sally watched Jim walk down the hall while he talked on his phone. If he'd walked away from Paul, the call must be important. Was it about Glynis or the car accident? He'd tell her later. She went back to Paul. "How are you holding up?" She sat next to him.

"I can't believe this. It was bad enough thinking some idiot, drunk by lunchtime, hit my wife and grandchild." He gestured at the door. "Do you believe him? Was Bronwen the target?"

"I don't know. But if she was, Trooper Duncan will find whoever is responsible."

"You and he are more than friends, aren't you?"

"He's my fiancé. But our engagement has very little to do with my faith in him as an investigator. I've known him for a long time and he's very good at his job." She poured a glass of water from the pitcher on the bedside table and handed it to Paul.

At that moment, a nurse pushed a wheelchair into the room. Bronwen sat in it, clutching a stuffed dog, a lost expression on her face. "Here she is," the nurse said as she parked the wheelchair. "She either has a very hard head or a guardian angel. No concussion or other trauma, just a lot of scrapes."

Bronwen looked up. When the nurse nodded, she got out of the chair and ran to her grandfather.

Sally watched them, then asked, "Can she go home?"

"Yes, we're drawing up the discharge paperwork now." The nurse smiled. "I advise playing hooky tomorrow. We'll give you a note for the school. A long day of rest, quiet games, and a couple of big bowls of ice cream is what she needs. I'll be back with the forms." She left.

Bronwen signed something to her grandfather. He nodded, and she hopped out of his lap. Then she came to Sally and reached out.

Sally wasn't sure what to do. "You want me?" She shot Paul a questioning look.

He nodded.

She opened her arms. Bronwen climbed up onto her lap. She signed, a gesture Sally vaguely recognized. "Dogs?" Again, she checked with Paul.

"She wants to know if she can see them since she isn't going to school tomorrow." He managed a grin. "I told her what the nurse said."

"I suppose I can bring them to you." Tanelsa wouldn't mind holding down the fort for a day. Besides, Sally doubted Paul wanted to leave the hospital until he was sure Eva was okay. "Do you want me to take her home?"

Paul brightened a little. "That is a great idea. Yes, please."

"Okay. Give me your keys. We'll stop for ice cream, and you can meet us later."

"Not our home." Paul paused. "Yours."

* * *

Duncan returned to the cubicle. Sally looked like she'd been hit in the face with a two-by-four. Bronwen curled in her lap like a cat. "Sally, I need to borrow your car. I'll be back soon."

Sally turned a frantic gaze at him. "Jim, tell him—"

"I will. Later. But I need to head over to the Zone 4 headquarters." There was something going on here, and he wasn't sure what. "They have some CCTV footage I need to see."

Sally blinked. "Yeah, sure. They're in my purse. You're not going to strand me here, are you?"

He rummaged around and found the key fob. "Nope. I hope this won't take long. After I get back, you'll drive me to HQ, I'll get my Jeep, and we'll head home. Call Marge and ask her to feed the boys." He looked at Paul. "Mr. Lane, if you have any questions, I'll be happy to answer what I can when I get back. Your wife is in excellent hands. I'll be pulling for her." He left.

The Pittsburgh Bureau of Police headquarters for Zone 4 wasn't that far away, but the evening rush hour traffic meant it was almost quarter to six before Duncan arrived. Inside, he went to the desk sergeant. "Trooper Jim Duncan. I'm looking for Officer Polson. She called me earlier."

The sergeant pointed. "Down that hall, first door on the right."

Duncan slapped the desk in thanks. He found the woman he was looking for inside a darkened room, a video monitor with the footage paused next to her. "Officer Polson?"

"That's me." She grasped his hand in a firm grip. "You made good time."

"You call almost half an hour to go ten miles good?"

"In rush hour? Yes." She pulled out a chair. "Reason I called. I also responded to the hit-and-run on Walnut. Two victims, an older lady, and a girl. At first blush, we thought it might be a drunk driver. Initial witness statements backed up that assumption." She checked her notes. "Then one guy, he said he thought it looked like the car deliberately mounted the curb, aiming for the woman and the girl."

Duncan unbuttoned his jacket and pulled out his own notebook. "Why'd he think that?"

"The car was rolling down Walnut real slow, like the driver was looking for a parking spot. Then he sped up, jumped the curb, hit the victims, and took off."

"This very observant witness get a plate?"

"Dodge Daytona. Brown with rust near the rear passenger wheel well. He thinks late nineties based on the taillights." She read off a plate number. Polson grinned. "Witness is a mechanic."

The kind of person who'd recognize a car. "I assume you ran the plate."

"I did. Car is registered to Leon Holder, who reported it stolen this morning. Five minutes before you walked in, we got a report of an abandoned vehicle in an East Liberty parking lot." She flipped her notebook shut. "It was Holder's. CSU is going over it now, but I'm not hopeful. The car's a garbage can. Dog hair all over the back seat, discarded fast food bags and wrappers, old coffee cups, grime everywhere."

"Probably a ton of fingerprints and none of them useful." Duncan leaned back in his chair. "Here's hoping we get lucky. You said something about CCTV on the phone."

"Yeah, check this out." Polson turned to the monitor. "This is from a store camera directly across the street from the incident. Here are the pedestrians." She pointed at the video of Eva and Bronwen, hand in hand, walking up the street. "At 13:07, the car is seen here. Now watch."

Duncan kept his eyes on the Dodge. It rolled into the frame, sped up, swerved, and jumped the curve. The front fender clipped Eva. She went down and pushed Bronwen out of the way. The car sped up and drove off. Duncan jotted down the plate number. "Crappy view of the driver. We won't get an ID off that. Was there any footage from when the car was stolen this morning?"

Polson shook her head. "No. It had been parked on a side street. If the actor had backed out, there was a camera there, but he—or she—pulled forward and went out the other side. No video. Our thief went in the same way, because there's no sign of anyone entering the street around that time either."

"Sounds deliberate to me." If the person who boosted the Dodge had known where the camera was, he might be from the neighborhood. "What's the address of the owner?"

Polson scribbled it down and handed it to him. "Ligonier Street, edge of Lawrenceville. Right where the trendy part stops, and the Strip District starts."

He was moderately familiar with the general location from visits he'd made over the years to the iconic Pittsburgh neighborhood. But there were two people who'd be intimately familiar with the area, and both of them were already on his suspect list.

Chapter Thirty-Four

A nurse had summoned Paul back to the OR recovery suite to see his wife, which spared Sally from having to immediately come up with a compelling counter-argument. While she waited, she rocked Bronwen. Sally didn't know any lullabies, but she needn't have worried. Not only could the little girl not hear them, she didn't appear to need them as she quickly dropped off to sleep. While Sally waited, she made a mental list of all the reasons why taking custody of a child was a very bad idea.

It was quarter after six when Paul returned. He collected their things. "They said we can go. Well, Bronwen and I."

"How's Eva?" Sally didn't rise from her chair.

"The collarbone was a clean break, but they had to put two screws in her leg. She'll never be able to go through a metal detector again without setting it off." He tried to smile at the weak joke.

"But she's alive and she'll recover."

"Yes." He straightened. "Have you thought over what we talked about earlier? You taking care of Bronwen? It would be doing me a huge favor, Ms. Castle. I got a feeling I'm going to be here at the hospital a lot for the next week or so. When Eva gets home, she's not going to be much use, all laid up. I can't take care of both of them."

"I have. I'm sorry, but I don't think I can do it." Sally's resolve faltered at his anguished look, but she would not break.

"Why not? Bronwen loves you."

"I'm happy to hear that, but I'm not qualified to take care of a child. Especially a deaf one." Sally brushed Bronwen's hair back. She looked so peaceful, head nestled on Sally's chest, eyes closed. "I don't know ASL. I can't communicate with her."

Paul waved off the concern. "Oh, you'll learn. Bronnie'll teach you. It's not hard, and in the meantime, you can make do with miming and pointing. Stuff like that. She's a good reader, too, so you can write things down."

"That's all good, but Bronwen will have to go with me to Confluence. I can't stay in Pittsburgh. I have work to do, and my office is in Uniontown."

He beamed. "But don't you see? That's why it's perfect. You said your fiancé is a cop, right? And you have dogs. If some lunatic is really trying to kill her because of what he thinks she knows, what better place to go than somewhere where no one thinks she knows anyone, with a police officer and two canines ready to protect her? And you, of course."

Sally thought of Rizzo and Pixel. Guard animals, they were not. "My dogs are more likely to lick an intruder to death than attack him."

"I bet they bark, though. And even if they don't, there's your fiancé."

"Rizzo barks quite a bit. Jim isn't going to be able to stay home all the time. He has work to do. He's searching for Glynis's killer, remember?"

Paul wouldn't let it go. "He'll be home at night. I bet a woman like you knows how to take care of herself. Don't you?"

Sally knew some self-defense moves. She'd gone to a shooting range exactly twice, since Jim insisted she know how to fire a gun and handle one safely if she was going to live with him. She switched tactics. "What about school? I can't drive Bronwen back and forth to Pittsburgh every day, and she can't miss class indefinitely."

"Aw, that's easy. They figured out the whole remote learning thing during the pandemic. I'm sure they'll come up with something." Paul held out Bronwen's backpack. "I'll get in touch with the principal and explain what's going on. In broad terms, of course. I wouldn't want to compromise the investigation. I'm sure she'll be fine with it."

Sally wasn't convinced, but she held her tongue.

At that moment, Jim entered the room. "How's it going?"

He'd back Sally's argument. "Jim, explain to this man why I cannot take temporary custody of his granddaughter."

Jim raised an eyebrow. "Well." He drew the word out. "It might not be a bad idea to get her out of the city for a couple of days." He faced Paul. "Do you have any other family you can call?"

Paul blanched. "It wasn't an accident, was it?"

"We can't rule out the possibility the act was deliberate. But we aren't sure."

"Then Bronwen was the target. Who'd want to kill Eva?"

Jim glanced at Sally.

He saw something on that CCTV. Sally tightened her arms around the sleeping girl. She didn't need him to say it. The mere fact he asked the question told her something was up, and he didn't want to alarm Paul any more than necessary.

"As I said, we aren't sure exactly what happened or who is responsible. They're still looking for the driver." Jim rested his hands on his belt. "I know everybody, including me, is sick of the phrase, but out of an abundance of caution, I think it's best Bronwen lie low for a while. I'll ask again. Do you have relatives who can help you out with that?"

"I just told Ms. Castle, no. My only option would be to put Bronwen back in foster care, and I won't do that." Paul crossed his arms, the pink backpack dangling from his hand.

Jim rubbed his chin. "How about this? We'll take her for a night or two. Maybe through the weekend. If it looks like things are going to go longer, we'll reassess."

Bronwen stirred and rubbed her eyes. She looked at Jim and smiled.

Sally kept her expression pleasant. Bronwen might not be able to hear them, but she'd pick up on any hint of argument from body language. "Jim, this is not a good idea."

"I don't want to get into specifics right now. Paul doesn't need the stress." Jim took the backpack. "Don't worry, Mr. Lane. Sally has your phone number. She'll keep you updated. Go take care of your wife."

Paul clasped his hand. "Thank you." He knelt down and signed to Bronwen while he spoke for Jim and Sally's benefit. "You're going to stay with Ms. Castle and Mr. Duncan for a bit, until Grammie is better. You can play with their dogs. I'll set up lessons with the school. Love you, sweetie." The two embraced. Paul left.

Sally fixed Jim with a glare. "I can't believe you did that. We are not—"

"We have to." He held up a hand. He told her what he'd learned in his visit to the PBP.

As he spoke, Sally bit her lip. "You're sure Bronwen was the target, aren't you?"

"It doesn't make sense any other way. Getting her out of the city right now may save her life. Paul certainly can't be two places at once." Jim crouched down and tapped his back.

Bronwen clapped and jumped off Sally's lap to climb on.

Jim stood and lifted her easily. "I know it'll be a challenge. We'll figure it out." He walked off, bouncing the child lightly as she shrieked with laughter.

Sally followed, surprised at his ease. Of course, he'd probably done the same thing with his sister Meg's kids when they visited. Jim was no stranger to children.

No, he'd be fine. The only person Sally doubted was herself.

Chapter Thirty-Five

Somehow, Sally made it through the night. Paul gave her Eva's keys to their house and the booster seat from his car, and she stopped to help Bronwen pack a bag for the weekend. The girl seemed cheerful, like the whole event was a big party. For her, it was probably true.

Paul turned out to be right about one thing. Bronwen quickly showed Sally some basic ASL as Sally pointed at items and Bronwen demonstrated the appropriate gesture. They weren't going to have any detailed conversations, but at least Sally would be able to ask the girl to put on her pants.

The dogs were delighted to have a new playmate who paid them endless attention. To Sally's surprise, Bronwen selected one of the DVD movies Jim kept for his niece after dinner. Jim turned on the closed-captioning, made some popcorn, and the trio of girl and canines settled in. Rizzo and Pixel even abandoned their usual sleeping spots to spend the night in the spare room on the bed with Bronwen.

Before Jim left the next morning, he reminded Sally to keep the doors locked and to pay attention to Rizzo's barking. "You're on watch, doofus," he said to the Golden Retriever, who managed to look happy and serious at the same time. "You hear anything out of order, you'd better sound the alarm."

Rizzo barked in reply.

Jim turned to Pixel. "I'm not even going to bother asking you to make noise. Just keep an eye on the kid."

Pixel tilted his head and perked his ears, his tongue hanging out of the side of his mouth.

After checking with Paul to make sure he had contacted Bronwen's school, Sally left her in the living room with some coloring books, crayons, and a spill-proof glass of water. Then she went to her office to call Tanelsa over Zoom and bring her up to speed.

Sally didn't expect it, but Tanelsa sided with Jim. "If anybody needs protective custody right now, it's that little girl. Don't worry. I'll hold down the fort here." Tanelsa sighed. "I thought kittens were a good test of whether someone was ready for parenthood."

"Don't even say it." Sally rested her chin on her hands. "The whole night felt awkward. I kept waiting for a major screwup on my part."

"Don't your brother and sister have kids?"

"Yeah, but I never took care of them overnight. I babysit for an hour or two on occasion. That's all."

"What about Jim?"

"Hell, he was a natural." Sally blew a raspberry. "You'd think he was around kids all the time."

"He does have a niece and nephew about that age."

"Yeah, who live on the West Coast, and he sees them maybe once a year. I'm the one who was scared shitless I'd make a mistake." Sally had second-guessed herself at every turn. Bronwen hadn't seemed to mind her fumbling around, but maybe the girl was being polite.

"Stop worrying. You didn't do as badly as you think you did. If you had, Bronwen would have said something. She's old enough to let you know when she's uncomfortable." Tanelsa aimed a manicured fingernail at the screen. "Being a perfectionist may help at work, Sally, but it will kill you when it comes to children. There isn't a handbook. As long as the kid is fed, warm, safe, and reasonably happy at the end of the day, you passed the test."

If only it was that simple. "When did you become a parenting expert?"

"My sister has kids. She tells me all about it."

Sally checked the time. "We've got that video call with Nithya now. You all set?"

Tanelsa switched from mirth to seriousness. "Ready when you are."

A minute later, Nithya's face popped on the screen. "Good morning. You are on early. Is everything all right?"

Sally and her partner had agreed not to say anything regarding Bronwen's location, but they did let Nithya know about the accident. "Fortunately, Eva will be okay, but she'll be in the hospital for a while. I think it best if we leave Paul alone as much as we can."

"Agreed." Nithya shuffled some papers on her desk. "I've read and marked up the contract. If absolutely necessary, I am prepared to go to court, but I hope we will be able to convince Mr. Tidwell to drop his suit, at the very least."

"I'd love to get him to relinquish representation of all Tyler's work," Sally said.

"Agreed, but that is a stretch. Unfortunately, we have already hit a snag." Nithya folded her hands in front of her.

Tanelsa's perplexed expression had to mirror Sally's. "What?" Tanelsa asked.

"I have been calling Mr. Tidwell since yesterday." Nithya read off a phone number. "That is correct, yes?"

Sally checked. "It's the number I have on file."

"He is not answering." Nithya shrugged. "I called twice yesterday and again before joining this meeting. I left a message each time. So far, no reply."

Sally tapped her desk. "I suppose he could be busy."

"More likely he's dodging us," Tanelsa said. "Maybe after your conversation yesterday, he looked you up, realized you weren't some random art buyer, and blocked your number."

"That doesn't explain why he's not answering Nithya." It was possible Tidwell had been spooked by learning his prospective client was a lawyer, but he should have answered Nithya's first call. "It's more likely he was tied up the first time she called, and once he listened to her message, he knew things were about to get hot for him. I hope he hasn't skipped town."

"Tell me about your meeting," Nithya said. After Sally finished speaking, Nithya continued. "This Delia Struthers. Did you not tell me she worked with Tyler Lane's widow?"

"She did. She said she's leaving Pittsburgh to take a job in Los Angeles with a gallery out there." Sally flipped through her notes. "The Los Angeles County Museum of Art."

Tanelsa typed and looked off the side of her screen. "Swanky place. Are we sure she's telling the truth?"

"No. I suppose we can find out. T, give them a call when we're done." Sally reread her notes. "Here's what confuses me. Delia told me she thought Tyler's work was overpriced."

"She is the expert. She would know." Nithya was also looking off to the side, most likely at a second monitor.

"Then why did she value a painting at twenty grand for Tidwell?" Sally asked. "Don't tell me that one piece is so special it's, what, ten times the price of one sold at The Glassworks?"

Nithya frowned. She picked up her phone and dialed. After a few moments, she hung up. "Ms. Struthers did not answer her phone. Did she mention when she was moving to California?"

"No." Sally's thoughts raced. "T, call the LACMA as soon as they open. See if they'll confirm she works there. Nithya, you should keep on Tidwell since you're up in Pittsburgh."

"I have some free time this morning." Nithya looked up. "If he continues to not answer his phone, I will try to go visit him, but I have other commitments this afternoon. Sally, you do not look like you are in your office."

"I'm not. I had something come up, and I'm working from home today." Sally heard giggling from the front room, so Bronwen must be okay. "But I can research Delia from here. I'll be in touch if anything comes up. I'll also continue to try to get in touch with Tidwell. I'll tell him I'm still interested in the painting he showed me yesterday." They ended the call.

Depending on what she found, she wouldn't be in a position to drive to Pittsburgh. But Jim had mentioned going up to see Tidwell. If necessary, Sally was fairly sure she could convince him to interview Delia Struthers as well.

* * *

The first thing Duncan noticed when he walked into HQ at eight the following morning was the fact that Abara was wearing the same sports jacket, shirt, and pants. Yesterday's tie was pooled on the corner of the desk. The second was that his partner clearly hadn't shaved that morning. "When did you get here?"

"I didn't leave last night. Got involved in my research." Abara looked up through slightly bloodshot eyes. "What happened at the hospital?"

"Have you eaten this morning?"

"Define morning." Abara waved his hand at a crumpled fast-food bag. "I had something late last night. I hit up the vending machine around four or five for one of those glazed things. I've been subsisting on energy drinks. Sit down and I'll show you what I've found." He picked up a tiny can, tipped it into his mouth, shook it to get the last drops, and threw it away.

From one extreme to the other. "Slow down. When I said you work the case until it's done, I didn't mean you sleep at your desk. How long will it take you to go home and shower?"

"An hour, maybe less."

"Okay. Tell me what you found. Then you're going to get cleaned up. You don't interview witnesses looking like you do. Take this." He shoved the bag containing his breakfast into the other man's hand.

"I can't eat your food."

"You need it more than I do. It's just a Sausage McMuffin, but you gotta have something in your stomach. I'll get something later." Duncan sat and rolled his chair over next to Abara. "Talk."

"Okay." Abara laid his hands on two piles of paper, presumably mulling which to talk about first. "Ned Tidwell. Bottom line, the guy's an ass."

"We figured that."

"Right, but remember how we didn't quite know if the victim actually threatened him?"

Duncan caught the gleam in the other man's eye. "You do now."

"It took a while, but I dug into his past, way into his past. Ten years ago, Tidwell was sued by a client for failure to…I forget the exact words." Abara unwrapped his McMuffin and took an enormous bite. "Basically, the client said Tidwell was reporting one sale number and resulting royalty to him, but actually selling for a much higher price and pocketing the difference." As Abara spoke, crumbs dropped onto the desk.

"Chew, swallow, then talk," Duncan told him. He waited until his partner complied, then continued. "What was the result?"

"The court found insufficient evidence to uphold the complainant's accusation, but it also warned Tidwell that, how did they phrase it?" Abara paused while he shuffled paper. "Right. His bookkeeping was shoddy and insufficient for a legitimate business, and he'd better get his act together before another client complained."

"A wrist slap, but one with some sting."

"Like the old-time nuns with their rulers." Abara crammed another wedge of sausage, egg, and muffin into his mouth.

"Are you sure you ate dinner?" Duncan had never seen anyone consume a breakfast sandwich in three bites, but he'd never be able to say that again.

"Yeah, but don't ask me what it was." Abara brushed off his hands. "They say caffeine is an appetite suppressant, but when it's almost all you've had in"—he checked his watch—"twelve hours, I guess it stops working like that. Anyway. Fast forward to about six months ago."

Which would have been last fall. "What happened?" Duncan asked.

"The tech guys were able to retrieve even more of the victim's deleted emails from her server."

"Besides the threatening ones?"

"Yes, but there were more of those, too. I'll get to that in a bit. Anyway, I read, oh, hundreds of them. At least it felt that way. She contacted Tidwell to ask if there'd been an accounting error, because a check she'd received was short. He said no and supplied the sales receipts. She said he must be mistaken, and they went back and forth, yada-yada, and finally, here." He cleared his throat. "Mr. Tidwell. Pursuant to our ongoing conversation over Tyler's artwork under your representation, I have contacted Haskins and Lowell, an art appraisal firm from New York, to evaluate your work. If their audit results in identifying misrepresentation and fraud on your part, as I'm sure it will, I am prepared to have my attorney serve you with a lawsuit seeking past royalties and indemnification. I will also report you to the authorities for investigation into any laws you may have broken. I am willing to drop the indemnification if, and only if, you admit to your fraudulent practices, but it is my intention to refer my findings to the police regardless of the outcome of the civil suit. Yours, et cetera."

Duncan raised an eyebrow. "Lady knew how to write. I have no idea if that meant anything in reality, but it sure sounded bad. When did she send that?"

"A month before she died."

"Did she contact that firm?"

"Yes, about three months ago." Abara handed over a sheet. "She emailed them again to get a status update, and they responded they hadn't quite finished, but 'we think you have a solid case.' They set up a meeting for this week."

Duncan skimmed the text. "Did she ever call Tidwell? I didn't find anything in the records I had."

"Only email. I think she wanted a paper trail, or whatever they call a digital record these days." Abara slugged down some coffee. "She heard from Haskins and Lowell last week, the Thursday before she died. She was supposed to meet with them this past Wednesday, three days after she died, and she'd proposed a get-together with Tidwell next Tuesday. He never responded to that proposal."

"Or he did it in person. What about the threatening emails?"

"I found four more of them. That tech guy, Andy, told me what to look for in the headers. They were sent from the same webmail address, but a different IP. Get this. It's the public WiFi at the coffee shop where Olivia Mueller works. She must have sent the first few, realized they could be traced, and changed locations."

Duncan stood. "Good work. Let's head to Pittsburgh and talk to Mr. Tidwell."

"But wait, there's more." Abara whirled to pick up another sheaf of paper.

Duncan sat again, wondering if water would flush the caffeine from the other man's system and how much it would take. "About Tidwell?"

"No, Christopher Janssen." Abara cleared his throat. "I found a picture of him online, and he fits the description the kid gave us, right down to the bird on his arm. Which is really amazing artwork, but that's beside the point." He pushed over several printouts. "He and Glynis were definitely an item. I had the tech guys take another crack at her phone, and they were able to retrieve some message records from a cloud backup. I think she and Janssen met when he worked for Craddock. This would be when Craddock and Glynis were involved, or whatever you want to call it."

"Based on what I'm reading, I think you're right. Glynis and Janssen definitely hooked up." Duncan skimmed through the messages. "Sounds like he got pissed at the end, though. Glynis wouldn't introduce him to Bronwen."

Abara crumpled the wrapper from his sandwich. "I'd take it personally as well. Yes, I know she says it's in the girl's best interest. But."

Duncan read from one of the more recent messages. "I understand. But what are we? It's been months. You're special to me. If you feel the same, I should meet your daughter. If all I am is your f-buddy, then I'm out. I won't wait forever, G. Make up your mind or I'll make it up for you." He looked up. "Is Janssen home or at work, do you think?"

"At this hour of the day, my first guess would be work. His employer is located in Stahlstown. Both that and Bear Rocks are an easy drive to Ohiopyle. And the best part?"

Duncan looked up.

Abara held out one more sheet. "He owns a Smith and Wesson 686. Revolver. The right size caliber." He cocked his head. "Want to head to Pittsburgh by way of Stahlstown?"

It sounded like a very good idea. After Abara went home and took a shower.

Chapter Thirty-Six

It was almost eleven by the time Duncan and Abara arrived at Logan Brothers HVAC, Chris Janssen's current employer. The company was located on Route 711. They pulled into the parking lot, which held two mud-spattered pickups and an older SUV. Abara ran the plates of all the vehicles. "The black Ram 1500. That's Janssen's."

Duncan got out of the unmarked Interceptor and took a moment to scope out the truck. Four doors, six-foot bed, not unlike dozens of other trucks in the area. He judged it to be less than five years old. Not the flashiest model, but hardly entry-level either. Janssen was doing okay for himself.

The troopers went to the main office, which was empty. Abara rang the bell on the counter while Duncan checked out the interior. Posters advertised the various models of HVAC equipment. An oversized calendar hung on the wall, the days up until the current date crossed off. It was not a showroom, but also not solely for the purpose of the crews.

A man came through the door at the rear. "Can I help you?"

Duncan knew at once it was Janssen. Every detail of his appearance matched Bronwen's description, from his shaved head to what looked to be a gigantic phoenix tattoo on his right bicep peeking out from under his sleeve. He wore work boots, faded jeans, and a plaid shirt over a t-shirt. A scabbed-over scratch marred his jawline. Even if Duncan knew the answer, he had to ask for confirmation. "Are you Chris Janssen?"

"I am. Who are you?" Janssen's voice was soft for such a big man. He wiped his hands on a dirty rag. His expression was more puzzled than alarmed.

"Troopers Duncan and Abara, State Police." Duncan held out his badge. "We have a few questions for you."

More confusion appeared on Janssen's face. "What's this all about? I haven't had any run-ins with the cops in a lot of years. Certainly nothing worth bringing the staties out here."

"Do you know Glynis Lane?" Abara asked.

"Of course. We dated." Janssen looked between the troopers. "Is this about her death? I read about her murder in the paper. Is Bronwen okay?" His forehead crinkled.

"You say you read about it in the paper." Duncan looked around the office. "You haven't spoken to her in-laws?"

Janssen's face reddened. "They, um, they don't know. About Glynis and me."

Abara pulled out his notebook. "Why not? We heard you two were close. Very close."

"You don't gotta beat about the bush," Janssen said, voice curt. "Cops don't ask questions they don't know the answer to, so you're already aware Glynis and I were sleeping together."

"How long had you been together? Or were you just..." Abara looked at Duncan. "How did he put it?"

"F-buddies." Duncan watched the suspect.

"Damn it. I never did learn to keep my mouth shut when I was angry. I shouldn't have sent that freaking text." Janssen rubbed his head. "Can we not talk right here? Customers sometimes come in. I don't want to do this in front of anyone who walks in. Bad for business."

Duncan raised an eyebrow. "You'd rather be seen getting into the rear seat of a police cruiser?"

"I hoped we could use the back office." He jerked his thumb over his shoulder.

Duncan pointed at his partner. "Abara, check it out."

He nodded, pulled out his sidearm, and left. He came back a minute later. "Clear."

"What, you think I'm gonna ambush you?" Janssen asked.

Duncan walked ahead of Janssen on the way to the office. "Can't be too careful." The room held a desk, phone, and some battered file cabinets. He placed his back against the wall and assumed a command stance. "Now that we're out of the public eye, how would you describe your association with Glynis Lane?" Far from being aggressive, he thought Janssen looked embarrassed.

"To me, it was a relationship. I loved her, and I didn't hide the fact. Glynis…" Janssen blew out a heavy breath. "She said she needed to take it slow. Especially with Bronwen in the picture. But Glynis was a healthy woman, you know? A widow, but with a lot of her life in front of her."

"Oh, we know exactly what you mean." Abara smirked. He took up a position that both blocked the door and allowed him to watch it.

"It was more than that, okay?" Janssen threw aside the rag. "You make it sound dirty."

"Let's back up. How'd you meet?" Duncan asked.

"I used to work for Whitley Craddock. I did HVAC consulting and design for him. Glynis, I don't know. She did interior work of some kind. They were involved, I knew that. At first, I only saw her in project status meetings. Then her thing with Craddock wound down. They had a big blowout fight one day at a site. She and I went out for drinks later. We hit it off, went out a couple more times, and"—he lifted his massive shoulders—"you know."

"You became intimate." Duncan couldn't detect any evasiveness in the answers. "But she wouldn't introduce you to Bronwen or the Lanes."

"Far as I know, she never let any of the men she got together with meet Bronnie. She said she wouldn't confuse the girl, and when the time was right, if it ever was, Bronwen would meet me. I don't know what she told the Lanes. I mean, she'd been married to their son. I assumed it was the same as with her daughter." Janssen sighed. "It wasn't that I didn't want to meet them, trust me. Hell, I learned ASL so I'd be able to talk to Bronwen. I begged Glynis. She didn't have to introduce me as a boyfriend, just a friend. I repeatedly asked when the time would be right, and she kept dodging the question."

"That made you mad."

Janssen leaned against the desk and crossed his arms. "I see where you're going. Yes, I was pissed off. Glynis would say she loved me, but she refused to let me meet Bronwen or the Lanes, her family."

"What about her parents in Philly?" Abara asked.

"She said she didn't speak to them." Janssen shrugged. "Anyway, I thought it was a lot of mixed signals. You've read the texts, so I'm not gonna lie. We fought about it, especially recently. I wasn't a one-night stand. We'd been together for nearly six months. I introduced her to my friends, parents, and brother. It hurt like hell she wouldn't do the same for me."

It was a completely understandable reaction. Duncan considered his next question. "When did you last see her?"

"The day she died." Janssen's reply was immediate. "She'd told me she was taking Bronnie hiking in Ohiopyle. I knew their favorite trail. I thought I'd just show up, you know? Glynis wouldn't be able to hide from me in the middle of the woods. Shows you what I know." He snorted.

"What happened?" Duncan asked.

"Glynis must have seen me coming. I mean, I'm not hard to miss." Janssen held out his arms. "By the time I got to her, Bronwen wasn't there. Glynis had sent her off somewhere. She got real mad, accused me of stalking her, what right did I have to interrupt their time together. It was a mess. I shouted at her, and she yelled right back."

Abara pointed. "That how you got that scratch?"

"Yeah. She slapped me. Cut me with her nails." Janssen dropped his gaze to his feet. "I told her…I said if she didn't trust me enough to introduce me to Bronnie, we were done. I said I'd always hoped we were more than friends with benefits, but apparently that's all she was interested in. I stormed off. Never saw Bronnie." He looked up. "Tell me, what else did I have to do to prove I was serious about her and I? I'd never met that little girl, and I already thought of her as special."

The anguish in Janssen's voice cut Duncan's heart. He didn't think the man was lying. "Did you know Glynis was pregnant?"

From the thunderstruck expression on Janssen's face, he did not. "When we first got together, I got tested for STDs. I asked if she wanted me to use a condom. She said her docs told her she'd never have another child, so it didn't matter."

"Maybe she wouldn't have carried to term, but she was about ten weeks along." Duncan kept his voice gentle. "Was it yours?"

"Had to be. I mean, I'm sure I was her only partner." Janssen choked back a sob. "You need my DNA for a paternity test, is that it? I'll give it to you. What do I have to do?"

Abara shifted his stance. "You said you were mad at her. How mad? You told her to make up her mind or you'd do it for her. By shooting her? Were you angry enough for that?"

"By leaving, you dumbass." Janssen's gaze was wild. "I didn't kill her."

Duncan held up his hands. "The day you confronted her, were you carrying?"

"Yeah. I do bank runs for the company on most days, so I got a carry permit. My truck doesn't have a lockbox, so the gun is almost always with me."

"Your weapon has to be concealed in a state park." How would Bronwen have seen the gun?

"I know that. You think I'd pull it out and wave it around?"

"Bronwen said she saw a man matching your description, with a gun, arguing with her mom." Bronwen had not mentioned the gun, but Duncan wanted to see Janssen's reaction.

"I don't know how she'd have seen my piece." He thought. "I wear a standard OWB holster, like you guys." He nodded at the holster threaded through Duncan's belt, which let the gun rest on his hip. "I was waving my arms in the air. I guess she could have seen it when my jacket lifted up. But I didn't pull it out."

Abara pulled a skeptical expression. "What would you say if I asked you to give us your .38 for ballistics?"

"I'll do whatever you want. You need the gun? It's yours." Janssen held out his hands. "You need to swab my hands for gunpowder residue, have at it. I already told you I'll give a sample for DNA. I loved Glynis. No matter how angry I was with her, I wouldn't kill her."

Duncan glanced at Abara. "You say you stormed off. Did you see anyone?"

"Not that stands out." Janssen thought. "I kept walking forward. No one else was on the trail."

Duncan hesitated. On the one hand, the suspect was being cooperative and not acting like a guilty party. On the other, he could very well know that the gunpowder test would be useless after so many days, so he had nothing to fear. *But he is willingly surrendering the weapon.* "Tell me one more thing. Where were you yesterday around noon?"

"On a work site. I was there from ten until two, two-thirty. New bid for an apartment complex in Pittsburgh."

"With anyone else?"

"No. Well, the building manager let me in and out. I didn't see him much in between."

Easy enough to sneak out, but Janssen would have had to steal the Dodge, too. Still. "Where in Pittsburgh?"

"East Liberty. Why?"

Duncan hadn't intended to say anything about Bronwen, but if Janssen was going to crack, this might do it. "Bronwen Lane was involved in a hit-and-run accident yesterday."

Janssen gripped the desk. "Is she okay?"

"She wasn't injured." Duncan paused. "We have reason to believe it was deliberate."

Janssen seemed confused.

Abara chimed in. "As in, she witnessed her mother's murder, and the shooter is trying to get rid of her."

The big man looked sick. "I would never, ever...look, you have to believe me. How can I convince you?"

"Ballistics on your Smith and Wesson and your DNA is a good start," Duncan said.

"I told you, done. It's locked in the safe in the main office. I'll go get it." Janssen pushed off the desk.

"I'll go with you." Duncan laid a hand on his weapon.

"I guess I'll get a swab kit." Abara left.

Duncan followed the suspect. It was true guilty people rushed to be helpful, but so did some innocent ones. Of course, a smart killer would have used a weapon that couldn't be traced to him. All Duncan knew was that if it turned out Chris Janssen was a liar and a murderer, Duncan's fragile faith in humanity might never recover.

Chapter Thirty-Seven

By noon, Sally was sure Delia was avoiding her. Every direct phone call went unanswered. No one at The Glassworks knew where she was. On a whim, Sally had even called The Juicery, but Delia wasn't in the store.

"I have to go to Pittsburgh," Sally muttered.

That, of course, raised other problems. She'd made it through the morning okay. Between miming and Bronwen demonstrating the signs for lunch, sandwich, bathroom, and juice, Sally managed to interpret the girl's wants and needs. The sign for dogs had been one of the first she'd learned, along with outside. Bronwen, Pixel, and Rizzo had spent several hours playing in the backyard under a sunny May sky.

But if Sally had to go to Pittsburgh, what was she going to do with the child?

Maybe she could take Bronwen along. No, that was irresponsible.

Sally was mainly concerned with Delia's role in any art fraud, but there was also the very real possibility that Delia had killed Glynis. "Mother of the year material, taking a kid to interview a potential murderer," Sally muttered as she watched Bronwen through the kitchen window. No, it couldn't be done.

The first option was Jim's neighbor, Marge, who often took care of the dogs when necessary. But Marge wasn't home. Sally called her sister, Noreen, but she couldn't come. One of her kids had pink eye. No use calling her brother Johnathan's wife. Reen had complained more than once their sister-in-law never wanted to watch any kid who wasn't her own.

Asking their mother was out of the question.

It left only one option.

"You have to be kidding, Sally." Tanelsa dragged Sally into the kitchenette after she entered the office, Bronwen in tow. "I cannot watch a kid, a deaf one at that, and run a law firm."

"I won't be gone any longer than I have to." Sally squirmed under her law partner's fierce stare. "I brought her crayons and coloring books. Park her at the table. You'll never know she's there. Besides, you aren't going anywhere today. Our next court appearance isn't until next week. It isn't as if I'm asking you to mind an infant."

Tanelsa huffed. "You owe me. I'm not sure what, but it's gonna be big."

"Whatever you want." Sally didn't care if she had to spring for a new pair of Louboutin shoes. She pulled out her phone. Briefly, she considered a video call, but instead she dialed. "Paul, it's Sally. How is Eva?"

Paul's tired voice said volumes. "Not much different than yesterday. She's asleep. I hope you aren't calling to talk to her."

Good thing I skipped the video. Bronwen doesn't need to see this. "No. Listen, something has come up, and I need to go to Pittsburgh. I'm leaving Bronwen with Tanelsa, my law partner. I thought you should know."

"If you think it's necessary, do what you have to do. I trust you."

"I do. I'd take her with me, but this is not something I can or should take a child to." Sally paused. "I promise Bronwen will be okay. I'd trust Tanelsa with anything."

Tanelsa mumbled under her breath.

"Tell Bronnie we love her."

"Will do." Sally hung up. "That's taken care of. T, did you call the LACMA?"

Tanelsa brewed herself a cup of coffee, then grabbed a bottle of water and a pack of crackers and cheese from the cabinet. "Yes. Delia Struthers may have a new job, but it's not in LA. They've never heard of her."

"Interesting." Sally followed her into the main office. "Is she even leaving Pittsburgh?"

"I don't know." Tanelsa held up the water and crackers in front of Bronwen, who nodded and signed.

"That means thank you," Sally said.

"That one I know." Tanelsa twisted the cap off the bottle and set it down on the table. "Anyway. Delia sure wants us to think she is. Something to bring up when you find her." She glanced at the clock. "You'd better be going."

* * *

As Sally drove, she pondered where the best place to look for Delia would be. Not The Glassworks. The woman had no reason to go there, and besides, Sally had already called.

It was early afternoon. Too late to accidentally run into her at The Juicery, and Sally had burned that ploy.

She decided to start at Delia's condo, where she pressed the buzzer for her unit. No response.

The building manager came by, hauling a bag. "Who are you looking for?"

Time to find out how well she could lie. "Delia Struthers. We're supposed to meet to go shopping, and I'm running late. She didn't answer her buzzer."

"She left an hour ago." He threw the bag into the utility room.

"Damn. She didn't leave a message for me, did she? We're supposed to go to Nordstrom's up at Ross Park."

"Not with me. But I don't think she was headed to the North Hills." He scratched his chin. "Come to think of it, she asked if I thought traffic would be bad at the Liberty Tunnel at this time of day, so sounds to me like she was going in the opposite direction."

What could possibly be of interest to Delia in the South Hills? Sally thanked the manager and went back to her SUV, where she drummed her fingers on the steering wheel. She called Tanelsa. "Delia may be headed south of the city. Did we find any known associates who live over there?"

"South? Wait a sec. Let me see what I can pull up." Tanelsa put her phone down. A moment later, she was back. "Looks like there is a new art gallery opening near the old Century III mall. Tiny. Specializes in modern works. Moderno. Could she be headed there?"

CHAPTER THIRTY-SEVEN

"I need to start somewhere." Sally paused. "How is Bronwen?"

"We're good. She's helping me shred documents."

"You'd better not get us in trouble over child labor laws."

"Worry about finding Delia and let me handle the kid." Tanelsa clicked off.

* * *

Sally greeted the girl at the front desk at Moderno. "I'm meeting someone. Delia Struthers. Is she here?"

"You just missed her," the receptionist said. "I'm so sorry."

Sally made a show of checking her phone. "I can't believe she didn't wait. We're going for a late lunch."

"I think she went without you." The girl gave Sally a rueful smile. "She asked for a good place to grab something to eat since she's not familiar with this area."

"What did you tell her? Maybe I can still catch up."

"I said Soup's On over on Liberty has a good lunch spread. I don't know if she took my advice, but she did turn in the right direction after leaving the parking lot."

Sally thanked the girl and left. It was a shot in the dark, but at least Sally would be able to fill her growling stomach if she struck out.

But when she pulled into the Soup's On parking lot, Delia's blue Tesla 3 was parked near the building. Jackpot. She went inside and scanned the dining room.

The hostess pulled out a menu. "Just you today?"

"I'm meeting someone, and I think I see her, thanks." Sally threaded her way through the tables until she stood by Delia. "Fancy seeing you here. Mind if I sit?" She glanced at the hovering waitress. "Could you bring me a glass of water? I don't need a menu."

Delia looked up. "God, you again? What now?" She glanced at the waitress. "Would you give me a few minutes, please?"

The girl nodded and walked off.

"I want to talk to you about Tyler Lane's paintings." Sally dropped into the seat across from Delia.

"I told you not to buy it. What are you tracking me down for?" Delia's phone lay on the table face down. When she noticed Sally glance at it, she put it in her purse. "I have nothing to do with that place any longer."

"But you did have something to do with Ned Tidwell." The waitress brought Sally's drink, which she accepted with thanks and took a sip.

Delia placed her order, and the waitress walked away. "Who?"

"Don't play dumb. Ned Tidwell was Tyler's agent. You priced paintings for him."

Delia ran her tongue over her ruby red lips. "I don't remember—"

"Cut the bullshit. I don't have time for it." Sally set down the glass and placed her hands on the table. "I called Tidwell pretending to be a customer. He presented me with a sales sheet that had your name on the bottom as the person who'd valued the painting."

"Asshole." Delia's voice dripped with disgust. "Okay, fine. Yes. He asked me to give my opinion on a good offer price for Tyler's work."

"All of it?"

"I priced six paintings. I don't know if that was everything he had."

Sally steepled her fingers. "The work we talked about earlier. You said it was overpriced at five thousand dollars."

"Yes. I valued the biggest piece for Tidwell at a maximum of two thousand, and that was mostly because it was oil on canvas."

"He tried to sell it to me for twenty."

There was a long pause. Delia's expression could have been carved from stone. "That's not what I told him. He tacked on an extra zero."

"Did you know he was doing that? Inflating your valuations?"

A muscle in Delia's jaw twitched. "No. Of course, he's free to ask whatever he thinks people will pay. He doesn't have to use my number."

"Your name is on it. Are you honestly telling me you that doesn't bother you?"

"That he's using my reputation to scam people? Of course I care. I can't do a damn thing about it, though."

The tone of Delia's voice was wrong. It was flat, uncaring. Sally would have expected her to be outraged. "Not true. You could take legal action. Sue him for misrepresentation or whatever they would call it."

Delia scoffed and looked away.

Either she doesn't believe me, or there's some reason she can't—or won't. Sally gambled. "You tell everyone you graduated from the Pratt Institute. But that isn't true, is it?" No response. Sally pressed. "Your degree is from Montclair State University. Why lie about it?"

"I think this conversation is over." Delia shook out her napkin.

"Did Ned Tidwell know? Did he force you to price paintings higher than their actual value? Or did he say he'd blow your secret if you turned him in?"

Delia fixed Sally with a dagger-like stare. "Get out before I have you thrown out. I can't imagine that would look too good for you. I can see the headline. *High-flying Lawyer Kicked Out of Local Restaurant for Harassing a Patron.*"

Sally held up her hands. "I'll go. But you should know I'm helping the Lanes defend against a lawsuit Tidwell filed. If I have anything to say about it, he's going to lose everything." She stood and shouldered her purse. "You can help me, or you can go down with him."

Delia picked up her phone and focused on it.

After a moment of silence, Sally gave up and left. If Delia didn't want to talk voluntarily, fine. She could blow Sally off in a restaurant. She'd have a much harder time ignoring a subpoena.

Chapter Thirty-Eight

Duncan drove down Butler Street, hunting a parking spot. In the city, especially at midday on a Friday, it would be a challenge. The warm weather meant people were out and about.

"There." Abara pointed.

The bad positioning of the car ahead of the open spot meant he'd be halfway in a no-parking zone, but there was no other choice. "Grab the placard out of the glove box." Duncan eased up to the curb and parked. "God, I hate city driving."

"Is there anything about Pittsburgh you do like?" Abara put the sign on the dash and got out.

Duncan followed. "Don't mind coming to a baseball or football game. Other than that, not really."

Abara shook his head. "Do you think Janssen will come up clean? He was awfully cooperative."

"That, or he knows he's handed us a big bag of nothing." Duncan had promised to call him with DNA results. "He seems like a good guy, though. This is one time I fervently hope our suspect is being honest."

"He mentioned contacting the Lanes. Will he?"

"It wouldn't surprise me." Duncan's attention went to a marked city patrol car with its blue lights on, and a white van parked in front of a building a couple blocks away. He glanced to his right and checked the number. "What's the address we're going to?"

"4509 Butler. Why?"

Duncan pointed.

Abara stopped. "That doesn't look good."

They picked up their pace. Sure enough, the action centered on their destination. The sign in the window identified the address as the Tidwell Artistic Advancement Agency. The inside swarmed with techs in Tyvek bunny suits, taking pictures and collecting evidence.

Duncan flashed his badge for the officer at the door. "What's going on here?"

"We aren't sure yet. I'd let you in, but it's kind of a mess right now."

Duncan held up his hands. "We don't want to complicate anything."

A man in a suit, wearing paper booties, emerged. "Who are you?"

Duncan identified himself and Abara. "What seems to be the trouble?"

"Detective O'Neil, Pittsburgh Bureau of Police." He shook. "Before I say anything, mind telling me why you're here?"

Abara peered over the detective's shoulder. "We're here to question Ned Tidwell in relation to a death we're working down in the Laurel Highlands."

O'Neil crossed his arms. "I'm afraid you won't be able to do that."

"Did you arrest him?"

"Nope. I'd absolutely be willing to let you question a witness in custody." O'Neil drew a breath. "Tidwell is dead."

* * *

After Sally left Delia, she navigated back through the Liberty Tunnel and crossed the bridge. Delia hadn't been forthcoming, and Sally didn't buy her story for a minute. Delia had absolutely known what Tidwell was up to. The question was why she didn't press the issue when Tidwell blew her off. If she'd been a victim, she had nothing to lose by going to the authorities.

Well, nothing except her reputation. Once she exposed Tidwell, there'd be no way she could continue the fiction of her education. Not having a degree from the Pratt Institute wouldn't sink her career. The entire Pittsburgh art world knowing she lied about it might.

While Sally waited in traffic, she dictated a text to Tanelsa. **How's it going?** She didn't see the reply until she parked on Butler, several blocks from Tidwell's office.

We're fine. Had girls' lunch out. Now decorating.

Sally was afraid to ask about that last bit. She paid for her parking via the app on her phone and set off toward her goal. The sight of revolving lights and a white truck stopped her. Now what?

She thought about messaging Jim, but how would he know what was going on in Pittsburgh? A young man wearing jeans, sneakers, and a hoodie stood on the sidewalk, holding his phone up. A glance at the screen showed he was filming the action. "Excuse me. Do you know what all the fuss is about?"

He kept his stare on the phone. "No clue. Cops got here half an hour ago. The white van showed up about ten minutes later. There's some kind of emblem on the door, but it's parked so I can't see it. There are words on the back, but the doors are open. I think it's some kind of medical team."

But it's not an ambulance. Sally thanked him and kept walking. She angled herself so she could see the side of the vehicle. The logo was from the Allegheny County Medical Examiner's Office, the words *death investigators* emblazoned on the side. Who had died? Had they caught Tidwell? Had there been a shoot-out?

A uniformed officer stopped her well ahead of her destination. "Sorry, ma'am. You can't go any further. You'll have to cross the street."

"I was headed to that building." She waved at Tidwell's place. "Is something wrong?"

"I can't say. I'll get one of the detectives." He turned and whistled. "Detective Suarez. This woman says she was going to where you found the victim."

A woman strode over. "Detective Emilia Suarez, PBP. You are?"

"Sally Castle. I'm an attorney from Uniontown." Sally fished out her court credentials and showed them to the detective. "I'm here to interview Mr. Tidwell about a case I'm working on."

"Castle?" The detective held up a finger. "Wait here." She walked back to the building and conversed with someone inside. She came back. "Ms. Castle, will you please come with me?" She held out an arm, clearly indicating Sally should proceed into an office next to the hive of activity.

Sally recognized an invitation that was really a command. "What for?"

"I'd rather talk to you where it's a little quieter."

"I'd rather know why we can't talk right here." Sally crossed her arms.

Detective Suarez eyed her. "Do you know Mr. Tidwell, or was this the first time you were coming to talk to him?"

"We've spoken before. I met him the other day in Connellsville. We discussed a painting from an artist he represents." Sally wondered if she should hedge. But the presence of the M.E.'s van changed her mind. "He filed a lawsuit against clients of mine recently, which is why I'm here today."

"Was that the last time you saw him?"

This was sounding too familiar to Sally. An interrogation, not a simple question. "I'm sorry. I need to know what's going on before I answer any further questions. Because this sounds like you view me as a suspect of something."

Detective Suarez sighed and tilted her head. "Mr. Tidwell's body was found this morning by his assistant. You had a meeting with him recently. There's a message from you in his voicemail, and your number is on his phone multiple times. What were you calling him about?"

"It's a legal matter. I'm not at liberty to say."

"Well." Detective Suarez pointed again. "Let me make this simple. You can talk to me here and get this cleared up, or I can take you downtown. But we're going to have a conversation. Your choice."

Sally recognized the ultimatum. It was absolutely ridiculous, but fighting wouldn't make it easier. However, if the Pittsburgh police thought they were going to bully her, she would show them how wrong they were.

* * *

Detective O'Neil had Duncan and Abara sign in before they accepted their paper booties and followed him to the back office. Tidwell was sprawled on the floor in a pool of blood. A congealed trail went down his neck onto the floor. Staying well outside the area, Duncan moved to the side. "Got the murder weapon?"

The young man kneeling on the floor didn't look up. "We retrieved a letter opener from over there." He nodded to a numbered spot just to the left of Tidwell's head. "It's consistent with the wound, but obviously we won't know for sure until we get him back to the office and open him up."

"How long has the body been here?"

The investigator shook his head. "Who the hell are you?"

"Relax, Coop." O'Neil made a shushing motion with his hands. "These two are state police troopers out of Troop B. They were coming to interview the decedent."

"Because that's what we need, more people in this shitstorm." Coop snorted. "Hopefully, you two aren't the type who expect me to perform magic and know every detail right here and now. I'm not gonna give you the hour and minute this guy died."

Abara opened his mouth, but Duncan forestalled him with a raised hand. "I have a good friend who works with the coroner in Fayette County. I don't expect details. Generalities are fine."

Coop muttered something but answered. "He's been here for a while. Twelve hours at least. Maybe more. Lividity is fixed, and he's in full rigor."

Duncan checked his watch. It was a little after two. Unlikely the man had been killed early in the morning. Why would he have been at work? "Thanks." He returned to O'Neil and Abara. "Who saw him last?"

O'Neil reviewed his notes. "The receptionist said she left a little before five. The victim was here, wished her goodnight, and told her to lock the door behind her. She told us she didn't know what he was doing, but there were no appointments on his calendar for last night."

Abara went over to the desk. "Nothing here but invoices, what looks like publicity materials, and a date book." He paged through it. "Nothing written on it for yesterday."

Duncan stepped back so he could see most of the room. Aside from the DB and the pool of blood, it was tidy. "Did the receptionist know about any problems or threats he'd had lately?"

"Nothing." O'Neil slipped his notebook back into the breast pocket of his jacket. "She did say some lawyer from Uniontown kept calling. Tidwell was definitely ignoring the calls. He told the receptionist to say he was unavailable."

Duncan figured he knew who that was. He masked his reaction. "Do you have his phone?"

"On the desk." O'Neil pointed. "The receptionist gave us his lock code, so we were able to look at recent texts and calls. We didn't see anything significant in the text history, but there are multiple calls from a 724 number between yesterday and this morning, including one voicemail." He looked up. "That's your neck of the woods, right?"

Duncan nodded. "What's the number?"

"724-555-4928."

Yep, that's Sally. She had most likely been calling about the lawsuit Tidwell filed against the Lanes.

Before he could say anything, a uniformed cop stuck his head through the doorway. "Detective O'Neil, your partner asked you to come next door, pronto. She has someone over there she wants you to talk to."

"On my way." O'Neil looked at Duncan. "Want to come along? If Tidwell was a suspect in your case, whatever is said might be related to your investigation."

"Works for me. Abara, stay here and see if you can suss out anything relating to Glynis Lane."

Abara gave a thumbs-up. "Copy that."

Duncan straightened his sports coat and followed O'Neil and the uniform outside. "The person we're going to see. Got a name?"

The uniform looked over her shoulder. "Sally Castle."

Chapter Thirty-Nine

While Sally sat alone in the empty office next door to the gallery and fumed, she shared the situation with Tanelsa. **Tidwell dead. Waiting to talk to Pittsburgh police.**

The response was swift. **Why? Have they shared info?**

No, but I've got a bad feeling about this.

Call me if you need me. You know how much to say.

Sally put her phone in her purse. She did indeed. She'd been in this situation often, not as the interviewee but as the person giving advice. Some cooperation with the authorities was good. But she'd represented too many people who thought they were being helpful but wound up getting themselves in hot water.

The door opened. A train of people entered, led by Detective Suarez. Before she could demand information, the sight of the third person robbed her of speech.

It was Jim.

Detective Suarez pulled over the two other chairs in the room and sat. "Ms. Castle, this is my partner, Detective O'Neil. Also, Trooper Jim Duncan. He's with CIS out of Troop B of the state police. We have a few questions for you."

O'Neil took the last chair, leaving Jim to stand. He gave her the tiniest of head shakes. He didn't want her to admit to knowing him. Not at that moment.

"Depending on what you ask, I'll be happy to answer them." Sally kept her focus on the city detectives. "I'm a criminal defense lawyer. I know how the game is played."

Detective Suarez lifted her eyebrows. "You've been calling the victim for two days. What is your business with him?"

"Mr. Tidwell filed a civil lawsuit against two clients of mine. I wanted to talk to him about some developments in that case."

Detective Suarez's response was swift. "I thought you said you did criminal defense."

"I do. I'm consulting with Nithya Patel. She is the lead attorney. I'm providing some assistance."

"What kind of assistance?"

Sally shot a glance at Jim, who studied his nails. "I'm not at liberty to say."

Detective O'Neil took up the questioning. "Have you ever met the victim?"

"In person? Once. As I told Detective Suarez." Sally paused. They'd find out about her previous activities. "We met yesterday morning. I had called to inquire about a painting by a man named Tyler Lane. At that point, I posed as a buyer."

Detective O'Neil turned to Jim. "Lane. Isn't that the last name of your victim?"

"It is." Jim put his hands in his pockets. "Tyler is her late husband. That is the tie to your victim I mentioned. Tidwell was Lane's agent before he died."

"Huh." Detective O'Neil focused on Sally. "Did you buy the painting?"

"No." Again, she paused. She had to make sure nothing she said put her or the Lanes in a bad light. "But from what I learned, I believe Tidwell was inflating the sale price of Tyler's art, reporting a different price to his widow, and pocketing the difference."

"How did you feel about that?" Detective Suarez fixed her with a sharp-eyed gaze.

"Offended. Especially considering the suit against my clients."

The three police officers were silent for a long moment. Detective O'Neil spoke up. "Where were you last night between five and nine?"

Here it comes. "Why?"

"Please answer the question."

Out of the corner of her eye, she saw Jim nod. "At home."

"Was anybody with you?"

"I am currently watching over Bronwen Lane. Her grandmother was in a serious accident, and her grandfather asked me to keep Bronwen until his wife is out of the hospital. I was with her." She didn't mention Jim's presence. If he wanted these two to know about their relationship, he'd say something.

"How old is Bronwen?" Detective Suarez made a note.

"She's six."

The two city detectives exchanged a look. "Old enough for us to interview her to confirm your alibi. We'll need to talk to her."

There it was, the line she wouldn't cross. "Like hell you will."

"You're not her legal guardian, Ms. Castle." Detective Suarez leaned on the table. "You can't tell us no. We'll get a court order."

"That little girl has been through enough. She lost her mother. We aren't sure if she witnessed that death. And she's deaf." Sally fought to keep her cool. No way would she and Tanelsa stand by and let them berate Paul into putting his already traumatized granddaughter through unnecessary police questioning.

"We need to corroborate your story, Ms. Castle." Detective O'Neil tried to sound conciliatory but failed. "Without that, we might have to detain you for the night, and who is going to watch the girl then?"

Sally slapped the desk. "This is ridiculous. You can't possibly consider me a serious suspect for Tidwell's death."

"You were angry with him. You admitted he's trying to work over your clients."

"I am a respected member of the Pennsylvania bar. I litigate. I don't murder people."

Jim stepped forward. "Let's take it down a notch. You don't need to talk to the girl. Ms. Castle was at home just as she said."

Detective O'Neil shook his head. "I'm sorry, Trooper. How could you possibly know that?"

"Because I was there. Ms. Castle is my fiancée."

Detective O'Neil's face reddened. "How come you didn't mention this earlier?"

"Because until now it wasn't relevant." Jim straightened and moved to face the city detective squarely. "When we walked into this room, I didn't expect you to consider her a serious suspect. If I did, I would have told you. Now I have, and I've saved you any number of wasted hours."

Sally held her breath as Detective O'Neil and Jim had their staring contest. The detective was shorter but wider. Jim had put on his implacable expression, the one that said he wasn't going to give way.

Eventually, Detective Suarez spoke up. "Let it go, O'Neil. What's done is done." She focused on Sally. "Was your desire to talk to the victim the only reason you came to Pittsburgh today?"

"No." Sally gave them the highlights of her meeting with Delia, including what she knew of Delia's connection to Tidwell.

Detective Suarez drummed her fingers on the desktop. "Hmm. And Ms. Struthers denied pricing the painting at twenty grand?"

"She did. I wanted to press her, but I also didn't want to cause a scene." Sally looked up at Jim. "Something's not right there. I'm sure of it. I haven't been able to figure out what, but I'd put money that if you go through Tidwell's papers, you'll find evidence of an ongoing scam."

Detective Suarez rose. "Thank you, Ms. Castle. I have your card. I'll be in touch if we need to talk to you further." She and her partner left.

As soon as the door closed, Sally sagged and blew out her breath. "What a crock of shit. I should call and file a complaint."

"They were doing their job. You know that." He sat on the edge of the desk.

"Thanks for the save. I can't believe you didn't tell them about us earlier."

"As I said, it wasn't relevant until they started talking like you were a suspect. Anyway." Jim ran a hand through his hair. "Is that all Struthers told you?"

"It is. I don't know whether she was giving me the truth about the prices. My suspicion is Tidwell held the whole fake credentials thing over her head."

"I agree."

"The question is whether she knowingly overpriced the paintings or whether Tidwell somehow attached her signature to a second sell sheet."

Jim appeared to mull over her words. "Either way, if Tidwell went too far, she may have decided enough was enough. I saw the scene. If the weapon was the letter opener they found, it's likely she lashed out. Spur-of-the-moment decision."

"And Glynis? Do you think Delia is the killer?"

"Not sure. You were right about Tattoo Guy." Jim told her about his meeting with Chris Janssen. "He gave up the gun and his DNA too willingly. He's either clean or he's incredibly clever."

"If he's innocent, that poor man." Sally thought about Bronwen, who probably would have loved having a father figure who adored her. She picked up her purse. "I have to get back to the office. I left Bronwen with Tanelsa. God knows what is going on. If those city detectives don't throw you out on your ass, look for any other sell sheets and check for forged signatures."

"I will." Jim followed her outside. "I'm sure Tanelsa is fine. You haven't gotten any panicked texts, right?"

Sally checked her phone. "No. Will you be home on time?"

"I have no idea." Jim threw a glance over his shoulder. No one was looking, so he kissed her cheek. "I'd walk you to your car, but I'd better go back to check on Abara. He overdid the caffeine last night. I hope he hasn't crashed and burned."

"Are things any better?"

"Some. Let's just say there's hope. See you later." He returned to Tidwell's office.

Hope. Sally walked down the street, deep in thought. Tidwell's death solved one thing. The Lanes would be off the hook. They might even get all of Tyler's artwork rights back. She dialed Nithya's number. She ought to feel happier.

But until Glynis's killer was behind bars, Bronwen—and by extension the Lanes—weren't out of the woods.

Chapter Forty

Duncan and the Pittsburgh detectives went back to Tidwell's gallery.

"You should have told us you knew Ms. Castle." O'Neil gave him a side-eye. "I wouldn't have asked you along."

"And you'd be wasting time on a dead end. I told you. If I'd known you were going to threaten to haul her in, I'd have said something."

Suarez's phone rang. She excused herself and walked off.

"Anything else we can do for you?" Detective O'Neil stopped at the door.

"If it's all the same to you, I'm going to check in with my partner and see what he's up to. I'll let you know."

O'Neil's expression said he didn't want to agree, but he couldn't object too strenuously. After all, Abara was already inside. O'Neil stepped out of the way, and Duncan proceeded back to Tidwell's office. In the intervening time, the body had been removed.

Abara stood behind the desk, going through sheets of paper in his gloved hands. He was moving his lips, but no sound came out.

"What have you got?" Duncan walked up beside him.

"I'm not sure." Abara spread out the papers. "I think these are sell sheets for all of the paintings Tidwell represented. Not just for Tyler Lane; for everyone. Take a look at this." He tapped the signature at the bottom.

"Delia Struthers. She worked for him more than once, and this is more than Tyler Lane's pictures. Sally was right. She was helping him inflate the prices."

"Don't be so fast." Abara picked up a sheet. "Check out the zero, the last one. What do you see?"

Duncan held it under the light. Sure enough, the last number looked a little out of place. "This was added on later."

"Yes, and not by the same hand." Abara used his pen to point out the differences. "It's very subtle. But see how the last number is fatter than the rest? I mean wider. It takes up a bit more space. I think it's a different pen, too."

"What do you mean?"

"Fine tip versus medium tip. The ink is the same color, same intensity. But it's like if you use two different pens from the same manufacturer. The line will be just a tiny bit different if the nib isn't the same size." Abara opened the desk drawer, removed a pen, and drew a line in his notebook. "This is one of Tidwell's, a medium point. I use a fine tip from the same company. Check it out." He drew a second line.

Abara was right. The difference was so slight, it wouldn't be caught unless the reader was paying close attention. "Good work."

"Thanks." Abara yawned.

Duncan looked at the other man closely. "You look like you're crashing."

"I'm fine."

"Did you get any sleep last night?"

Abara yawned and shook his head.

"As soon as we're done here, we'll head back to the barn. You go home and get some zzz's." Duncan slipped one of the sell sheets into an evidence bag. "The PBP folks aren't happy with me, but let's see if they'll let us take one of these."

Abara smothered another yawn. "Why aren't they happy?"

"I shot down one of their suspects." Duncan looked up. "I wonder why they haven't pulled the CCTV footage. It had to have a clear view." Duncan pointed at the camera in the upper corner of the room, its red light blinking down at them.

"I wondered the same thing. Turns out, it's not hooked up. All for show. Cheap bastard. However." Abara shook his head before continuing. "There is a city traffic cam not too far from here. I overheard two of the uniforms saying they were able to identify a person coming into the office around seven last night. But he, or she, was wearing an oversized hoodie. All they know is it's a Caucasian of slight build dressed in black."

Which matched half of the city's population and probably three-quarters of the people who were in Lawrenceville last night. "I guess if you're running a scam from your office, you wouldn't want yourself on record." Duncan initialed the bag.

"Uh-huuuuh." Abara dragged out the last sound as he gave his biggest yawn yet.

Duncan clapped him on the shoulder. "Come on. We need to try and find Struthers while we're here. Think you can hold out, or do you need to nap in the back seat?"

"I'll manage." Abara slapped his cheek. "But you're driving. If I do fall asleep, wake me when we get there."

* * *

The first thing Sally heard when she got back to her office in Uniontown was raucous laughter, both from Tanelsa and Bronwen. *What the hell is going on?* She stopped in the doorway to the main space. "Well. It looks like you two had quite the party."

Shredded paper lay all over the floor. In between the piles were pathways created from colored Post-it Notes stuck together in chains. Pieces of printer paper lay at the ends of the paths. They were drawings. Looking closer, Sally saw they were of various destinations: the dragon's cave, the castle, the Dark Forest. The handwriting was Tanelsa's, but the drawings were Bronwen's. Tanelsa had many talents, but art wasn't one of them.

Tanelsa, wearing a paper crown, sat in the corner, her hands bound by a paper chain. "Hey, you're back! Just in time to help the princess free me." She pointed her chin at Bronwen.

The girl held a cardboard sword decorated with multiple colors and glitter. She rolled a pair of dice and held up four fingers. Then she took four careful steps along the path of pink paper, which brought her to Tanelsa. She raised her sword over her head and brought it down, severing the paper chain.

"I'm free!" Tanelsa threw her hands up and gave Bronwen a hug. Then she clambered to her feet. She looked at Bronwen and mimed sweeping.

The girl nodded and started to gather up the shredded paper.

Sally had been prepared to find Tanelsa tearing her hair out. "What the heck are you two doing?"

"We had all this shredded paper." Tanelsa waved her hand. "It seemed like too good of an opportunity to waste. So we made up a game. Well, Bronnie made it up. I just did what I was told."

"Told?"

Tanelsa removed her crown. "She's smart as a whip, Sally. All I had to do was mime. Once she understood, she showed me the ASL sign."

"I noticed that last night."

Tanelsa smoothed her hair. "If that didn't work, I wrote it down. She can read pretty well for her age."

Great. Everybody seemed absolutely comfortable taking care of the child. Everyone except Sally. It wasn't reassuring and made her feel even more inadequate. What was wrong with her?

Her feelings must have shown on her face because Tanelsa rubbed her shoulders. "Sally, your problem isn't that you don't know what to do. It's that you don't have any confidence in yourself. And you should. Bronwen isn't helpless. I've learned more ASL today than, like, ever. Immersive learning. You should give it a try."

"Kids make me nervous, all right? What do I even say to her?"

"She's a small human, not an alien. She wants the same things you do. Snacks, something to drink, affection, and to feel secure. You can do all of that." Tanelsa found her shoes and slipped them on. "Go get a trash bag."

Sally obliged and the three of them spent the next fifteen minutes cramming shredded paper and used sticky notes into the bag. Sally saved the illustrations, including the dragon with its detailed sparkly green scales. "We don't have glitter, do we?"

"We do now. Bronwen and I went shopping." Tanelsa tied off the bag. She looked at Bronwen. "Water?" she asked as she signed.

Bronwen nodded and skipped off. She returned a moment later with three bottles and gave one to Tanelsa and one to Sally, who signed "Thank you."

The child signed back.

"That's you're welcome," Tanelsa said.

"I learned that one last night." Sally swigged. "Ned Tidwell isn't going to be a problem."

"Did you get him to cave?"

"No. Someone killed him last night." Sally proceeded to give Tanelsa all the information she knew, including her interrogation. For once, she was grateful Bronwen couldn't hear them.

"Those idiots honestly thought you were a suspect? Thank God for Jim." Tanelsa recapped her bottle.

"I don't think it would have gone very far, but at least he managed to cut them off at the pass. Otherwise, who knows how long I'd have spent up there." Sally pursed her lips. "I don't think they were very pleased with him."

"Too damn bad." Tanelsa took her seat. "What does that mean for us?"

"I'll have to check with Nithya, but I think the lawsuit will be dead in the water." Sally watched Bronwen, who had returned to the table and was coloring. "I guess we'll have to learn how Tidwell's contracts get transferred. That's something for Nithya to figure out."

Tanelsa made a note. "I'll call her in the morning. If a civil lawsuit is outside our expertise, probate is way, way outside."

"Exactly." Sally checked the time. It was almost five. She went over to tap Bronwen on the shoulder and wrote "pizza" on a scrap of paper.

The girl's face lit up. She tapped the word, made a V with two bent fingers, and drew a Z in midair. Then she drew a slice with little red circles, made a circle with her thumb and forefinger, spread her other three fingers wide, and moved her hand in a circle.

"Pepperoni. Why not." Sally nodded. She sent a text to Jim, letting him know she was heading home and that she'd get food. She thought a moment. She got Bronwen's attention again and made the sign for dogs, then mimed eating, and driving.

Bronwen nodded and made more gestures. She gathered her paper and crayons and put them in her bag.

Sally looked at Tanelsa. "Think all that meant let's drive home to feed the dogs and eat?"

Tanelsa held up her phone. "I've been following along. Based on the app I downloaded earlier, I think so."

"Wonderful. Call me tomorrow after you talk to Nithya." Sally held out her hand and Bronwen clasped it. "I'll call Paul when we get home and get another update on Eva."

"Will do. And Sally?"

Sally glanced over at her partner.

"You're going to be fine."

Sally's gaze went to the child at her side, who looked at her with an expression of absolute trust. Bronwen's hand was warm and small. At that moment, Sally only had one wish. *God, please. Don't let me fail her.*

Chapter Forty-One

Although Sally had mentioned talking to Struthers over in the South Hills, Duncan didn't bother driving all the way across the city. It was nearly dinnertime. If she wasn't at her condo, he'd get Abara back to HQ and send him home. The younger man dozed in the passenger seat, not quite asleep, but not awake either. Not for the first time, Duncan chastised himself for not being more specific about what "work the case" really meant.

The fact that it was nearly five did not improve the parking situation around Struthers's home. He parked and checked on his partner. "Are you sure you don't want to stay here and rest?" Duncan asked.

Abara jolted awake. "No, I told you. I'm fine."

"Yes, because when you're wide awake, you always snore."

"I don't snore."

Duncan rolled his eyes. Once inside the building lobby, he pushed the button for Struthers's unit.

"What?" Despite the fuzziness of the system, her voice snapped.

"Delia Struthers?"

"Go away. I'm busy."

"I'm afraid I can't do that. Troopers Jim Duncan and Kevin Abara from the Pennsylvania State Police."

A pause. "I don't have any business with the state cops."

Abara rubbed his eyes. "I'm too tired for this shit," he muttered.

Duncan pushed the intercom. "We need to talk to you about your dealings with Ned Tidwell."

Another pause. "Oh my God. Why does everybody want to talk about that jerkwad today? I priced some stuff for him. End of story."

"He was murdered last night." The silence went on for a long minute. "Ms. Struthers? We need to speak to you. And you'll most likely get a visit from Pittsburgh Homicide as well. You can brush us off now, but we'll be back tomorrow. Might as well get it over with."

She didn't answer, but the door clicked open.

Duncan and Abara took the elevator to her floor. Duncan rapped sharply on her door.

She jerked it open. "Come in. But I don't have anything to tell you."

They followed Struthers into a space that was all high-end decor but lacked personality at the same time. Dressed in leggings, an oversized fleece pullover, and wearing sherpa-lined slippers, she grabbed an insulated water bottle as she passed into the kitchen. Her orange-tipped hair was pulled into a messy bun. No makeup. "Let's get this over with, huh? I'm busy." She snapped the lid of the bottle open and closed.

Duncan held out the evidence bag with the sell sheet they'd been allowed to take from Tidwell's office. "Do you recognize this?"

Her gaze flicked to it and back. "I'd say it's one of the forms Tidwell has for the art he sells."

"Look at it closely."

She huffed and leaned over. "Yeah?" *Snap, snap, snap.*

The sound grated Duncan's nerves, but he controlled his face. "Is that your signature at the bottom?"

"Duh. I told you I priced some art for him."

He was used to dealing with recalcitrant witnesses. But Struthers's voice was brittle, a bit too harsh. Was she naturally tough or hiding her nervousness behind bravado? "I'd like you to look at the price. Did you write that as well? Don't glance at it. Really look."

She grabbed the bag and peered at the number. She bit her upper lip. "I did. Well, most of it. Maybe. Tough to tell through the plastic."

"Hold it under the light," Abara suggested.

She shot him a look and flicked on the light over the island. Her gaze roved over the sheet. "I remember this one. I priced it at five hundred, not five thousand." She gave back the bag.

"Where'd the extra zero come from?" Duncan took it from her.

"No clue. Not me." She took a drink.

"Ned Tidwell?"

She flicked a piece of hair from her forehead. "Could be. I don't know who else would have the opportunity. He has a receptionist or secretary or something, but she only does filing and answers the phone. At least that's all I've ever seen her do."

Abara, all trace of sleepiness erased from his face, cocked his head. "Did you know about it? Him changing the prices."

She closed her eyes. When she opened them, her gaze drifted off to the left, somewhere over Duncan's shoulder. Her expression was still. "I didn't know. But I suspected something was hinky."

She's too calm. And yet she's still playing with the lid. Duncan took out a pen and pad to take notes. "Why do you say that?"

"I heard things. The art community is pretty tight. And of course, I worked with Glynis Lane. She bitched all the time about Tidwell." Struthers hesitated. "It was a feeling, nothing definite."

"Did Glynis know Tidwell was messing with the prices of her late husband's paintings?"

Struthers's shoulders twitched. "No clue. She didn't talk to me. We weren't friends."

"Did Olivia Mueller know?"

Silence.

Abara spoke again. "Did Tidwell know you faked your degree from the Pratt?" Struthers's gaze went to him, and he smirked. "Yeah, we know all about your game. Making it seem like you went to some high-flying art school when you really graduated from a state-run university in New Jersey. Is that what got you fired from the Met?"

Struthers lifted her lip in a snarl. "Screw you."

He continued. "Did Glynis know? Did she threaten to blow your secret? Is that why you hated her?"

Struthers growled and stepped forward.

Duncan stopped her by putting his hand between them. "Just answer the question."

She took a deep breath and retreated. "That bitch had no business poking her nose into things that didn't concern her. Yes, dammit. She knew, okay?" She took a drink. "It didn't matter. I quit before she could do anything. I'm going to LA."

"Where?" Abara crossed his arms. "Before you answer, remember. We can check your story."

She opened her mouth, then closed it, lips pressed together.

"What about Olivia?"

Delia gave a sharp laugh. "Little Miss Mouse wasn't as meek as people thought. That woman knew more than she let on."

"Did Ned Tidwell know?" Duncan asked.

"Yes." The word came out in a hiss. "You people kill me. All right. You want the truth? I knew he had altered my pricing. I confronted him. The bastard laughed at me and said it was in my best interest to keep my mouth shut. Otherwise, he'd let everybody know I was a fraud, and that would be the end of my career." She swallowed hard. "I decided what the hell. If people want to overpay for artwork, it's not my problem. I didn't work on commission, so it wasn't as if he was taking money from me."

Duncan doubted that had truly been her reaction. "Where were you last night between five and nine?"

Her face turned brick red. "I met some friends at a club down in the Strip. You want their names?"

"That would be great." Abara smiled. "You didn't happen to be with them last Sunday afternoon, were you?"

Calling the look she sent him dagger-like was an understatement. "No. I was at home. By myself. I don't hike, if you're thinking I followed Glynis and her brat. I'd have shot her in the parking lot, not some damn tree stand in the middle of nowhere."

Duncan handed her the notebook and pen. "No need to get snippy. If you'll write down the names and phone numbers of your friends, we'll get out of your hair."

She scrawled the information and practically threw the notebook back. "Happy?"

"For now. Thank you." Duncan jerked his head toward the door. He and Abara left. From the sidewalk, he looked up at the windows to Struthers's condo. "She wasn't very happy to talk to us."

"They never are." Abara smothered another yawn. "Think she has an EZPass?"

"I think we should check. And it'll be interesting to talk to her friends." Duncan slapped the notebook across his palm. "Before we leave town, we'll look for Mueller."

"I'll get on the EZPass as soon as we get back to HQ."

They arrived at their parked Interceptor. "No. You'll go home and get some sack time. We don't need sloppy mistakes caused by muzzy thinking."

"What are you gonna do?" Abara got into the car and buckled up.

Duncan followed suit and pulled away from the curb. "I'm not sure, but it will involve food. And finding out just how much Olivia Mueller knew about what was going on around her."

Chapter Forty-Two

After dinner, Sally set up a FaceTime call with Paul. Eva was not able to join them, but at least Bronwen had been able to talk to her grandfather. "It'll be a few days before Grammie can go home," Paul said. "You'll have to help me a lot."

Bronwen signed, but the only thing Sally recognized was "dog."

Paul laughed. "No puppies until your grandma is off crutches. We'll talk about it when you get here."

After that, Sally and Bronwen worked on ASL lessons. They sat on the floor in the front room. The girl signed, and Sally copied it. She looked at the iPad next to her and signed again. "How are you?"

Bronwen smiled and responded.

Sally took another peek. She recognized the question Bronwen asked. "Basic conversation isn't so basic." She rewound part of the video. "Ah, here it is. That was the sign for good. Okay. We're making progress here." She pointed at Bronwen. This time, she asked the question, and Sally responded. The girl corrected her, and Sally tried again and received a smile.

Sally heard the crunch of gravel. Rizzo and Pixel, who had been lounging nearby, scrambled up and dashed for the back door.

"The boss man is home." Sally leaned forward and tickled Bronwen.

A moment later, Jim appeared. "This looks cozy."

Bronwen signed, got up, and ran over to give him a hug.

"That was hello." Sally gathered up her tablet and the throw pillows scattered on the floor.

"Someone's been practicing." Jim repeated the sign.

"What else was I going to do? I can't rely on miming forever." Sally rose to her feet and came over for a kiss. "She's a good teacher. I downloaded an app for learning ASL, but on-the-spot correction helps."

Bronwen seized Jim's hand and tugged him toward the kitchen.

"Clearly, I'm supposed to follow her." He obliged.

Once there, Bronwen climbed a step stool, took out a plate, and put it on the table. She patted the seat. Then she pushed over a pizza box.

Jim looked over at Sally. "How do you say thank you?" She demonstrated, and he copied her. Bronwen responded. "I'm guessing that means you're welcome."

"It does." Sally set a bottle of Edmund Fitzgerald in front of him. "Do you want me to warm up the pizza?"

"It's good." He took a bite, the cheese still soft enough to stretch before breaking.

Bronwen pointed at the dogs, herself, and the back door.

Sally nodded. "Here." She handed the girl two leftover pizza crusts. "Otherwise, I doubt they'll go after her."

Bronwen waved the bread in front of Rizzo and Pixel. She went outside, and they trotted behind.

Sally sat. "You're home early."

"We hit the wall. I wanted to interview Olivia Mueller, but she's in the wind. She quit her job at the coffee shop, and I learned today she's been fired from The Glassworks."

"Why?"

"Poor sales skills, or so Virginia Ridgemont said. We swung by her apartment, but no joy."

"What's Olivia got to do with anything? Or can't you tell me."

"She was behind the poison pen emails Glynis received. She knew about Janssen. She knew more about Glynis's campaign against Tidwell than she first let on. What else did she know?" He took a bite.

"The old fly on the wall routine." Sally rested her chin on her hands. "She might have known about Delia and Tidwell's scheme."

"Exactly." Jim set down his slice and wiped his hands.

Sally watched him. "How pissed were those Pittsburgh detectives this afternoon?"

"They were more irritated than anything." He gulped some beer. "Maybe I should have said something about knowing you, but I didn't think they were going to threaten to drag you downtown. Sorry about that."

Sally waved it off. "So Tidwell's dead."

"As a doornail."

"Shot?"

"No, looked like he was stabbed with his own letter opener." Jim crammed the pizza into his mouth. When he had swallowed, he continued. "The scene had all the earmarks of a crime of opportunity, not planning. My guess? There was an argument, someone got desperate, and killed him."

"Did you find anything on the Delia-Tidwell connection?"

"We did." He told her about the sell sheets in Tidwell's files and Delia's confession. "Delia gave us an alibi for last night, but it's shaky. Her friends were so drunk by the time she arrived that they can't remember exactly when that was."

Sally sat back. "She admitted to knowing about the fraud?"

"I guess she doesn't have a reason not to at this point." Jim reached for a second slice. "It's too much to try and convince us she wouldn't have heard all about the pricing from Glynis. They may not have liked each other, but they did work together."

"Yeah, but Delia has to see this gives her motive. Tidwell was holding it over her head. He'd have blown her story about being a Pratt graduate."

"I think that was done anyway." He took a giant bite. He covered his mouth while he spoke. "Glynis knew. I'm sure of it." He washed the pizza down with a pull from the beer bottle. "I don't think she'd be the type to keep quiet, either. Hell, she might have known about the pricing scam. Both Tidwell and Struthers would want to keep that under wraps."

Sally drummed her fingers on the table. "Do you think that's why she was fired from the Met? Delia? They must have found out about her fake credentials. How did they not know?"

"Abara found out she was an intern, not an employee, so she wasn't fired as much as let go. I don't know for sure, but that might have made it easier for Struthers to pull it off. Or hell, maybe someone from HR got lazy."

"A small operation like The Glassworks would take things on face value. I don't think they even have an HR department."

"It would explain Struthers moving from a major city museum to a small gallery in a midsize market." Jim finished off his pizza and grabbed his bottle. "What does Tidwell's death mean for the Lanes?"

"Tanelsa talked to Nithya. Tidwell was a one-man operation, so there's no one to pursue the lawsuit." Sally gathered up the plates and put them in the dishwasher. She wrapped the last two slices of pizza in foil, put them in the fridge, and threw out the box. "Nithya is going to file for a dismissal on Monday. That leaves Bronwen and the threat against her."

"How was she today?"

Sally went to the door and looked out. "Pretty much what you see. Tanelsa watched her while I was in Pittsburgh. Ever since we got home, she's been helping me with my ASL."

"No problems or strangers hanging around?" Jim stood beside her and leaned on the doorframe.

"None. She might as well be on vacation."

Jim wrapped an arm around Sally. "How are you doing?"

"I feel…lost." Sally leaned into his warmth. "Bronwen is happy. She spent a great day with Tanelsa, who has less experience with kids than I do. Why does it seem like I'm making everything up as I go and failing miserably?"

Jim laughed. "I think that's called parenting, Sally. My sister has talked about it. Meg says not only isn't there a playbook, every kid is different. Just as you think you've got it sorted, the whole game changes and you're lost again." He squeezed her. "I'm sure you're fine. Any problems on the wedding front?"

Sally's phone rang. She picked it up. "Great. You spoke it into existence." She answered the call. "Hi, Mom. Yes. Yes. I've been busy, sorry. Yes. Tomorrow. Got it. Bye."

Jim put the empty bottle back into the case for recycling. "More shopping?"

"Another dress store." She put her phone away. "Want to come along?"

"Not in a million years."

"Coward." She stuck out her tongue. "I'll have to take Bronwen. Who knows? She might find it fun."

Jim's expression sobered. "Shit. I just thought of something."

Sally waited. She had the sinking suspicion that whatever had crossed his mind had nothing to do with their wedding.

"When we talked to Struthers earlier, she referred to Mueller in the past tense."

Sally didn't have to work to follow his thinking. "And now Olivia's missing. Coincidence?"

Jim grabbed his phone from the table. "Yes, Detective Suarez. It's Jim Duncan with the PSP. Have you talked to Olivia Mueller? Yeah, I couldn't find her either. Based on the statement from Delia Struthers, I'm worried. You might want to amp up your search. Great. I'll call you tomorrow." He set down the phone and rubbed his face.

"You're going back to work."

He looked up. "I have to. I should have caught the past tense thing earlier. I'm sorry."

"Understood. What about Abara?"

"He spent all night at HQ. He fell asleep on the way back from Pittsburgh, so I sent him home."

"Did you ever think *you* might be beat, and that's why you missed the past tense reference?"

"Maybe, but now that I caught it, I can't ignore it.

Sally sighed. "Bronwen and I will think of something to do."

"I can help with that." He grabbed a ball from the bucket of dog toys and held open the door.

"What are we doing?" She stepped outside.

Jim let the door bang shut behind him and tossed the ball to her. "Two dogs, a kid, and a ball. I see a massive game of catch in your immediate future. I'll get you started before I leave."

Chapter Forty-Three

Duncan was back at his desk by nine-thirty Saturday morning. Friday had been a bust. Cops in Pittsburgh reported Mueller's apartment was empty, but there was plenty of evidence she'd left in a hurry. Using an exigent circumstances argument, they'd been able to locate her phone, tossed in a dumpster down the block from her building. Friends and family listed in her contacts denied seeing or hearing from her in the last twenty-four hours.

"I think she was worried about something, though," her mother said when Duncan reached her.

"Did she say what?"

"No. She was always a little stressed about money. But this sounded like something different." The mother paused. "I asked if I could help. She said she was handling it and would be in touch. That was Thursday afternoon, and I haven't heard from her since."

Abara showed up a little later, dressed more casually than he normally would be, but holding two large cups of black coffee. "You sounded like hell when I called, so I figured you could use this." He set down a cup. "You look like shit."

"Thanks." Duncan seized the cup, for once not caring about the source of the liquid inside. "I didn't get home until after midnight. No one knows where Mueller went. Last contact with anyone was her boss at the coffee shop late Thursday afternoon when she quit."

Abara sat. "She give a reason?"

"Said she was leaving town. That was it." Duncan blew on the coffee.

"Pittsburgh police called an hour ago. Her bank accounts have been emptied, but there's no record of her buying a bus or train ticket. They've put airport security on notice, but she hasn't shown up there, either."

"How much cash does she have?"

"A couple thousand bucks. Not much, but it's enough to buy a one-way ticket somewhere." But where? Duncan stared at his dark computer monitor, willing it to give him an answer. It didn't cooperate.

"What about her car?"

"She left it behind and hasn't rented one." Duncan thought over the possibilities. Hitchhiking the Turnpike would be dangerous. But if she was desperate, she might have gone that route.

"It doesn't look good, that's for sure." Abara tapped on his keyboard. "You don't pull this kind of disappearing act because you sent a few nasty emails and got caught. She's running from us."

"She's fleeing from someone. There's a statewide BOLO out for her. Neighboring states are looking, too."

Abara pawed through a pile of reports. "Ballistics are back on Janssen's .38."

"Don't bother with them. No match. Negative for gunpowder residue, not that we expected anything from that. But he is a DNA match for the epithelial cells under the victim's nails, and he is the father of her baby. Just like he said." Duncan rubbed his eyes. "I don't think he's our guy. I read the results when I came in and called him. He sounded near tears."

"Poor bastard." Abara set aside the reports. "I assume the Pittsburgh cops went back to Struthers."

"She's also gone. Car is still outside, but she's in the wind. I put out an alert for her."

"What do we do now?"

"There are the other loose ends, such as Gareth. We need to lock down his alibi, because I don't think he's the killer either." Duncan rotated the coffee cup, absently noting it was not from a major chain. "Struthers or Mueller. Both missing, both have motive."

"Neither have a gun."

Duncan waved the words away. "You said it before, though. It's easy enough to get one. We find them, we'll find the murder weapon."

"Pennsylvania is a big state." Abara raised his eyebrows. "By now, either woman could be in West Virginia, Maryland, New York, Ohio, or New Jersey. Those aren't small states either, except maybe Jersey. And they could have gotten further."

Duncan didn't need the reminder they were searching for a needle in a haystack. Unfortunately, all they could do was keep looking.

***

It was one o'clock before a tidbit of news crossed their desks by way of a call from the Holiday Inn Express in Donegal. "Strike Gareth Beddoe from the list." Duncan put down his phone.

Abara looked up. "Who was that?"

"The hotel where he was staying. He hung the privacy sign, but an alert housekeeper got suspicious because it's been there since Wednesday night. She looked, and his car is gone."

"Nice."

"Yeah. Anyway, she got into the room on her master key, and the place is trashed. There was a pile of receipts in the garbage, one of which is from a local restaurant, timestamped *after* when we think Glynis was shot in Ohiopyle. Too close to the time of the murder for it to be him."

Abara raised his eyebrows. "She thought to look and contact us?"

"She was on duty when we visited and saw us." Duncan cracked a grin. "She's been following the story in the paper. She also watches a ton of crime shows on TV. Once she knew he was gone, she rifled through what he'd left behind, found the receipts, and called."

"Smart woman. Helpful, too. Wish everyone was that way. By the way, Craddock's wife called while you were on the phone."

"What did she say?"

Abara cleared his throat and read from his notes. "Quote, as much as I'd like to see the philandering son-of-a-bitch in jail, he was with his current plaything that day. I guess I'll have to settle for taking him to the cleaners in divorce court."

"Ouch. Craddock might have preferred being arrested." Duncan leaned back. "Now we need the ballistics for Beddoe's .38 so we can tick all the boxes."

Abara pointed at his monitor. "I was about to tell you that we got it."

"And?"

"No match. If he didn't know about the nastygram emails, he wouldn't know about the art fraud. Even if he was still in town, you're right. He's not our guy, either."

Duncan stood and went to the conference room. He'd already drawn a line through Janssen's name on the whiteboard, now he did the same for Beddoe.

Abara followed him. "Still no update on our missing women." He worried a fingernail. "Isn't there something else we can do?"

"We already put out the word to other departments. All we can do is wait." Duncan replaced his marker and stared at the board. Three down. Two missing. He knew it was only a matter of time.

Here's hoping it's not too much longer, though.

* * *

Sally met her mother outside Michele's, a bridal shop in downtown Pittsburgh. Tanelsa couldn't go with her this time, but hopefully, Bronwen's presence would make the expedition a little more enjoyable. More than if Sally had to deal with her mother alone. She'd toyed with the idea of asking Marge to look after the girl, but opted to keep her close. A terse text from Jim earlier had let her know that both Delia and Olivia were still missing. It was unlikely either of them would show up in Confluence, but Sally wasn't willing to take the chance.

For Bronwen, once she understood the purpose, the trip was another adventure. She held Sally's hand and skipped along the sidewalk. Every pigeon that crossed her path elicited a smile. As a city resident, they couldn't be a new experience. Maybe she simply liked birds.

Louise waited on the sidewalk in front of the store, arms crossed and foot tapping. "You're late. Again." She glanced at Bronwen. "Who is that?"

"This is Bronwen." Sally laid her hand on the girl's shoulders as she signed hello. "She's deaf. That means hello."

Louise froze, a tiny frown on her face.

"You don't have to worry about doing anything special for her," Sally said, correctly interpreting her mother's expression. "Just make the same sign. It's the polite thing to do."

"Oh." Awkwardly, Louise returned the greeting. She focused on Sally. "Where'd she come from?"

"I'm watching her for a friend. I thought she'd enjoy looking at fancy dresses, so I brought her along."

"You'll babysit someone else's kid, but you don't want your own?" Louise *tsked*. "Sarah Marie, what am I going to do with you?"

"Nothing. Because that's all you can do." Sally lifted her chin. "It's not that I don't like kids. I do. You're right. I don't want my own children, and I don't feel the same motherly desire that Noreen did. But Bronwen needs me. I can help her, and I'm going to. Because that's what I want." A thunderbolt realization struck Sally. "There are so many kids who are looking for a good home, safety, and love until they get into a good situation. If that's what I can provide, then that's what I'm going to do."

"He, Jim, is okay with this?"

"I haven't told him. But he will be." At least Sally was pretty sure he would. "Do you want to debate my life choices or look at wedding dresses?"

Louise huffed but went into the store.

Shopping with Bronwen turned out to be quite the experience. She loved the princess-style dresses, but every time Sally tried one on, Bronwen's face scrunched up and she gave a thumbs-down sign. The clean, elegant lines of the gowns Sally preferred garnered more approval.

Louise, initially pleased by Bronwen's selections, turned sour. "I can't believe you're taking dress advice from a five-year-old."

Sally changed back into her street clothes and shook out her hair. "She's six, almost seven." Sally winked at the girl. "I happen to think she's got great fashion sense." Sally made the sign for thank you, and Bronwen gave *you're welcome* in response.

Bronwen signed again and put on a hopeful look, complete with puppy dog eyes.

"Don't tell me you understood that." Louise fussed with her purse.

"Of course I did. She wants to know if we can stop for ice cream." Sally signed yes and ruffled Bronwen's hair.

Bronwen clapped and hugged her around the thighs.

Louise heaved a theatrical sigh. "You've got all the time in the world for a stranger's child, but—"

"Let it alone." Sally shouldered her purse. "I love you dearly, Mom, but it's past time to face facts. I am a grown-ass woman, as the kids say these days. I'm going to make my own decisions. That includes my family, my career, and my wedding. You are welcome to join us for ice cream. If not, I'll be in touch about scheduling another shopping trip."

"I think I'll pass." Louise pushed past them and out the door.

* * *

Duncan drained his fourth cup of coffee and threw the empty cup in the trash. The brew from the HQ break room tasted almost delicious. It was a mark of how desperately tired he was. Two o'clock. Time jumped forward in chunks. On the one hand, he felt like he'd been awake for days. On the other, he couldn't believe it was afternoon already.

"Why don't you head home and spend some time with your fiancée?" Abara screwed the top back on the giant bottle of sports drink he'd bought an hour ago. "I'll call you if anything breaks."

"She's up in Pittsburgh, continuing the hunt for a dress." At least Sally had Bronwen with her as a buffer against Louise. Duncan briefly wondered if the child's presence made the trip better.

Sally had eased into her role as caretaker since Thursday night. Last night, she appeared to relax enough to enjoy herself and be less anxious.

She'd always been adamant about not wanting children, something Duncan supported her in even though he'd always seen himself with a family. *Maybe Bronwen will change her mind.* Doubtful, but possible.

"I don't understand why you two don't elope." Abara set aside his bottle. "Or at least go to the courthouse. I mean, it's not really my business, but from everything I've overheard about it, her mother is a candidate for one of those reality TV shows about weddings."

Duncan shrugged. "Sally only intends to do this once. She deserves a big day." His cell phone rang. "This is Duncan. Go."

"Trooper Jim Duncan?" asked a female voice.

"That's me. Who is this?"

"Carla James. I'm a nurse at Upper St. Clair Hospital. A patient was admitted early this morning with a gunshot wound in the abdomen. We finally got her stabilized enough to go through her personal effects and found your card in her pockets."

Duncan snapped his fingers to get his partner's attention. "What's the patient's name?"

"Her driver's license identified her as Olivia Mueller. Do you know her?"

Duncan tapped the speaker button on the phone. "Yes. She's a suspect in a homicide we're investigating. I've been looking for her since yesterday. What's her condition?"

"Critical." James paused. "She's in the ICU. Frankly, it's astonishing she survived long enough to be found. The bullet missed any vital organs, but she lost a lot of blood before she was picked up."

A million questions crowded through Duncan's mind, but he only asked one. "Did she say anything?"

"She maintained consciousness long enough to identify the person who shot her, but only by first name. Delia."

Abara grabbed his desk phone and dialed.

Duncan took his phone off speaker. "Anything else?" He heard Abara saying something about the existing BOLO on Delia Struthers. Confident that was under control, he focused on his own call.

"It was barely audible, but one of the other nurses picked up the words

Bronwen, next, and maybe 'said something,'" said James. "I'm sorry it took so long to get in touch with you, but it's been a crazy morning."

"I'm on my way over now." Duncan glanced at Abara, who was still on the phone.

"Don't bother. She's unconscious. If she comes to and says anything else, we'll call you."

Duncan thanked her and hung up as Abara did the same. "What'd you find out?" Duncan asked.

"That was the PBP. I called to update them that Delia is armed and presumed dangerous." Abara checked his notes. "A patrol unit went to her condo again and called in while I was on the phone. Her Tesla is still in its spot, but no answer on her intercom or her phone. The uniform talked to another resident, who said he'd seen her come in late last night. She brushed past him without a word, and she looked agitated."

"Ten to one she was coming from shooting Mueller."

"Speaking of, is Mueller alive?"

"Barely." Duncan stood and stretched while he gave Abara a summary of what he'd learned from the nurse. "This resident. He say anything else?"

Abara glanced at his notes. "Yeah. Struthers left early this morning but didn't take her car. He thought that was strange because she's not a big walker." Abara's desk phone rang. "Abara. Yeah. Yeah. Wait, say that again? Shit. Yes, armed and dangerous. Anyone you can spare to search is appreciated. Thanks." Abara hung up. "They broke into Struthers's apartment. They found a notepad on her table with Sally's name and your address on it. There was also a city address that turned out to be a bridal place downtown."

Ice trickled down Duncan's back. "What's the name of the store?"

"Michele's."

Exactly the place Sally and Bronwen intended to visit. Duncan raced out of HQ, dialing for backup as he ran.

Chapter Forty-Four

Sally held Bronwen's hand as the girl hopped next to her. There was no particular reason to rush home. They found an ice cream store and ate their cones while sitting on a bench in Market Square. Bronwen had fun chasing pigeons. They window-shopped around the square and enjoyed the warmth of the spring sun, accompanied by a refreshing breeze. People were out in force, casting the dreary days of winter into memory. Occasionally, the back of Sally's neck tingled with a sensation of being watched, but every time she looked, no one was paying attention to them. Both Delia and Olivia were still out there, but surely neither of them would be so stupid as to try something in broad daylight.

Okay, Sally had to admit the car incident had been in the middle of the day. She kept an eagle eye on passing cars, but all of them obeyed the traffic laws, in all the ways that were important, and passed without incident.

Around three, Sally stopped. "How about we head home?" she asked Bronwen, although the only sign she used was home.

Bronwen nodded and signed.

Sally laughed. "Yes," she replied. She hadn't understood all the signs, but "food" and "dogs" were quite clear.

Sally brushed hair from her face as she looked around, trying to reorient herself and pull up the memories of downtown geography from when she had worked with the Allegheny County District Attorney. The fastest way back to the parking garage off Market Square was to go one block farther on Fifth and cut over on Wood. But the spring construction season had started. From where Sally stood, she could see the signs indicating the road and sidewalk were closed. She could continue down to Smithfield, but that would take her a couple city blocks out of her way.

People brushed by as Sally considered the pros and cons of walking through the construction zone. Finally, her feet made the decision for her. "What the hell, right?" she muttered to herself. City residents, notorious for jaywalking, also wandered down closed streets all the time. She wouldn't get in trouble. She tugged Bronwen's hand and pointed toward the intersection with Wood.

They made the turn and were about halfway down the closed block of Wood between Fifth and Forbes when Sally saw Delia approach from the opposite end of the street.

Delia's hands were buried in her pockets. "I thought I saw you two," she called. "I hoped I'd be able to catch up to you here. Nice day, isn't it?"

Sally jerked to a halt. "Sure is. What are you doing?"

Delia casually looked around. "Window shopping. How'd the dress hunt go?"

The offhand question put Sally on edge. "How'd you know we've been dress shopping?"

Delia blew out her breath, ruffling the orange-tipped strands on her face. "I saw you come out of the store, and I've been following you."

"Yeah? Why didn't you say anything earlier?"

Delia gave an exaggerated shrug. "I was waiting for the right time."

Every nerve in Sally's body screamed at her to run, but she knew that was the wrong move. The sidewalk was too torn up for Bronwen to move quickly. "This is the right time? On a semi-deserted street?"

"Best I can do." Delia's right hand came out of her pocket. She gripped a handgun and aimed it at Bronwen.

The girl sidled closer to Sally.

"You're going to shoot us in the middle of the city? Pittsburgh has Shotspotter tech." Sally mustered up a bravado she didn't quite feel. "The cops will be on you before you get two blocks away."

"I parked my car around the corner." Delia's hand trembled. "Not the Tesla; that's too noticeable. I'll take my chances. All I have to do is take care of you and the kid, and I can leave permanently."

"You really want to shoot a child?" Sally stepped in front of Bronwen.

"I didn't want to kill anyone." Delia clenched the gun butt. "But she saw me that day, in Ohiopyle. She's the last loose end."

Sally pushed Bronwen farther behind her. "She didn't see anything. Glynis sent her away when Chris Janssen showed up. He was the person she saw, his gun. She never mentioned seeing a woman. And of course, she wouldn't have heard you. Walk away, get in your car, and leave." Of course, Sally would immediately call the police, but no sense saying that.

Delia licked her lips. "You won't let me do that. Not with two murders on my hands. Even if they weren't my fault."

Sally had faced people with guns before. They usually possessed a calm, resolute air. Delia didn't. Her eyes darted from Sally and back, and there was a definite tremble to her hand. Lack of composure didn't make her less dangerous. Keep her talking, Sally thought. The longer they spoke, the more likely it was that someone else would come onto the block, construction or no. "Tell me, why'd you shoot Glynis in the first place?"

"I didn't mean to." Delia's hand trembled, and she gripped it with the other. "She knew I wasn't a Pratt grad. I tried to argue with her. Who was I hurting? No one. Then she found out about my involvement with Tidwell." Delia half laughed. "I tried to tell her I hadn't helped him scam her and all those other people, that I was as much of a victim as her, but she wouldn't believe me. She'd accumulated enough information to go to the cops. I tried to talk her out of it. She wouldn't listen."

"How bad would it have been, though? As you said, you were being used."

"Don't you understand?" Tears streamed down Delia's cheeks. "I could have gone to jail for fraud. He knew about my degree. That's how he got me to sign the valuations. Maybe if I'd said something earlier, I could avoid arrest, but who would hire a liar? I'd never have my gallery, never be as important as Stein. I'd lose everything I worked for. I might even have been sued, which would wreck me. I can't afford that."

"She wouldn't listen."

"Nope." Delia swiped at her cheeks. "I knew she'd be at the park that day.

I went and took my dad's old gun with me. I just meant to wave it in her face. But it didn't scare her. She *laughed* and said I didn't have the guts. Next thing I knew, I'd squeezed the trigger, and she was on the ground."

Set up the conditions for tragedy, and odds are it would happen. That's what Jim would say. Did he know yet? Was he on the way? Sally gripped Bronwen's hand. "What about Tidwell?"

"That asshole." Delia tilted her head to look at the sky. "I went to his gallery to tell him I was done. Somehow, he figured out what happened with Glynis. He said if I wanted him to stay quiet, I'd work for him for as long as he wanted me. I thought going to jail for fraud would be bad? Try murder. I grabbed his stupid letter opener and jabbed him. I was blind with rage. I didn't even know where I'd hit him. The next day, I found out he was dead. Now I was on the hook for two murders, neither of which I meant to commit."

If Delia hadn't been pointing a gun at her, Sally might have felt bad for the other woman. "So you came for Bronwen. How'd you find us?" If Delia hadn't fired yet, chances were she wouldn't. At least not intentionally. Her finger was on the trigger, after all. But it was an awfully big chance to take.

She let go of Bronwen, held up her hand against her back, and hoped the girl understood the message. *Don't move.*

"I broke into your house on Friday while you were gone." Again, the gun wavered, and Delia steadied it. "I can't believe you don't have a security system."

Something to fix on Monday.

"I was afraid I'd have to hurt the pooches, but I threw them a few snacks and they were my new friends." Delia took a breath. "I saw you'd written the dress shopping thing on your desk calendar. I figured the odds of successfully getting you out of the way unseen were much better here than in Confluence. I've been keeping an eye on you since you left the store. When you headed this way, I figured you were going back to your car, so I hurried around the block to cut you off. And here we are." She widened her stance and lifted the gun.

"Delia, look. I can tell you aren't a killer at heart."

"Haven't you been listening? I murdered two people. Maybe three by now." She snorted. "Olivia thought she could get money out of me. She figured everything out. Joke's on her. I left her bleeding on the ground."

Sally brushed off the news. She couldn't worry about Olivia right now. "But not intentionally. You've been talking to me all this time. I bet you're finding it hard to pull that trigger in cold blood. Especially when the victim is a child."

Delia sucked in her breath as though she'd been punched in the gut.

"Turn around. Leave. Bronwen hasn't heard anything. I need to stay with her. If you're lucky, you'll get away."

"The first thing you'll do is call your fiancé." Delia shook her head. "Sorry. You and I might have been friends under different circumstances. But it's too late for me now."

While Sally had been talking, she'd surreptitiously inched closer to her attacker. She'd manage to close the gap to a manageable five feet. Delia might have noticed, but she hadn't said anything, and she hadn't moved. More evidence she didn't want to pull the trigger?

Maybe.

Not quite close enough. Sally's approach was slightly off-center because she had to stay between Delia and Bronwen. Sally sensed the girl hadn't followed her. "What about the car accident?" *Just a few more feet.*

"That was a little spur-of-the-moment, too. I stole the car so I could follow her. Like I said, the Tesla is too noticeable. I'd started to think the kid hadn't said anything. But when I saw her on the sidewalk, the idea leapt into my mind. Just another hit-and-run by a drunk driver." Delia's laugh sounded a bit desperate. "Everything is Glynis's fault. Why couldn't she leave it alone?" Delia squeezed her eyes shut.

Now. Sally moved a quick half step closer and pivoted to her left. She brought her hand up and slammed Delia's arm away, while wrenching the hand holding the gun around so it pointed back at Delia, who gasped in pain. Sally jerked the gun out of Delia's grasp, then retreated out of range.

Delia grabbed her hand and sank to the ground. "You bitch! I think you broke my thumb."

Sally held the weapon in the teacup hold Jim had taught her, finger near the trigger but not on it, and pointed the gun downward. "You're lucky you didn't get shot. Stay there." While Delia glowered from her kneeling position, still grasping her hand, Sally fumbled her phone out of her pocket, voice dialed 9-1-1, and explained the situation. While she did, she felt Bronwen press up against her from the back.

What seemed like a ridiculously short time later, two Pittsburgh police black and whites screeched to a halt at the end of the street, and multiple officers piled out. Two went over to Delia, heaved her to her feet, and cuffed her.

A third officer came over with his hand outstretched. "I'll take that, ma'am."

Sally handed over the gun, which she now recognized as a .38, without argument. She fought the urge to collapse now that the threat was over. She reached around and squeezed Bronwen's shoulder. "You got here quick."

The officer made the firearm safe before dropping it in an evidence bag. "We were already on our way when the call came from the EOC."

"How'd you know where I was?"

"State police gave us your GPS location and said you were in immediate danger." The officer gave her a lopsided grin. "You must have friends in high places." He walked away.

It had to have been Jim. Whether he'd used the Find app or located her some other way, she didn't care. She pulled Bronwen around and held her tight. The girl pressed her face against Sally and sobbed. "Shh, it's okay, sweetie. She can't hurt you now." Sally stroked Bronwen's hair, hoping the motion provided the reassurance the unheard words did not.

The officer returned. "You'll have to give a statement. Are you okay to come to the station now?"

"Let me call my fiancé to get Bronwen. I don't want to upset her more than she is." Sally took out her phone again. Her hand shook so much, she dropped it.

As the officer picked it up, another car pulled up next to the Pittsburgh patrol cars. Jim leaped out and ran down the street, dodging construction debris.

"Sally! Are you hurt? What about Bronwen?" Jim halted next to the uniformed officer. "I've got it from here."

The officer touched the bill of his department-issued ball cap and moved off.

"We're okay." Sally could feel the adrenaline drain out of her. She stumbled.

Jim grabbed her elbow. "Come with me." He led her and Bronwen to the car. "What happened?"

Sally told him the whole story. "How'd you get here so fast?"

"You'd be amazed at what lights, a siren, and a high rate of speed can do to travel time." He proceeded to sketch out the details for her. "Once I learned Delia was on to you, I left everything in Abara's hands and hit the road. I notified PBP and gave them your location using the app on my phone. Are you sure you're okay?"

"Scared half to death, but otherwise unharmed." Sally rubbed Bronwen's back. "Is Olivia still alive?"

"Last time I checked. I haven't called for an update. She's not exactly my priority at the moment."

"They want me to go in and give a statement. Can you take Bronwen home?"

"I'll do you one better and take you myself." Jim pushed off the car. "Because if you think I'm letting you out of my sight, either of you, you're out of your mind."

Chapter Forty-Five

Duncan made the executive decision not to take Bronwen back to Pittsburgh until Sunday. Both Sally and the girl were emotionally exhausted after their confrontation. What they needed was quiet and a little canine love, which Rizzo and Pixel were happy to provide once the three of them returned to Confluence. Both Sally and Bronwen fell asleep early and didn't wake until mid-morning. Duncan provided a hearty breakfast of blueberry pancakes, eggs, bacon, and toast. Afterward, they set off for Pittsburgh under a perfect blue sky.

Paul stood on his porch when Duncan eased up to the curb. Bronwen jumped out of the back seat of the Jeep and ran to her grandfather. Duncan and Sally followed at a slower pace.

"Think she's excited?" Sally asked, her eyes on the pair.

Bronwen's hands flew, and Paul smiled as he took in her story.

Duncan wrapped his arm around his fiancée. "Yeah, I think she is. But I think she was pretty content with you, too."

Sally smiled, but there was a bit of sadness there as well.

Duncan kept an eye on her. *Who'd have thought?* Four days ago, Sally had been terrified at the idea of caring for a child. Now he'd bet anything she regretted seeing their young charge leave.

Paul met them halfway up the sidewalk. "I can't thank you enough." He held out his hand. "Bronwen's been telling me all about your adventures."

"Yeah, sorry about that last bit." Sally winced. "I didn't exactly cover myself with glory there."

"Nonsense." Paul brushed away the apology. "You can't control everything.

It sounds like you did exactly what I'd have expected you to do in that situation. I knew you wouldn't let any harm come to Bronnie. It's who you are."

"And that is?"

"A protector." Paul put his arm around Bronwen, who stood beside him. "She might not be your blood kin, but you'd have done anything for her. It's why I asked you to watch over her."

Sally wiped her thumb over her eyes.

Duncan squeezed her. He didn't miss the fact that Paul hadn't spoken to the police officer. No, his gratitude was all for the woman beside him. "How's Eva?"

"Better." Paul moved his attention. "She's got a long recovery, but I'm hopeful she'll be home by the end of the week."

Bronwen stepped forward and tugged on Sally's shirt. Then she signed a question.

Sally dropped to her knees and signed slowly. "Yes. You can come visit and play with Rizzo and Pixel."

Bronwen glanced at Paul, then turned back to Sally and signed, "Thank you. I love you."

Duncan noticed the watery gleam in Sally's eye as she responded.

"I love you, too." She clasped the girl in a tight embrace.

* * *

Sally didn't bring up the topic of Bronwen again until after dinner. She and Jim sat in the back yard on a wicker love seat while they watched Rizzo and Pixel gambol around the yard. "What a weekend."

"That it was." Jim held a bottle of porter in his right hand, his left snug around her shoulders. "You still have Bronwen on your mind?"

"Yes." She rested her head on his shoulder.

"She's a good kid."

"She is. The whole thing got me thinking."

"About what?"

She looked up. As she looked into his eyes, she could tell he knew exactly what she was talking about. But true to form, he let her say it in her own words and time. "Family. Kids. What I want."

"And what is that?"

She took a deep breath. "I know it's important to you, Jim. I appreciate the fact you respect my stance on that. Not wanting children, I mean."

"I told you before. I'd rather have you without kids than kids without you."

"But I've realized there are a lot of children like Bronwen. They need a place to stay and be safe for a while."

He gazed down at her. "What are you saying?"

"I want to be a foster parent. Not as in birth to adulthood. But short-term. For kids who need a temporary home." She held her breath. She wouldn't have brought up the subject if she wasn't fairly sure of his answer. But there was always the chance he'd surprise her.

He set down his bottle and cupped her face. "If that's what you want, that's what we'll do. You know, assuming two people with a habit of getting into trouble the way we do will make acceptable foster parents."

"Oh, come on. We've got jobs, dogs, a house. What more could they want?"

He raised an eyebrow. "People who don't come face to face with violent criminals on a regular basis?"

She poked him in the side. "I swear I'll behave myself."

"Oh, Sally." He kissed her. "Don't make promises you can't keep."

Chapter Forty-Six

Duncan rolled into headquarters Monday morning around nine and found Cavendish seated at her desk. "Well, look what the cat dragged in."

She took a gulp of coffee and set the cup down with a thump. "Who the hell has been messing around with my stuff?"

"Aren't you a little, what's the word? Testy?" Duncan sat. "The new guy used your desk while you were off having fun with the family."

"Fan-freaking-tastic. Bad enough that I spent ten days cooped up on a floating torture chamber with dozens of kids running around screaming. And not just my nieces and nephews. No, it was a *family-friendly* cruise." Cavendish continued to root through her drawers. "I come back to find everything out of its place. Testy is not the word."

"Quit your bitching." He knew his partner wasn't as pissed off as she sounded. "It couldn't have been all bad."

"Well…" She stopped and grinned. "The eye candy at the pool made up for a lot. New guy, huh? Did you talk to him much?"

"Hell, I had to partner him." Duncan aimed a pen in her direction. "And solve a murder. The next time I go on vacation, I'll talk to Ferguson and make sure your experience is as eventful as mine was."

"The next time you go on vacation will be your honeymoon. This will be the last place you think of." Cavendish stuck out her tongue. "Speaking of that, how's the planning going?"

"I swore on every holy book in existence that I would meet Sally and her mother this afternoon to go over reception meal options. If we catch another case, you are taking point. I will not leave Sally holding the bag this time." Behind him, a door opened, and he heard Ferguson say something.

"Psst. That him?" Cavendish lifted up in her chair.

Duncan turned. Abara stood at the lieutenant's door, exchanging a firm handshake. Then he headed toward Duncan. "Good morning. You must be Trooper Cavendish. Thanks for the loan of your desk."

She waved him off. "Don't mention it. Welcome to CIS."

Duncan spun his chair to look at Abara. He held a cardboard box on his right hip. The flaps were folded shut. He was wearing a button-down shirt and slacks, but no coat and tie. "Why do you look like a man on his way out the door?"

"Can't put anything past you, huh?" Abara put his free hand in his pocket.

"It's his super-power," Cavendish said.

Abara rocked on the balls of his feet. "Well, you're right. I'm not staying."

Duncan watched him closely. His temporary partner didn't look angry, upset, or disappointed, which made him think it wasn't the job that drove Abara away. "I hope it wasn't something I said."

"It was, but not a bad thing. You were right." Abara faced him squarely. "I took this position because I figured it was a way to build a resumé and get to a place where I didn't have to talk to people. I realized that was wrong. Police work is never a place where you work solo. Even if you move up the chain, there's management, press conferences, public relations…it's not for the faint of heart."

"You leaving the PSP?"

"No, just this location. I'm transferring out near Philly. Somewhere I can start over." Abara grinned. "You know, where I haven't made a bad impression yet and people don't think of me as an asshole."

"I understand." Duncan stood and offered his hand. "For what it's worth, I wish you luck. You ever need something, call."

"Thanks." Abara gripped the outstretched hand. He faced Cavendish. "Has he told you how much you owe him yet?"

Cavendish's expression soured. "No, but I'm sure he will."

* * *

Monday evening, Sally parked her SUV outside La Belle, a new upscale restaurant in Uniontown. "Are you sure you want to do this?" she asked as she sat behind the wheel.

"I've missed enough." Jim patted her hand. "Besides, based on what you've told me, Louise needs to be reminded of my name and what I look like."

They got out and approached the building, hand in hand. Louise stood outside the door, scrolling through her phone.

With Herculean effort, Sally kept from rolling her eyes. "Hello, Mom. I hope you haven't been waiting too long."

Louise sniffed. "Long enough." She eyed Jim up and down. "I see you decided to come for once."

Apparently unruffled, Jim nodded. "Nice to see you too, Louise."

She tossed her head and entered.

Jim squeezed Sally's hand. "Stay cool," he murmured.

Inside, Louise looked around for the coordinator they were meeting. "Before we get started, let's get our game plan settled. We're going to need at least five courses. I was thinking we'd start with—"

"Hold it right there." Sally made the time-out sign. "It's time we got a few things straight."

Louise folded her arms and narrowed her eyes. "Like what?"

"No five-course dinner. We're going to do a cookie table, like they do in Pittsburgh, for a starter. Dinner is salad, a choice of chicken, beef, or vegetarian. Chicken and beef will come with veggies and a starch. Dessert will, of course, be cake and whatever is left of the pre-meal cookie table."

Louise raised her eyebrows. "A cookie table?"

"Next. I do not want a hundred strangers at my wedding. I want to know them, or at least be familiar with the name. The limit is one fifty. If every guest brings a plus-one, that's seventy-five invitations."

Louise's face reddened. "I can't possibly—"

"Finally." Sally spoke over her mother's objections. "I will have a maid of honor, Noreen, and two bridesmaids, one of whom will be Jim's sister. Jim will have his best man and two groomsmen. No phalanx of people. I want to be friends with my attendants."

Louise wheeled to face Jim. "You put her up to this."

He held up his hands. "I did no such thing. This is her day, and I support her one hundred percent."

"Mom." Sally's voice softened. "I appreciate that I'm your baby and you want to throw a big bash. But that isn't me, and it's not Jim. You don't need to impress anyone, and I certainly don't. I hope you respect and love me enough to go along with my plans." *And if not, I'm going to make them anyway.* But Sally didn't want to push her luck and say the words aloud.

Louise fumed, her jaw working as though she was chewing the inside of her cheek. "Fine." She whirled and stomped off.

Sally heaved a sigh. "Why do I think I'm going to pay for that?" She watched Jim put his hand in his pocket as his gaze followed his future mother-in-law as she went to berate the restaurant's event coordinator for being tardy.

He pulled Sally close with his free arm. "She'll get over it. I think. I hope."

Sally hoped so, too. Otherwise, it was going to be a long time until September.

Acknowledgments

For the past several years, I've written two sets of acknowledgments a year. For 2025, I wrote three. So, if it sounds like I'm repeating myself, well, I am.

A million thanks to my critique group: Annette Dashofy, Jeff Boarts, and Peter WJ Hayes. If I've grown as a writer since that first book was published, a lot of it is due to your input, patience, and encouragement.

Many thanks to editor/writer Susan Helene Gottfried for giving the book that final sparkle before it leaves my hands. If you are a fan of books about real people living real lives, you should check out Susan's Tales from the Sheep Farm novels.

Thanks to the Dames of Detection, Shawn Reilly Simmons, Verena Rose, and Deb Well, for all you do: from great covers, to production, to answering my emails at any time.

Thank you to everyone who picks up a book and leaves a review. Writers are like small children: we thrive on praise – at least this writer does. I once told a book club that if readers understood the true power they hold in publishing, they'd never refer to themselves as "just a reader." Without you, the whole business falls apart.

When I talk to people who say they want to write a book, I ask what professional organizations they belong to. If they give me a blank stare, I immediately point them in the direction of Sisters in Crime and Pennwriters, in my not-so-humble-opinion two of the best. I'm honored to have been part of the National board for Sisters in Crime for the past three years. It's not impossible to publish a book without belonging to a group of like-minded people, but it sure is harder. Thanks also to the blog communities at Jungle Red Writers, Wicked Authors, and Chicks on the Case, including the "back-bloggers" who comment. It's always a thrill when I get to meet one of you in person.

Last, but definitely not least, thanks to my family – especially my husband, Paul (who knew you were so good at writing back-cover copy?). Love you to the moon and back.

About the Author

Liz Milliron is the Shamus award-nominated author of the Homefront Mysteries, set in Buffalo, NY during the early years of WWII, the Laurel Highlands Mysteries set in the scenic Laurel Highlands of southwest Pennsylvania, and the Jackson Davis Mysteries set in Niagara Falls, NY. Her short fiction has been published in multiple anthologies including *Murder Most International, Murder Most Historical,* and the Anthony award-winning *Blood on the Bayou.* Liz is a past president of the Pittsburgh Chapter of Sisters in Crime and the current Secretary, as well as the Education Liaison for the National Board of Sisters in Crime. She is also a member of International Thriller Writers, Pennwriters and the Historical Novel Society. Liz lives in the Laurel Highlands with her husband and a very spoiled retired-racer greyhound.

SOCIAL MEDIA HANDLES:
　　Facebook: https://facebook.com/LizMilliron
　　Instagram: https://instagram.com/LizMilliron
　　Threads: https://www.threads.net/@lizmilliron
　　Newsletter: https://www.subscribe page.com/newsletteridyllic

AUTHOR WEBSITE: https://lizmilliron.com

Also by Liz Milliron

The Laurel Highlands Mysteries
Saving the Guilty
Thicker Than Water
Lie Down with Dogs
Harm Not the Earth
Broken Trust
Heaven Has No Rage
Root of All Evil

The Homefront Mysteries
The Lies We Live
The Secrets We Keep
The Truth We Hide
The Lessons We Learn
The Stories We Tell
The Enemy We Don't Know

The Jackson Davis Mysteries
Shattered Sight